THE CINDRA CORRINA CHRONICLES
BOOK 1

THE GOLD CAT'S DAUGHTER

MARK RUDE

All persons, gods and monsters appearing in this work are fictitious. Any resemblance to real individuals, living, dead or immortal is purely coincidental.

Conversely, if any of the gods or monsters described herein turns out to be real after all, the author takes no responsibility.

ISBN 978-0-615-52736-9

Printed in the United States of America.

To all those who Believed.

Acknowledgements

A special "Thank you" goes out to:

My mother and sister for their invaluable input and encouragement.

Jason and Tanya, my test audience and best supporters. Thanks for putting up with me.

My friends in the Nerd Herd who gave me encouragement when I was unsure and feeling overwhelmed.

The old bookstore café that isn't there anymore, for giving me a place to write and enjoy good company and a lovely beverage.

Contents

The City of Portsbia, 1114 A.O.

Chapter One

The Arrangement

Lady Cindra Corrina sat wrapped in a blanket upon a cushioned bench in the window alcove as she watched the clouds drift by. Though the window might have provided a spectacular view had the castle been higher or the walls lower, it still offered a chance to watch the sails of tall ships entering and leaving the harbor. She would often spend hours at this seat, writing her poems or just practicing her hand in ink and quill, but today she had no words she wished to commit to parchment. She had far too much to think about concerning her future, as it all seemed bleak and dismal from this day onward.

Cindra was small for a girl of fourteen, but still had some growing to do if her mother's height was any indicator. The maiden had inherited her mother's longer nose and soft, sculpted jaw, and her father's hazel eyes and olive skin. She had strong legs from a childhood of

1

running up and down stairs and all about the castle, but to her dismay she was not blooming as early or as noticeably as other girls her age. Surely she ate better than the servant girls, but suspected her breeding was partly to blame. It was often a source of insecurity, and her mirror knew her image well.

Lady Cindra's auburn hair shone with streaks like burnished copper in the sunlight. Upon her brow she wore a thin circlet of gold that served to mark her as nobility, should anyone in her father's service not be aware of her station or existence. At least, that is what she told herself on some of her more disheartened days like today. It was the 28th of Kraamoth, 1114 in the Age of Omens, and it was Cindra's birthday.

Not that this was usually a bad day, but on this particular birthday she was faced with the prospect of a feast in her honor and the announcement of her upcoming nuptials. It had been her fate as a girl-born to be married off at a young age, lest the best of her childbearing years be wasted, leaving her husband with no heirs and her unable to have more.

Now only a few scant months after today, she would be packed aboard a ship with her baggage and a dowry to be deposited in a foreign land and married to a man she had never met, all to seal an alliance painstakingly forged by her father for reasons of state. It was as if her world was coming to an end.

"I hope you like sailing Rufi," she said to the small cat upon her lap as she parted the blanket. Rufi poked his black calico head lazily out of the blanket and looked up at her with disinterested eyes. "You were never happy to wander anywhere but in my rooms. I couldn't imagine leaving you here all alone." Rufi sighed in feline manner and laid his head upon his paws once more.

"He's hardly alone, milady." Mineth, Cindra's young handmaiden, came through the curtains separating the day room from the bower, two dresses folded over her arms, "He has his whole family about, brothers and sisters to play with, and more space here than he'd have aboard ship, to be sure."

Mineth adjusted the dresses in her arms and smoothed them against her ample hourglass figure, over which she wore a simple gray dress. She had dark hair and pale skin with large brown eyes that managed to balance a rather protruding but elegant nose. She wore her hair in large braids under a veil and a small flat cap. She smiled reassuringly with broad, full lips.

Cindra petted the drowsy cat in her lap. "It's possible to live with one's family and be alone, Mineth."

Accustomed to her mistress's moods, Mineth laid the dresses carefully upon the sewing table and sat opposite the girl. She had known Lady Cindra most of her life, which counted some twenty-six years. Mineth was the daughter of the countess's handmaiden come from Aurilon, and was given charge of young Cindra once the child no longer needed a wet nurse. She had very nearly raised the girl twelve years her junior, and knew her ways all too well. "Don't be like that, milady. You'll always have me about, and things are not so very bad. The count and countess love you, and they'll miss you sorely."

"Not as much as my brother, I think." Cindra knew it was a mistake as soon as she said it, for Mineth stiffened and took on her scolding tone.

"Your brother is dead, milady! A child can break a parent's heart in many ways, but dying is the worst! You've no right, begging your pardon milady, *no right* to wish for that kind of pain upon your poor parents. They're sending you off to be a duchess after all, not to die."

"I know," Cindra said quietly, "It's just that sometimes," she heaved a sigh and hugged the cat to her chest and it mewed in annoyance, "sometimes, I feel like we all died with him; like we're just unfeeling ghosts drifting through the halls." She returned her gaze to the clouds, adjusting the blanket about her shoulders.

There was a knock on the door beyond the curtain dividing the day room from the bower. Mineth stood and gave her lady a stern yet sympathetic look, patting her shoulder comfortingly before hurrying off to answer. A moment later the curtain parted and Mineth reappeared, bowing and holding the fabric open for the countess.

Zara Corrina was willowy and statuesque, with a regal bearing and gliding walk. Her mouth was generous, her emerald eyes seemed to smile even when her lips did not, and her skin was like fresh cream. She wore her golden hair braided and topped with a bonnet of soft white fur. The collar of her dress was embroidered with the seashell and pearl symbols of House DuMaylione. She glided across the floor with even steps and her daughter rose to meet her, first depositing the disgruntled cat upon the cushion and discarding her blanket.

"Mother," Cindra said, giving the countess a curtsey. The girl wore a pelice of gray silk lined with rabbit fur over a dark blue, high-necked gown.

"I hope I am not intruding?" The countess gazed at the sewing table, "I see Mineth has picked out some dresses for your approval." Her voice was lower and more compelling than many women were gifted with, but soft and measured, capable of much tenderness. Her Aurilonian accent, with its longer vowels and lisping quality, made her all the more elegant.

"No mother, I had not looked at them yet," the girl said, trying to seem happy on this, her least anticipated birthday.

"Your father has heard that you have been playing on the battlements again, making the sentries nervous," the countess said as she walked to the window alcove, her eyes following the window's tracery crafted in the shape of a rose of the goddess Selvina, "I think he believes a seagull will snatch you up."

"I could only wish," Cindra said, wistfully.

The countess turned and regarded Cindra with saddened eyes. "He only worries for your safety, kitten. You are his only child."

"I am his *daughter*," she said, a little louder than she had intended. Then softer, "If I were a boy, things would be different. As they are, he hardly notices me. And now he's going to get rid of me." She felt a catch in her throat, her emotions rising significantly as she gave voice to her thoughts.

Mineth made a loud "tsk!" and turned away to busy herself with the dresses. The countess stared at the ornate carpet, her eyes seeing only a tiny face from the past and not the colorful embroidery. When she spoke again, her voice was lower than before, and unsteady, "Do not despise him, child. He has lost much... *we* have lost much. Now all his hopes for the future are pinned upon your marriage. It is so very important to him."

Cindra turned to look into her mother's moistened eyes as her own began to fill with tears. "*I* want to be important to him."

The city of Portshia had endured for twelve centuries upon the Crimson Bay on the southern coast of Calilon. To the east rose the sheltering mountain slopes of the Casselvane Range, where rich veins of silver had been discovered; to the north and west was the edge of the Shadowood, a dark and ancient forest through which the Joshian River flowed. The river had long ago been diverted to a large canal system, which irrigated crops in the northern lands and formed a moat and waterway about the city walls.

Towards the southern end of the city was the Highcourt, enclosed by a wall that encircled a cliff as it rose towards the sea. Upon the sea cliff was raised a low and humble castle, not very much higher than the wall surrounding its bailey; Casselvane Keep was a thick ring of stone that enclosed a small inner courtyard.

Having been restored after many battles, it was found that a low profile was more defensible against the new powder cannon that had risen to prominence in the last century. Its lime-washed ramparts were an impressive sight, but the keep itself was mostly hidden from view by the encircling curtain wall. The front of the keep presented a gatehouse through which all would enter; a double portcullis between two imposing arms of masonry.

The main banquet hall was arrayed in splendor for the evening's celebration. Flames burned high in the hooded fireplaces, warming the great hall against the winter chill. Feminine sky blue banners draped the arched doorframes and hung from the walls; the rest of the city was adorned in much the same way with ribbons and streamers. It was so on the week following Cindra's birth, and again when her brother was born, except those banners were masculine burgundy. Now the town and castle were festooned with colors to mark her engagement and the success of her father's efforts.

The grand chandelier glowed with enchanted light that would shine until morning, neither flickering nor waning. Life-sized portraits of Corrina ancestors were dusted and cleaned so their paint shone with fresh vibrancy, and incense was burned in the galleries.

From the tall supporting arches of the main hall were hung banners of the Corrina Family coat of arms: a field of blue upon which posed a rampant golden cat, below was a golden half-sun/silver half-moon, and above the beast's head were arrayed three silver crowns in the three-pointed style of Arathus, the King God.

The dining table formed a large circle; open at the far end to allow servers to move about the center area. The table was draped with a dozen sections of linen, all embroidered with images of game animals, fish and fowl. Chairs with lavish red cushions lined the outside of the table.

Guests were first led to the audience hall in the east wing, there to be entertained by minstrels, dancers, and wizards from the Mystic College. When all had arrived and been given time to mingle, they were guided into the lavish west wing to be seated at the circular table. The count and countess were announced and made their entrance, walking hand in hand as was the custom. The minstrels had taken up their places in the gallery along the inner wall and played a lively melody to accompany them.

Count Corrina was an impressive man, being neither overly tall nor broad; yet he possessed a steady, measuring gaze and lordly self-assurance. His hair was chestnut brown and graying throughout, and receded at the brow, which was creased as one who spends much time in deep thought. He wore rich burgundy garb, a golden circlet upon his head, and about his neck was a pendant bearing the device of a boar and mountain peaks, symbol of the province of Casselvane.

The countess wore a blue gown with airy sleeves of gauze and a necklace of pearls on which hung the DuMaylione family crest of silver shell and pearl. Her braided hair fell down her back and was crowned with a silver comb in the form of an open net. She also wore a golden circlet at her brow, set with an emerald to match her eyes.

Once the count and countess took their places at the head of the table, the herald called out "Lady Cindra Corrina!" All heads turned as the young noble girl was escorted into the main hall. Cindra had chosen a gown of bright yellow and upon her brow was a gold circlet set with a large ruby. She wore no other jewelry, and was happy to not be burdened with an engagement ring yet.

The lady's escort was one of the count's most trusted knights; Sir Fedrick Dunlorden was an aged man, but still spry and full of voices when needed. He wore a knight's formal attire with the Corrina coat of arms upon the chest; he walked with a slight limp, smiling despite a few missing front teeth and a scarred eye, white and useless. All were badges of service, and he wore them with pride. His hair was white where it still clung to his head, and his beard was wiry and stiff, like the bristles of a boar's back. Sir Fedrick took his place beside his son after seeing the young lady to her chair, and the castle pages poured the toast.

The formalities dragged on as the count took his daughter's hand and raised it, proclaiming, "Friends and honored guests, negotiations have been completed and the arrangements have been made." He turned to Cindra, "My daughter, Lady Cindra Corrina, shall marry his grace, Haynyyd Syn DeKaard, Duke of Kyshmeryyk, three months hence in the kingdom of Rokvynnar!" He pronounced the difficult foreign words with practiced ease. The assembled guests raised their goblets and cheered in praise.

Cindra wore a smile that barely concealed her disgust; the guests were mostly bootlickers and social climbers, caring nothing for her happiness, but saw only opportunity and riches for themselves. *They would cheer so if my father told them his favorite hound had puppies*, she thought bitterly, *Besides, he got the duke's name wrong. It's Hammyd.*

Once the meal service had begun, Cindra allowed herself to relax a little. Soon the noise of the diners reached a jovial buzz as the winter mead flowed, and Cindra began looking at the guests to try and remember just who they were. Her mother had gone over the guest list with her a few days before, since it was her duty to be educated about the workings of court, but she had taken only outward interest at the time. Now she made a game of it.

The woman to her right she knew well enough. Reverend Sister Lyneth, the local head of the temple of the love goddess Selvina, was a common sight in the castle, being a good friend of the countess. The Reverend Sister wore a stiff white veil tucked and shaped artfully about her head, and set like a gauzy pavilion over her braided blonde hair. Her blue gown gave only a slight nod to modesty, but such was the way of the Selvinians.

Lyneth was a great beauty herself, full of figure and graceful, and possessing a delicate nose which Cindra often envied, and large brown eyes that made her look far more innocent than she was.

She recognized the albino Lord Clavemont beside the priestess, though they had never met; his pale skin, light blond hair, and pale blue eyes were unmistakable. He was perhaps thirty or more, dressed in gray velvet and bearing the emblem of a golden wyvern.

He was accompanied by a young woman who seemed to laugh at the wrong times when listening to his humorous stories. She had a large, ornate headpiece that was nearly as broad as her shoulders, and her head seemed to veer to and fro as she turned about. The woman looked a bit drunk already; Clavemont would occasionally place his hand upon hers, as if politely reining her in.

Next to Clavemont was a married couple that Cindra guessed were Master Theenix, chairman of the Trade Guild, and his pinch-faced wife. The count had invited them to gauge the support of the city's trades, should they be required to supply a war effort.

She paused in her game and returned to her meal for a moment. War was the reason for this banquet, these pleasantries, and her marriage. Her tutors had explained this to her over a year ago, when her father's overtures to Rokvynnar began at the bidding of Calilon's king. Alliance with Rokvynnar meant trade and wealth, but also fast ships, and an ally instead of an enemy in the western reaches of the kingdom.

Cindra knifed a bit of eel and swirled it in sauce, wondering if her future husband had to like her, or she him, for this arrangement to work to everyone's satisfaction. *Probably not*, she mused.

Cindra looked to her left and recognized one man by his pendant: a serpent weighed upon merchant's scales. Some commoners were wealthy enough to purchase their own coat of arms, and such was Kobus DuChat. He was a handsome man with thick, curly, black hair and a trimmed beard, and immaculately fitted attire. Cindra wondered where he acquired the cut on his eyelid that caused it to lie more heavily than the other. DuChat was known to be sympathetic to the crown and the status quo, and was being courted for his resources, as well as his rumored spies among the trade routes, many of which crossed into unfriendly lands.

Cindra marked the difference in behavior of the couple farther on, commoners also, but trying all too hard to start or enter conversation. The man was Julen Gordon, a ship owner and opportunist. He ruined Cindra's game by giving his name and business freely, and his wife Lemorea was no better. They had seemed to rehearse their stories and conversation for the benefit of the other guests, trying to bring attention to their business connections or form new ones. If they had not been invited, they might have wheedled their way in the door. They toasted too loudly and frequently, and Cindra was put off her dinner.

To the left of the merchant couple was Sir Fedrick, the worn old knight who had once been a commoner himself. His son, Sir Jaron, was seated beside him, speaking quietly. She had not seen Sir Jaron before now and wondered how he had avoided her notice. He was perhaps eighteen with a light beard trimmed thin along his angular jaw, and large, deep-set eyes of blue-gray over sculpted cheeks. His hair was dark brown and cut with forelocks that framed his brow, and was otherwise pulled tight behind his head and tied in the knight's traditional *tipok* knot. His skin was olive and tanned from a life outdoors, looking warm and radiant under the chandelier. He finished speaking and turned his attention back, directly to.... her.

As their eyes met, Cindra felt a flush in her cheeks; the young knight held her gaze with boldness beyond his station, with an intimacy that startled her. Her stomach fluttered with butterflies, and she remembered that the love goddess Selvina had a fondness for those creatures. Small wonder.

The young knight smiled and saluted her with his goblet, a slight, private smile on his full lips. Cindra's heart began to pound and she felt lightheaded. She blinked and flicked her eyes about the room, seeing if anyone noticed the exchange. He was still looking! She smiled despite herself and reached for her own goblet, almost knocking it into the pudding. Her hands were unsteady and beginning to tremble.

Reverend Sister Lyneth spoke to the girl, "Does milady Cindra enjoy the mead? The food is most excellent, is it not?"

Cindra blinked and turned bodily in her chair to face the sister, desperate for the distraction. "I... yes! It is quite good. Quite fitting for... for this occasion. My birthday, that is." Cindra felt as empty-headed as Lord Clavemont's giddy escort. She tried to recall how much mead she had drank, and found it was not much at all.

Sister Lyneth gave her a knowing smile as she lifted a bite to her mouth. "Milady has a good eye," she said, and took a nibble.

Cindra braved a glance at the young knight and found he was eating too, looking often in her direction. She decided to act natural and eat, but suddenly didn't want him watching her while she ate. She fluttered her hands about her plate indecisively. "I don't know what you mean, Reverend Sister."

"No, of course not," the priestess said, looking from the girl to the knight.

Sir Jaron noticed the woman's attention, stole one more glance at Cindra, and proceeded to call for more mead.

The priestess smiled to herself and felt the hand of the goddess at work. "If milady attends the Festival of Devotion in a few months, you shall no doubt see him in the joust."

"Hmm?" Cindra asked innocently, "See who?" She blinked a little too much.

"Sir Jaron Dunlorden, the handsome young knight across the table," she said knowingly, "It's only but a few short years since he earned his spurs, and already he is gaining a reputation as a masterful fighting man. He's very popular with the festival crowds."

"Is that so?" Cindra replied, looking to him as if she had only just noticed, "He seems very..." she groped for the right word as several inappropriate ones passed across her mind, making her blush, "...very confident."

"It is said that fortune favors the bold, milady."

"The same is said about the foolish, is it not?" Cindra replied.

"Even so," Lyneth answered, "I could introduce you if you wish."

Lyneth's plans were interrupted by the count himself, who leaned towards them pointedly so Cindra would pay attention. "Reverend Sister! My daughter will favor the young duke, I think. Do you agree?"

Turning her big, innocent eyes to the count, she proclaimed, "Yes, I am sure she will, my lord. His grace is quite accomplished and worthy... for a lad of twelve years." She turned back to her food; the goddess's will be done.

"TWELVE??" Cindra exclaimed, spinning in her seat to face her father, "Twelve? The duke was supposed to be twenty-three!" The party conversation died rather abruptly.

The count looked quite embarrassed, as though he had felt beneath the table and realized he had forgotten his stockings. Clearing his throat, he started, "Well, Hammyd Syn DeKaard *was* twenty-three..."

Cindra was livid, caring nothing for the eyes around her. "When I heard you say *Haynyyd*, I thought you said it wrong! Who is Haynyyd then?"

The count raised his voice, both to gain some measure of control and make his case to the curious and cowed party guests. "Hammyd *was* the duke. Unfortunately, his grace died a few months ago, under unknown circumstances. I..." Another clearing of his throat, "I managed to salvage the marriage arrangement with the dowager duchess; her younger son Haynyyd is the *new* duke. She accepted the terms." The count looked about the table, avoiding his daughter's coal-hot eyes.

There was a bit of murmuring about the table as the guests took in the news. It was not so much a concern that the groom had been substituted, but that the first duke had died under "unknown circumstances." Such was the spark that began a brushfire of rumors at elegant parties.

Cindra abandoned her game of guess-the-guest and cried, "What kind of marriage is this? Will my husband pull my braids and throw stones at me? Will I have to wipe his snotty nose and his spotty behind?"

"Oh no," said the Reverend Sister, "I'm sure he has servants for *that*."

"Ugh!" Cindra fumed, her braids feeling too tight and her appetite utterly destroyed.

"That will be enough, Reverend Sister Lyneth," rumbled the count under his breath, regretting inviting the meddlesome priestess, then wondering why he had done so in the first place. *Ah yes*, he recalled, *the countess had insisted on it.*

Hoping to break the tension, and of course, to call attention to himself, the merchant Julen Gordon raised his voice and his goblet. "A toast! To a prosperous union between the Lady Cindra and the young duke, and to her wise and adept father, Count Casselvane."

His wife, Lemorea, beaming with pride at her husband's social prowess and tact, smiled with approval and raised her glass as well. "To the Lady Cindra and the Count!" she intoned.

The guests all raised their goblets at the toast, hoping to defuse the powder keg that was the young noble girl in braids. The count accepted the toast in good form.

"Granting more than just secure trade and the alliance of the Rokvynnar, this union will serve to send a message to the Dissenter Houses: the king has a strong naval ally and full command of the Red Coast. They may think twice before making a treasonous mistake." At the word 'treasonous,' the room went silent.

Lord Clavemont, cocking his white head in concern said, "Are things truly so unstable in the kingdom, my lord?"

The count paused, weighing his words carefully. "His majesty has reason for preparation. The eastern provinces have suffered the ambitions of their barons for many years. Far from the sight of the crown, they seek to carve out their own kingdoms. The king has tried to regain control, but marching on the rival barons may, in fact, unite them to a common cause."

The threat of civil war voiced so clearly gave pause to all, even the pages who scurried to clear away the empty plates and trays.

Only Cindra was unmoved, for she had heard all of this before; the number 'twelve' was floating in her vision like an insect that could not be fanned away. She had to leave the table before she threw a fit again, or worse, broke out into tears before the insensible dinner guests.

She rose from her chair. Her father and the men at the table rose with her, as was customary, but her father took her hand and held it tightly, turning to Cindra and catching her off guard. He said to her, "Friends are becoming scarce, and His Majesty desires that such alliances will bring hope in times of great need." He looked into her eyes and with surprising sincerity, said, "My daughter, you wed with the blessings of the king, and with all of our hopes. May your beauty and grace strengthen us and foster peace."

The gathered guests applauded and Cindra tried to leave as gracefully as her bearing required, and quickly too, lest she scream in frustration before reaching her bedchamber.

Chapter Two

Black Will

"PEACE!" She cried as she stormed about her bower, the stoked fire matching her mood and the light giving flame to her brushed-out braids. "He wants *peace*, does he?"

Mineth wrung her hands in worry as she tried to think of something to calm her lady but was at a loss in the face of the storm. Instead, she went about collecting the shoes Cindra had flung at the walls.

Cindra stalked back and forth at the foot of her poster bed, punishing her braids out with a silver brush and shaking her fists in rage. "Marry me off to a twelve year old boy!" She stomped about wanting to kick a chair, but some better sense told her she would only hurt her toe. "Send me to live in Rokvynnar! Duke Kyshymuck, Heinous Sin DeKaard!" She stopped suddenly in the middle of the room, and Mineth sensed it was safe and appropriate to get close.

Cindra began to cry, holding her brush close to her like a holy relic and choking on her sobs. Mineth put supportive arms around the girl's shoulders and muttered in Aurilonian words of comfort she had picked up from her own mother, handmaiden to the countess, "*La shupú, fellí, mesha shupú.*"

"It's not fair Mineth," Cindra sniffled, "It was bad enough as it was... now, a boy.... twelve!"

Mineth put her arms around the girl and led her to the vanity table so she could brush out Cindra's braids in a less violent manner.

"I've never been anywhere, I've not seen the world at all, and now I'll be sent off to another castle to be cooped up like a hen." She sat at the padded stool and slumped in despair as Mineth tended her hair.

"See the world, milady? Few people truly see the world. Even your father rarely travels far from his lands. Merchants travel all about, but only where their business leads them. Pilgrims journey to temples and holy sites, but with their heads bowed and eyes turned inward, and soldiers march for miles and miles, but go where they are told and have death as a constant companion. No one really travels just to see the world." Mineth had a way of looking at things simply, making them easier to bear.

Cindra was not convinced. "The Galindri go where they please. They sleep under the stars, and go from town to town and province to province."

"Does milady wish she had been raised Galindri?" Mineth smiled at the thought of her noble born lady traipsing about in a caravan and selling blankets.

Cindra smiled in spite of herself, her mood lightened a bit by the idea. "That would be a sight, would it not? But my skin is too light and my eyes are not nearly green enough." She gathered her hair in a topknot that spilled down about her face, like the pictures she had seen of Galindri traders. She added, "It's said they steal children to raise as their own, but no one would be fooled by me." Her mind lingered a bit on the thought of the disguise.

Mineth continued working on Cindra's hair; she was pleased to see it had its usual calming effect. "Well, the guests will be leaving soon enough, and things will be peaceful here again."

Cindra was still looking into the mirror on her vanity table, an idea turning in her head. *The guests would be leaving soon... all the commotion and activity... it would be a perfect opportunity...*

"Milady?" Mineth glanced at the distracted maiden, wondering what had taken her so far from her sulking. She had a distant look in her face, as if she was seeing something unfold far away.

"Mineth!" Cindra finally said, "Mineth, that's it! The guests are leaving, and no one will notice! It's perfect!" The girl got up and began pacing the room, looking to and fro.

Mineth was rightly confused and a bit worried, for she sensed that whatever thought had entered her lady's head was leading her into nothing but trouble. Once, Cindra had concocted a new game to play with the servant children that involved running in a serpentine formation all about the outer battlements and whacking the guards' halberds with sticks. This looked worse.

"A disguise!" Cindra exclaimed, turning on Mineth with glee, "A simple disguise, something no one would notice. I can slip downstairs and out to a carriage, and ride away with no one the wiser."

Mineth was aghast. "Ride away, milady?? What nonsense is this?" She put her hands on her hips in her resolute, unmovable stance.

Cindra was not discouraged. "I'll need a cloak, and a simple gown, nothing fancy, maybe one of yours, and something warm for my feet... oh, and my purse. Where is my purse?" She began rummaging in her dressing drawers.

"You cannot leave the castle, milady! Absolutely not! Your father and mother would worry so, and what if something were to happen to you?" Mineth tried to keep her voice stern but quiet, not wanting to draw attention if this disaster could be contained.

"If anyone finds out, tell them I put you up to it on pain of death or something." Cindra said helpfully as she searched Mineth's dressing chest in the corner.

"Pain of death?" The handmaiden said in alarm. *Was it some kind of threat? What had gotten into the girl?*

"Or something," Cindra said distractedly, picking out a simple but warm wool gown of blue, "I will go out into the city and come right back, once I've had a look around." Cindra took the handmaiden by the shoulders and looked her in the eye, her intensity overpowering. "This may be my last chance for an adventure before I spend the rest of my life locked in another castle. I have to do this, Mineth."

"An adventure? What do you need with an adventure? What's gotten into you, milady?" *The girl was mad!*

Cindra gathered her disguise onto her bed and began to undo the bindings of her yellow party gown. "I don't know how to explain it, but all my life I have felt that something more is waiting for me outside these walls, and I must go and see for myself. This is my chance, and I cannot allow it to pass. All I ask of you is to take my place in the bed until I return, and tell no one. It will be alright, trust me!" She continued undressing, and Mineth began helping her out of habit, "I shall ride on a carriage, then call for another to take me back to the keep. I shall pretend I am you if they question me at the gate." Cindra had worked it all out in her head, confident that her plan was foolproof.

She was also sure that Mineth was beginning to weaken. Her handmaiden had a strong sense of what was right and wrong, but also found it impossible to deny the girl that was like a baby sister as much as a lady she served. She might worry endlessly until Cindra returned, but she would not stop her or alert her parents to the plan. All that was needed was a bit of assurance to keep her conflicted, a sworn promise to immobilize her. She felt a pang of guilt at manipulating her handmaid, but she was a servant after all, was she not?

Cindra took Mineth's hands in hers and made her voice steady and solemn. "Mineth, I promise I will return safely. The gods will it; I can feel it. All I need from you is your sacred promise that you will keep it a secret, and not spoil their plans for me." The gods had a special influence over Mineth that Cindra could not match, but could invoke when needed. Perhaps such manipulation would weigh against her soul one day, but Cindra figured she had plenty of time to sort it out before her day of judgment.

The poor handmaid did not know what to do. Did the gods really mean for her lady to put her life in danger and wander the city this night? Was there something divine at work in her mad plan? Or was this more like the time she had explained to her enraged father that Balkon, the god of war, had told her in a dream to fire off a cannon at the west bank and shatter a tree? "I... oh milady Cindra, you mustn't ask me to swear."

Cindra pressed her advantage home, "But Mineth, if you don't swear, I will not know if you've betrayed my trust. How could I fulfill my destiny if my parents are waiting for me at the gate when I return? Please, will you swear?"

"I... I suppose," Mineth said weakly.

It was all Cindra needed, and she tossed the yellow party gown on the bed. The cold air tingled against her skin through the thin undergarments, but it was nothing like the excitement racing up her spine at the thought of slipping away into the night, unmissed and unnoticed. She climbed into the woolen gown and began pulling on her hose and boots. She fastened her coin purse to her belt, and after securing her hair in a kerchief, draped the dark blue cloak with its deep hood about her shoulders. Looking in her large polished mirror one final time, she bade Mineth to dress in a nightgown and pretend to sleep if anyone should come calling.

She left Mineth behind in the bower to climb into bed and mutter recriminations to herself. She carefully closed her chamber door and looked over the railing of the second floor hallway, which overlooked the base of the stairs inside, and the courtyard without.

Carriages were lined up to cart away the party guests who had begun donning cloaks and coats at the foot of the grand stair. Cindra made her way down as calmly as possible, keeping her face down and her hood up. Some of the guests and servants looked up at her curiously before returning their attention to meet the cold air. *So far so good*, thought Cindra, quite pleased that she was so easily ignored.

As she reached the base of the grand stair, she stood off to the side to give the guests room to depart. The wealthy commoner couple the Gordons were currently pulling on fancy gloves and scarves and chatting away about the prospects of trade with Rokvynnar. Cindra waited until the large ironclad doors were opened to let them out and she started to move around one of the carved pillars that flanked the decorative stonework of the portal. She followed the Gordons out until a voice stopped her dead in her tracks.

"Tsst! Hold up a minute, miss." It was a doorman in burgundy and gold, who was suddenly at her side, a restraining hand on her arm. Cindra's terror turned to shocked outrage at being grabbed so by a servant, but then she recalled that she was in no position to mind, being as she was, disguised as a servant herself.

The doorman gave her a harsh whisper before releasing her, "Give the departing guests a respectful distance, now." Cindra relaxed as she realized that her disguise had worked perfectly.

She waited for the footman to help the Gordons into their carriage, and she hurried down the stairs past the stonework cats at the base of the wide banister, which held aloft globes of magically illuminated crystal. The Gordons were still flaunting their business, though it was being wasted on the teamsters and horses.

Julen was saying, "This is quite an opportunity! I shall leave tomorrow on a packet ship bound for Rokvynnar and try to feel out the situation. No doubt the merchants there will have heard the news as well."

Lemorea asked, "Is it not too soon? The wedding is not for another few months." She situated herself in the seat and her husband followed.

Cindra slipped around the footman and quietly folded down the baggage shelf so she might sit on the back of the carriage. She could still hear their conversation through the curtained back window of the covered passenger compartment.

Julen was saying, "It's never too soon to take advantage of a good thing. I don't plan to sign any contracts, but I might still make some inquiries."

Lemorea replied, "Very well, my dear. That poor girl didn't seem too happy with the situation, did she?"

Julen turned to her and said, "What poor girl?" The carriage pulled away as Cindra mentally knifed the boorish man in the back.

As the back of the carriage moved into view of the footman, he noticed the extra passenger and raised his arm to call out to the driver. Cindra quickly dug into her purse and tossed some silver coins at the footman, holding her finger to her lips to beg for his silence.

The jingling of coins caught his attention immediately and he thought the better of raising an alarm. The footman stooped to pick up the silver, muttering to himself in amazement, "Three silver Calimarks? That's about five days wages!" He looked up at the departing carriage. "Well, when you need a ride, you need a ride."

Cindra held her breath as the carriage crossed the courtyard and passed through the gatehouse. As it moved under the portcullis and into the bailey, she felt a laugh bubble up inside of her, quiet and potent, making her shake. She leaned over the side of the luggage shelf and looked around to see forward, watching as they moved under the large gatehouse and into the Highcourt. This was farther than she had ever traveled unsupervised, and she counted herself lucky that she had hitched a ride with the Gordons, for they were commoners and no doubt lived farther into the city. Her journey might be a long one indeed! To improve matters, they had ceased to speak in such loud voices since there was no one about to impress.

The chill of the night was hard to ignore, but Cindra did her best. She was for all purposes alone and on her own, and it was better than she had dreamed. The ground was receding just inches below her dangling feet, and the bumps along the road made her feel as though she might be dislodged any moment. The spinning wheels tossed up dirt and grass, and the clip-clop of the horse's hooves brought to mind a song, but she could not remember the words. The noble residents of the Highcourt went about their nightly lives, unaware of the great caper unfolding outside their doors.

The stars shone brightly and the moon was full, and the world was bathed in a new light. The castle grew smaller in the distance as the carriage bore her away, and Cindra began to wonder if this excursion was entirely wise. After all, the city at night was an unknown, more so than the day, for there were fewer people about after sunset, and their intentions were... questionable.

She decided that as long as she kept her wits about her and stayed on the main streets, she would be all right. After all, she was highly educated, as many noble women were. She could read and write Aurilonian, her mother's language, as well as a bit of Rok, Norsican and Celvestrian. She knew her history, her numbers (as much as were needed for the care of household finances), and she was well versed in law, being as she was, somewhat in a position of authority. She was certain that she was up to the challenge of exploring her own city, for the common people did it all the time.

Tonight was Nixy's night. He'd spent the last few years trying to prove himself to the rest of the lads, and to Dexer, and tonight was his big test. He'd be going alone into the streets, no bushers, no dodgers, and no help. He'd pass or fail, live or die. Well, maybe not die, but one never knew. At worst if he got away without the grab, he'd be made to sleep out o'doors, and that was bad on a night like tonight. Cold, it was, but not so cold he couldn't keep his fingers warm. All he needed was quick hands and a sharp knife.

His knife was the sharpest. *Cutter*, he called it, simple name for a simple fact; it could cut leather like butter, never grew dull as long as he'd had it, and was his most prized possession. It was his only possession too, except for the clothes on his back, for the knife belonged to his mother, and it passed to him when he left home. Now he'd put it to work and show them all he was ready.

Cricket and Daymi were there, watching him like dogs, like he was a sausage. They'd been made brothers years back, and were set to watch the test. They'd tell Dexer how he did, and let him know if his training and trust had been wasted or not.

Nixy never wanted to cross Dexer, for he was just as likely to beat you as look at you if he was in a foul mood. Nixy was one of his favorites, if the others were to be believed, but that made things more dangerous. Cricket and Daymi might let their jealousy get the better of them and let him take a fall. Nixy wasn't made yet, so anything could happen.

"You got yer nerves up, Nixy?" said Daymi, the pushy one with dark, curly hair, "You ready to do what's needed, night rules and all?"

Cricket chirped in with his pinched little laugh, "Night rules. Stab's as good as grabs," he grinned, picking skin off his lower lip and staring at Nixy through long greasy hair.

Nixy was defiant, saying, "I don't need no stabs. I can skin a mark with my blinkers closed, and him none the wiser." He gripped the black, raven-headed handle of

Cutter, but kept it sheathed; he didn't show off his prize knife to these two.

The two watchdogs weren't impressed. "We'll see about that, DuQuayne," said Daymi, using Nixy's family name.

Made brothers didn't have family names, because they caused trouble for the people back home. Nixy wasn't that worried; his mother was already dead, and his father lived far from the city, probably didn't even know his son was in Portshia. He had no other kin, so Daymi using his family name was no threat, except it was a reminder that he wasn't one of them yet. He decided to keep quiet, because it was always the best idea.

The watchdogs led Nixy down the wide alleys to the Market Square, with its tents and stalls closed for the night and the shops all locked down tight. There were a few places where people sat with their fires and blankets, having too much to move for the evening or no place else to go. Nixy was sure there would be a chance to prove his skills here, and he told the watchers he would work the area. They laughed at him of course, for the Market Square was used to thieves, pickpockets and greedy hands, and was always on the lookout for suspicious types. No matter, Nixy was firm on the idea, and slipped into the shadows.

The watchdogs looked at each other, a bit more impressed. Nixy could be a pompous little bastard sometimes, but he had a knack for the shadows that the two had never seen. Dexer was impressed too, and that meant something. Nixy would come back with a grab, or a grab and a bloody knife, or not at all, if he was smart.

Cindra's carriage was rolling through the dark streets, passing wizard lamps. The glowing orbs of blown glass were suspended from scrolled iron hangers at every street corner. There were people going into taverns and warm looking apartments, people standing in doorways talking and smoking pipes, and a few striders about going no place in particular. The scene was perfectly ordinary and perfectly thrilling to the young girl's eyes.

The two and three story buildings were angular and simple, with plastered walls, curved red brick shingles, and arched doors and windows. Balconies and empty planters adorned the upper floors, waiting for warmer weather and use. Shop windows with heavy shutters and colorful awnings gave distinction to the uniform streets, and trees with winter bare branches cast skeletal shadows along the moonlit avenues.

The main streets themselves were wide and paved with flat stones, and gutters fed rainwater into sewers, like those used in ancient Celvestria. The sewers led to the canals that surrounded the three smaller districts of the city, providing protection from invasion once the bridges were raised and the gates shut.

Cindra's carriage was now turning and passing through one such gate and over a bridge. Over the tops of the buildings Cindra saw the Tower of the Silver Moon.

The structure was among the tallest freestanding towers in the world. It was built a century ago over a period of ten years by the Order of Astrellaris, using the finest masons and craftsmen, and held fast by mystical building and binding techniques acquired from many lands. The tower was wider at the base and tapered as it rose until it widened into a bulge, narrowed again, and widened at the summit. The utmost pinnacle was topped with a great orb three times the height of a man, and formed of copper. It glowed brightly, mimicking the phases of the moon by means of a special enchantment. Twelve stone ribs that ran from bottom to top supported the tower, and were covered in copper plates which had since turned to greenish patina.

Cindra had only seen the edifice this close during the day, on family outings to the cathedral. At night, its full splendor made her eyes water in the chill air.

As the driver slowed to take a turn onto the bridge, Cindra thought she heard one of the Gordons mention her name in their quiet conversation. A tingle went down her spine as she suspected they were aware of her presence, but nothing followed to confirm this. She decided they were only discussing the banquet and had not detected their passenger. Cindra strained her ears to listen to what they were saying about her but the driver had completed his turn and began across the bridge; the noise of the wheels on the stones made eavesdropping impossible.

The carriage crossed over to the Harbor District, with its warehouses, raucous taverns, and bawdy houses. She caught a glimpse of masts and sails, and barges tied up for the night. She could hear the lowing of the water oxen as they drifted and splashed about at their moorings. Then the carriage turned and was crossing another bridge farther north into the city, heading for the Temple Walk and the Market Square.

The keep was still visible in the moonlight, its whitewashed walls gleaming, but it was so very far away now. She imagined her mother and father, unsuspecting of her absence, getting sleepy on winter mead and boring conversation. Her mother would turn in first, leaving the count to chat with the important guests a little longer and plan for the future, or just drink. They would likely not check on her until morning, and Mineth was taking up the bed in case anyone looked in to see if she was all right.

For the time it took her to conceive and execute this plan, it was an amazing success. She wondered if perhaps the ruse about the gods willing her to leave tonight was not entirely false, for her adventure seemed charmed or blessed from the start. She decided to say a little prayer of thanks as they passed the cathedral, if indeed they were going that way. And so they were.

As the carriage rolled on between the temple of Obamir and the darkened Market Square, Cindra saw the fires. There were people, probably merchants or vagabonds, camping in the open on the cobblestone plaza.

One fire caught her attention, and as the carriage slowed a bit to more easily navigate the sparse crowd, she followed the impulse to leap off the luggage shelf. She stumbled a bit but regained her feet quickly, and took a moment to straighten her belt, purse, and cloak. It was bitter cold, but more bearable now that there was no breeze from movement, and the fires looked inviting. She walked cautiously towards the arched columns that lined the square and took to the shadows to watch what caught her attention.

There was a caravan in the square, a horse-drawn wagon with a curved wooden roof, gaily painted in the colors of autumn. It bore trim of angled designs and images of frolicking horses, and the sides were hung with baskets and barrels, pots and pans, and many items that the owners were likely selling. The fire was lit in a standing brazier, for the night watch forbade campfires on the street, and a family of Galindri was tending its warming glow; real Galindri, the people of the plains and forests who traveled with the seasons and the furdeer herds and who once held great favor with Kraal himself. The ancient king had given them exclusive rights to go where they willed and live as they once did before the coming of the empire, and the Galindri were the most free willed people of Calilon. Cindra moved closer for a look, smelling the exotic food being prepared and listening to their strange tongue.

There were five adults, two men and three women. They all had dark skin; the color of wet clay, and emerald green eyes that seemed to shine in the firelight, piercing against their dark faces. The men and women kept their hair in long braids or thickened strands that they tied into topknots, all save one, a younger woman of perhaps sixteen years, who wore her hair unbound.

The men wore loose fitting shirts of bright colors, and trousers with knee-high wrapped boots of leather. The women wore layered skirts and loose blouses that left the midriff partially uncovered; it was a style that carried over to the bolder members of Calilonian society, though often not polite society. One of the women, fuller of figure, was serving a man whose gray hair and lined face

27

marked him as an honored elder. Next, she served the younger man, whom Cindra assumed was her husband by the way they interacted. The youngest woman was tending her hair, which seemed dark gold in the firelight, and the last woman... she seemed to be standing watch, watching Cindra as she spied on their meal.

This one was tall, perhaps as tall as the countess, and had a stern but beautiful face. About her brow was a burgundy strip of cloth or leather, divided by a dark line or pattern. Her topknot was bound in a crimson cloth, and her clothing was the color of coral and the red sands of the coast. She wore skirts that stopped at the knee, and fur lined boots of leather; about her waist hung two knives or daggers in sheaths, and her wrists were wound with leather straps, making her look almost... warrior-like. Perhaps she was a hunter?

Cindra did not know much about the Galindri or their ways, but had assumed that the men hunted and the women tended their caravans or tents, or whatever they lived in at most times. This woman did not look as though she cooked much; unless it was something she caught herself.

The dark, imposing beauty made a rapid hissing noise and waved her hand at Cindra, as if scaring off a dog. The others looked up from their meal at the lone girl, hiding in the half light. Caught off guard and unused to being treated like a mere pest, Cindra backed up a bit and moved on, petulant but still fascinated. The soft chuckling of the Galindri let her know that her trespass was not serious.

She had seen real Galindri and their caravan! This night was getting better by the moment. She walked further on, avoiding the other fires, and headed out of the Market Square and towards the Tower of Sight, another one of her tourist destinations.

Nixy had a mark in his sights, an easy one, by the looks of it. She was alone and wandering, with no clear purpose, and that told him a lot. New in town, or lost, she was staring at the wizard's tower without a care in the world. He'd wait till she turned the corner, out of sight of the fires, and out of earshot if something went wrong. There was a tavern up the street a bit so there might be folks about; he'd have to choose his time careful. Night was different than day, when there were so many people wandering the streets it didn't matter if someone saw; you could lose yourself in the crowd and be off before they knew you'd grabbed their coin. But at night, you had to be good with the escape, and make sure there was no one around to get in the way. Tricky, but Nixy was up for it. Day grabs were kid's stuff, anyhow.

He edged around the corner of the market, watching the girl gaze at the tower. Nixy didn't really care for the Tower of Sight, it was grand enough with its white ivy-covered walls and shiny dome, and the lights up there were unnatural but pretty. What disturbed Nixy were the times he had slept nearby in an alley or doorway surrounding the tower. Dreams came to him those nights, dreams that were strange and sometimes made him wake with a start: the raven in the woods, the beautiful woman with the strange eyes, the black wolves hiding in the shadows, the man and the monster, the dragons. He'd only have those dreams when sleeping near the tower, and figured there was some magic there that was to blame. He used to sleep there out of curiosity to see what his dreams would show him, but that was before they got too terrifying. He slept elsewhere now.

The girl was moving north and east towards the festival grounds. Nixy followed at a distance, his cloth foot wraps barely making a sound. He'd have to strike soon or she might turn onto a busier street. The tavern was up ahead, and he prayed for a moment that she didn't go in. She didn't look like a pub doxy or serving wench, but you never knew. She paused at the door as a man entered, greeting his friends within. Nixy held his breath as she peeked in the windows and lingered a bit after the door shut, but he relaxed when she kept on walking. Nixy nodded his head in thanks to Obamir the Luck Giver, and smiled at the carved symbol of three tumbling coins that was set above the tavern's doorway. Just a few more steps, just a few more....

He drew *Cutter* from its sheath, and the cold metal flashed in the shadows.

———————

Cindra wanted to go inside. The tavern looked warm and inviting, as she assumed taverns would be, but she thought the better of it. There were no girls her age inside, and the large, sturdy woman holding a tray gave her a stern look before closing the door. It was probably best to avoid drawing attention to herself, she decided. If anyone found out who she was, she could be in real trouble, and all of her plans would be for naught. She moved away from looking in the tavern window and continued up the street towards the corner light.

It occurred to her that if someone truly recognized her walking the streets alone at night, they might have other things in mind besides turning her over to her father. If someone was bold or stupid enough to try and ransom her back to the count, they might make her a hostage and steal her away to another country. This idea did not give her comfort as she went along, and she resolved to find a carriage and hire a ride back to the keep as soon as possible. She glanced nervously over her shoulder, and to her dismay, saw a shadow move against the wall. Either her mind was playing tricks on her, or she was in a very bad situation. Cindra quickened her pace towards the light around the corner.

The street opposite her corner was lined with trees and beyond in the moonlight she saw the walls of the king's Winter Palace. He would normally be in residence there, but for a sickness that made him unwell to travel from the capitol in the west. The trees lined the grounds where festivals were held, and the breeze blew a bit more briskly here. She made her way around the corner and found herself standing under a glowing street lamp, its enchanted fires burning cold and bright within the glass orb. As she looked about to get her bearings, she heard a scuffling sound behind her. Terror hit the pit of her stomach and all her skin went cold, and she felt a hand move at her waist under her cloak. A knife blade flashed in the light, white against the shadows surrounding the street lamp. There was a slight tug at her waist and a burst of motion beside her, and as she spun about with a shriek on her lips, she saw her attacker bolting towards the trees.

He was a child, clad in rags and tatters and clutching her purse to his chest as he ran. His mussed blond hair flew wild as his hood blew off, and his shabby cloak fluttered in the wind of his passage. Cindra's fear turned to outrage and shame; she had been robbed by a street urchin! Her arms went stiff at her sides and she shouted in a voice reserved for frightening servant children, "Hey! Stop!" It did not have the desired effect. She would have to run the little brat down.

She hiked up her wool skirt and sprinted after the fleeing child, her longer legs giving her an immediate advantage. The boy hazarded a glance behind him, and his eyes widened in shock as Cindra matched his pace. He made for the fair grounds and scampered under the wooden stands built at one corner of the jousting field. He waited for the girl to follow him in where he seemed trapped, then he ducked under some low support beams and escaped into the open, hoping her height was fouling her up in the confined space. Cindra cursed and removed herself from under the stands, now resolute to catch him since she had been tricked. She gulped the chill air and ran until her legs burned, closing the distance with the little thief as she passed through the grandstand portal.

Nixy was confounded. Who *was* this girl, fool as she was, chasing him through the streets? If it weren't for his test, he could have led her right to the bushers, and they would have slowed her up permanent if they had the mind. But he was alone, and the watchers wouldn't help, probably laughing at him right now, but *she* didn't know that. Was she really that stupid? Or was there a lot of money in this purse? It felt like it held more than a few coins. He could hear her running behind him, getting close. He had to get away from open ground, into narrower alleys and places with quick turns, even a crowd of people where he could lose her. She was just too fast, like a cat on a mouse, a mouse with no bolt holes. He didn't like being a mouse.

Cindra passed under the high boxes of the grandstand and into the street, where the little thief was heading into a gated plaza. Many of the buildings in the city were arranged in rectangular blocks enclosing a central courtyard, each side having at least one gateway onto the street. The boy was heading into one such enclosure that contained a small temple with a high steeple, topped with a round orb. It was likely a temple of Lieutrella, goddess of the moon and Lady of Secrets. The area ahead was illuminated, but she saw no worshipers around to call out to, no one to stop the thief's progress. Luckily, Cindra was right behind him.

Nixy was jerked back by the neck, a strangled choke escaping his mouth. Cindra had reached out and grabbed his cloak, yanking him off his feet and forcing him to tumble to the ground. He dropped his knife and the stolen purse as Cindra stumbled over his prone form. The impact was harsh on the cobblestones, made more so by the cold, and the two children were stunned for a moment, out of breath and jarred by the fall. Cindra regained herself first and seeing the boy's knife, lunged for it. Nixy rolled onto his back to get out from under her legs when suddenly she was upon him, pressing the cold metal of his own blade at his throat.

"D-don't kill me!" He gasped, realizing that he had not only failed his test, but might die before Dexer ever got his hands on him. The anger in the girl's eyes was not decreasing his fear.

Cindra, panting and furious, leaned in close to further frighten the little thief. She had no desire to kill him, and wondered at herself that she seemed so inclined to act like it. She assumed it was her sense of justice that made her want to scare the boy into an honest life, but there was also a thrill coursing up her spine that felt almost primal and savage. She pushed that feeling aside and focused on the cowering child beneath her.

"I am not going to kill you," she breathed a few times before continuing, "But I want my purse back."

"Oh, this? Sure, here ya go." The boy reached over and retrieved her purse, offering it up to her. The fear in his eyes was rapidly diminishing.

She snatched the purse from him and sought a way to reattach it to her belt, her fingers fumbling in the cold as she tried to keep hold of the knife. Finally she fastened it to her satisfaction and stood, letting the boy up.

"Pestilent little vermin, I should see you whipped!" She rearranged her cloak and skirt, trying to make herself presentable should the city watch arrive.

Nixy was on his feet, looking up at her with his head level to her shoulders. She'd caught him, but he wasn't done with her yet; she still held his knife, his mother's knife. He figured, since she said she wouldn't kill him, it might be all right to try and make conversation.

"You talk kinda funny," he said, still trying to figure out what 'pestilent' might mean. Probably nothing nice.

Cindra was shocked at the impudence of the boy, who was in no position to be cheeky. "I do *not* talk funny," she said, looking down her nose at him, "I'll have you know I speak perfect Calilesh."

"See? Tha's funny." Nixy thought she was a bit snooty for a... whatever she was. Her clothes weren't nice, but weren't shabby either. Maybe she served in a good house? She didn't smell bad, so she must bathe once in a while too.

"So... if ya just gimme my knife back, I'll be going," he started hopefully. She ignored him. "Maybe I can show you around if yer lost. You look lost."

Cindra was looking about, trying to get her bearings. She turned to him and said defensively, "I am *not* lost. Go away before I turn you in."

Nixy remembered his watchers and wondered if he still might save his test. "Ya know there are more out there, and bigger than me. I can guide you so you'll be safe." Cindra started wandering off and he followed, not letting his knife and his grab get away so easily, "There's baggers out there, and cutthroats and slavers," he embellished a bit, "...and ghosts and trolls. You don't wanna be out here alone."

"Are you to be my bodyguard now?" Cindra sniffed at him, beginning to feel weak in the knees from her run and tumble. She wondered where the best place to find a carriage might be, but she wasn't going to lower herself to ask this scamp.

"Naw, I'm just saying, I can keep you out of trouble." Maybe she would give him some coin for being a guide, he thought.

Cindra was having none of it. "Look, you little cutpurse," she said, pointing his knife in his face, "I wasn't in trouble until you came along. Now get yourself lost before I call the city watch!"

Nixy faced her, hands on hips. He was going to get his knife if he had to get her to stick it in him. "Stab me with it if you hafta, but leave me my knife! You got yer stupid purse back."

Cindra opened her mouth to retort, ready to give the boy a lecture he would not soon forget, but the words did not come out. Her voice died in a squeak as a shiver ran down her body, for just behind the boy was a shape moving down the wall of the temple. It was the shape of a man, but it moved with a crab crawl, picking its way down the sheer wall onto the street below. Upon touching the ground, it lurched into the light with twitching, stuttering movements, long bony fingers outstretched and shoulders hunched, like an obscene puppet. He moved too fast.

The man was dressed in rags, filthy and stained, and his dark hair was wild about his head. His black beard was bedraggled and tangled, and his hollow cheeks supported large, staring eyes that seemed to bulge with each raspy breath. His flesh was stretched tight across his bony frame, and was the color of tallow. His feet were bare and clutched the cobblestones with long toenails, and his fingers ended in similar ragged claws. He was boring his eyes into the back of the boy's blond head.

Nixy felt his blood go cold at the look on the girl's face. He was about to glance behind him when a strong, bony hand grabbed his shoulder and claws dug into his skin. The boy let out a scream that died in the air as soon as it left his mouth, and the hand wrenched him around to face his attacker. His worst nightmare was clutching him in an unbreakable grip: Black Will, the one who killed helpless people in the dark of night, the one mothers warned their children about to make them obey. But he was just a story. He wasn't right here, dragging him into a dark alley behind the temple. He was just a story.

The nightmare man spoke in a hoarse, doubled voice, like two people rasping through one throat, "*Need you boy... need your blood, scream won't help.*" He walked backwards into the alley with his lurching gait, dragging the poor doomed child along. Nixy screamed for all he was worth, but Cindra, being mere feet away, could barely hear him. She raised her voice as well, looking around for someone, anyone, who could help. There were shadows of people walking by just outside the courtyard gate, but her voice was useless. All she could do was stand and watch, the knife hanging forgotten in her hand.

"*Need your blood, father's blood, Blood Magic, Blood Magic...*" Black Will rasped.

The knife? She had a knife! She forced her eyes down from the monster man to her shaking hand, where the boy's purse cutter was held. It was sharp and beautiful, with a Shadowood handle carved into a raven's head. The blade was irregular, with a curved, pointed spine and a wicked tip, and the metal looked white in the moonlight. The primal, savage feeling rose within her again, and she resolved not to let this boy be slaughtered before her eyes. She found a well of courage in the pit of her stomach that rose and spread to her arms and legs, giving her strength and motion. Before she could think or plan, she was rushing at the man as he hunched over the terrified child, and with all the strength in her arm, she thrust the blade into the small of his back.

A howl of pain arose in his throat, two voices crying out at once, like a pair of dogs baying at the night. Cindra looked up at the man's head and was horrified, for a shape had leaped from his body as if the knife had driven it out; they were his bones, or the shape of his bones, black and wraithlike, as if they were made of solid smoke. The bones twisted in pain, the eye sockets glowing like furnaces. The black skull turned to grimace at her and then leapt back into the man's body as he spun and caught her by the throat.

When he spoke again, his voices were more distinct; a man's raspy tone, strained by pain and thirst, and a voice from the darkness of the Abyss, torturous to hear, oozing dread.

"Girl... soon dead girl. Girl hurts with pretty knife."

The fiend's talon tightened about her neck, and Cindra felt the blood welling in her head, her ears pounded and her eyes bulged as he threatened to pop her head from her shoulders. In desperation she crossed her knife arm over his wrist, and using her last ounce of strength and breath, slashed the nightmare man across the cheek.

The point cut deeply below his left eye, metal flashing and ringing with the stroke. He released his grip and stumbled back into the boy, who was trapped in the alley. A horrible cry of pain and anguish arose from the man's chest, and the ghastly bones leaped forth again, towering above them all. Within the ribcage was a glow like a distant fire, and where her blade had struck upon the left cheek were plumes of red flame, spewing forth sparks and smoke from the ashen skull. Black Will's cheek bled freely from his damaged flesh, and his lurching movements echoed those of the blackened bones hovering above him.

"Girl cut through flesh! Girl cut... ME!" it cried out, the spectral wound flashing upon its terrible visage. Its furnace eyes glowed with hatred, and Cindra thought, something else. She coughed and gagged as she readied her blade for another attack, when the specter did something she was unprepared for. The bones leaped back into the man's body, and in a blur of speed and inhuman agility, he jumped and spun in midair, clutching the wall and scurrying up to the roof like a frightened lizard; in a moment he was out of sight. The boy shuffled over to her, not taking his eyes from the rooftop. "Is he gone?" he said, now able to speak and be heard.

"I think so," Cindra offered, holding the knife above her like a shield, "I think it got... scared." The idea was preposterous, but she was grateful.

"You saved me. He was gonna kill me, and you saved me." The boy began to cry, and like the frightened child he was but could seldom be, he clung to Cindra and sobbed freely on her dress. She placed her arms uncertainly about him, trying to be of some comfort; though she was at her wit's end herself. It seemed the proper thing to do.

Still, something was not right. She felt hopelessness and fear sinking into her skin, as though this night's actions were all for nothing. The boy would die, despite her heroics, and she would be unable to stop it. The boy felt it too, for he stiffened and his sobbing grew choked, as if waiting for a killing stroke to fall. Cindra had had enough of this.

"I'm going to call the watch, but don't be afraid. Call them with me. Yell as loud as you can." She took him by the hand and they ran towards the nearest gateway, shouting loud enough to wake the dead, not that they would have wished to, for they had enough to worry about.

Above the courtyard, perched on the moon orb atop the temple spire, a shadow hissed in dismay. The cowardly Black Will had fled in pain over the rooftops, leaving Paugh to fend for itself. Leathery skin stretched over bony joints as the horned head peered below. It had sent a pall of despair upon the children to paralyze them, but the girl was braver than most.

No matter.

If the Guadim had learned anything in its countless years, it was patience. With a sickening pop and creak, it unfolded vast wings of putrid flesh, and leaping from the spire, it began to follow the children as they ran shouting towards the light.

Chapter Three

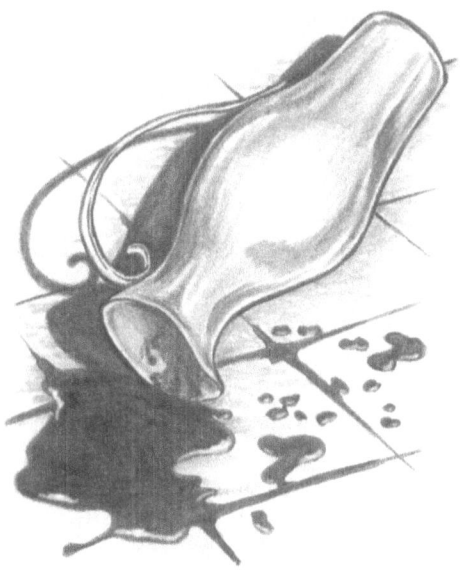

Distractions

"The watch never believes you," said Nixy, looking back through the carriage window at the guardsmen. Cindra had her arms folded over her chest and was pouting, but was happy to be on her way back home. The pair had told their story to the men, leaving out the part about the purse snatching and chase, and bade them to search for a man creeping about the rooftops with his skeleton popping out occasionally. The guards had not been amused or inclined to help, but they did get the children a carriage to take them home. That was something, at least.

The ride was taking them past the temple of Obamir, with its tall relief sculptures of toil and reward, and the offerings laid about the temple doors. Cindra said a silent prayer of thanks, for she had received more than her share of good fortune this night, and wondered if there was a tradeoff to be made somewhere. Luck, prosperity and benevolence were the coins of Obamir, and few people had all three in any abundance. Perhaps she had paid for her luck by losing the good will of others. Did this mean she'd be caught and punished? Not if she could help it.

"So, what do I call ya?" said the boy, fidgeting in his seat. He had never ridden in a carriage, and was unsure how to conduct himself.

"La-, Cindra. You may call me Cindra." She had almost used her honorific title of 'Lady', but decided that she would maintain her disguise for now. "And you are?" she asked.

"Nixyalderthor DuQuayne, Prince of Portshia!" It was a mouthful, and Cindra was glad she had kept the 'Lady' to herself; it seemed the carriage was becoming crowded with nobility all of a sudden. She recognized the given name as Old Norsican, roughly meaning "Elder Fairy Gift," but his surname was Aurilonian, from the southeast across the Great Bay.

Taking her pause as confusion, Nixy said, "I ain't really a prince, ya know. My dad always said, 'Grand deeds needs a grand name,' so I got one. Don't know what he expected for me though."

"Where is your father now?" If she could drop him off at home things would be much easier.

"I suppose he's home at the farm in Syngmore, up north." He fidgeted a bit more, "When I left, uh, I walked fer days, until a red hat, one o' the Obamitte priests, picked me up. I rode on his wagon all the way here and he talked about how Obamir made Portshia rich. When we got to the city, he even blessed me, but said it wasn't a strong one 'cause it was free."

Cindra nodded, "The Obamittes like their donations. How does that one go? 'May you not die in debt?'"

"Yeah, tha's the one," said Nixy.

"How long ago was this?" asked Cindra.

Nixy thought and answered, "Oh, 'bout two winters past, when I was... eight, I think? I started beggin' over at the cathedral, and then I got a proper job as a runner. But the man who gave me stuff to deliver would hit me if I were late or slow. So I ran off fer good. Then I got a job in a stable, brushin' horses. I love horses. They don' care where you came from, just like dogs."

Cindra couldn't believe the things this ten year old had done in his short life. He had traveled across the province and worked for his food, and this was *her* first night out alone.

"When did you start to steal?" She asked, feeling the raven head of the boy's knife that was secured in her belt.

Nixy looked down at his hands in his lap and mumbled an answer, "I met some lads... they said they thought I'd be good at pinching and they was right. So I took up with them and their boss. Now they'll be missing me, but I won't miss them much." He looked up hopefully at Cindra. "Where're we going?" He asked.

Cindra was torn, for she couldn't take the boy home and his only family in town was a pack of thieves; besides, there was a monster after him. She decided that they would both be safe in the castle, but that meant explaining his presence to her father in the morning. "We're going someplace safe," was all she said, and Nixy relaxed in his seat.

The carriage rolled along as Cindra tried to concoct a likely story for the boy, one that left her blameless. Perhaps she could say that Mineth found him while on an errand for her? Claiming divine providence would not work again she was sure, since she had tried that once after the cannon incident, and was paddled for blasphemy. *Blame the gods for not speaking to us anymore*, she thought.

There was little trouble getting into the Highcourt and the castle grounds, since carriages were coming and going for the guests, but the main gate was presently closed. The driver pulled around and let the children off, leaving the boy and girl to face the gatekeeper. He was a tall, scar faced man with a stern countenance, and watched them closely.

Nixy had his first look at the castle, and could only stand there agape. The gateway was arched and barred with a heavy wooden gate shod with iron, and the Corrina coat of arms adorned the keystone. Above the portal was a large sky blue banner draped from the central arrow slits, and torches illuminated the upper floor and its watchmen. Twin braziers lit the entrance and kept the gatekeeper warm, and cast him in an imposing light.

"You actually live here?" Nixy asked, following her towards the gate.

"Yes." She said.

"Must be a pain to clean, huh?" He observed.

As if she would know. She said, "I suppose so."

The gatekeeper stood leaning against the wall, halberd within reach. "Where do you two think you're going?" he demanded.

Nixy stepped forward, using his most charming smile. "We are with the cleaning staff, so if..."

Cindra cut him off saying, "Please let us pass. We are here on official party business."

The gatekeeper folded his arms across his chest. "Oh, really now, does the party need beggars that we're taking them off the street?"

Nixy was sure that was meant for him. He was about to say something mean about the man's scar, when Cindra interrupted again. "I am bringing one of the lady's friends from town. Surely she may have her *own* guests for her birthday feast?"

The man was not impressed. "And who might you be?"

Cindra realized that the gate guards might know Mineth, so she took another name. "My name is Loreth, and I am a maidservant of the lady. Mineth is busy, so she sent me instead."

The man reacted, so she decided that name dropping was the key. She just wished she knew the names of more servants. "You may ask Mineth's mother, the chambermaid Vanetha, if she is not too busy seeing to the countess's bath. But please hurry, the lady must be to bed soon, and I'd hate to arrive late with her guest, for she is in a foul mood tonight, but you didn't hear that from me, mind you."

The gatekeeper looked from the girl to the boy and back again, wrestling with his judgment. After a moment, he decided that these two, if lying, could not cause too much trouble. If they were not, he could be in trouble indeed. "Alright, in with you," he said, and opened the smaller sally gate to let them pass.

Once the gate closed behind them, Nixy whispered to his rescuer, "I thought you said your name was Cindra?"

She hissed to him, "It *is*, but don't call me that here. We could get in trouble."

Nixy wondered what Cindra had done wrong, but chose not to ask. He wasn't always proud to let people know his business either. He looked across the round courtyard at the large doors, and tugged Cindra's sleeve. "How are we getting in?"

She thought for a moment, and the smell of food drew her attention. Nixy smelled it too. "We can go in through the kitchen and avoid the departing guests." She headed to the right to a small door under the covered walkway. The kitchen was one of the few basement rooms that led up to the main floor without having to pass a guard post. She pulled the door open and went inside, Nixy in tow.

The aroma of the evening's banquet was overwhelming, and the uneaten remains of several courses were piled up on the tables in the scullery. The kitchen staff was mostly cleaning now, and eating their fill from the leftovers. They saw the picked over trays of cheese, beef and pork, pheasant and goose and honey breads, pastries and pies, fish and eels.

Cindra removed her cloak and wrapped it about the boy's knife; her appetite had returned, and she stopped to pick a bit of meat off a roast. She remembered to offer some to Nixy and as she turned, she saw that he had frozen in place.

Nixy's senses were under a delicious assault. Sitting before him was more food than he had ever seen, and all of it having been brought *back* from the meal, waiting to be finished by the servants lest it spoil. His eyes were as wide as saucers and watered with joy, his nose was tingling with a hundred different aromas and his mouth was dripping like a slavering dog's. His stomach made a loud and obnoxious sound, demanding and deep, but turned up at the end like a plea or question.

Before Cindra could retrieve him, a plump woman in an apron approached her with an ornate serving pitcher wrought of silver, the kind used to serve fine vintage wines. Minerva, if Cindra remembered her name correctly, was a cook mistress. Cindra had made her children part of a few of her more memorable games, for they were always looking for a way to get out of menial work. Now, however, it seemed that Minerva had some menial work that needed doing, and Cindra was right in her path.

"You girl, I don't remember you. What're you doing here?" Minerva squinted at the girl, trying to get a good look in the dim light. Her eyesight was poor, which perhaps explained her association with the squat and lumpish stable master.

Cindra tried to back away, turning her head to avoid being recognized. "I'm... er, I was just going upstairs to help with the cleanup," she lied, wondering where Nixy had disappeared to.

Minerva said, "There's nothing that needs a cleanup anymore, you're late for that missy. But here, you can be a help and take this up to his lordship and the remaining guests. There's a good girl." She pushed the silver pitcher into Cindra's hands, exchanging it for the girl's bundled cloak.

"Remaining guests?" Cindra was alarmed, her back literally against the wall, "But, I thought the banquet was over!"

Minerva was getting annoyed now, for she had no time to argue. "Some of the nobles stayed to talk. Now get up there before I take a switch to you! Go!" She shooed the girl upstairs.

Cindra bit her tongue and chose not to spoil her disguise, for it had gotten her this far. Instead she carried the pitcher up the stairs to the main hall, peeking over the stone railing at the banquet table to see just how much trouble she was in. A line of pages were walking past her, carrying trays laden with picked-over scraps, so she was unable to pass her burden on to one of them.

She slowly walked to the table with her head bowed, hoping her father was intoxicated enough for her to go unnoticed, for he liked the sound of his own voice more than usual after he had imbibed a good amount of mead. She walked to the young knight Sir Jaron, who was seated farthest from her father and began to pour.

This got the young man's attention, and he turned to look at her in surprise. As their eyes met, his mouth opened as if to say 'My lady!' or some other such disastrous exclamation.

Cindra gave him a pleading look and shook her head, glancing at her father. Sir Jaron recovered himself in time, and his expression turned puzzled, then amused, and he assumed she was playing at some game. He then corrected the breach of custom that took his attention in the first place, whispering, "The count is served first, then the peers by rank."

Cindra pulled back the pitcher, cursing herself for not recalling something she saw on a regular basis, but then, she never had to pour drinks at the table.

She edged around the table towards her father, but tried to keep out of his line of sight, not an easy thing to do at a round table. During the meal, drinks were poured from the open center, but with so few diners at table, she figured she could pour from behind them easily enough. Currently her father was going on about the state of the world, and sharing his theories of statecraft. This was a topic surely saved for when the common guests had departed.

"...The old ways are fading and the king knows it, as I am sure you all do." He was saying, toying with his goblet while he spoke. "The guilds are becoming more prolific and their wealth and political power is formidable. Soon, they may displace the noble class entirely."

Constable Fingelm, a peer in the family's service, spoke, "But how are we to maintain control when commoners have so much power, milord?"

Needing no excuse to continue his lecture, the count said, "The commoners *are* the power. They always have been though they do not realize it. Keeping them content and distracted is the key to control, and that is where the nobility comes in."

Cindra tried to disguise her voice, making it deeper and improvising a servant's manner. She spoke softly, "Wine, milord?"

Her father, thankfully, blathered on without doing more than raising his goblet. "Some of those merchants have greater wealth than we do, and taxes can only be levied so high. So we must work with the guilds and keep them contented, and they will keep the rabble happy."

Lord Clavemont spoke, his pale blue eyes twinkling in the light reflected off his goblet. "Casselvane, is it not strange that the wealthy commoners would keep the poor in line? Are they not an elite class unto themselves, no better than we?" He refused more mead from Cindra with a polite smile, looking her straight in the eye. One of his rank did not do this with servants, and it caught Cindra off guard. Had he recognized her?

The count took a sip and said, "Another illusion! The guildsmen are wealthy and powerful, but they are not *nobles*. Therefore, the common people see them as something to aspire to and so, feel more empowered."

Cindra poured for the constable, who surely would have known her had he looked, and moved on to Sir Fedrick, keeping on his blind side.

The count continued, "The masses can be distracted. Give them festivals, entertainment, trade fairs. The ancient Celvestrians had their arena sports, the Maanok clans make constant war with each other, and the temples do their part as well. Why, even young Sir Jaron provides the service of distracting the masses. His skill at the joust is well known."

Sir Jaron nodded to the count as Cindra poured his wine. He said, "I am honored that I can be of service, milord, but I do find it a bit troubling…"

The count asked, "What is that, Sir Jaron?"

Cindra had finished serving and was about to return to the kitchen to collect Nixy and try another route upstairs, when Jaron answered, "It seems that the act of serving can sometimes include deception." He glanced at the retreating girl, speaking to her back, "From the highest noble to the lowliest serving wench."

Shoulders clenched and hands shuddering at the remark, Cindra dropped the pitcher with a ringing impact that resounded about the hall and beyond. Fine wine sloshed to the floor. Cindra stumbled to recover the pitcher and waited for the nobles to reprimand her clumsiness, exposing her, when a young man's voice shouted from the kitchen stairs. "STOP THIEF!"

Cindra looked up, almost dropping the pitcher again, and she was not sure to be thankful or horrified. Nixy, his arms full of pilfered food, was racing up the steps and across the main hall with two older pages in pursuit. The boy had a bun of honey bread in his mouth and was trailing sausage links behind him and slices of ham were dropping here and there to the delight of a pair of cats who had been dissuaded from begging in the kitchen.

The pages stumblingly halted their pursuit for a moment to bow to the nobles, mumbling apologies, before continuing the chase. Cindra replaced the pitcher on the table and used the spectacle to slip behind her father, who was looking about in confusion. She made good her escape by hurrying in the direction of the chase. Before she knew it, she was out of the main hall and before the grand stair; Nixy was nowhere in sight. She started up the stairs and could hear her father's words from the table beyond the wall.

He was laughing. "It seems the masses have begun the revolt in my own kitchen!" The nobles chuckled merrily, too full of food and drink to pay it any mind. "Now, where was I?"

Sir Jaron smiled, sipping his wine. "I think milord was talking about the value of... distractions."

Cindra ran up the stairs and made her way to her bedchamber, careful to make as little noise as possible as she opened the door. Once inside she quietly closed the door, latched it, and let out a silent laugh at her victory. She removed the kerchief from her hair and bent over to shake out her locks.

The fire was warm and cozy and Mineth was keeping her bed warm. This would be the best sleep she had ever had, for she was returning home after a grand adventure and she would remember it always. She changed into her pelice and went to rouse Mineth who, despite her trepidations, had fallen fast asleep.

She awoke with a start, first unsure of where she was, then in fear that the worst had happened. When her eyes focused on her lady she sat straight up in the bed. "Oh, milady!" She hugged the girl and reprimanded herself, "Forgive me, I must have fallen asleep!"

Cindra was shaking with excitement, her eyes wild and her fists clenched before her, as if to hold the feeling tight and not let go. "I made it Mineth! I made it out of the castle! I rode a carriage all the way to the Market Square and saw people and looked in windows and, and... OH! I saw a real Galindri caravan! With real Galindri! They were magnificent, and they shooed me away, but then... then, I got mugged!"

Mineth was trying to keep up, but heard the last part clearly. "Oh milady! Are you alright?"

Cindra nodded, "Yes, I caught him and made him give it back, and oh, the cook mistress, you know, the one who can hardly see? She has your cloak and the boy's knife. Be sure to get them for me."

"Boy, milady? What boy?" Mineth was confused again.

"The boy who robbed me! Pay attention." Cindra chided her. "Oh, and we were attacked! It was horrible, *horrible*! Nixy, that's the boy, called him Black Will, and he had these claws and ratty hair, and his eyes were bulging out of his skull!" She extended her arms in a pouncing posture, leaning into the poor handmaid and causing her to creep back under the covers. Cindra continued her tale, "And then... his black bones jumped right out of his very skin when I *stabbed* him!"

"Oh milady Cindra!" It was all Mineth could say, for she was as yet unsure if the girl was giving a true account or one of her more colorful versions, but either way, she did not like this story, real *or* imagined.

Cindra started swinging herself around her bedposts, making the curtains sway. "I'll need you to go down to get the cloak and knife, and find the boy too. Some pages were chasing him, but I don't think they caught him. He's a quick one."

"You brought a boy, a thief, into the castle, milady?"

"The thing that attacked us was after *him*," Cindra explained. "When you find him, bring him to one of the guest rooms. He's staying at least for the night."

"How will I know him when I see him, milady?" Mineth said, donning a house robe.

"He's thin, fair-haired, arms and mouth full of food pinched from the kitchen." Cindra said as she put her hair up. "He answers to Nixyalderthor."

Nixyalderthor had lost his pursuers for the moment, but he'd had to run almost the length of the main floor and double back to do it. He was currently hiding under the minstrels' stage, which was shrouded in the shadows of the darkened audience chamber. The older boys were still looking for him, out of breath and sounding none too happy. *If they used their noses instead of their eyes, they might have better luck*, he thought, and chewed a sausage link in silence.

There was another set of footsteps coming from the big staircase, and Nixy wondered if Cindra or Loreth or whatever she wanted to be called, was coming for him at last. As the footsteps reached the base of the stairs and walked towards the darkened chamber, he heard an unfamiliar voice call his name in hushed tones. "Nixyaldrer, Nixyal- oh, phooey, Nixy? Are you there?"

He was about to answer, but the pages came back across the hall, still breathing hard. The blond one asked, "Evening ma'am, did you happen to see a young scamp run past? Arms full o' food he pinched from the kitchen?" The dark haired lad was still panting.

"Er, no," said Mineth, holding her robe closed.

"Well if you see him, give us a shout," said the page.

Mineth looked back towards the laughter coming from the main hall; "Have the guests all left, then? The count is off to bed?"

The pages looked at each other, a bit guilty. "Why, ah. No, ma'am."

Mineth took the blond page by the ear and led him in the right direction saying, "Well then get back to your duties! Off with you!"

The pages made ugly faces at her and scurried back to work, leaving the handmaid standing in the shadows of the audience hall. "Alright," she said to herself, rubbing her temples, "I chased off the hounds, little rabbit. Now come out so I can get some sleep." Did she smell sausages?

"Thanks," said the boy, as he appeared at her elbow. She jumped with a start and almost yelped, for she was sure she was alone. He was thin and blond, and his arms were full of food. "Nixy?" she said, and he nodded.

"Lady Cindra has sent me to collect you. She wishes that you be put up for the night. Follow me, if you please."

"Can I keep the food?" he asked around a mouthful.

Cindra found the boy in one of the guestrooms farthest from her parents' chambers. He was sitting by a fireplace in one of the high-backed chairs, his knees pulled up to his chest. He turned nervously as she came in the door, but smiled once he recognized her.

She was in a fur-lined pelice with a silk dress beneath, and she wore fur and leather slippers. Nixy was prepared for this finery, for Mineth was good enough to explain to him that his former victim and current protector was, in fact, the child of the count of the whole province. He was also told to keep his mouth shut about the whole thing, and that was always the best idea anyway.

Nevertheless, he could not contain a grin as she entered and sat in the opposite chair. "This is a nice castle you have here, yer ladyship," he said.

Cindra looked into the fire and sniffed, "If you say so. I always thought it was very dark and gloomy."

Nixy looked about him and said, "It's a good bit better than other places I've slept," and Cindra had the sense to see his point. Regardless of the décor, she slept with her own fireplace and curtains, and was safe in the high walls. Out in the city, anything could happen.

She leaned forward and spoke in a hushed tone saying, "That... thing that attacked us tonight. We must tell my father about it, or rather, *you* must tell him."

Nixy gaped. "ME?" Then more quietly, "Why me? He's yer father, and he's the count!"

Cindra tried to explain, "I can't tell anyone I was out, or everything will be ruined. We have to have a story to tell him."

Nixy was unconvinced. "Why tell him at all?"

"Because that thing is still out there, and might attack someone else. *Didn't you see what came out of him*, the black bones of smoke and fire? It was a monster, maybe a *demnox*!" she said.

"Don't say that!" Nixy hissed. He knew the stories about the evil spirits of chaos that could possess like-minded people, and he knew they never died. He didn't want to think about that.

Cindra knew the stories too, but was learned enough to know that they were real, and not just fairy-stories made to frighten children. The ancient Norsicans, from whom part of her family line descended, used to invite into themselves spirits of insane bloodlust, to give them advantage in battle.

"It was Black Will, that's what they call him; when kids disappear or they find people torn up by the docks or in the alleys... there's a rhyme they made about him," Nixy began a singsong recounting in a nervous voice.

His will is black,
His hands are red,
Find Black Will and wind up dead.

He paused and made as if to recite more, when Cindra stopped him. "That's all I care to hear," she said, "Anyway, there was some kind of dark magic at work, and my father can call upon the city's wizards to help find him. Surely they will know what to do."

Nixy crossed his legs and looked Cindra in the eye. "I'm not gonna stand in front of the count and lie to him! He'll know, and he'll toss me in a dungeon with... with a dragon!" Thoughts of dungeons and dragons made him tremble.

Cindra frowned, "We don't *have* a dragon."

Nixy threw his hands up. "Still! No one's gonna believe me, no one ever does. Besides, you saved me! Won't he be proud of you? Yer a hero!"

Cindra shook her head, frustrated with the boy's ignorance. "He will hardly be pleased that I left the castle and almost got killed. The whole kingdom is depending on me apparently, and you aren't the young boy I'm supposed to impress."

Nixy had no idea what she meant, but he sulked in his chair until he remembered something else that had been nagging at him. "Did you get my knife? Can I have it back? It was my mother's."

Cindra was happy to change the subject, and reached for a pocket to retrieve the thick cloth she had wrapped the blade in for lack of a proper sheath. She unrolled it and handed the blade to Nixy; handle first, as she had been taught. "Here you are. I had Mineth get it from the kitchen." She sensed the sadness in his voice and asked, "What happened to your mother?"

He took the blade carefully and examined it in the firelight. "She died giving birth. I never knew her, but dad said she was really beautiful, with gold hair and blue eyes. When he talked about her, he'd sometimes get sad or real mad. I think he... blamed me that she died."

Cindra felt little wonder that he had run away as young as he did. She reached out to pat his knee for comfort. "I'm sorry Nixy," she said.

He sniffed, rubbed his nose, and gazed lovingly at his knife again. "Dad said this would be mine when I was old enough, and he used to hide it in the thatch. I snuck it before I left. It was the first thing I ever took without askin'."

Cindra knew it was impolite to pry, but her curiosity was getting the best of her, and Nixy had told her much already, and freely. Besides, he seemed to be aware of very few manners anyway. She asked him, "Nixy, why did you run away from your father?"

Nixy looked into the fire and let his mind drift back to the night he decided to leave. "I got scared of him," he said.

He remembered it had been a hot day, and his father had come home late from the tavern. Nixy had made sure he did his chores and had a bowl of mash waiting, like always, for his dad could get foul if he thought Nixy had been dawdling.

It was dark in the shack's single room, and the mash was fair cold, but Nixy had lit a candle when in came his dad, who sat down to eat it without a word. He ate half the bowl before just sitting there, staring ahead at the chair across the table.

Nixy was waiting for his father to finish with his mash so he could clean up, when his father began to cry. Afraid, Nixy went to him and tried to ask what the matter was, when the man got angry. Nixy smelled the ale and remembered what day it was, and too late, he began to back away. The man grabbed his boy by the shirt and glared in his face. "You!" he shouted. "It's always you! Why did you have to take her?" Nixy knew he had to get away until his father fell asleep or passed out. Today was Nixy's birthday.

His father wasn't through with him though, and he stumbled to the corner where he kept a switch, an arm's length of thin flexible wood. Nixy darted around the table, muttering apologies and pleas, but his father kept coming, holding the stick high. Nixy was in a panic, and he dove for a dark corner to curl in a protective ball. He watched his father through his hands as the man staggered for the boy's corner.

Something was different, for his dad seemed about to panic too. He started shouting Nixy's name and grabbing for him, but Nixy backed farther away, and the man just couldn't reach. His dad's eyes became wild and frenzied, his switch forgotten.

The next thing Nixy knew, he was running through the moonlit field, running for the edge of the woods, where he would sleep until morning. He'd come back and grab his promised knife before leaving, and he'd be off to find a new life.

Cindra watched the emotions play across his face in the firelight, and was resolved to act. She feared her father's wrath, true, but knew that it was born of worry for her safety. She feared her father out of respect, but not for any cruelty beyond tolerance.

She would not run from her father's house as Nixy had done, for she was noble born, and so had responsibilities. One was to her father and his will, and another was to the people who depended on her strength, whatever that might be. Yes, she had triumphed over tremendous odds tonight, and no one was the wiser, but there were more important things at stake than her pride and blamelessness. Nixy needed her to be strong if this monster was to be caught; she would not risk the boy's safety on one of her convoluted stories, which might fail to convince of the danger he was in.

She stood from her chair, her back straight and her head held high in the face of her duty. She gazed into the fire, into her soul, and made the bravest decision of her young life.

"I shall tell mother," she declared.

Chapter Four

Butterflies in Winter

The enemy army stood defiantly upon the western bank, their jeers and battle cries making the blood of the defenders boil. Something had to be done and soon, or all might be lost as the city fell. It was left to the great general and her elite guard to win the day. There were spies about that would alert the enemy if they weren't careful, but the general had a cunning plan.

Cindra led the children all about the bailey, secretly gathering what they needed for the attack. The servant children were her most trusted allies, for they knew that they could get into no real trouble if they were with her, just following her orders. For her part, General Cindra answered to a higher authority than mortal man, for she had received her orders from the god of war Himself. At least that would be her story. The army of bedraggled youths made their way, parade-like, into the western cannon wall.

The outer walls were reinforced against cannon fire but also housed mighty cannons themselves, which could be prepared to fire under any weather conditions, as the battlements sheltered them from above. The sentries had been lulled into carelessness, for Cindra had led the children around chanting and marching until the guards paid them no mind. Now they carried precious cargo: a powder charge from the armory. They toiled now at the ropes and pulleys to draw the loaded weapon forward into the rounded opening in the outer wall. Chanting and yelling covered the sounds of the effort.

The general led her troops out of the wall passage and up the steps to the battlements. Now was the time to raise the siege and let the enemy know that they were doomed. General Cindra stood behind her troops, now arrayed in a volley line across the battlements. The two nearby sentries, spies for sure, looked at each other in amusement at the innocent play of children. The general raised her legendary sword, still bearing a leaf or two, and shouted to her troops, "Let's give them a volley! Draw..." The children raised their arms and pulled imaginary bows, aiming at the phantom army. Cindra cried, "Loose!" and the arrows flew, blotting out the sun, or would have had they been real. She surveyed the enemy army, frowning as they raised their shields and deflected the attack.

"Did we get them?" asked one brave soldier, the young son of the pole turner.

"No, they evaded our arrows!" cried the general, and the troops groaned in despair. The general had no option; she would have to unleash the fury of the gods upon the invaders. "Prepare to give fire!" She shouted over the battlement wall to her most trusted soldier, the eldest of the miller's five children. She could smell the cannon fuse.

The sentries could smell it too and looked at one another in mild alarm, their eyes going to the general as she again raised her sword.

"FIRE!" she cried, and a moment later the bailey shook with a deep BOOM! The general watched eagerly as the ball flew to the west bank of the channel, smashing a tree into bits and terrifying birds out of their rest. As her soldiers cheered, she heard another noise, and looked behind to her father's castle. It was ablaze, and the walls crumbled into heaps of blackened stone. The outer wall was falling, and the grand homes in the Highcourt were ignited like kindling. The towers of the city and the twelve spires of the cathedral were collapsing as well, as the sound reverberated across the landscape. As the heat swept across the bailey, Cindra's heart was racing; what had she done? It was not supposed to be like this!

She awoke on her window bench with a start, the late morning sun shining on her face. Her favorite cat, Rufi, leaped from her lap in dismay and the writing pad slipped from the bench, scattering her parchment. She hated dreams when one's own mind was a betrayer.

It was one month from the day she had awoken and told her mother about her 'indiscretion' in town and the attack on the child. The countess had responded with soft fury, and once she had regained herself and met the boy Cindra had saved, she had taken the report to the count. Cindra had endured a cannon roar of curses and recriminations, and even the threat of a whipping, but the pleas of her young houseguest saved her. Instead, she had been banished to her bedchamber for an entire month, with only her handmaid and whatever cat could sneak in for company.

She reached down and gathered up the parchments and padded writing board, arranging them on her lap. She had been writing a poem to commemorate her imprisonment, and now gave it a reading.

Young Lady Cindra of the House of Corrina
Had escaped from her father's keep.

She sought to enjoy an adventure in town,
And got herself in too deep.
Young Lady Cindra of the House of Corrina
Had saved a young boy from his doom.
Her mother she told, but her father did scold,
And had her confined to her room.

It was not a masterpiece, but few of her poems were. They were a means of expression that she cherished, for they helped her work out her innermost problems and recorded her state of mind. Such a thing was helpful to review from time to time, as milestones of mental and emotional progress. She hoped she would look back on this and laugh one day, but doubted it.

Mineth was at the sewing table, mending a skirt and humming a morning song. She had been Cindra's only companion (that could speak) and they had maintained a truce for the last week. The lady's complaining about the injustice of her sentence had finally grated on the nerves of the handmaid, and there had been a number of arguments. Cindra had not imagined her father could be so pitiless in restricting the freedom she cherished, and Mineth continually reminded her that she had gone much farther than he had ever imagined she would on her 'adventure,' and perhaps a severe punishment was just the thing she needed, begging her lady's pardon. Mineth had settled the arguments by making the girl realize how much she had worried her, and how she would have died of grief if something had happened to her lady. Cindra had actually apologized to her handmaid, which was a rarity.

Now the girl put away her writing set in the compartment under the window bench, and began to pace her room, awaiting a visit from her jailers. She had read every book and scroll in her possession, and had used up much of her ink on letters and poems. She only had the view out the window from which she could watch the other children play and the castle carpenters go about their duties.

To lighten her mood, she had Mineth hang up a tapestry Cindra had received as a token from the Trade Guild chairman for her birthday. It was a lovely piece depicting ponies prancing about in open fields, and flowers growing wild for them to feast on. It was bordered by a pattern of twisting knots that she followed with her finger to pass away the hours. She loved horses, but did not believe she would ever be allowed to ride one unless her future husband allowed it.

There was a knock at the door of her bower, and Mineth hurried off to answer, seeing the look of anticipation on the girl's face. She returned through the curtains from the bedchamber, holding them open for the countess. "I have come to see the prisoner. Have I found the dungeons?" the tall noblewoman asked.

"Yes, mother. We have banished the mold and rats and hung up curtains," Cindra said in good humor, curtsying to her mother. Rufi jumped on the sewing table to greet the countess in his cat-like manner.

Cindra waited for her mother to say the words, 'You are free,' but they did not come. Instead her mother began patting the cat and scratching behind his ears, as Rufi purred with pleasure. "I have come to discuss the terms of your release."

Cindra felt a quiver in her stomach and said "Terms?" She was afraid to ask.

Her mother said, "You thought your father would release you without securing a promise from you? He would have you swear to take great care in all your choices, and to abandon your foolish 'adventures.' Also, he will have you assigned a bodyguard to watch you wherever you will go. In return," she paused, stroking the cat's back, "you may go into the city if you wish, so long as you behave as suits your station."

Cindra blinked and took in the meaning of her mother's words. "I-I can go into the city? I can leave the walls of the castle and go into the city?" It was beyond belief. Something must have happened to her father; she was half expecting to be forced to wear a ball and chain.

She looked at Mineth, eyes wide, and saw that the handmaid had heard the same words and was just as shocked as she. How could she refuse? Behave and use better judgment and she could be truly free; at least, as free as one could hope to be, what with an armed man following her around.

Something else occurred to her. "This bodyguard who is to be given such a perilous duty," she began with a hopeful heart, "Is he anyone I've met before?" Thoughts of the handsome Sir Jaron swam in her mind, as they often had the last month. She not only wanted to see him, but also to make him answer for his deplorable lack of discretion while she was trying to sneak past her father at the table. It made her more comfortable to have something to press him about, putting him on the defensive.

The countess said, "Just one of your father's poor knights, chosen for his watchful eye and even temper." The countess scratched the cat under his chin.

Cindra turned her back to her mother to hide her hopes. "And his name?" she asked.

"Ah! Tssk," her mother exclaimed; the cat had decided to bite her finger and run. "Sir Earnold Greenfellow. Do you know of him?" She massaged the punctured finger gently.

Cindra was crestfallen. "Oh... no I don't." she said. She changed the subject, "How is Nixyalderthor, the boy I brought back?"

The countess smiled. "He has spent the entire month in the stables and kennels, working, sleeping, and eating a great deal."

"Good..." Cindra walked to the window and looked out to sea. "What of... Black Will?"

The countess joined her, folding her hands before her. "Your father had the watch search the city for him, looking for anyone with the look and the wound you described, but have found no one so far. However with Divine Alchemy, such a deep cut could have been much mended by now." Assuming any priest had treated such a man, the art of Divine Alchemy could greatly hasten healing. The gods had long since left humans to their own devices, denying them the miraculous powers of old, but had taught their faithful some of the secrets of nature. Healing draughts and oils were a healthy source of income for many faiths.

Cindra thought back to that night, her eyes going blank. "He moved like an animal, and we couldn't cry out. There was some kind of magic there, something more than human."

The countess nodded, "The Casting Guild seems to agree, although they could offer little help. Your father has contacted Master Ildric himself, but the wizard has informed us that telling the evil spirits from the evil men is difficult in a city such as this, especially if they share a body." The wizard Ildric Finnael was the greatest Diviner of the age, so the news did not cheer her.

Cindra examined the extent of her window view saying, "I didn't know he had returned. I can't see the towers or the city, only the lighthouse and ships at sea." She sank onto her bench. "And I have only two more months here before I leave this city, this country, probably forever. I'll never see you again. Or father either."

The countess, who knew exactly how her daughter felt, sat beside her; Mineth sniffled back tears at her lady's words. "Now kitten," the countess said, stroking her daughter's hair, "You may yet visit us, for Rokvynnar is not so very far along the coast. Your duties may allow you time, that is if the duke allows..."

Cindra turned, crying now, "If the dowager duchess allows! She will run the household until he is grown, and he will likely ignore me for the next several years... I hope."

The countess hugged her daughter close, something she only did in times of great trouble. "These things will pass, kitten. When I was wed to the count, I barely spoke a word of Calilesh; and things were so foreign here, so unlike my home."

Cindra sobbed, "What if they are cruel to me? What if they keep me locked up in a tower, or make me scrub the floors all day long? What if they refuse to feed me if I disobey? Who can I turn to if things go wrong? I am afraid, mother."

The countess took her daughter's chin in her hand and raised her head, looking into the girl's eyes. "No one will mistreat you, kitten. You are to be the duchess, mother of the heirs. You may write to us often, or we can even send Gavagul to take messages back and forth, if he is at liberty." Gavagul was House Corrina's Ember Swallow, one of the bizarre creatures that appeared in the Time of Chaos over a millennium ago. Ember Swallows were avian messengers, capable of understanding simple instructions, and delivering messages with great speed and in the voice of the speaker. Gavagul had hatched in Casselvane Keep when Cindra's grandfather was a young man, and the bird showed no signs of slowing down.

The girl took heart from the words, and as her mother wiped her tears away, she asked, "So if they are torturing me, father will send a fleet of ships to raze their castle?"

"I shall see to it myself." said the countess, smiling.

Mineth kneeled at the girl's feet and took her by the hands. "I shall be with you, if you'll have me, milady." She said.

Cindra laughed and said, "Oh, Mineth, I don't know what I'd do without you!"

The countess sat back and favored the two with a shrewd gaze. "At the least, she could help you hatch escape plots."

Cindra had dressed in a shoulderless gown of violet and blue, with her hair braided to the sides and gathered in an ornate hairnet in the back. It would be a bit cold for the fashion, but she wanted the sun to touch her skin today. She followed her mother to the count's private study, where he held appointments with his administrators. As they entered, she prepared for the worst, but the study was unoccupied. Well, almost.

Standing at attention next to the desk was a tall and powerful looking knight, with a dark heavy brow and deep-set gray eyes that scrutinized everything they set upon. His nose was straight and pointed, and hung over his thin, cheerless lips like the beak of a predatory bird. His dark blond hair was braided in a *tipok* knot, with forelocks that sought to cover the nasty scar that marked his left cheek. A small beard adorned his pointed chin, and at his waist he wore an expensive looking sword. The blue and gold beret of a Corrina knight sat upon his head, bearing a large white feather that was perhaps a bit too showy. He bowed as they entered.

The lady and her mother gave a nod to the knight, and Cindra said, "I thought father would meet us here." She looked around the room as if he might be hiding behind the tapestries.

The countess took a seat behind the desk and folded her hands upon the surface, where Cindra had expected her father to be. She gave her daughter a measuring look, losing some of the compassion she had shown earlier. It was her authoritative face and Cindra rarely saw it while her father was in residence. "Mother?" Cindra asked, her confusion growing.

The countess spoke, "The count is not here. He left two weeks ago on his annual visit to the north of the province."

"He's been gone for two weeks?" Cindra felt a spark of anger rising but it was extinguished as the countess raised her eyebrows slightly, brooking no argument.

"He made it clear that your punishment should not be made lighter by his absence, and I agreed. This foolishness you engaged in was far too serious this time."

Cindra lowered her eyes in shame, genuine for the most part. So her mother had held out against her so long? It must have been serious indeed.

"Your father wished for you to be confined until your ship departs, but he relented in time." The countess sat back in the chair. "It was due in no small part to the testimony of our young guest. Nixyalderthor made much of your heroism in the face of grave danger."

Cindra made a little smile, vowing to repay the boy in some small way.

The countess rapped her knuckles on the desk, making the girl jump, "But in the face of grave danger is no place for a count's daughter! You put the fate of the kingdom at grievous risk because of your 'adventures,' and it was a miracle that you made it home at all."

The girl was truly ashamed now, for her mother had fear in her voice as well as anger, and this made it so much worse. Besides, the countess had chosen to berate her in front of a subordinate, and that was never good.

"Before I set you loose upon the city," the countess said, "I shall have assurances that you will behave as a lady of your station, and defer to your bodyguard in all matters of your safety. Swear now to me and so to your father, and you will be freed."

Cindra bowed her head and placed her hands over her heart. Behave. It seemed like such a small price to pay for independence. "I swear to you mother, and so to father, that I shall do so."

The countess smiled and motioned to the knight, who stepped forward with military flare. "I present Sir Earnold Greenfellow, who is to accompany you and keep you out of trouble." The knight took to one knee, bowing deeply.

"Milady, I pledge my life to your safety and honor." He said with great weight.

Cindra looked at the top of his head and waited for him to move, and wondering what was expected of her, mumbled "Well, alrighty then." The knight rose and stood behind her. She again curtseyed to her mother and said, "You have been more than kind, mother. I shall strive to be an obedient daughter." She truly believed the first statement since hearing of her freedom, but had her doubts about her second statement.

"It is all I ask of you, kitten. Remember, bravery and foolhardiness, being strong-willed and being reckless, they are but shades of each other. Be mindful." She rose and straightened her robe.

Cindra said, "I should like to take my leave and visit Nixyalderthor."

"Of course, my dear," said the countess, and Cindra departed, knight in tow.

The girl flowed down the great stair and out into the courtyard, and ran out of the main gate towards the stables along the western wall. Sir Earnold was rushing to keep up, but she had no concern for him within the castle walls. She arrived at the stables and looked among the horses and grooms, searching for a mop of blond hair. "Nixy?" she called.

"Cindra!" came a cry from behind a chestnut pony. Nixy ran out to greet her, arms wide, a groom brush in one hand. He looked well; his cheeks had filled out, and his hair was trimmed close about the ears and back of the head, but still made an unruly mess on top. He wore the hooded tunic and trousers of a groom, and his feet were clad in real shoes, instead of his old swaths of cloth tied at the ankle. He ran into her and hugged her with delight, and that was when the smell hit her.

"OH! Nixy, you need a bath!" Horse smells and child sweat and dirt and gods knew what else surrounded him like an aura. She held him at arm's length and turned her head to gasp a breath of fresh air. "Father says I have you and my mother to thank for my early release, and she tells me you are doing well here with the horses and hounds." She coughed for air.

"Yeah," Nixy agreed, "it's a lot of work, but I love it. Stable master's a bit of a mean cuss though."

Cindra remembered the stable master's temper, but humored the boy. "Oh? How so?" she asked in mock ignorance.

Her answer was forthcoming. "NIXY!" shouted a stocky little potato of a man, dressed in a tunic and leather apron, and wearing trousers and thick boots covered in muck. He stormed out, pointing his finger accusingly. Just the kind of charm Cindra had come to expect from Stable Master Gorin.

"What's all this chatter? What'd I tell you, boy? Yer here ta work, not flap yer jaw." He came right over and tweaked Nixy's ear, making him squeal.

Cindra intervened, saying, "It is my fault, stable master. I came to talk with him."

"Who asked ya?" The little man didn't even look at her, spinning Nixy towards the stables. He was bald on top, but the hair around his dome was long and bound in back, making him look a bit, Cindra thought, like a horse's behind. She frowned as the man continued to berate the boy, who was rubbing his ear in pain. "Yer a bit young to be chatting up the maids, ain't ya boy? The only fillies you need ta worry about gots four hooves, not two. Ha!" He turned to Cindra, pleased with his joke.

She looked him directly in the eye, for they were of a height. "My mother sometimes calls me a kitten, but I've never been called a filly before." The stable master started to make a crude retort, when he saw Sir Earnold stalking up behind the girl, glaring at him. Only then did recognition set in and he began fervently groveling. "F-forgiveness, yer ladyship, I-I'm, I meant no harm." He stammered, his face going red from bowing at such a depth.

"Nixyalderthor is here at my request, so if you can spare him, Master Gorin, I would like for him to give me a tour of the kennels." Cindra was at her most regal, hands folded before her and head held high. The other grooms stopped their labor to watch the spectacle, giggling and tittering among themselves. Master Gorin was at quite a loss, for in another time he might have been whipped or even killed for his impudence. All he could manage was to mutter, "Yes, please, take him yer ladyship." He thought his eyes would pop out onto the ground if he had to keep bowing so low, but he dared not look up.

Cindra turned and flourished her hand saying, "Splendid! Lead the way Master DuQuayne. I shall no doubt see you again, Master Gorin." Nixy took the opportunity to make a very rude face at the bowing man, to the delight of the other grooms. He then led the noble girl and her guard off to the kennels across the bailey. Master Gorin rose with a groan, the blood rushing back into his feet. He turned to the grooms, who were all busy tending the horses. *At least they have the sense to pretend*, thought the miserable man, stalking to the back of the stalls. He determined for the hundredth time to look and think before speaking.

The kennels were the home of the count's enormous hounds, each as tall as Nixy at their shoulders. The boy walked right in amongst them, patting and scratching them roughly, and they licked his face a great deal. Cindra was not overly fond of dogs, for they chased her beloved cats, but she could approach them. Nixy had a very different level of familiarity with them, as if he had raised them himself. *Some people are dog people*, Cindra thought.

"Besides the lovely Master Gorin, how have the others been treating you this last month?" She asked him, standing in the kennel's arched doorway.

Nixy checked their water as he spoke. "Well, the other lads can't believe I was attacked by Black Will, and they wanna see the knife that stuck him, but I won't show it around. They been all right, I suppose. Better than I'm used to."

"My father inquired with the city's wizards, but even Ildric Finnael himself said it would be hard to find Black Will." She didn't want to worry the boy, but had to let him know that people were taking them seriously at least.

"Finnael? Ain't he the one they call *Talon*? Cause of his metal hand?" Nixy clawed the air to demonstrate.

"That would be him. He lives in the Tower of Sight in the Silver District. Lots of pickpockets around there, I hear." She smiled.

Nixy blushed a bit in the shade of the kennel, but declined to comment. Instead, he asked, "What about the other ones, the ones that light the lamps and blow the dung off the streets? They always act so important, they can't help?" Nixy had wanted to be a guild wizard, but found the education was a bit out of his means.

Cindra sighed, "The Casting Guild and the Mystic College are only concerned with making money. They focus on training wizards for trade jobs, not for higher magic. That's what I understand, anyway." She held out her hand for a curious hound to sniff.

Nixy shrugged, "I guess everyone wants into a guild, huh? It's the only way to work in a city like this." He thought back to his failed test, and wondered if he'd ever have to go back to that life again.

Cindra nodded, "There's a guild for every trade, and their envoys get together and meet with my father every few months to complain."

Nixy looked up, somewhat interested. "Complain about what?"

Cindra said, "I'm not really sure. Father just said they complain a lot. I'm never allowed to attend the meetings."

Nixy blinked and asked, "Cause yer a girl?"

Cindra nodded, wondering how this boy could be so annoyingly insightful sometimes. She turned away from the kennels and looked out into the sunlit bailey. There was so much she wanted to know just for the sake of knowing. Maybe it was because she wasn't supposed to, the lure of forbidden knowledge impossible to resist. Maybe it was because she wanted her father's approval, and he was robbed of a male heir. Maybe she just hated her lot in life. Cindra had long wondered if there was some magic that could change her sex, making her a beloved son instead of a devoted daughter. It was a fantasy. Even if such a power existed, it would have had to be used at her birth, before anyone was the wiser. The other option was even more fantastic: if she could not change herself, she would have to change the world. *Simple*, she scoffed.

Well, she thought, *if I cannot change the world, I may as well enjoy what I can.* She turned to Sir Earnold, who was standing back at a respectful distance. "Sir Earnold, I should like you to see that Nixy is excused from Master Gorin's gentle voice for the day. We are going into the city!" Nixy leaped to his feet, and Cindra strode off in excitement, making a list of the necessities for a proper daytrip on her fingers. "We shall need an open carriage to enjoy the sun, and some spending money... and see about a map." Nixy marched happily after her as the knight strode to keep up and listen, "...and snacks, we shall need snacks. Or can we buy snacks? Yes, lets. And find out if we can get a peek into the wizard towers, and... and..." She spun on Nixy, wiping the smug expression from his face as the knight called for the stable master. "And see that Nixy here gets a *bath*!" she shouted with glee. The boy blanched in betrayal.

One of the white, elegant open carriages was prepared for the excursion, a horse was hitched, a teamster was summoned, and the boy was bathed. Cindra was helped into the fine conveyance and took a seat, cushy and comfortable, made for luxury. Metal suspension bars underneath caused the cab to creak and tip as she shifted her weight, but the overall effect was a ride free of the jarring bumps and ignoble rattling about one could expect in a simple cart. Nixy hopped in next to her, and Sir Earnold mounted his own horse to follow behind.

The driver guided the carriage out of the courtyard and past the villas of the Highcourt, heading for the heart of the city. The fine houses were an assortment of architectural styles, built to the tastes and means of the wealthy owners, although many were only occupied in the winter. The king himself had a palatial dwelling in the city for the colder months, far from the royal seat in the northwest.

The carriage left the Highcourt Gate and crossed the bridge to the Lowcourt, where many of the wealthier merchants and tradesmen lived apart from the bustling market. The sun was warm and the winds were cool and bracing and smelled of the sea. It had been a dry winter and there was very little snow upon the distant peaks, and the rivers were running lower and the canals had a bit more of a stink about them, but nothing dampened the joy of the day. Cindra took in the busy people going about their lives, working, buying, selling and talking. She had spent much of her time in isolation thinking about her one night of true freedom, and the thrill she felt as she rode into the night, and she had remembered the travel song that had eluded her before.

Wheels roll, horse to pull me,
Sun is high, wind to cool me,
See the road out before me,
Travel far, roll and soothe me.

Roll and away, roll away with me,
Watch as the road rolls out before you,
We'll see together what one would never see,
With the turning of the wheels, every turn is new.

Wheels roll, now I find you,
Come along, I won't mind you,
See the way out before you,
Travel far to unbind you.

Wheels roll, tree to shade us,
Dine on the wine and cakes I've made us,
Soon it's time to look behind us,
Turning back, our joy delayed us...

She hummed the tune as they rolled through town, drawing an inquisitive glance or two from the street's onlookers. Cindra admitted that she and Nixy made an odd pair, as he was dressed in a clean groom's woolen tunic and her in simple finery. It didn't hurt to have some attention, and she found Nixy waving to some of the more curious striders.

70

The route she had chosen would take them past many of the places in town she longed to see beginning with the Lowcourt, also called the copper district, so named for the copper-covered Tower of the Silver Moon.

The greenish patina of the tower starkly contrasted the terra cotta rooftops of the tan and ochre buildings surrounding it. The copper orb shone brightly in the sun, being the only part of the exterior protected from the effects of age. Whether it was kept so by some spell, or by constant polishing, Cindra had no idea, but the dizzying height made her guess the former.

As she and Nixy watched, a family of pigeons roosting on the first tier of the structure was scattered by a Dweedragon, long of neck and tail, with bat-like wings as wide as an eagle's. Dweedragons were among the few remaining kin of the ancient dragons who once ruled over the entire world. Legends told of a Great Sleep that overcame them; whether this was a true sleep or a euphemism for death, none could tell. Cindra had no idea any lived in Portshia.

The wizards of the Order of Astrellaris were gathered in a rare session to discuss matters of great import, so the tower was not available for a tour. Nevertheless, Cindra had the carriage circle its base a few times, just in case there was something interesting to see. Gatherings of wizards were boring it seemed, at least from the outside. Finding nothing overtly magical to gawk at, Cindra ordered the teamster to drive on.

The carriage rolled over one of the many bridges to the Gates District, where they would pass the Grand Portshia Theater. The structure was commissioned by her great-great grandfather, Mathas Corrina, when plays surpassed arena sports in popularity. The round, domed playhouse was a symbol of culture and enlightened civilization, shunning the bloody games of the old empire.

These days it was more likely to present bawdy comedies and scandalous tragedies of questionable taste. Rarely was something exceptional seen there, if the vocal patrons and critics were to be believed. It was closed this early in the day, but perhaps later they might tread upon the stage.

The carriage turned onto the northwestern end of the Temple Walk and headed to the left around the massive cathedral and its surrounding temples. This road was the most beautiful and thriving of all the streets of the city, lined with trees, evergreen bushes and lush lawns.

Not so impressive in the winter, Cindra thought.

But the temples made up for the lack of greenery by their stunning architecture. Celvestrian-style pillars supported domed or angular roofs, and fantastical relief sculptures depicted the god or goddess to whom the temple was devoted. Seven temples in all surrounded the walk, along with their more contemporary dormitories and utility buildings.

Also along the Temple Walk was the tower of the Mystic College, home of the guild-sanctioned wizard school. There were less than a hundred students at any given time, magic being an expensive endeavor even for most noble families. Most of the major cities in the kingdom had a branch of the Mystic College, though Portshia had one of the largest in Calilon. The tower itself was unimpressive; neither being great in height or outstanding in form, but the roof was crowned with a large statue of a dragon clutching a golden rod, the symbol of the college's authority.

In the heart of the city was the Cathedral of Twelve, the temple seat of Casselvane. Devoted to twelve of the gods and goddesses revered in the city, the cathedral was a tall, vast space of arched majesty supported by twelve towers and their flying buttresses, the two largest and thickest towers at the front.

The face of the building was adorned with great relief statues of the deities, and near life-sized statues of kings and prophets of old lined the rooftop and tips of each tower. A semi-circular stair led to the large doors, which were recessed in an elaborate stone arch. Beggars sat upon the stairs, begging alms from the passing parishioners.

Cindra had been inside the cathedral, but did not long to return. Her family's private services and devotions were held within the castle's chapel. The last time she had set foot inside the cathedral, her brother was being mourned by the city; the time before that, he was being named and blessed by the archbishop.

The way before the cathedral was the open expanse of the Market Square and the temple of Obamir standing across from it. Cindra had last been here a month ago and at night, but the difference was profound. The square was now a sea of people, moving in little tides and currents, driven by the winds of commerce.

This was Nixy's element, and he would have been relaxed but for his unusual position in the carriage. He found himself picking marks out of habit, noticing who had their hand on their purse and whom the sights and sounds were driving to distraction. He felt strangely exposed, sitting in an open carriage and seated above the heads of most of the shoppers. He was used to being short and beneath notice.

Cindra was eager to get out and enter the throng, but Sir Earnold intervened. "I could not protect you in such a crowd, if someone were to wish you harm," he said from the saddle of his horse. She grudgingly agreed, remembering her father's wish that she listen to the hawkish man when it came to matters of her safety. Instead, she asked the driver to pull over near the line of street vendors selling food.

Once Sir Earnold had made sure the common folk had temporarily relinquished their place in line, the mismatched pair stepped off the carriage and Cindra bought them each a hot portion of stew, served in a large hollowed bowl of bread. They then sat in the carriage and ate greedily with their fingers, bowl and all.

A thought occurred to Cindra as she wiped her fingers on a kerchief. "Driver, is there an entertainment in the

Commons today?" She knew it was nearby, for she had chased her purse that way.

The driver turned and said, "Might be, yer ladyship. There's preparation for the festival."

Cindra perked up and spun on Nixy. "I forgot! The Festival of Devotion! It's one of Selvina's holy days, when couples have their engagements blessed or get married." Her eyes took on a dreamy haze as she looked towards the spires of the Winter Palace that loomed over the tournament field.

Nixy was unimpressed. "Bleah, that's girl stuff. What's ta practice? Kissing?" He made a face at the notion.

The driver turned to him and replied, "No young master, there's a jousting tournament on festival day!"

Cindra made up her mind then and there, remembering something she overheard about a particular young knight...

"Let us go there, then! We will see the jousting practice." She sat back in her seat, smiling to herself.

"Milady," said Sir Earnold, forcing a grim smile upon his lips that was not reflected in his eyes, "It may not be the safest place to be, for jousting is a dangerous sport."

Cindra looked at him with raised brows; she was having none of it. "We are going to watch, not to joust, Sir Earnold." And with that, the carriage moved through the crowd.

Up ahead was a crowd of people gathered around an animal seller from a far off land, possibly Rasha by the man's wrapped head and strange voluminous silk jacket and trousers. He was holding the reigns of a creature Cindra had only read about; it was a tall, two-legged beast with a large hooked beak and eagle-like eyes. A feathered crest topped its head and short, thick tail, and it had grasping arms that ended in talons. The creature had pebbly skin that was colored in stripes yellow and green, with red legs and a blue head. It made a bizarre cry, a throaty warble backed with a high pitched whistle, making the crowd flinch back and widen the circle about the animal.

Cindra turned to admire the creature as the carriage rolled by. "A moku!" she said, recalling her lessons. "They ride them in the deserts and jungles of greater Gozhia, and Hibland too." She was practically hanging over the back of her seat now.

Nixy had seen one before, and it made him uneasy. Instead he looked ahead to the street, where his eyes set upon a familiar face; one he didn't want to see. Daymi, a youth of about sixteen, with dark curly hair and a natural sneer, was staring right at him in shock. He reached next to him and hit the arm of another boy, about the same age, getting his attention. A greasy head of stringy hair turned and revealed a rat-like face with a bruised eye and cheek. Cricket stopped picking his lip and chirped in amazement.

As the carriage rolled by, the boys took in the situation and decided now was not the time for a reunion; instead, Daymi sneered and made a subtle gesture, opening his left eye slightly with two fingers. Nixy shuddered and desperately searched for something else to look at. It was a code: *Dexer's looking for you, and you're in trouble.*

Cindra turned back to Nixy and saw the frightened look on his face, and nudged him saying, "It's not so scary, just a big bird-lizard." She then settled in to enjoy the ride up the street to the fairgrounds. Nixy kept silent.

The fairground was abuzz with activity. Carpenters were constructing little chapels for the blessing ceremonies as Selvinian priestesses supervised. Some of the market's traveling food vendors had come to sell to the spectators who were gathered to watch the jousting practice; knights rode by with lance and shield, striking at targets held by their pages. There were a disproportionate number of young women about, and most of them were seated in the stands beneath the shade of the high boxes. The Winter Palace, white and gleaming in the high morning sun, loomed over the proceedings, its row of evergreens adding height to the outer wall.

At least a dozen knights were about the field, all preparing their equipment and supervising their servants with their duties. There were coarse jokes being traded, and ale being consumed, but all were here to check out the competition and potential trophies, for the old custom of winner-take-all was still observed at such an event, and a defeated knight might be ransomed by the victor, or have his horse and armor taken as prize.

Sir Jaron Dunlorden was currently making a run against a series of wicker rings held high by six young lads standing but a few gallops apart. He called out with a "Hey!" as he speared each ring successfully, and then wheeled his horse around in a leisurely trot. He tossed his lance to one of the boys and returned for a fresh one.

Cindra and Nixy had departed the carriage and were making their way for the field, when Sir Earnold came to her side, firm resolve in his voice.

"Milady," he said, "This place is unsafe."

"That is Sir Jaron, is it not?" she asked, ignoring his warning.

"*Dunlorden*, yes." His voice held a sneer that drew Cindra's attention.

"You don't seem to approve of him, Sir Earnold." She said, looking up at him for an explanation.

"He is not the sort your ladyship should be associating with. He's naught but trouble." The knight's brow drew together as he watched the jousting practice.

"Will you be jousting in the tournament, Sir Earnold?" Cindra asked, knowing the answer already.

"No milady," said the dour knight, "I have other duties from now until your ladyship leaves for Rokvynnar."

"Ah, that's right," she said, pretending to remember. Then, she added, "You're supposed to keep me out of trouble!" And with that she ran to the railings and called out to Sir Jaron as he rode by. Greenfellow was aghast, and strode forward in checked anger.

Jaron heard his name and turned, and upon seeing Lady Cindra, quickly recovered from his surprise and eagerness. He affected a casual manner and rode his horse to the railings, and many of the gathered women in the stands pouted and folded their arms as his attentions were so rudely taken. He looked down at Cindra and said in a loud voice, "Who is this gentle maid who hails me as if calling for a carriage?"

Cindra was at first put off; then thought '*I can play his game.*' "If you cannot remember *me*, sir knight, than perhaps *you* are beneath my notice as well." She raised her eyebrows in mock offense.

Sir Earnold stood behind her and said, "He *is* beneath your notice, milady. Let us leave this place and be done with him." His hand was resting on the hilt of his sword.

Dunlorden stared at the tall bodyguard "So glad you could join us, Greenfellow. We thought you had forgotten your way here." He dismounted and passed the reigns to a pageboy, who began leading the stallion off the field.

Greenfellow glared back and said in a low voice, "I forget *nothing*, Dunlorden."

Cindra became acutely aware of a deep animosity between the men, and stepped aside to observe them both. Jaron snapped his fingers and said; "Now I remember! You're one of the count's serving girls! Fetch me a drink, wench, and don't drop it this time!"

Cindra was genuinely shocked at his insolence, but was learning his game, and was intent on beating him at it. Sir Earnold, however, was not amused. He lurched forward as if ready to strike the man. "Watch your tongue, Dunlorden! This is the lord count's daughter!"

As if berating a child, Sir Jaron raised a warding hand and said, "Oh peace, Greenfellow. It is a private joke between the lady and I regarding a party to which you were *not* invited."

Cindra turned to put her guard at ease and avoid an argument, saying, "It's all right, Sir Earnold. I can handle myself." She turned back to Jaron to continue their duel. "Sir Jaron, my father should be informed of your appalling lack of manners!"

Jaron straightened and put on a haughty air. "The count retains me for my fighting prowess milady, not my tact."

Cindra placed her hands on her hips and did her best to look down upon the taller man. "A true knight should have prowess and tact, both in equal measure."

Jaron smiled, "Is it better to favor one's strength or strengthen one's favor? Take from my prowess to fill my manners, and I would be meager in both." His eyes were laughing.

Sir Earnold was not laughing. He was standing to the side and glowering at the curious knights, who were distracted from their practice by the scene. Some of the knights of House Corrina, who were either competing or watching the events out of professional interest, were now keeping a close eye on the two known rivals and the storm brewing there.

Cindra was greatly amused at this game, and found the young knight to be a more competent player than she had given him credit for. She giggled at him and said, "You tease me! You are too clever to be a mere brute."

He leaned on the rail, drawing closer. "Ah, but some poor brutes are able to weave charms as strong as any wizard's, milady." He smelled slightly of sweat and leather, a combination Cindra had not, until now, considered pleasant.

She drew back a bit at his boldness and said, "Why, Sir Jaron, do you really imagine that you are *charming* me?" She thought, *let him recover from that.*

Jaron stepped back and bowed his head slightly, not taking his eyes from hers. "I could only hope to, for it would be a fair exchange."

Cindra could not think of a pithy reply, but just stared at him, smiling.

Sir Earnold had had enough. "*Milady,*" he said, a bit too forcefully, "Your father would not wish us to stay overlong."

Jaron, still looking into Cindra's eyes, said loudly, "Surely the lady can decide for herself. Are you a bodyguard or a wet nurse, Greenfellow?" He turned to match the taller man's glare.

Earnold placed himself between his charge and the interloper, putting a finger in the other knight's face. "I'm warning you, Dunlorden..."

Jaron rested his fists on the rail and retorted, "Your warnings have never troubled me, Greenfellow."

Even Nixy, who was watching the horses go by, started to pay attention to the armed men and their raised voices. Cindra was about to try and talk sense into them when a great voice boomed out from behind. "HOLD!" it cried, and everyone in the commons froze for an instant.

Another man, a knight by his blue and gold beret, was crossing the grounds with long strides. He was bear-like, broad of chest and wide of shoulder, and wagged a thick finger at the two men, as if he might separate them by disturbing the air with it. He had blond hair, trimmed and bound in a knight's style, and a full beard, and he wore a short red cape fastened with a chain between two round clasps, bearing the device of a hound's head. His shirt, shoes, and voluminous trousers were deep orange, with black stockings beneath, and he had an elaborate leather vest dyed tan with russet design. A trusty sword hung at his hip.

"What a sight this is!" he bellowed, "Two knight companions about to come to blows, and all in front of the lord count's own daughter!" He stopped before Cindra and bowed, removing his beret.

Jaron gestured to the new arrival saying, "Lady Cindra, allow me to introduce you to my overly punctual comrade-in-arms, Sir Cord Freekirk. Sir Cord, Lady Cindra Corrina."

Cindra gave him a nod, and said, "Sir Cord. Have we met before?"

The knight righted himself and replaced his cap saying, "No, milady. I simply make it a point to know my betters."

Jaron sneered, "Sir Cord knows a great *many* people."

Cord turned to him as if seeing him for the first time. "Do I know *you* sir?" He acted offended.

Cindra watched the banter between the two men and smiled, for she could see that they were good friends who, like many men, showed their affection for one another by way of verbal abuse. She decided she liked the big man, for he had a calming, jovial manner that made one feel at ease. Sir Jaron had been defused almost immediately, leaving only the looming form of her bodyguard.

Sir Cord drew the angry man aside to calmly speak with him, leaving Jaron to apologize to the lady for his poor behavior and continue their conversation, before Cord came back and decided it was over.

Nixy, for his part, went back to watching the horses.

————

There was so much preparation, so much to organize. Reverend Sister Lyneth had been busy all morning, and would be so throughout the week, as the tiny chapels were built and consecrated for the Festival of Devotion. Many couples would either be joined in matrimony, or more often, have their betrothals blessed by the sisterhood in attendance, to be wed in warmer months.

The festival was also a time for reflection, but Lyneth tried to avoid much of that. Her life was devoted to the goddess of love and passion, yet she herself had been bereft of such emotions for a long time. It gave her joy to encourage it in others, yet she had none to share.

Instead, she turned her passions towards her faith and tried to leave her own deficiencies behind. As the holy writings read, 'Be a light to kindle other lights, and share in the light of others. Above all else, know thine own heart and renew thine own soul.' The passages from the Songs of Selvina were a comfort to her when her mind dwelt too long on her loneliness.

She wrapped her deep-hooded cloak more tightly about her, for the traditional dress of the sisterhood was normally an elaborately wrapped sheet of white linen, bound and fastened about the waist and shoulders, but leaving bare the arms and throat. She wondered what her northern sisters wore in the colder climes. The sound of galloping horses and pounding mallets continued, and she cast her large brown eyes at her sandals as she walked about the field.

Suddenly, a fluttering of color dashed before her eyes, and she lifted her head to see two large butterflies flitting before her face. They had golden wings with long tips and red and green patterns on them that almost resembled little flowers as they beat in the cold air.

The beautiful creatures danced with one another as they drifted across the jousting field, drawing the eyes of the priestess to a pair of figures talking by the rail on the opposite end of the field.

Immediately she recognized Sir Jaron, who had been practicing earlier, but as he moved to the side she saw the face of the Lady Cindra herself! How could she not have noticed? She called one of her fellow sisters to her side with a conspiratorial whisper.

"Sister Avyth," she said, motioning with her head to the couple. "Look there. It is the lord count's daughter and young Sir Jaron. Do you remember what I told you about the banquet last month?"

Sister Avyth, a woman of fuller figure and greater years, turned her dark haired head to peer into the distance. "I remember you told me you were there to bless her engagement..." Avyth was perhaps a bit more prudent and practical, thus making her unsuitable for higher rank. Still, she was good council.

Lyneth was not dissuaded. "*And* I told you she fancied the young knight. He seems to feel the same, yes?" She smiled as she watched the young couple talk quietly, ignoring the two arguing knights behind them.

Avyth stepped closer, so not to be overheard, "But Reverend Sister, dare we encourage anything more between them?"

Lyneth bowed her head, letting the deep hood cover her face. "If it is the will of the Goddess. Love and Passion amongst nobility are like butterflies in winter; precious and delicate things that must be treasured while they last, for they don't belong."

The hawk spun lazily over the city spires, enjoying the morning sun as it warmed the air currents. She beat her wings and caught an updraft, letting it give her lift. The open grounds below were good hunting spots, for there were many burrows in the grassy field and nests amongst the trees, and the high spires of the palace made perches for tasty pigeons. It was more difficult to hunt in the city, with the dragon-kin claiming a wide territory between the tall towers. *Things on this side of town taste better anyway*; the hawk consoled herself as she drifted on the ocean breeze.

The beating of tiny wings caught her attention. Few other birds flew this high, and the hawk looked about anxiously for another predator, or perhaps an Ember Swallow, for they loved to taunt larger birds with their speed and smoke trails. Seeing nothing, she continued to listen.

The wing beats were getting closer and faster, if that was possible, and the hawk strained her eyes to find the source. Suddenly from below, two tiny flutters of light went whooshing past at a great speed, climbing towards the morning sky. The hawk was almost tumbled in the wind of their passage, and lost a feather or two to the encounter.

She craned her neck around to see if she had imagined it, for what she saw soaring past was impossible. Just before the luminous creatures disappeared with a crack of the air and a puff of smoke and ash, the hawk confirmed what she had seen. *Strange days*, she thought, *when butterflies act like that*.

Chapter Five

Family Matters

Sir Cord walked across the jousting field, his arm around Sir Jaron's shoulders, leading him away from the count's daughter. Cord Freekirk had fought his greatest battles with his words, and had triumphed again, this time averting a duel between his younger friend and the lad's old archrival. It was all in a day's work.

"Once again, you owe me lad," said the big man. "I came here to arrange an exhibition for the school on festival day, and I find you about to start your own." Sir Cord was the headmaster at Freekirk Academy; his family's fighting school, where warriors trained in the *Daerbrik* style of fencing and shield fighting. Jaron had been one of his finer students.

Jaron was craning his neck around to watch the maiden retreat, and to see if she did the same. Cord shifted his arm from Dunlorden's shoulders to his neck, nudging his head forward in a less than gentle way. "She's far above your station boy. You're out of your depths," Cord poked a warning finger at Jaron's nose.

Jaron said wistfully, "Ah, but to drown in those depths..." He chanced another look back and caught her watching his retreat.

Cord knew how to cool the lad's passions. "I mean it. Even the maiden's droppings outrank you!" He chortled, pleased with the double meaning.

Jaron threw off the larger man's arm, jabbing up with an elbow. "Damn your forked tongue, Freekirk! I get the point!"

"Good," said Cord, giving Jaron a slap on the back as he walked off, "I didn't want to have to get vulgar."

Jaron had little gift for vulgarity, and was at a disadvantage when dueling with a fluent speaker. "You... your mother was a sailor and your father was a mop!" He shouted at the big man's back. Such an insult, clumsy though it was, would have brought death to another man if delivered in true or jest, but Cord held Jaron more like a brother than a student or comrade.

"Aye," Cord said, waving, "And the finest mop in the navy was he! Farewell lad!"

His attack effortlessly deflected, Jaron set to grumbling at his feet as his friend departed. "I'll have you one day, old hound. One day I'll get the last word on you. Dressed like... like a cheap rent boy..."

"Finer than that, I think." The voice was gentle and feminine and came from his shoulder.

Jaron spun and found he was facing a Selvinian sister, a Reverend Sister by the look of the delicate silver circlet at her brow, crafted as intertwining roses. "I, er, I was just..." he stammered, realizing he had been swearing surrounded by priestesses and consecrated shrines.

"Yes, I heard." She smiled and gave him a wry look. "May we talk for a moment?"

Jaron was utterly flustered, but had no means of escape. He was sure this would get back to his father somehow. "Why, uh, of course." He began walking by the Reverend Sister as she adjusted her hood and moved on.

It was a few steps before she spoke again, and when she did, there was no hint of rebuke. "Sir Jaron," she began, "have you ever been lonely?"

"Lonely, Reverend Sister? I suppose so..."

"I mean truly alone, as if no one cared for you or thought of you. So alone that one could stand in a temple full of people and feel invisible, as if not even the gods were watching." She looked to the sky. "I speak of a lack of affection; no one reaches out to you and you fear to reach out to others, unsure of your own worthiness." Her voice quavered in the depths of her hood.

Jaron was uncertain where her thoughts were going. "I must confess I have not felt so, not to such an extent. Why..."

"Lady Cindra," the priestess said suddenly, turning to face him. "She has spent her whole life being sheltered away, and now she faces an uncertain future, far from all she knows and loves." Reverend Sister Lyneth stopped and favored him with her large brown eyes. "Life is but fleeting moments of happiness. Do not be afraid," she placed a hand on his cheek, stroking his beard, "do not be afraid to be her friend. It is what she needs most."

She walked away, leaving the young knight speechless and bewildered. If his heart were true, he would understand and act. The goddess's will be done.

———

Nixy was tagging along behind Cindra and her guard, keeping a distance while she scolded the man. The knight was pulling his horse along as they walked to rejoin the carriage, and Nixy was still wondering what he had missed. Something about the other fellow had set off the bodyguard, but Nixy hadn't been paying attention.

"Really, Sir Earnold, I do not approve of your actions. I can handle myself!" She was saying, sounding angry. The knight was muttering apologies, while trying to look alert and imposing. "Imagine my father's reaction if two of his own knights shed blood over me on my first day out! It would be my last!" She scowled at him before turning back to board the carriage.

If the knight said anything after that, Nixy never knew it. He was grabbed about the arms and waist, a hand clamped over his mouth, and before he could thrash or struggle, he was stuffed through a doorway on the busy street. Few people took notice, for the attackers were boys themselves. It looked to be just fun and games.

The door closed behind him and he was in the dark, the scuffling of footsteps around him. The hand was removed from his mouth and he knew better than to yell for help; keeping quiet was always the best idea anyway. The room was part of a candle shop, and he could just make out the lengths of beeswax drying on the racks, looking almost like swinging bones in the dim light seeping through the shutters. The scent was sweet and cloying, and Nixy had always liked it before, but he had the notion he would never feel the same way about it again. The shop had been closed and deserted in a hurry, for he could still hear the bubbling of the melting pot, could smell the burning firewood. The owners did what they were told, when the right person was doing the telling.

A lamplight approached from the shadows at the back of the shop, and Nixy's eyes fixated on the face it illuminated, pale and skull-like under a wide-brimmed hat. The gaunt man wore a cowl under the hat, which exposed only his face; they said his head was scarred or burned, but Nixy knew of no one who had seen it. A deep maroon cloak draped his shoulders, and he wore a matching vest over a long black robe, which went almost to the floor. Velvet gloves with wide cuffs hid his hands, and a simple knife was worn on his hip. Nixy was sure that there were more knives hidden on the man than he had fingers and toes.

"Dexer!" he choked, looking up at the looming specter. The inevitable moment that had nagged at the back of his mind this last month was here at last.

Dexer placed the lamp on a countertop, and pinned the lad with his gaze, rubbing a gloved fist with the other hand. His heavy-lidded eyes, gray and unfeeling, bulged out under a thin brow bereft of hair. A smile creased his face, like the cracking of ice under foot. "Nixy. Boy. It's so good to see you..." he motioned to the other boys, Daymi and Cricket, his abductors. "We were so worried."

"I-uh, I can explain, Dexer-" Nixy began, desperate to make amends, but Dexer stopped him with a raised finger.

"Oh, let me start." His voice scraped out of his throat and across Nixy's ears, and he closed on the lad slowly, going down on a knee to get face-to-face. "One of my most promising students goes out for his test, his big test, to show me he's ready to be trusted... only to run off with some girl. A girl, and at *your* age!" His face laughed at the notion as he poked the boy's chest, but his eyes remained deadly. "Next thing we know, you and your little friend are hollering for the night watch..." He gripped the boy's collar as Nixy shook his head in denial, "and you ride off in a carriage while the count's *own men* spend the next few weeks looking for... suspicious types." He lifted the boy to his feet with a jerk, murder in his eyes.

"No, it weren't like that!" Nixy stammered, trying not to cry. "She was the mark! I made the grab but she ran me down, and we was attacked by Black Will! She stabs him and we calls the watch to catch *him*! Not ta look for *you*, I *swear*!"

There was a knife at Nixy's face faster than he could see, and his toes went cold. Dexer glared at him and snarled, "Black Will. And my ma's a twelve-titted weasel. Lie to me again, boy..." The blade was pressed cold against his cheek.

87

"She's the Gold Cat's daughter!" Nixy blurted in panic, "I been at the castle fer a month, working for the lord hisself! She's right outside... an' her guard with her."

Dexer paused and spoke to the two older boys, not taking his eyes from Nixy's. "That true, Daymi?"

The curly haired lad folded his arms, and beginning to look worried, said, "Seems might be so, Dexer. The carriage we saw him on is fine enough fer fancies, and she's got one o' the Cat's men with her."

Cricket looked out the store blinds to the street, letting in a shaft of daylight. "They's looking about for him, and the carriage has the Gold Cat's arms on it," Cricket chirped as he peered at the coat of arms emblazoned on the side. "Sword-man's with the girl, getting nervous."

Dexer appraised Nixy with admiration and said, "My my, you know how to pick 'em, boy. How lucky for you, that you fell into such fine company. I'll be telling the Boss what a unique situation we have here, and I'm sure he'll have a thing or two to say."

The Boss. Nixy didn't want to have nothing to do with the Boss. Dexer was bad enough, but when Nixy found out there was one that had say over *him*, Nixy made up his mind never to put himself across the Boss's ear. Now it was too late, and Nixy would be mentioned to the leader of the Circle of Gold, and plans would be made that he was sure he wouldn't like, and he wouldn't be able to say no. This was bad.

"We don't wanna keep the pretty and her sword arm waiting, do we?" said Dexer, brushing the boy's shoulders off and making him look less roughed up. "I'm gonna send you back to the keep, and you'll play nice and pay attention to all you see." He handed Nixy a candle from the rack, "A present for the lady," Dexer said as he smiled like a proud father, waving the boy towards the door. Nixy wasn't sure if this was better than a beating, but made for the door while he had the chance. His hand was on the latch when Dexer hissed, "Nixy! Just remember... who your family is." Nixy nodded as a shiver ran down his spine, and he rushed out into the busy street.

Sir Earnold had stowed Cindra in the carriage and was on his horse, circling the area for the boy. Cindra spotted him coming out of the candle shop and waved, shouting, "Sir Earnold, he's here! Nixy, where were you?" She opened the carriage door and the boy hopped inside as the driver prodded the horse into motion. Earnold rode up beside the carriage, scowling at the troublesome child.

Nixy handed Cindra the candle, almost reluctantly as he explained, "I bought this for you." She took the candle and looked at him in puzzlement.

"We were worried about you Nixy, we thought you might have been in danger," she scolded.

"I was worried too," said Nixy. "Can we just go back now?" He looked pale in the sunlight.

"I suppose so... we've had quite a first day out anyway. Thank you for the gift, but please remember that until we find Black Will, it's not safe for you here." She found herself feeling very protective of the boy, as if he was her responsibility. Cindra thought it was a bit odd, for no one had made Nixy her charge, but she had taken on the duty to mind his safety. She wondered, *perhaps it is part of growing up?* She had a sneaking suspicion that Mineth would know just how she felt, and a bit of guilt nibbled at her for taking her handmaiden's cares lightly.

———

Dexer rarely had such interesting news for the Boss. One of his own protégés, his most promising boy, had managed to find a nest with the count himself. He was a 'man on the inside,' as it were, and that could be useful indeed. He quickened his pace through the courtyards, avoiding the main streets and the day watch.

Daymi and Cricket had been sent back to the Warren to inform the lads that Nixy was on a special job, and not to ask questions. Whether the Boss would make use of the boy in the castle or not, Dexer had to let the others know he was in control. Nixy hadn't escaped or found a better life elsewhere; he was right where Dexer wanted him.

The Warren was a secret hideout in the Silver District, from where the boys could take advantage of the market's traffic and the main avenue traveled by most newcomers to the city. Pickpockets were a common sight, but Dexer's were a well-trained team. They never got caught with the goods, and always came through for him. He made sure they knew the price of failure, and it was a high price indeed.

Dexer was heading elsewhere though, and he needed to take care. It was easy to go about unnoticed as long as you didn't have a sense of style; Dexer did, and cultivated his distinctive presence to strike fear into those who had right or reason to know his name. His clothing was neither rich nor poor, but somewhere in between, like the fashions created and worn by city folk to set themselves apart from their pastoral fellows. The dark colors, cloak, and wide-brimmed hat gave him a menace that reputation alone could not. As he was therefore not beneath notice of wary watchmen, he made a point of taking the indirect route to the nicer side of town.

A winding carriage ride took him around the city and past the temples, by the theater and towards his destination: a large and fashionable household taking up a two-story block and courtyard. Trees and ivy hugged the walls, giving the ivory plaster a cool and comfortable look, and high balconies draped hanging flowers over the street. *The more to make unwelcome entry difficult and noisy,* Dexer thought.

Keeping an eye out of the back to make sure he was not followed, Dexer pulled aside the curtain covering the side window and revealed his face to the guard at the gate. The iron-shod wooden doors swung wide, parting the heraldic device of Serpent and Scales, and the carriage entered the lush courtyard, rolling past pear trees and grape vines, and stopping near the fountain topped with a patina statue of Obamir, pouring endless water from a pitcher. Dexer got out and paid the driver well, and strode into the cool shaded foyer.

Larger than many noble houses in the city, DuShonmaer, *the House of Triumph* in Aurilonian, was a testament to the power of the merchant class. The master of the house, Kobus DuChat, walked in the best of circles, and in the worst as well, Dexer mused. The house he lived in was a fortress and sanctuary, and kept its master's secrets.

The DuChat family had been a modestly wealthy and honorable one, until the young Kobus returned from studies abroad. Tending to his blind and ailing father, the young man took over the family holdings and dealings and tripled them in the space of five years. Upon his father's death, Kobus DuChat ruled a business empire that bridged the Crimson Bay and stretched north into the continent. He was one of the wealthiest commoners in the kingdom and many said that Obamir had showered more than his share of blessings on him, but Dexer knew better. DuChat's house was soaked in blood, and few knew the truth.

Dexer was one of the few. Taken on for his ruthlessness and skill, the gaunt man had served as DuChat's hidden dagger. Through Dexer, DuChat became aware of the Blood Circle and Golden Hammer gangs; the Circle dealt in whores and protection rackets in the Harbor District, and the Hammers worked the Silver District gambling and rolling people for coin. DuChat saw the possibilities and arranged a meeting with the leaders of the gangs, uniting them into a single band of thieves called the Circle of Gold, with DuChat himself as its secret leader. Running a vast business empire together with a deadly and formidable guild of rogues, House DuChat became a force to be reckoned with.

And that wasn't all. Some, who knew the boy who came back a man, had sworn that he had changed too much, that something was too very different about him, not just in character, but in appearance. He never spoke of the scar on his left eyelid, and distanced himself from his boyhood friends. Many of them either took ill and died, or met with a tragic accident. One of them even drowned washing his face in a fountain; no one saw that coming. Well, Dexer might have.

A house servant met Dexer in the foyer and escorted him into the residence, down a pillared hallway adorned with paintings of foreign lands and exotic views. The smell of incense wafted into the hall from a burner set in a small alcove, and glazed arched windows let in the light from the noonday sun. Dexer padded on the imported tile, making as little noise as possible. His nose was twitching and his eyes watering from the overbearing incense, and Dexer wondered what DuChat was trying to cover up. Best not to ask, for Kobus would tell him if he needed to know. Curiosity was a bad trait for a killer.

The servant knocked twice and opened the door when he heard the master bid enter. He let Dexer in without comment or introduction and returned to his duties, his eyes seeming to take in nothing. *A survival trait, no doubt*, thought the gaunt man.

The right wall of the study was shelved in bloodwood, its rich, dark-red finish contrasting with the green paint, and the shelves were decked with books and scrolls, no doubt ledgers and contracts and other legitimate records. The left wall held a collection of prized artwork and crafts from many lands, some with practical value, and some items that Dexer could not begin to identify. Swords, masks, pelts, sculptures, vases, and dozens of other sundry articles were displayed to impress visitors with the extent of DuChat's wealth and reach.

The man himself was standing behind a polished dark wood desk at the end of the study. Above the desk was a portrait of DuChat's late father and above that was a single arched window, glazed and wrought with iron bars in a fan pattern; the light coming in from the street made Dexer squint.

DuChat was studying some sheaves of parchment on the desktop and looked up at Dexer, motioning him forward. He was dressed in a robe and undershirt, but still cut a more elegant figure than Dexer. His black curly hair and trimmed beard were immaculate, despite his dress. "To what do I owe the pleasure, Lintroth?" DuChat asked the gaunt man, using his family name. How he had learned Dexer's real name so many years ago, Dexer had never learned, but it nettled him when it was spoken. "I expect this is not a social visit?" DuChat never let down his social manner, and thus was not as plainspoken as Dexer liked.

Dexer stepped forward, removing his hat and nervously rotating it by the brim as he spoke. "One of my boys, Nixy DuQuayne, has found himself in, ah... an interesting position. It seems he's fallen in with the count's daughter; I'm not sure how, but they have him working in the castle." Dexer watched DuChat as the elegant man straightened his embroidered house robe and went back to his parchments, seemingly uninterested. "I had a talk with him..." Dexer offered quickly, "and he knows not to cross me. I told him to keep his eyes and ears open..."

DuChat looked up and stared at Dexer, his heavy-lidded blue eyes locking with the gaunt man's unfeeling gray. "You have a spy in the count's household? Impressive. I have two myself." He looked bemused at Dexer's expression and reached for a silver snuffbox, releasing the sweet earthy smell as he opened the lid. "If you think he'd serve better slopping out stables for the count instead of earning you a living that is your business. It so happens," he took a snuff into each nostril, working his face to accommodate the sensation, "that I have another job for you, something that involves travel and a spot of intrigue." He replaced the snuffbox on the desk without offering, knowing that his associate didn't appreciate the finer things in life.

Dexer looked almost disappointed at the Boss's lack of interest in his news, but the prospect of a mission brightened him again, and his eyebrows would have risen with curiosity, if he still had them. "Ready as always, Master DuChat," he said and waited.

DuChat sat back in his upholstered chair and ran his fingers through his beard before speaking, "There is a merchant from Minael who has offered to sell me a prized amethyst, one of the largest found. He will take a ship from the port of LuQuivost, across the bay in Aurilon," he regarded his manicured fingers as he continued. "See to it that he is parted from the jewel before he leaves port. Don't kill him if you can help it, but I want that stone here before the end of next month."

Dexer's eyes narrowed, already forming a plan. His talents were wasted governing the Warren and its budding thieves, but since DuChat had consolidated his power, there was little need for truly treacherous work. A caper was just what Dexer had been waiting for, and his pulse quickened. *The day has taken a good turn*, he thought. Nixy wasn't that important after all, and the upcoming voyage would require all of his attention.

Nixy was an important part of the puzzle, Ildric Finnael was sure of it. The wizard studied the scrying crystal, looking for clues in the swirling mists. Solving the puzzle had occupied much of his attention since the count had entreated him shortly after the Lady Cindra's birthday. The noble girl had gotten herself into trouble in the city, a scandal in itself, but she and the child Nixy had encountered something horrible in the wizard's own neighborhood, and it wanted the boy specifically, but why? Ildric had studied the darker creatures of the spirit world, and he had faced many of them before, but few of the monsters of Chaos were so particular with their prey. Demnoxa varied widely in power and temperament, but one terrified victim was just as good as the next. What made this boy special?

The wizard ran his left hand through his receding white mane and then rubbed his eyes wearily. Scrying into the past, present or future was trying at best, but he had been at it for many hours of many days. The children's paths had crossed in the streets of Portshia and it sent ripples across the pond of possibility, leading to many strange futures. Ildric scratched absently at his trimmed white beard, the fingers of his gauntlet-like right hand tapping on the desktop. It had been a long and trying session, and his flesh ached where the metal hand joined his arm.

The ruination of his right hand had been the price of gaining the Eye of Omithys. He looked thoughtfully at his silver replacement. The limb resembled an armored gauntlet, though clawed and talon-like. It began partway below the wrist where it joined the flesh, and was animated by powerful charms to move as he willed. The clever construction allowed for delicate tasks like writing, for Ildric was right handed. Again for time uncounted he chided himself for using this hand to grasp the dangerous magical treasure. Well, there was nothing to be done for it now.

Ildric Finnael continued to study the Eye of Omithys embedded in the palm of the silver hand, surrounded by binding glyphs. This, his greatest treasure, allowed him to extend the range and power of his divinations beyond that of any mortal, perhaps farther than the ancient Ilves, but at a cost: he could see his own death. He knew his destruction would be at the hand of the great adversary to come, and beyond that final battle he had no visions.

But this was not the mission he had been given; he had a monster to find and questions that needed answering. He took a deep breath, inhaling the incense and alchemical mixtures that adorned the shelves of his study. Once again, he would dive into the currents of time and try to glean some wisdom from them. He closed his eyes, and opening his inner eye, placed his silver talon over a crystal orb upon his desk.

He saw the boy's home in the north of the province, saw some of his sad childhood with the simple, broken man who was his father. He even glimpsed the boy's mother, a beauty with fair skin and pale hair, before she succumbed to the rigors of a difficult birth. He saw the lad steal and run, earning a harsh living on the streets. But for all his searching, he found no answers. Perhaps he would have to speak with the lad directly...

"No luck then?" said a high and sleepy voice. Drahnizhlomazhith had arrived perhaps an hour earlier making himself comfortable in one of the cushioned chairs by the fire.

"I'm afraid not," said Ildric, a bit distracted. Drahn, as he liked to be called by those incapable of pronouncing his proper name, was wise and intuitive and an excellent scholar but sadly lacked the ability to entertain himself while others worked.

"I suppose the twail has gone cold by now," Drahn said, stretching and yawning. "It has been mow than a month since the attack." His tongue became even lazier when he was tired, and his speech suffered for it. His meager lips didn't help matters either.

Ildric's frustration began to grow and it carried to his voice. "A month or a year, the time matters not. There are forces at work that are hiding things from my sight. I can see them in the corners of my vision, but when I focus on them, they vanish. A dark shroud is being pulled about this boy, hiding the answers I seek." He sat back in his chair and straightened the folds of his dark robe, absently flicking off the crumbs of his breakfast.

Drahn had been up late practicing his spell weaving, and was anxious to show his mentor what he had learned, but he first had to wait for the wizard to tire of his latest obsession. Divination was a complicated art, and Ildric was a master, but even masters could make a mistake now and again. Drahn sat up and fiddled with his long tail, and looking as sheepish as a Dweedragon could, asked, "Are you sure you are doing it wight?"

Ildric thumped his metal hand on the desktop, making Drahn jump in his chair. "Of course I'm doing it right!"

he said. The wizard grumbled something under his breath.

"Sowwy," Drahn said contritely and he lowered his head. He then offered, "Maybe you'd have better luck focusing on the count's daughter?" He shifted his wings and waited for Ildric's reaction. "Tomowwow, maybe?" he added hopefully.

Ildric sighed and nodded in agreement. It had been a time since he last set his efforts on the noble girl's part in all of this and maybe something had changed.

"I shall have a look now..." the wizard said, and Drahn let out a sad groan, his neck drooping as his cat-sized body slouched in disappointment. His purple scales turned a deep crimson before reverting to their usual color.

Ildric Finnael prepared for another scrying trance, clearing his awareness of any distractions. He structured the framework of the spell in his thoughts and drew upon the magic energies that flowed from the spirit well upon which his tower was built. He then channeled the power into his body and mind, letting it wash over the spell of vision he had prepared, giving it form and purpose. He spoke the words of initiation, "*Thit weviss, aram thimas mevos thimas,*" and opened his inner eye, placing his silver hand over the crystal orb...

Water. Rippling light above and darkness below. Air bubbles. Sinking. The surface was receding as the sunlight cast beams of radiance futilely into the depths. Something was drifting in the sunbeams, flowing to and fro as it seemed to reach for the sky beyond the swelling veil.

Linen and auburn hair.

Chapter Six

The Warrior's Spirit

The Lady Zara Countess Casselvane sat in her day room, doing her needlework and listening to her friend, Reverend Sister Lyneth, read passages from the *Songs of Selvina*. It was her pleasure to have the priestess visit one or two days a week as her duties allowed, and they both enjoyed the gossip and conversation that women of their station had access to.

The countess was a devout Selvinian herself, and deeply believed that one must have passions in life to make everything worthwhile. Romantic love had not entirely escaped her, and she had been fortunate to marry a man she had grown to respect and care for. Such a luxury was rare in noble marriages, where a lady could find herself displaced by a younger or prettier mistress. Depending on the age and manners of her husband, she was often happy to be relieved of the bother so long as she could maintain her station and dignity.

Because paternal bloodlines were more favored, married lords had a freedom to engage in 'affairs of state' that their ladies did not share. Such were the ways of her adopted country.

The countess was also fortunate that her husband was honest and true, and had not indulged in such dalliances. She knew this because she trusted him, and because she had other eyes and ears to keep her informed.

Such precautions were not uncommon in political marriages where an older wife (of perhaps thirty years, like the countess) who had not produced a surviving male heir (again, like the countess) could be annulled and sent packing.

There were times when she was amazed at her husband's devotion, forsaking a chance at a new wife and possible sons, choosing instead to well-marry his daughter and trust in his king to set matters aright in the unforeseen future. It was for these reasons and others that she channeled her own passions into her faith and creative pursuits, instead of risking scandal and shame in amorous affairs of her own.

Besides, Lyneth was able to provide plenty of salacious gossip, so that the countess could live vicariously through the tales of others. It was a guilty pleasure to be sure, but much more diverting than needlework. Lyneth continued their shared favorite passage:

> *Hail the venturous spirit! Hail the seeking heart!*
> *For those who wait in silence know not the joy of song.*
> *Those who suffer in silence know not the comfort of healing.*
> *What famished man seeks not food?*
> *What child does not cry for its mother's arms?*
> *Woe unto those who choose despair over hope,*
> *and seek to extinguish the flame of desire.*
> *For they will walk alone in the dark,*

and their fellows will not see of them.
Be not afraid of the paths ahead,
for every land hath both hills and vales,
every sea hath great waves that will break upon a
shore.
Nothing is without both joys and sorrows,
and every life begins and shall end.
Look you to the times ahead with hope,
for none can see all ends.
Go forth as a ship that follows a star,
trusting it will find its way upon dark and troubled
waters.
Be a light to kindle other lights, and share in the light
of others.
Above all else, know thine own heart and renew thine
own soul.

The countess tried to live her life by such words, filling her soul each day with hope and love anew. Such devotions had become much more important, and more difficult, after the loss of her dear baby boy. Selvina was also the patron of motherhood, and the countess had felt betrayed by the death of her child. She had hidden away all traces of her faith for months, although many remained to haunt her; the rose symbols in the wrought iron windowpanes and stained glass pieces that she had commissioned were by the count's word not to be removed, for the cost was prohibitive.

It was her friendship with Lyneth that had brought her back from the brink. The caring and comforting presence of the priestess, and her sensitivity to the grieving mother's anger at the goddess, had made it possible for Zara to find her own way back over time. She had never really lost her faith; it had just been shaken to the core but made stronger by the ordeal.

Tapestries and icons of the goddess and her blessings once again adorned the day room, and the thoughts of the countess turned to her daughter. Young and vibrant, with her life ahead of her, Lady Cindra was soon to enter a marriage without even the guidance of an older husband. What chance was there for even a taste of true love in such a circumstance?

No doubt the dowager duchess, the widowed mother of Cindra's husband-to-be, would only make things worse. She would want to see grandchildren before she died to insure the progression of the line, making Cindra feel more like a brood mare than a duchess, and her young son would no doubt learn to see his wife in the same way. Boys seldom developed desirable traits like kindness and compassion until well into their teens, if properly guided. It would be a lonely life indeed.

The countess had consulted her friend with her worries when Cindra was confined to her rooms, and the priestess had told her to pray for the child. 'Some things,' she had said, 'were in the hands of the goddess alone.' It was Lyneth's way of saying that fate must intervene, and lately, it seems that it had. A smile formed at the corners of the countess's mouth, and the priestess looked up from her book.

"What seems to have lightened your mood milady?" The reverend sister asked happily, "Surely not my reading."

Zara looked up from her needlework and said, "It seems as though my prayers have been answered."

The priestess raised her eyebrows in question, waiting for the countess to offer more. After a moment, she said, "Well, don't keep me in suspense! What has happened?"

The countess removed a formal letter from her robes and handed it to the priestess. "It is an offer from a young knight, Sir Jaron Dunlorden, to escort my daughter to the theater this evening."

Lyneth looked up from the letter, her brown eyes wide. "Such an audacious request! What prompted him to make such a proposal?" Her thoughts went back to her exchange with Sir Jaron yesterday and she silently praised the goddess.

The countess looked into the priestess's big, innocent-seeming eyes for a moment, but they remained unreadable. "In the letter he states that the lady mentioned to him, upon meeting at the *festival grounds*," the countess indicated, "her desire to see a play, and writes that 'a more prepared excursion would make the amusements of the city more presentable.' What do you think of that?"

Lyneth was impressed. "He is well spoken for a knight, especially one of his breeding. One wonders how long it took him to compose it."

Zara wondered if the priestess was teasing her. "I meant what do you think of the *proposal*? Allowing Cindra to go to the theater in the company of this young man?" Her voice held excitement and caution, for although such a thing was not unheard of it could have unwanted consequences if the public or peerage were to have the wrong impression.

Lyneth seemed to consider for a moment and said, "So long as all is handled well, and proper arrangements are made, it should be harmless enough. They will need a chaperon of course..."

"Of course!" the countess said, acting scandalized that it even needed to be mentioned.

"And it best not be one of my order, for that would truly give the wrong impression." Lyneth smiled at the thought of the uproar it would cause in certain circles.

The countess refused to be baited further. "Mineth is surely up to the task."

Lyneth placed a finger to her chin in thought. "What would the count think of this? After all, he chose her bodyguard with great care, and I do believe that Sir Earnold and Sir Jaron are not fast friends, to be mild about it."

Zara said, "I have heard of the feud between them as well, for it is a family matter as well as a personal one. Sir Earnold may have the evening to himself. As for my husband, he is away to the north to view our holdings and to visit his brother at Syngmore Castle. He may rail about it when he returns."

Lyneth's eyes returned to her holy book. "Do you not fear that something may develop between them?"

The countess folded her hands in her lap and looked at the fruits of her labor: a satisfactory arrangement of roses in needlepoint and a scroll of text from the *Songs of Selvina.*

Above all else, know thine own heart and renew thine own soul.

"I can only hope that she may have a love to take away with her to that far-off land, to give her happy memories and warmth during cold nights. It may be all she ever knows."

———————

Cindra had nothing to wear!

Mineth had pulled out every dress in the wardrobe, and *still* Cindra was at a loss. What color was best for the theater? What will Jaron be wearing? And what about her *hair*? There was more to consider than she imagined, and she almost wished she had declined his offer, in order to give her a week to plan. Now she had... how much time did she have?

"Mineth? What is the time?" Cindra's voice was pinched and frantic.

Mineth looked towards the window to check the shadows in the courtyard. "It's about one in the afternoon, milady. There's plenty of time if you would just pick a dress."

Cindra began her search anew, going to each dress laid out upon table, chair, and bed.

Her mother had delivered the proposal at eleven that morning and Cindra had to have her read it again before she believed it. An engagement at the theater! Dinner in town! It was too much to take in. She had run back to her room with the letter and set Mineth to turn out her closets as Cindra went through scrolls of hairstyle pictures. The afternoon had seen a flurry of fabrics and accessories strewn about, most rejected as either too simple or too fancy.

"What is the play we are seeing, Mineth?" Cindra asked while laying three dresses side by side on the sewing table.

"I think I heard it was to be a foreign play, milady, something from overseas. I hope it's done in Calilesh; I think a chorus is distracting."

"Imagine if they made you read along and follow the words as you watch." Cindra had narrowed her choices down to two dresses

"Oh dear, I'd be happier with a puppet show than that, milady," Mineth shook her head and came over to see the lady's choices. "But I suppose if the costumes are colorful and there's a lot of flash, it would be entertaining enough."

The remainder of the afternoon was spent making a hundred little decisions, each seeming critical to the night's success and the impression the lady sought to make. As Cindra sat at her vanity and her hair was done up in the chosen style, Mineth made clear what was expected of a lady and made sure that Cindra was in full knowledge of the rules and customs of courtship, even though they did not exactly apply to the situation. She was betrothed after all, and Sir Jaron was beneath her station, but the formalities of courtship were meant to preserve the honor of both man and woman in the eyes of the families, the public, and each other. Mineth would be present at all times, and would serve as the social arbitrator, watching the young couple's behavior as they enjoyed themselves in perfect restraint. Cindra grew a bit glum as an evening of thrills and spontaneity was plotted out for her in dull detail.

She had thought it best not to mention to anyone the details of her meeting with Jaron at the fairground. She had made herself quite a fool, and he had made himself an ass, and Sir Earnold was right to be affronted for her sake. There had been no proper introductions; the talk had started loose and familiar, and had grown more unbridled with each turn, dangerous flirtation couched in flowered speech. It was the single most thrilling conversation Cindra had ever had. Her heart had been racing, and at the time she thought it was because of the short sprint to the rail, but it had grown steadily stronger as she had stared into his eyes. Deep eyes the color of rain clouds...

She felt a flush and Mineth stopped her lecture, looking at the maiden's face in the vanity mirror. "Are you not listening, or are my lessons on table manners making you blush so?" The handmaid raised her dark eyebrows in question as Cindra squirmed under her look.

"I was just..." she struggled to change the subject, and instead found a doubt. "Why... why do you think Sir Jaron asked to escort me tonight?" Cindra said to Mineth's reflection.

"Well," Mineth began, uncertain of the lady's mind, "I expect he wishes you to enjoy the finer things in the city, seeing as you may leave the castle."

"But *why*?" Cindra pressed. "I know so little about him, but that he has a quarrel with my bodyguard, and his father was once a commoner."

Mineth continued to set the girl's hair; "What is there to question? He is an attractive young man, and you are a beautiful young lady of high station, betrothed and completely unobtainable. That makes you impossible to resist." She smiled at the jest, but Cindra was not amused.

"But what if his intentions are not honorable?" Cindra protested. "What if he is attending me to torment Sir Earnold? What if he is only looking to impress his fellows? Oh Mineth, what if he doesn't-" she cut herself off.

"Care for you?" Mineth finished her lady's words. "Is that what is troubling you, *fellí*? You want him to care for you?"

Cindra looked down at her hands clenched in her lap. "I... I wouldn't mind so much," she said meekly.

Mineth brought a stool around to sit by the maiden's side, taking her hands to comfort her. "This night will only be enjoyable if you live in the moment. Do not think on his feelings for you or yours for him. Just enjoy each other's company and make the most of it. If his intentions are less than honorable, or if he indeed cares for you, milady, you will learn in time." She primped Cindra's hair as she spoke, "Besides, this is not a courtship, only a diversion to pass the time. It's not as if either of you are free to act on your feelings. It is better to keep them private and enjoy his company for itself. If he feels the same, it is the best you can hope for."

Cindra toyed with a silver hair ornament from the vanity, turning it in her fingers as she moped, "Thank you Mineth, now I shall be miserable."

Mineth sighed saying, "I know it is not what you wish to hear, milady, but it is the truth. Even were you not betrothed, it would be impossible to marry the man, and anything else would just be... scandalous."

Cindra briefly entertained the idea of causing a scandal, but pushed the thought away. It would do her no good to sully her honor or bring wrath upon Sir Jaron, to say nothing of the poor diplomatic message it would send to her husband-to-be. Not that she cared what the boy duke thought, but she had her father to think about, and her mother, and the king, and the stability of the realm... if she could only disregard her *own* desires, she would be happy. Or at least she would be indifferent, blissful and indifferent, rather like a cow.

She suddenly pictured herself standing in a field in an elegant dress, dull-eyed and chewing grass, as dozens of snotty children ran about her feet. She shook her head to drive the vision away and Mineth chided her.

"Oh! Careful of your hair, milady."

———

Jaron had hired an expensive carriage for the evening, with springs for a smooth ride and an extending cover lest it rained. The sky had gone a bit gray as clouds rolled in from the ocean, threatening a light sprinkle. The air was cool but not bitter and the evening would be perfect for the theater, where the bodies of the crowd provided most of the heating.

He tugged at the voluminous shoulders of his velvet jacket, adjusting it for the tenth time that day. He was not used to wearing finery, although he was told it suited him. The green jacket was embroidered with dark ivy patterns and laced in front of a fine linen shirt. The stockings were a little itchy, and the short trousers felt far too roomy for his tastes, but it was the style. His shoes were pointed at the toes, but thankfully the fashion had moved away from toes so long they needed to be hoisted out of the way. A burgundy cape, flared gloves and a beret completed the ensemble, and Jaron had decided against jewelry for fear that it would appear too pretentious. He had nothing impressive after all, and it would only look like he was trying to dress above his means.

He announced himself at the gate of Casselvane Keep and was shown to the entrance, where he was to await the lady at the foot of the grand stairs. He found himself sweating in his garments regardless of the cool weather, and wondered if he was doing the right thing. This was, after all, one of the most socially precarious engagements he had ever entered into.

The priestess of Selvina had asked him to allow himself to be Cindra's friend, and Jaron was sure there was more to her request than she let on. He could not deny that he felt more than affection for the girl, although he was in no position to pursue it. Also if his senses did not deceive him, she beheld him favorably, perhaps more than favorably. The priestess must have seen this, and decided to bring the two of them together, but to what end?

There was nothing unusual about the engagement at least as far as society was concerned. Women of nobility did not always have a husband or male family member to escort them; while an escort was not required of them, it

107

was more seemly. Therefore she might choose a knight or suitable escort from her household to accompany her so that she might have the benefits of chivalrous companionship. That was the thinking of society.

The impolite truth was that such escorts often had the role of lover as well, and society turned a blind eye to these improprieties. Tongues might wag, but there would be little action taken to discourage the affair if they were at least discrete. Husbands often had their mistresses as well, and many noble households maintained a carefully cultivated illusion of fidelity and honor, in spite of reality.

What worried Sir Jaron was that the Selvinians preferred such an arrangement to the alternative of faithful, loveless marriage.

Lady Cindra was not yet wed, but as good as, and Jaron was not a suitable suitor. That left little room for alternatives. Either the priestess had intended for them to spend time together in innocent pleasures, or she was doing the will of her goddess and trying to make them into something more, something that could not be.

All of this had passed through Jaron's mind the night before, yet here he was.

"Lady Cindra Corrina!" announced the door servant, as the lady appeared at the top of the stairs. She descended the north flight and paused at the landing where Jaron was able to take in the results of the lady's efforts.

She was a vision to behold, her face as radiant as the moon, beaming with happiness scarcely contained. Her dark auburn hair shone under the enchanted house lights, and was set up in two full and cascading tails high upon her head, curling at the ends and fixed with gold. A thin golden circlet crossed her brow, and her earlobes sparkled with small diamonds. Her throat was draped with a necklace of her mother's pearls and family seashell emblem. The cut of the neckline was pointed downward slightly and trimmed with gold and silver embroidery, as were the outer sleeves and hem. The dress itself was the blue of the ocean at noon, with a dark navy bodice and yellow trim. Her shoes were deep blue and gold, and peeked out from under her hem as she stepped down the dark wood stairs.

Sir Jaron had scarcely noticed that the lady's handmaid had joined him carrying their evening cloaks.

Jaron bowed low as Cindra reached the foot of the stairs and said, "Milady Cindra. You are a vision of Haven itself." He had used that particular compliment with more than one young woman, but this time he truly meant it.

Cindra gave him a slight curtsey as her cheeks flushed, and she said to him, "Thank you, Sir Jaron. You are looking far better than I have come to expect." She wanted him to know that their game had not ended. She had told Mineth in advance about the opening remark, and the handmaid was suitably inattentive to the girl's poor choice of compliments.

Shocked, Jaron took only a moment to recover and smiled knowingly at the lady. With a chaperon at her side to keep things proper, Cindra had a tactical advantage that he could not hope to overcome. It would be wrong to be brash anyway, so he chose to present himself as an even bigger target. "It was not for your ladyship alone that I am polished so; my horse had refused to let me ride him lest I bathe."

"And have you appeased your horse, sir knight?" Cindra asked.

"He gave me leave to attend you tonight milady."

Mineth smiled at the exchange; Cindra said, "I am glad that you value your horse's opinion so highly," she formally presented her hand for him to take, "and that he deemed you fitting to escort a lady."

"He even picked out my clothes for me." Jaron said impressively.

He was pleased to hear the girl laugh for the first time.

The carriage rolled through town as the sun painted the sky in the rosy hues of dusk. The robed wizards of the Casting Guild could be seen making their rounds through the darkening streets, raising their staves to touch the small hanging orbs of glass found at each street corner. Speaking the words to invoke the light-giving spell, they moved from orb to orb, illuminating the city for the coming night. Brighter than torches or lamps and needing no oil, the 'wizard lamps' would only be extinguished if they were broken and could no longer contain the spell. The radiance endured for twelve hours by design, ensuring that the guild wizards were employed each evening.

Jaron was telling the women of their dinner plans. "We will be taking supper in the finest establishment in Portshia. It is poor and modest without, much like myself," this brought a smile to the lady's face, "but within is a charming feasting hall that serves the most tender meats and baked delicacies you have ever tasted. And the wines, oh the wines..." His eyes closed in remembered pleasure.

Mineth leaned forward, wagging a finger, "I must insist, no wines, at least no more than a glass. A small glass."

Jaron raised his hands in appeasement, saying to Mineth, "My dear lady chaperon, I assure you there will be no overindulging." He turned to Cindra and assured her, "Milady Cindra, your honor and dignity are in good hands. You are under the watchful eye of one of the count's most trusted and vigilant guardians..." he turned back to Mineth saying, "and I shall be here also."

Cindra giggled at Mineth who blushed furiously, smiling in spite of herself.

The Grand Portshia Theater was abuzz with activity as barkers advertised the evening's performance and patrons lined up to gain entry into the large round playhouse. Street sellers had migrated from the Market Square to feed the waiting spectators with a variety of burnt things-on-a-stick and fresh baked goods. Children ran about in the courtyard surrounding the building, playing games that only made sense to the young, as their parents congregated in the doorways to watch them and comment on the gathering crowd.

Jaron's carriage was one of many that rolled up to the front of the hall in a loose line, the riding passengers preferring to exit where all could see them. As the driver pulled the reigns to stop the horses, Jaron hopped down and unfolded the step, and helped both of the women out of the vehicle. He spoke to the driver briefly as Cindra took in the scene.

There was a gathering crowd of people, mostly people of lesser means, who were being corralled to one side behind a wooden barricade, awaiting access to the floor. Noble patrons and well-to-do commoners, who had tickets for the upper levels, were being allowed to take their places first among the balcony seats.

The building itself was simple and grand, functional and beautiful. Cindra's great-great grandfather Mathas was credited with building it, but he had been no architect. He had commissioned the finest artists in the realm and beyond to submit a plan for the new theater, and this was the chosen design.

The playhouse was circular and some four stories in height, with arched portals on three sides and a small stage door behind. The roof was circular as well, covered with overlapping clay tiles, and topped with a wide copper-shod dome. Drainage between the tiles and the dome was channeled to eight large animal-headed waterspouts spaced evenly under the eaves. From her vantage, Cindra saw the stone heads of a lion, a bear, an eagle and a wolf, all stained from over a century of runoff.

After Jaron presented their tickets, the trio passed through the portal and immediately turned to the left, ascending a wooden staircase between the outer and inner walls. This led to two levels; Jaron led them to the first balcony and they exited the dark passage into the wide expanse of the theater. The balcony was two rows deep with a wooden rail and short benches to sit upon.

To Cindra's delight, they were at center stage and had a perfect view of the entire playhouse; the round stage was at the far end of the chamber and it had a balcony built along its back wall, over the rear curtains. The walls above and to the sides were draped with swaths of rich-looking fabric, and gilded relief sculptures adorned the corners.

Jaron produced two red cushions for Cindra and Mineth, allowing them to sit in comfort. They arranged the benches as their fellow audience members filed in, with the scuffling of feet above them signifying that the top balcony was being filled, and the commotion below at the final admittance of the groundlings. Cindra's eyes rose from the filling of the floor space to the high ceiling, taking in the banner-draped rafters and the inner curve of the dome, plastered and painted like a night sky full of stars. The apex of the dome had a round aperture as wide as a man was tall, and let in what light the heavens chose to share.

"What is the name of the play?" asked Cindra, for though she had seen a sign posted outside the front door; she had been too distracted to remember.

Jaron turned so that Cindra, and Mineth behind her, could hear him and said, "It is called *Princess Moon*, and it is from the kingdom of Onkanshu. The story is about a princess, named Moon, who lives with her uncle, the local warlord... I shall tell you what I know, for I have seen it twice before."

Cindra looked in surprise at the young knight. "I had not imagined you would have such an interest in the theater, Sir Jaron."

Jaron smiled and watched the musicians, with their foreign robes and instruments, move onto the balcony over the stage. "I have a passing interest in the ways of the eastern empires, and I yearn to watch anything authentic from their lands."

Cindra too had heard of wild tales from the great eastern continent of Gozhia, where it was said that the land stretched from the top of the world to the bottom, and all manner of strange and exotic people and creatures were to be found. She remembered her thrill of seeing the bird-lizard mount in the market, and imagined a land where such a creature might roam free with its fellows.

The audience was mostly settled as the house-mage began lighting the wizard lamps on the stage, signaling for the crowd to grow quiet. Everyone watched with casual interest as the young man in red robes and two-tailed cap created a fiery glow in each orb. Upon finishing, the caster departed and the theater presenter entered the stage to a polite applause. He wore simple finery and a blue and white-striped cap, which he removed with a flourish.

"Ladies and gentlemen, masters and mistresses, good people of Portshia and the wide world, welcome to our theater!" His voice resounded inside the hall, and people cheered. "We offer tonight, for your entertainment and enlightenment, a story of love and betrayal..." His dramatic presentation went on for several minutes as he built up the story, whetting the appetites of the gathered throng. Finally, upon the cusp of being shouted from the stage, he concluded his oration and called for the play to begin, using what Cindra thought was rather weak verse: "Now that we are joined within, let the evening's play begin!" There was brief cheer, then expectant silence.

The musicians began with the beating of a strange drum, which increased in pitch even as its beat grew faster and faded away. A strong single chord was strummed from some kind of elongated lute, laid flat before a kneeling musician. As the chords continued and the drum joined in with an eerie rhythm, the lilting voice of a flute wavered across the hall and stirred Cindra's heart.

It was the most bizarre arrangement she had ever heard, so different from the cycles of verse and chorus and the overlapping melodies of her native music. She realized that she would not be able to recall the tune, as seemingly disjointed and free as it was. *Perhaps it is only meant to be felt, not remembered*, she thought.

The actors took the stage in their costumes, presumably from a noble court in a far-off land. There was a man in a robe with a tall hat, and whiskers framed his face with the intensity of a wild boar. His skin was powdered pale and his eyes were the shape of almonds, accented in theatrical fashion with dark and curved lines. The man took a seat upon a low table, arranging his robes under him with skill. Next came two similarly dressed men, seating themselves on the floor and kowtowing to the man. *The warlord and his retainers*, thought Cindra.

The center curtain opened and from the darkness beyond came a small figure of extraordinary beauty and grace. Princess Moon was a dainty young woman, or might have been; her thick robes and their long floor-sweeping sleeves hid much. There were no female actors in Calilon, although things might be different abroad.

The princess walked to the side of the warlord with tiny steps, her sandals flicking from under her robe in deliberate strides. The robe was embroidered and dyed like a tapestry meant to be worn, with a long-plumed bird of many colors perched on a branch on each sleeve. The hem of the outer robe, for it was multilayered, depicted ocean waves, and the twisting form of a sea dragon undulated in the swelling surf. The princess withdrew a paper fan from her broad sash and fluttered it before her porcelain face. There was awed silence in the crowd, and the groundlings shuffled slightly forward.

The warlord held a fan of metal, painted with symmetrical symbols of flowers. He motioned with it as he spoke in a slow, deep voice, his unfamiliar words flowing together in time with the odd music.

When he finished, a young man of proud noble bearing strode from the side of the stage. The newcomer wore robes with some kind of leafy pattern, had dark hair pulled up in a topknot, and his almond eyes were painted with a fierce aspect that offset his gentle and strong face.

A long-handled and curved sword was worn at his waist, stuck through his black sash. He wore a kind of partial tabard like a knight of Calilon, but it had much wider pointed shoulders and hung down the back, and the front was open and long. It bore the flower symbol of the lord's fan and clothing. The man, obviously a warrior, bowed low and presented himself to his warlord.

Jaron leaned close and said, "This is Sun, greatest warrior in the land and the love of the princess. He is recounting his deeds to her uncle, before asking for her hand in marriage."

The play held moments when a chorus, speaking Calilesh, would give such key information to the audience, but Cindra preferred to listen instead to Jaron's whispered narration.

The warlord made a speech as the young lovers looked at one another, growing restless, and the music took on a staggered, melancholy tone. As the couple left the stage, each bowing to the lord and going separate ways, the music grew quiet. Then a sharp crack of the drum and the warlord's head whipping towards the crowd drew a start. His face held malice and his eyes were crossed in fury. He held up a shaking fist, as the lone drumming grew ominous.

Mineth leaned forward saying, "I'll bet he's the villain, milady."

Cindra nodded in agreement.

Jaron explained, "Sun can marry her if he defeats the lord's enemies, but the lord desires Princess Moon for himself, and is sending Sun to hunt for assassins while the lord has his way with her."

"His own niece? Vile villain, he is." Mineth was appalled.

Cindra could only watch in silence.

The close of the first act saw Sun and Moon talking together and declaring their love, and their worry, for each other. The second act began with a feast or party of some kind, complete with dancers. As the warlord became drunk, his intentions to the princess became more apparent, until he ordered the other revelers off stage. The tension rose between the two actors, predator and prey, making Mineth squirm. The music became spiked with harsh notes and cracks of wooden percussion. Just when things seemed to reach a fever pitch and the princess cried out, the hero Sun appeared and beheld his lord and his love. She ran to him and the lord made as if nothing untoward was happening, ordering them both out of his sight.

Jaron leaned in again and said, "The next scene is what the play is famous for. It caused somewhat of a scandal in its native land." Cindra waited for him to elaborate, but he only turned back to the play.

Sun and Moon, meeting in a forest (for there were thin trees in pots added to the stage) sang in argument back and forth, her pleading and desperate, and the warrior showing his frustration and torn devotions. The music was like a reedy breeze in the background, offering no clue to the untrained ear of what might be coming. The warrior Sun stood helplessly, with his head hung low in shame, and the princess slowly drew herself upright.

Suddenly, she reached for his sword and drew it, causing the audience and the warrior to start in surprise. Larger, deep drums began pounding like thunder from somewhere off stage and Cindra felt the beat resounding in her ribcage, like the heart of a storm dragon stirring the violent sea. The musicians let out a united shout and the drums all beat in unison, as the princess held the sword aloft. Glaring at the hero, she began swinging it with remarkable grace and skill, her robes flying, long sleeves parting to reveal a great colorful bird in flight upon each arm. Her long, silky hair slashed the air like brushstrokes of black ink, sandaled feet moving deftly under the concealing fabric.

Cindra felt a flush rising to her face, and the skin upon her arms prickled with excitement. She found she had forgotten to breathe, and inhaled sharply. Never before had she seen a woman (or a 'stage woman' for that matter) wield a sword. It was not so much a revelation to her that it could be done with such skill, for she had seen female acrobats and performers doing amazing feats. No, this was something entirely different.

Only in her imagination had she entertained the notion of stepping out of her female skin and into another, forbidden role. Many of her books told tales of valor and honor, heroism and sacrifice, taking up arms against an adversary. There was usually a maiden involved, but she always had a knight to fight for her. Helpless and at the mercy of the cruel world, her role was to await rescue and reward the bravery of another.

The sword flitted about the stage, as if it were guiding Moon's body, and the princess only following in its wake like a flowing ribbon of color twisting in coils of pure expression. Then subtly, she took the lead again and was guiding the sword, her will and intent clear upon her face. No longer lost to the dance, she locked her eyes upon her lover, teaching and berating him as she flourished the weapon.

Finally, as the warrior stood unmanned and the music crashed to an end, she dropped to her knees in front of him, offering up his sword with head bowed. There was a collective gasp in the theater, then began a thunderous applause.

Cindra was on her feet, clapping her hands furiously as the actors froze in place, ending the act. The swell of applause from the crowd was the most powerful she had ever experienced, raw and genuine, the roar of the common people, unrestrained and starving for spectacle. As Jaron rose and touched her elbow, she turned to face him, eyes alight and a great smile upon her face. He gestured with his eyes to the rest of the balconies, and Cindra saw that others were following her lead and standing as well. Slightly embarrassed, she reigned in her applause to a more genteel display and looked a bit sheepishly at her peers.

"Such an ovation is usually reserved for the end of a play," Jaron smiled, immensely pleased at her enthusiasm and appreciation.

The actors quickly left the stage and the applause died down as jugglers and tumblers burst upon the scene, giving the actors a chance to change costume and prepare for the third act. The audience regained their seats and the groundlings began to mill about, and Cindra started chattering excitedly with Mineth and Jaron, asking questions and sharing impressions. Her comments kept returning to the sword dance, and her heart beat faster as she relived the scene in her mind.

She felt the desire to lock herself in her room upon returning home, and find a stick to swing about, doing her best to mimic the graceful movements she had witnessed. Maybe she could even find a real sword, and practice with it? A part of her mind told her that nicks and cuts in the furniture and bedding would not go unnoticed, and she would rather not have to explain them to her parents, or to Mineth for that matter.

The third act began in a forest, perhaps a different forest as the trees had been moved, and three men in funny reed hats like upturned baskets were sharpening swords, talking silently. Princess Moon entered from the side of the stage, wearing a cloak and concealing hat. The men drew their swords in surprise at having been discovered, but she held up her hand to put them at ease, the music growing suspicious and the wooden percussion clacking like frogs and crickets.

Her song was low and scornful, and her face held disgust and cold resolve. Their faces hidden by the basket-hats, the men looked at each other in puzzlement. She then produced the warlord's metal fan and tossed it noisily before the assassins, its meaning clear in the suddenly quiet theater.

Mineth hissed, "She's given the warlord over to the killers!"

Grim betrayal was a common theme in tragedies, and the concept was not new to Cindra, but the noble in her shuddered. The lord was a villain and a beast, but he was still the lord, and she was kin. It was a cold and bloody act the princess had committed, no different than murdering the warlord herself.

She thought back to the sword dance and wondered why the princess was not able to protect herself from her uncle's advances. Was it because she was a woman after all, and defending her own honor was not her place? Frustrated, Cindra shushed her handmaid's mutterings and concentrated on the unfolding drama.

The final scene of the tragedy, typically where everyone dies, was a spectacle worthy of the stage. The three assassins were led to the sleeping lord by the princess, and they set upon him as the music swelled, sharp chords and shrill flute notes emphasizing each bloody stroke. There was no blood of course, but crimson ribbons spilled forth from his bed clothes and drew cries of shock and alarm from the more squeamish in the audience.

At the last moment, the hero arrived and drew his sword, slashing with fury and precision, sending red ribbons of theater gore flying everywhere. As Sun and Princess Moon faced each other amidst the carnage, realization dawned on the hero. She had betrayed the man he was sworn to protect.

The two shared a final song charged with anger and despair, with the princess trying to take her lover into her arms, and the warrior pulling away, shamed at his failure and her betrayal. The music took on a slow even cadence, like the pulse of a dying heart. The warrior Sun knelt center stage, a knife in hand, and the princess pleaded gently with him. At last, she turned her head as he plunged the knife into his own heart, unable to live without honor and unable to love without trust.

As Princess Moon took up her fallen warrior's sword and held it high to the domed heavens, Jaron said to Cindra, "His sword is all she has left of him. They believe the sword is the warrior's spirit, and she will care for it always."

Mineth was sniffling into her kerchief, and Cindra found herself blinking away moisture from her eyes. It was sad and tragic, as all tragedies are, but deeply frustrating as well. Was life really this unfair, or was it an indulgence of playwrights and poets?

She understood Princess Moon's situation perhaps better than most in the theater. Trapped by fate and station, and bound by promises that others had made, she was left to rail against her cage and hope that someone would untangle her life. But was it really for *another* to untangle? Was she afraid to take up the sword and handle it *herself*, taking the responsibility and blame?

Perhaps that explained why she found the young man next to her so attractive? He was audacious and brave, and had an air of danger about him; not a danger to her person, but danger to her carefully structured life. He could make it all fall down around her ears in the best way and very well might, but it would be a deadly blow to his honor if he did. What would it help her to gain a love that had sacrificed his honor? She would be better off nursing a memory, caring for a keepsake and leaving her love pure and unsullied.

She applauded mechanically as the players came back to life on the stage and bowed, oddly clapping for the audience in return. Slipping into a reflective state and feeling a bit hungry, she thought, *why couldn't we have seen a comedy?*

The carriage took them to a courtyard that connected to an alley, which was slightly narrow and ended a few doors down. There were some potted ivy plants that had grown their vines up the cracked plaster of the wall and over the door, entangling a decorative wrought iron receptacle for the wizard lamp.

Over the doorframe was carved the three-coin symbol of Obamir, and a large wooden sign was hung above the door, carved into the shape of a hawk in flight holding an arrow in its claws. Cindra read the framed menu by the door, which was the only outward indication that a tavern lay within.

Jaron explained that the Hawk and Arrow Tavern was one of Portshia's better-kept secrets, serving a discerning list of customers, both gentle and base, so long as they paid a yearly fee for membership. The owner had lured some of the most talented cooks in the city to work for him, and he hired the prettiest girls as servers (on the condition that they could serve food and drink). He managed to get first pick of the finest ingredients, slipping generous extra coin to those who brought him prized goods. As for his outstanding wine collection, rumor had it that he was connected to some of the famous family vintners in Aurilon, though none could say quite how.

As Cindra and Mineth stepped beyond the modest door and into the tavern, the aromas of dozens of meals stirred their cravings, carried on the currents of a warm fire and good company. The tavern had a large main floor with close to a dozen small tables and a few for larger parties near the fire. A stuffed hawk bearing an arrow in its claws was mounted above the mantle, and several hunting trophies were tastefully arrayed along the walls.

To the right was a short hall leading to the kitchen, and to the left was a desk at the foot of a staircase, which led to the second level balcony. Some of the wealthier diners ate there, where they could watch the merrymaking but not be in the thick of it. The banister was lined with creeping ivy, and life-sized wooden carvings of game animals stood at the railing junctions, a squirrel here, an owl there, a beaver and a fox.

At the desk stood a balding man of middle age with dark hair and beard, and a healthy paunch upon his waist, a mark of good living. Jaron removed his beret and hailed the man, who smiled and welcomed them.

"Good evening to you, friends!" Adric Minhollow, the owner, spread his arms in greeting, "Welcome to the Hawk and Arrow." He had the manner of the perfect host: jovial, warm and accommodating. Cindra felt strangely at home in his presence.

Jaron stepped forward and returned the man's greeting, asking after a table. "Good evening to you, Master Adric. Have you an upper table for three tonight?"

"Ready and waiting, Sir Jaron, ready and waiting. This way, my friends..." He led them up the stairs to a square table by the railing, with a window view just opposite. Candles had already been lit and a serving girl was standing at hand. Jaron and Cindra were seated opposite one another, and Mineth was seated at the middle, so she might mind them both.

The serving maid, who wore a short skirt just above the mid-calf and a long sleeved, midriff baring blouse and vest, recited the selection of house wines and ales, before sauntering off. Cindra watched her go, and commented to Jaron, "I think I see why you prefer this place."

Jaron insisted, "I swear, milady, it is the food which is the greatest draw. Wait until you taste the flatbread pie and the redfish; they are but simple dishes as well-prepared as anything at the count's table."

But she gave him a look, saying, "I suppose the girls make the food that much better?"

He considered it, smiled and said, "They don't make it worse."

Jaron ordered for the ladies, choosing dishes and a wine he had tried on earlier visits. Cindra was again impressed by his refined tastes, especially from a family so new to the peerage. She asked, "Are many of my father's knights so knowledgeable in the culinary arts?"

Jaron grinned, "No milady, there is little room in a knight's training for cultural refinement. I have taken it upon myself to explore such things. In truth, there are few I can share my tastes with. Even good Sir Cord is more at ease in a noisy tavern with warm ale and chunk of mutton."

"Well, I would not wish for anything less, Sir Jaron. You have shown me a delightful evening, and if the food is as good as you suggest I am sure it will only get better."

"It is only the first of many I might show you, milady," Jaron offered, but Mineth made a deliberate throat clearing noise and he quickly amended, "If the count and countess will allow, of course."

Cindra sat up straighter in her chair and said, "I don't see why they would not allow it. You have been far more agreeable than my father's choice of company, that stifling Sir Earnold." She noticed Jaron's smile fade at the mention of the name. "And there is so much more to see and do before I leave for Rokvynnar... like horse riding! Could we learn horse riding?" She grew more excited and hopped in her chair as Mineth tapped her finger on the table, calling for restraint. "And a picnic! We could make a picnic of it, perhaps out by the coast or near the edge of the Shadowood..."

Jaron rolled the base of his goblet around in circles as Cindra chattered on, and when she stopped for a breath he said, "It may not be so simple. I think perhaps the countess made an exception for tonight, allowing me to escort you without your... bodyguard."

Cindra stopped and blinked at him, wondering what he might be getting at. "Are you saying that you will not be pleased to accompany me if he is present?" The idea was childish.

Jaron sighed, "It is more complicated than that, I'm afraid." He smiled at the serving girl as she brought the first of the dishes, still unused to the idea of ignoring servants.

When she had finished and departed, Jaron continued, "Sir Earnold and I... we have a past. It may make things difficult, to say the least, but what I fear is what people might say... about your ladyship and I..."

Mineth squirmed a bit and Cindra shared her discomfort. She had not intended for things to truly become... *improper* between her and the knight, but to hear him speak of it made her wonder what others had been thinking. She said, "You had best explain what you mean, sir."

Jaron took a long drink of his wine and thought for a moment before continuing. "Let me begin at the beginning, and perhaps it may help you judge what is best.

"My father was once a foot soldier in your grandfather's service. He fought in the Battle of DuKort in Aurilon in 1066. Sir Earnold's father, Sir Waliss, was one of the count's own personal guard, sworn to his safety. As the story goes, my father was there when the count entered Castle DuKort and Baron LuKravore ambushed him within. Sir Waliss dropped his blade and fled, but my father came to the count's aid and slew the baron."

"Baron LuKravore was my third cousin, twice removed." Cindra said in a matter-of-fact way. "The union between House Corrina and House DuMaylione ended that feud."

"But another feud had begun," Jaron said, "Sir Earnold's father was dishonored and stripped of his holdings in Casselvane, and his license to run a fighting school in the province was revoked. *My* father was given a knighthood and Greenfellow's duties as the count's personal guard, and other honors besides."

Cindra chewed a bit of her steamed redfish as she listened. "So this is the source of the bad blood between Sir Earnold and yourself?" She thought family feuds could be so tiresome.

Jaron began to squirm a bit now, "That's a part of it."

Cindra's interest was piqued and she leaned forward. "There's more? Do tell, please."

Mineth tapped Cindra's arm and said, "It's impolite to pry, milady." However, in the following silence, she glanced at Jaron herself, waiting to hear more of the sordid tale. He took a bite of his flatbread pie and cleared his throat.

"I have a bit of a reputation... undeserved for the most part, but nevertheless," he stammered, searching for the right way to broach the subject.

"You're a philanderer," Cindra stated, waiting for him to deny it.

"I- now I wouldn't put it that way," he blushed. He actually blushed! Cindra smiled and leaned forward intently.

"So you have a sweetheart, then? One woman to whom you are honest and true?" She asked with sincere curiosity as well as wry humor.

"No! Er, well, no..." He sat back uncomfortably in his chair.

"So you have taken a vow of chastity then?" She whispered the question with a dramatic air.

"No, I just... well, now and again..."

"So your reputation is not undeserved." She stated firmly. Her face was calm but her eyes were laughing.

Jaron regarded her and said after a moment, "You're enjoying this, aren't you?"

"Oh, immensely!" Cindra said, clasping her hands before her.

He took a moment to compose himself and said, "I am no guiltier than the next man of a dalliance once in a while, depending who is asking or how much I've had to drink..." He stroked his beard with his fingers and continued, "But in the matter of Sir Earnold, I am afraid he has a legitimate grievance with me."

Cindra and Mineth were silent and attentive, not wanting to alter his talkative mood. This was better than spinners' gossip by far, right from the horse's mouth, as it was said.

"Sir Earnold and I came up in the same school, training in the *Daerbrik* style under the Freekirk family. We had our run-ins before, but Sir Cord always kept us in line. That is until Sir Earnold announced his engagement."

The women exchanged a look and sat in rapt attention, even as the food cooled.

"He made a point of showing her off, trying to impress his cohorts, and she made an impression." His eyes focused on something far away, seeing the vision of beauty that had been burned into his mind. "Her name was Deliah. She had hair as black as night, and skin like fresh cream, perfect and smooth. She was graceful and elegant, like no woman I had seen before. And her eyes... there was something about her eyes that were enticing and strange; they were the gray of spring rain clouds and had flecks of gold and blue, and when they beheld you... they made you helpless to look away."

Cindra raised her eyebrows in slight annoyance. "Was she wearing anything?"

Jaron broke out of his remembrance and turned to her saying, "A yellow dress with... frill trim."

"Just wondering," Cindra sniffed.

"Anyway, we were always in competition, Earnold and I, and well... I was young and stupid." He took another sip of his wine, letting it burn down his throat.

Cindra said, "So, you stole her away. You stole another man's betrothed." It was not a question.

Jaron nodded, looking glum. "Honestly, it was not much of a challenge. She was perhaps not so true as Earnold had believed, and before I could think for the better, we were undone. Sir Earnold found us behind the stables, engaged in a kiss, and he challenged me to a duel on the spot."

"Behind the stables?" Cindra asked with wrinkled nose.

"They had just been cleaned," Jaron clarified defensively. "Anyway, the entire school was present and he made the whole thing public. He set a time of day and made it all perfectly unavoidable. So... we fought.

"The duel was rather heated, since we had so much more of an argument than the lady. It went on for... I don't know. It seemed like an hour. He was trying to kill me, and I was trying to think of a way not to kill him, since I was in the wrong. Finally I scored a blow upon his cheek, giving him that charming scar he carries under his left eye.

"I was able to disarm him and make him yield, but it cost me a great deal. I was scorned by half the school, and earned a reputation as 'one not to be trusted with another man's wife.' They called me the 'Rose Knight,' among other less pleasant things. I carry the shame of it to this day."

Selvina's intertwined roses were not meant to stand alone. The name 'Rose Knight" spoke of one who toys with love, but also spoke of loneliness. Cindra remembered her food and took a bite, eyes downward. "What happened to Deliah?"

"Eventually she married an officer in the Portshia Casting Guild, forsaking us both for some... bookish wizard; no sense to it, really." He finished off his wine with the thought.

Cindra and Mineth ate their meals in silence for a while as Jaron poked at his long rice. Finally, Cindra broke the uncomfortable silence and put down her knife saying, "Well, I shall not have my last months of freedom and happiness hindered by the squabbling of my father's knights or by the wagging tongues of gossips. I intend to enjoy myself and I will ask that you attend me, whether my bodyguard likes it or not. You may kill each other after I am gone."

Jaron stared in surprise, but then smiled and bowed his head in deference. "As my lady commands," he said.

Chapter Seven

Old Scores

Sir Earnold Greenfellow had rarely visited the house but he knew the way by heart. He had ridden through these streets on other errands, sometimes passing the doorway, but had never stopped. Still he marked its location on every visit. There was a woman who lived there who owed him a great deal, and it was time to call upon her again.

The first time he met her he had saved her life or rather, he saved her from a fate worse than death. After putting her up in the city and learning more about her, he had asked his first favor. Since then she had managed to make a life for herself in town and Earnold left her to it, but always kept her in his thoughts. She was too special to let go.

He dismounted and tied his horse to a post in the courtyard that the woman's house shared with her neighbors. It was a decent area, walls were plastered when cracked and plants were kept from overgrowing. The woman's husband had done well for himself after all. He approached the door and reached for the brass knocker, which bore a device of heraldry that had been purchased rather than passed down. It was the symbol of a tower encircled protectively by a dragon, and from the tower ramparts sprung the head of a cat. Master Wyngaard held an office in the Casting Guild, and provided magical wards for the count and many other wealthy patrons. Being a commoner, he was only allowed to display a family crest if he paid for the privilege.

Sir Earnold struck the knocker three times, waiting as his breath steamed in the night air. After a moment the door unlatched and opened, spilling a warm light and the scent of lilac into the courtyard. The woman within was attired in a fur cloak and heavy dress against the cold; her skin was pale and perfect, and her hair as dark as raven's wings. A cozy fire burned within but the pair of captivating gray eyes that met Earnold turned icy cold as they took in his presence.

"Sir Earnold," she said, keeping the door open only enough to let him know he wasn't welcome.

"Deliah," he said, removing his beret. "Is your husband home?"

"It is Madam Wyngaard, if you please. And no, he is not at home. The council has him chasing phantoms on the orders of your count." She shifted her weight to her other foot impatiently.

"Good," he said, pushing his way inside. "I need to talk to you about another favor."

She began to protest but since he was inside already, she decided to hear him out before doing anything drastic. "Would you like some tea?" she offered.

"If you have any, please."

"I don't," she sneered and took a seat by the fire. "What is the favor this time?"

Earnold frowned at her, making his deep eyes sink even further into the room's shadows. He stood before the fireplace, leaning on the mantle and staring into the flames. "It's Dunlorden," he said simply, venom filling his voice.

"Of course it is! It could be no other. Your voice has that particular amount of loathing and hatred reserved only for him." She reclined in the high backed chair and glared at him, looking like a frost queen holding court. "I am married now, and I have my own future to think about."

He smirked and said, "Oh, don't worry. I would not ask you to violate your vows. I need something more subtle, something worthy of your secret skills."

Her eyes narrowed and she flicked a glance at the door, making sure it was shut and they were alone before she spoke. "I can't. If my husband was to find out, he would never trust me again, I'd be marched before the guild council and..." she shifted the focus to her husband, since Earnold didn't seem moved by her plight, "The council would think that *he* instructed me. The scandal would destroy him."

The knight ran his finger over the lip of a silver goblet on the mantle, bearing the mark of the Casting Guild. It had been given to Master Wyngaard as a token of good service, and was polished regularly. Earnold held it up and said, "Yes, that would be a pity. You'll just have to be careful."

"Say what it is you want of me and get out." She stared into the fire, her rage burning.

Earnold stood before the fireplace, blocking her from its light and warmth. "I was chosen by the count to guard his daughter until she leaves to be wed. But Dunlorden has managed to weasel his way into her company, trying to supplant me again! I want him to make a grave error, something I can call him out for..."

Deliah sighed, "Not *that* again. As I recall, it didn't work out for you so well last time. Besides, I told you I am married now."

"I don't need *you* to throw yourself at him again, but Lady Cindra will do."

Deliah just stared for a moment and said, "*What?*"

"It should not be so hard to encourage, with your abilities. Make them a public spectacle, the more public the better. I will be on hand to defend the lady's honor and dispatch the villain." The knight's mind turned with possibilities. "And you could tip the scales in my favor as well, so he doesn't get away with giving me another scar and slinking away alive."

Deliah barked in mirthless laughter. "Why not have him burst into flames at the sound of your voice? Or have him hand you his own head when you ask him?"

"Nothing so dramatic, Deliah dear. I will enjoy beating him into the ground before a crowd."

"And if I refuse to manufacture your great victory, what then?" She had to ask.

Earnold stared at her, enclosed in shadows, looking into her silvery eyes as they eerily caught the light on the walls. "Don't forget, I know what you are Deliah. I could do much worse than ruin your marriage and your husband's career. There are those who would pay dearly to add you to their collection of oddities."

Deliah's blood froze at the threat; her thoughts returning to the day Earnold came across her in the woods, running for her life. Now he was offering to return her to what she had been fleeing from. "Get out," was all she could say, and the knight knew he had struck a nerve. She would do it.

"I will provide you with the lady's schedule, and you may be as creative as you wish. Until then, I bid you good night." He turned and showed himself out.

Deliah sat alone in her house, staring into her fire, surrounded by the comfort of the most stable life she had led in a long while. Ultimately it wouldn't last, but she was determined to hold on to it as long as she could. She would wrestle with her conscience another time.

The hoof beats of Sir Earnold's steed faded into the night, and the fire no longer gave her warmth.

The scent of wood burning in a thousand hearths filled the city streets as the moon rose to its zenith. The smoke and haze caught the glow of the wizard–lamps below, spreading a soft orange blush over the rooftops. The watchmen made a slow patrol along the canal walks, pausing at the shadowy alleys to intimidate anyone who might be lurking there, and testing their own courage in the process. Drunks stumbled home in groups for protection, keeping to the lit avenues, while ladies of the evening, showing as much flesh as they dared against the cold, beckoned them into dark corners. It was a typical night in the city.

The man stumbling through the shadows was not out of place. Dressed in rags and smelling of filth and well-aged sweat, he resembled many of the poor wretches that haunted the alleys and doorways of any large city. His hair was shaggy and matted, and his bare feet scuffed along the cobblestones, finding occasional warmth in a steaming horse pile as he stepped haphazardly along the streets. He ignored the whores and drunken sailors as they turned up their noses at his stench. They were not his concern tonight. Tonight he had an important meeting. His eyes flickered to the rooftops, searching for a sign.

Seeing movement above, he slunk into a dark alley and clawed up the side of the three-story building in less than six seconds.

Black Will pulled his wiry form over the eaves and gripped the red clay tiles with his fingers and toes, walking insect-like towards a dark figure that was hunched on the pinnacle. He sat beside it and it stirred, as if noticing him for the first time.

"You are as worthless as a man," it croaked in a deep, gravelly voice. "I thought you could handle a child."

"*He was not alone,*" Black Will snarled in his dual voice, man and beast sharing one throat.

The hunched figure rasped with scorn, "Yes, a girl was with him. *Two* children, *very* formidable."

The filthy man turned his body to face his accuser, and bones of dark smoke leaped out of his flesh; a fiery plume issued from a gash on its cheek below its hateful burning eyes. *"She cut me! I have never been cut! The flesh, yes, but not me."* It pointed a bony finger at the wound as it smoldered and sparked, as new as it looked over a month ago.

"Welcome to the world of pain," the hunched figure rumbled. "Maybe it will remind you of the price of failure."

The smoky skull retreated into the flesh and Black Will absently rubbed his cheek, which barely bore a scar. *"Easy for guadim to talk of failure. Failed long ago and almost all gone now. So few, they asking us for help now, eh?"* A watery laugh issued from the man's chest.

"Silence," said the guadim as it flexed its muscles and looked to the night sky. The creature was taller than a man, even with its back and neck hunched forward. It had mottled gray-green skin that stretched over its bones, making it look like a starved moldering corpse. Frills of bone protruded from its spine, and on either side of its backbone were jointed, fleshy folds that sparkled with sickly moisture in the moonlight. The creature's head was horned and grotesque, with a large spiny brow and an over-long nose and chin, which were pockmarked and warty. Its large frilled ears swept back and up, as did its ribbed, twisted horns. The guadim's eyes glowed with an unnatural light born of hatred for all life, and its vertical pupils narrowed at the glare of the stars.

"You didn't grab the boy either, Paugh. You watched and did nothing." Black Will accused and hugged his knees to his chest.

Paugh smiled with its needle-like teeth and said, "She managed to wound a demnox like you, so I wasn't taking chances. This is my only body, and I must care for it. I still bear wounds from the First War."

Black Will was unmoved. *"So what now? The girl has taken the boy to the castle, where he is much safer. I cannot reach him, cannot get away with so much blood intact."*

Paugh looked over the rooftops to the distant keep, glowing white in the light of the moon. "The girl will not remain long. She is to travel away and leave him alone, and that is when he will be vulnerable. If I cannot take him within the walls, I will force him out into the streets."

Unconvinced, Black Will asked, *"Force him how?"*

The guadim folded its fingers and brooded. "I shall sing a song for his mind, a song of loneliness and pain. It will make the safe castle walls close in around him like a prison, and he will yearn for the open streets and his brotherhood of thieves. I will send him out into the night, and you will find him for me."

"And I will rip him, tear him," Black Will began, raising his claws in anticipation.

Paugh grabbed the top of the man's head and twisted his neck, making a sickening crunch of bones and looking him in the face. "No! We must bleed him and bleed him well. You may do what you wish when I have taken what I need. If you spoil him..." The guadim released the man's head and left him to sort out his damaged neck.

"Hrrm... Blood Magic, I remember." Black Will mumbled through his beard as he adjusted his twisted vertebrae.

Paugh stood, unfolding its sinewy frame and stretching its back; a wet popping noise issued from its shoulders as the sticky folds of flesh and bone unfurled. Long skeletal digits extended with a membrane of yellowish flesh stretched between them. They formed wings like those of a bat, through which the moonlight shone and illuminated a web of veins. Its voice rumbled into the night, "Once we have the blood, we will have the father at our mercy, and the coming war will be all but won."

At least, that was the plan. It leapt from the rooftop and beat its wings, catching the night air.

Black Will watched as the guadim flew across the moon, vanishing into the blackness. Once the guadim were numerous enough to blot out the stars, and now there were but a few left. *Just as well*, thought the demnox within the man as he crept headfirst down the wall. *Some things were never meant to blight the world.*

The morning air was cold but not uncomfortable, and the sun was warm, heralding the likelihood of an early spring. The Festival of Devotion, only a day away, would be more pleasant without the morning frost underfoot and the chill air making young couples' teeth chatter. Cindra was looking forward to her first, and probably last, attendance. She would be blessed by the Selvinian Sisters who would ask the goddess for a happy and successful marriage for her, but her own thoughts and feelings would be with the young man who rode beside her now.

The past several days had been spent learning to ride on horseback, something that Cindra had always yearned to do. Like most young girls, she had a love of ponies and horses, and wished to ride in the open with the wind in her hair. They began life so delicate and awkward, yet soon became graceful and beautiful creatures, able to carry kindred spirits on their backs to run free. Cindra had learned over the last few days however, that the romance of equestrianism had some harsh realities, for example, the sidesaddle.

Since ladies' dresses were not made to straddle a horse, and such an action would be unseemly, women had to learn to ride sidesaddle. It consisted of a single stirrup for the left foot, and a curved saddle horn used to anchor the knee of the right leg as it draped to the left.

Cindra had managed to overcome her fear of falling off the right side of the horse, trusting in her growing balance and ability to read her mount's intentions, but Mineth was not so lucky. She had taken a tumble or two, and thankfully had escaped injury, but her fear and mistrust of the animals did not help matters at all. Nevertheless, the handmaid was inclined to join them in the day's excursion, holding her duties as chaperon more important than the risk of bodily injury.

The Coast Road began from the city's southwest gate and crossed the canal way, heading west past the foothills of the Casselvane Range and eventually spanning the true Joshian River mouth before hugging the coast for hundreds of miles. It was a well-traveled road, but unlike the northern thoroughfares, it was less densely populated and boasted of more open spaces and fewer trees. All the better to keep an eye out for trouble.

The party of four riders trotted up the second gentle slope from the canal and neared a turn, passing a stone mile marker set in the roadside. Sir Jaron led the way upon his chestnut mount, followed closely by Lady Cindra, with Mineth and Sir Earnold taking up the rear. Cindra had been directed by her mother to allow Greenfellow to join them, since the count had made it a stipulation of her release.

Cindra's argument that her father was not at home carried little weight, and she knew it. Actually the grim knight had been very patient and well-behaved, and mostly ignored Jaron, preferring instead to chat with Mineth. Cindra could still sense the tension between the men-at-arms, but so long as the boys behaved she could not complain.

She patted the muscular shoulder of her mount for the tenth time, reassuring herself that she was really here. The clip-clop of hooves on the road stones made a soft music, and the sway of the creatures gait was calming. Jaron spoke of saddle sores being a problem for a frequent rider, but Cindra figured she would not get to do this very often anyway.

"Are you doing alright, Mineth?" Cindra called over her shoulder to the handmaid, who was lagging behind.

"I'm doing well enough, but this hairy beast is being difficult." Mineth held the reigns uncertainly.

Jaron spoke up, "I protest, madam, I have been a perfect gentleman!" Cindra laughed at his jest, but Mineth was too preoccupied to enjoy humor. Earnold just scowled.

"Oooh, just go straight!" She huffed at the horse.

"There is a disagreement as to who is in charge," said Earnold.

Mineth risked a glance at the knight riding beside her, afraid to look away from the animal's neck. "I don't know how you manage to ride around all day, Sir Earnold. My backside is killing me sitting up like this, and my poor foot is asleep."

Earnold looked at the road ahead and pointed to a teahouse under the boughs of a large tree. "Perhaps we might stop at the house ahead and give the poor woman a rest?" He called forward, not caring who made the decision. The teahouse was the last stop before reaching the city, and travelers often paused there to gather themselves and enjoy the relative quiet before heading into the urban scene.

Cindra looked back at her handmaid and asked her, "Mineth, do you wish to turn back?" Her eyes held concern for her friend, but she hoped the woman would manage to hold out and not cut the day short.

"I would like to stop milady, but we need not turn back just yet," Mineth said and squirmed a bit in the saddle.

The teahouse had a short front porch and a sitting room with large windows facing the sea. Jaron dismounted and tied off his horse to the hitching post, helping the women dismount as the owner of the teahouse came out to meet them, smiling and nodding in welcome. Sir Earnold ordered drinks for Mineth and himself, and spoke quietly to the woman as she massaged her tingling foot.

Cindra asked the handmaid if she was able or willing to continue, and Mineth answered, "There is no need to wait for me, milady. Sir Earnold has offered to stay with me while I recover myself. You and Sir Jaron can ride ahead." Earnold brought Mineth her tea and sat on the porch beside her, sipping his own drink. He seemed quite content.

Cindra and Jaron exchanged a look, resolving to take advantage of this turn of luck before either the chaperon or bodyguard changed their minds. Jaron readied their mounts and helped Cindra into the saddle, saying, "We shall ride to the top of the far hill and no further, staying near the road. If you feel able, you may follow and join us." He mounted his steed and looked to see if Cindra was ready.

"Shall we make a race of it?" She asked. When he only smiled and set his horse to walking, she spurred on her bay mare into a gallop and shot past him, drawing a protest from his lips as well as from the poor handmaid sipping her tea.

Jaron sought to reach her horse and bring it back under control, but as he neared the girl, he saw her turn and smile at him, her face filled with excitement and joy. She was a quick learner and showed no fear, reveling instead in the thrill of the chase. He smiled at her in turn and relaxed, falling into a pace behind her so that she would not drive her animal any faster.

The wind was whipping her braided hair and setting her riding skirt flowing about her ankles as her body settled into the rhythm of the galloping horse. She had watched her instructors closely, paying more attention than she ever had for any other course of study, and it was well worth it.

Her spirit was set free as the grass and stones blurred under her, fresh air and the smell of the sea filled her lungs and made her eyes water. She watched her shadow on the road ahead, confirming in its silhouette that she was really here, now, in this moment. She could not contain her glee as she passed peasants on the road, pulling carts and leading animals of their own, moving to give her room. She looked at all of them as she rode past, seeing her smile returned in most of their faces.

Her horse was beginning to slow and Jaron rode beside her, nodding in approval. "Very good milady, one would not know you had only learned this week." She laughed and let the animal make its own pace as she guided it off the road towards a tree upon the top of the nearest rise. When they reached the shade of the thick branches, just beginning to show spring buds, she turned her steed back towards the city and took in the view.

Portshia was but a few miles away; its towers were visible above the hills and trees, but the castle that was her home looked like no more than an outcropping of white chalk upon a seaside cliff. She slid from her saddle and walked towards the vista, feeling the breeze blowing at her back, the locks of hair at her ears tickling her cheeks. A tear spilled down her face unexpectedly, elation and awe filling her chest. She wiped it away as she heard Jaron walk up beside her.

"I have never been so far from home," she said, "I knew the world was a big place; I've seen maps and charts, I've read books... but to look back on the city and see it so small... to know that this is just the beginning..."

Jaron wanted to place a comforting hand on her shoulder, wanted to give her support, but he dared not touch her. Even alone, with no one to see but the birds and squirrels, he had to maintain his sense of propriety. The lady might or might not complain, but that was not for him to chance. He stood beside her, gazing at the city as he folded his arms and asked, "If your life were a song or story milady, how would you like it to be written?"

Cindra thought for a moment as she stared at the mountain range, seeing how far it stretched to the northeast when viewed from a distance. "I think I would like it to be an adventure, full of travel and new things. I would want a story that led to new and wonderful discoveries without end." She hugged herself as she spoke, warming her arms in the shade of the tree. "What about yourself, Sir Jaron? What kind of a song or poem would be written about your life?"

The knight smiled to himself, thinking on how his answer might have been the same as hers once. He walked to the tree and sat down, leaning his back against the smooth bark. "I think I would want something with an ending, I mean a happy ending like 'and he lived happily thereafter.' I would like a family one day, a quiet life, perhaps a country home and some children..."

Cindra turned and walked to the tree, a questioning smile on her lips. "Hearth and home at your age, sir? You are too young to settle down into a quiet life, surely?"

Jaron said, "I have had my share of adventure, and a brush with death or two can make a man yearn for a quiet life. Besides, it is easy enough to find trouble if you truly wish to."

Cindra sighed and sat next to him, leaning her head upon his shoulder as the wind rustled the branches. "Yes it is," she said as she closed her eyes, feeling her heart beating in her ears. "It is indeed."

Jaron forced himself to relax as she snuggled at his side, a blush rising in his face that he was happy she couldn't see. He looked down the hill towards the teahouse and found it obscured by the trees and distance. Still, someone riding up the road could espy them if they knew who they were looking for. He was about to suggest that they head back so their companions did not worry, but decided instead to enjoy the moment, knowing it would likely not come again. *As long as we don't fall asleep*, he thought to himself.

He felt warm despite the shade, and the tree blocked the nipping of the breeze. He listened to the horses grazing and the sound of the wind, when something else caught his notice: soft footfalls from behind, and a scent like... lilac? At first he thought it was his imagination, but then he heard a voice on the wind, light and airy and relaxing, calling for sleep.

Drowsiness overtook him, and his head drooped and nodded, and it seemed as though the entire world went quiet for a moment, only to become clear again. He looked at the lady leaning on his shoulder and heard her breathing grow heavier and deeper, and the weight of her body leaned more into him as sleep took her. Again, the heaviness of his own head made him nod as his eyes became weary, until he could resist no more. The musical voice on the breeze was lovely and irresistible.

Deliah Wyngaard stepped quietly around the trunk of the tree, drawing a small curved knife, like a tiny scythe, from the sleeve of her dress. She could hear the measured breath of sleep coming from the two figures before her, and she knew that her spell was in full effect. Looking around to insure there were no witnesses on the road or surrounding fields, she kneeled down beside the knight and noble lady, taking a moment to look upon their faces.

Jaron was just as she remembered him, perhaps a little older and more mature, but not much. He had been so easy to lure in: flattery with a word, a secret smile, an overlong glance. Sir Earnold had judged him correctly, but since their 'engagement' had been nothing more than a trap, she felt Jaron was the more honest of the two men. Pity.

Lady Cindra was a pretty girl, though not a classic beauty. Her face did not have the delicate curves and subtle features that recalled childhood innocence after it had passed. Like her mother, the lady would have a face that radiated wisdom and nobility, intimidating lesser men rather than captivating them. For now, however, she was an innocent. But that was about to change.

Deliah raised the knife.

———

"What is keeping them?" asked Mineth, having recovered somewhat and finishing her tea. She looked on the high horizon, trying to see beyond the sparse trees and farmhouses near the western road.

Sir Earnold was becoming a bit restless himself, but made no move to ride after them. He said, "Perhaps they've stopped to rest their horses. The poor beasts can't run full-out and uphill like that for long."

Mineth made a disapproving clucking of her tongue and began pacing the porch, causing the housekeeper to step outside and inquire if she needed anything else. She declined and as the man took away her empty cup, she turned to Sir Earnold with her hands on her hips. "Are you certain she will be... alright? With him, I mean?" She had time to think on the story of Jaron and Earnold, and the animosity between them. It seemed strange to her that he had been so ready to let them out of his sight, although she held her opinion for now.

Earnold looked up at the handmaid and his face darkened. "He is a knight companion and she is the count's own daughter. I doubt even Sir Jaron would put a foot out of line," he crossed his arms and looked up the road, "but if he did, I would personally see to it that he received his judgment."

Mineth was not appeased. "Of *that* I have little doubt, begging your pardon sir knight," she said, "but I don't want to wait for him to 'put a foot out of line' if there's a chance he might."

Earnold frowned and looked at the shadows of the trees. It was almost noon and the pair had been gone for nearly an hour. He stood to stretch his legs and give the appearance of action, lest the handmaid be inclined to rant on. He walked around to where the horses were tied and began fiddling with the reigns as he heard the trotting of hooves on the road, nearing the teahouse from the west and heading for the city. He peered past the hanging branches to see who it was.

Mineth too heard the noise and walked out past the tree to look up the road. She saw the single rider and huffed in frustration; it was a woman in her mid-twenties, with long black hair and pale skin. She slowed as she neared the teahouse, her silver-gray eyes falling on Mineth and making her start, for they were beautiful eyes but strangely piercing, almost ghostly. As the woman saw Sir Earnold, she nodded to him, and he returned it with a tip of his feathered beret.

Chapter Eight

The Festival of Devotion

The festival was better than Lady Cindra had imagined it. The perimeter of the park was lined with colored pavilions and ribbons hanging from posts, and miniature temples built over the last week which had been decorated with white silk and roses from the temple hothouses.

The Selvinian Sisterhood presided over the ceremonies and events bestowing blessings upon lovers and those seeking true love. There were minstrels, jugglers, acrobats, and even a dancing bear, which Cindra thought looked rather out of place as it walked upright behind its handler. It would be tragic if someone were mauled during his or her marriage because a dancing bear decided to retire and become a predator again.

Cindra sat with her mother in a high box above the grandstands, their backs to the morning sun and a roof overhead to provide shade for most of the day. Their view of the tournament field was wonderful, and they could enjoy all of the sights and sounds of the jousts without worrying about being covered in dust and flying grass. Mineth had a seat next to Cindra, and Mineth's mother was next to the countess.

Because her father was absent, the countess was in the chair reserved for the count, and Cindra got to sit in her mother's chair. It was a strange feeling if she thought about it, for although they were only chairs, they were symbolic of high station, with cushioned backs rising above the head and bearing the boar and mountain device of Casselvane Province. For the first time she felt like she was presiding over an official function rather than simply attending one.

She absently fingered her hair, feeling for the lock that had refused to be pulled back into a braid. It was a bit too short, as if it had been cut, and now it stuck out loosely and had to be tucked under a longer strand. Her hair was done in a pair of double braids that joined in the back; a yellow ribbon tied part way down. Her dress was quartered in blue and gold, bearing the cat and half sun/half-moon symbols of House Corrina, and upon her elbows were bound long false-sleeves of yellow silk, indicating her state of betrothal. Available women seeking a love of their own wore green ribbons at their sleeves and in their hair, and married women wore red.

The countess wore a bejeweled dress of blue and seafoam green, woven with strings of pearls and mother-of-pearl in swirling patterns upon the bodice, hem and sleeves. Her golden hair was pulled back into an elaborate braid, with a jeweled cap and veil trailing behind. She often saved her best and most beautiful dresses for Selvina's holy days, and today was no exception.

The countess leaned over to her daughter and asked, "You seem to be enjoying yourself, kitten. Why did you not ask to attend last year?"

Cindra spoke to be heard over the cheers of the crowd as a pair of knights made a noisy pass of lance on shield. "I thought if I told father I wished to go, he would have made me stay home. So I pretended not to be interested."

The countess smiled and said, "Men are not so complex, and they are easy to confuse. Be careful how often you play such games."

Cindra smiled and turned her attention to the field, where another pair of knights was waiting beyond the railings for their turn at the joust. Cindra recognized Sir Jaron by his livery, for he wore a helmet and heavy armor that obscured his form. His shield was green and bore the symbol of a brown antlered furdeer, and his helm bore an antlered crest. His steed had been draped with colors of green and white, and many colored ribbons hung from its saddle horn. They were the favors of ladies for whom the knight was dedicating his combat.

Cindra realized that she had given him no favor; in fact the idea had not occurred to her until this moment. She wondered if she might remove one of her ribbons when she heard a voice from below the high box. It was clear and feminine but wavered with age, carrying up to the box with practiced delivery. "Roses for favors, favors for the brave knights! Buy a rose and give your heart, let him carry your favor into battle! Roses..."

Cindra leaned over the railing and looked below to see a woman clothed in a peasant's dress with a warm but shabby cloak pulled over her shoulders and a kerchief and hood over her gray wiry hair. The old woman looked up at the lady and her milky eyes twinkled as she caught the girl's attention. She called up to the high box, "A rose for a knight, milady? Show your favor and give him strength in battle?"

Cindra smiled at her luck and called, "Yes please, for Sir Jaron Dunlorden." She pointed to him on the far side of the field and motioned for Mineth to get her purse.

"Very well, milady, very good." The old woman called, catching the silver coins dropped into her basket. She then withdrew one of the roses and tossed it up to the lady saying, "One for the lovely lady as well! May its fragrance bring you joy!" The woman moved off through the crowd, heading for Sir Jaron.

Cindra caught the rose and sat back in her seat, her face flush with joy and more than a little embarrassment. She had just given away her feelings for Sir Jaron in front of her mother and the entire crowd, had they been paying attention. *Perhaps a bit more discretion,* she thought, *for next time.* She inhaled the rose's fragrance, breathing deeply.

Her head became light and swirled with feeling, a wave of euphoria moved through her as she let out a sigh and sank into the ornate chair. She closed her eyes and one face leaped into her vision, a pair of deep blue-gray eyes under a strong brow, full lips and angular jaw, chestnut beard and hair pulled back into a *tipok* knot. Jaron's scent filled her being, and the warmth of his body felt so near, like a beam of sunshine upon her neck. Her heart pounded in her chest and she felt the pull of desire rush down her spine. She placed the rose to her lips, breathing in its scent, *his* scent, and riding the wave of sensation again and again.

Sir Cord Freekirk was standing by the lance rack, hefting each of them for weight as he watched a pageboy check the harnesses on Jaron's steed. Cord had yet to don his heavy jousting armor, and wore the light mail and tabard of House Freekirk, a black mace and chevron set upon a field of red.

His own combat was set for later in the day, but it was his tradition to attend his friend before a fight, so they might take their minds off of the impending danger. Time enough for that once the battle began. It was only a joust, but jousts were hardly safe, and more than one competition had been lost before the mounts had been even set to galloping. Serenity of mind was half the battle.

"How are you feeling in there, lad?" Cord asked Jaron for the fifth time.

Jaron turned at the waist to look down from the saddle, since his jousting helm was not made to allow head motion. "For the fifth time, I'm fine. At least I will be until the visor goes down. I hate these things." He tugged at the straps securing the helmet to his breastplate.

"Better than losing face, literally." Cord said, patting Jaron's horse.

A kindly female voice called to him from the railing, "Sir Jaron Dunlorden! A token from Lady Cindra Corrina! A token to carry into battle. May its fragrance give you strength!" An old woman approached with a basket, and offered him a rose.

Jaron looked at her in surprise and took the rose, looking up at the high box for the lady. He saw her sitting back in her chair beside her mother, a somewhat foolish smile on her face as she waved to him, holding her own rose to her lips. Jaron took the rose from the woman and saluted Cindra, smiling winningly and taking a sniff of the flower before tucking it into his gauntlet for safekeeping. He closed his visor as the herald called for the next joust to begin.

The feeling took him. Jaron experienced a rush of warmth and dizziness that had nothing to do with the metal that enclosed his body or the anticipation of competition. A single image swirled in his mind: the face of the lady, the young woman who had captured his heart and set his world spinning; Cindra, noble and lovely, soft and strong, so full of life and expectation. He turned his body toward the stands to see her through the visor, and he found her sitting forward, watching with rapt attention. Her scent and essence swam about inside the helmet and set his heart to thundering, the smell of her skin, her hair, her breath as she leaned in close...

Trumpets sounded, signaling the beginning of the joust. Training and instinct kicked in and Jaron spurred his horse forward, his mind barely registering the danger he was about to face. He had only seconds until he met the other knight in the center of the field, and he raised his shield and set his lance only just in time. The roaring of the crowd filled his ears, but through it all he could hear a solitary voice calling his name, half in fear for him, half in desire.

The impact threw him from the saddle, unhorsing him with a shattering of his opponent's lance. Cheers turned to cries of shock and dismay as the favored local champion was run into the field, but Jaron only heard the ringing in his ears and he gasped and choked, regaining the breath that was knocked from him. His ribs felt bruised and tight, but he was able to force his lungs to fill with dusty air. Staggering, he regained his feet and fumbled with the latches and straps of the helm, trying to remove it. Sir Cord was at his side, and the confusion and concern in his voice was all too plain.

"Jaron, lad! Are you hurt? What in blazes happened?" He helped the knight out of his helmet as the trumpets sounded the victory of his opponent.

"Jaron!" Lady Cindra shouted, as she ran down the steps from the high box. She was almost to the ground before the countess or Mineth could react, but Sir Earnold was close behind, his hand on his sword.

"Mineth! Go after her!" cried the countess, trying to remain composed. The handmaiden sprang up and followed as quickly as she was able. Her daughter's actions were reckless and ill-founded, and the countess wondered if allowing her to spend time in the young knight's company was not a profound mistake.

Cindra pushed past the startled guards at the foot of the stairs and ran out towards the field, where the victorious knight was riding a tour around the arena, holding his shattered lance high for crowd to see. The sight of the noble lady rushing to the fallen knight, dress and ribbons billowing, detracted from the praise he was hoping for, and the victor looked about in bewilderment.

At the sound of her calling his name, Sir Jaron spun and stumbled towards the Lady Cindra as she fell into his arms at the edge of the jousting grounds. The crowd let out a collective gasp as the young maiden reached for the knight's head and pressed her lips to his. He embraced her in return, his mailed hands soiling her dress and hair as they lost themselves in the kiss.

Mineth stopped dead in her tracks. The countess stood from her chair and let out a choked cry, as her own handmaid fainted where she sat. Sir Cord was at a loss for words and stared at the back of Jaron's head, the lady's fingers were entwined in his locks, her one hand still clutching her rose. The gathered spectators mumbled or gaped in awkward silence, and even the Selvinian Sisters were taken aback by the display, and whispered to one another urgently.

Cindra melted into the knight's arms, the scent of sweat and leather, dusty and musky, and the undercurrent of sweet roses filling her and intoxicating her. Her head was pounding and she could barely breathe, giving herself to his mouth and caresses. Her legs felt limp and her knees buckled but he held her to him, sending a tingle down her spine as her passion shut out all else, even the sound of booted feet stomping across the field from behind.

Rough hands parted the lovers and sent Cindra stumbling back into the arms of her handmaid. Jaron opened his eyes in time to see Sir Earnold's large fist heading straight for his face, and he moved far too slowly to avoid it. For the second time in minutes he was knocked to the ground, pain across his lips that had only just tasted the sweetness of his lady's kiss. He felt Cord's arm's picking him up, helping him to his feet, and the man's deep voice said, "You've done it now, boy."

Sir Earnold had drawn his sword and was standing before the smitten knight, tall and upright in righteous fury, his chin held high as he proclaimed loudly to the countess and all in attendance, "The honor of House Corrina and the young Lady Cindra has been soiled by the filthy hands of a Dunlorden! She is betrothed to an ally, but he has besmirched that pledge with his wicked words and temptations!" He raised his sword towards the countess in salute, shouting, "I demand the right to fight for the honor of the lady I swore to protect! I, Sir Earnold Greenfellow, hereby challenge Jaron Dunlorden to a mortal combat!" The crowd went dead silent.

The countess stared at the tall warrior, his face full of the disgust and outrage that she herself should be feeling, but all she felt was a cold lump in the pit of her stomach. Her face was passive but her eyes were intense, witnessing the scandal that she had unwisely brought upon her family. She had wished for her daughter to learn true love, but only to keep in her heart and hold close when loneliness closed in upon her.

Selvina cherished the unrequited love, for it could be nourished from afar and kept ever in bloom. But this... this was unbridled passion, unabashedly reckless and open, like the pages of a tawdry fantasy acted out before a festival crowd. Her own daughter...

Sir Earnold was still waiting, his sword raised towards the high box. "I offer my sword to restore the honor of House Corrina!" Jaron and Cindra turned to look at the countess, just realizing what was happening.

The countess had little choice. She looked at the faces of the assembled crowd; then to her friend and confidant, Reverend Sister Lyneth, whose large eyes held fear. She looked into the eyes of her daughter, now watering with tears, and she looked into the smoldering gaze of Sir Greenfellow.

She nodded her head.

"No!" Cindra cried, trying to run to Jaron's side, but Mineth held her back. Jaron pulled away from Cord and went to her side, but they only briefly clutched each other's arms before being pulled apart. Their roses fell to the ground and were trampled in the dirt as guards moved in to secure the fallen knight, now under watch until the duel. Mineth led Cindra back to the high box, leaving Sir Earnold to prepare for combat. He was already dressed in protective mail and had little more to make ready, as if he were anticipating such an event.

And of course, he was.

The old woman had faded into the crowd after delivering her roses, and moved behind the grandstands to watch the joust. She drew little attention from anyone, now that she was silent and had discarded her basket. The remaining roses became as wispy smoke and blew away, leaving the basket empty. Only the two real roses remained, fallen on the field.

The old woman spoke a word in a long dead tongue, and her disguise fell away. Years shed from her face and her hair became black and thick, and her skin lost its wrinkles. Her milky eyes became clear and bright, like gray and silver clouds flecked with gold and blue, and they moved over the scene from under her hooded cloak.

Deliah had planned for days, gathering the needed materials from her husband's stores, and preparing her spells in secret. She had even acquired some fresh roses from the Selvinian hothouses, and that had taken some doing. Now her plans had come to fruition, and Sir Earnold would have his fight. The enchanted roses could not have worked if Jaron and the lady had not felt love for one another, for such spells could only enhance one's feelings, not create or alter them. With a lock of hair or a similar token from the subjects, the existing feelings could become far more potent. Deliah hated this manipulative kind of magic, but she knew it well enough. Sir Earnold would have his fight.

And then we shall see.

From within his small pavilion, Sir Cord Freekirk removed Jaron's heavy jousting armor and helped him get into some of the lighter leather guards that would allow for better movement. Cord had never seen the lad like this, and wondered if the fall and subsequent punch had not addled his wits. He seemed to have no focus and was distracted easily by thoughts of the count's daughter, forcing Cord to drag him back to reality. Cord even had to slap him once on the cheek to make him stop mumbling about love and not being able 'to live without her.'

"You won't have to worry about that if Greenfellow kills you!" Cord said, "*She* will have to live without *you*, and maybe she *should*." The older knight shook his head and fastened the leather shoulder guards across the younger man's chest. "I don't know what's gotten into you, but you're acting a bigger fool than I ever thought you to be. If the count were here, he might well have had you executed rather than give you a fighting chance."

"I'm sorry," Jaron mumbled. It was all he could think to say. Telling Cord what was in his thoughts would only get him reprimanded again, maybe slapped. He could not stop thinking of the kiss, of Cindra's warmth and beauty, of all that he had dreamed of coming to pass in one fleeting moment... before he was struck in the face. His mouth still stung and his upper lip was swelling and cut. *Ah yes*, he remembered, *the duel*. That had been the price of his dreams, the consequence of forbidden love. He swam in the gloomy depths of his emotion, so raw and unfathomable. Oh, how he longed to-

"ARE YOU LISTENING?" Cord shouted, jerking the young knight out of his stupor. "You have to fight for your life, and you aren't even here!" He gripped Jaron's head in his hands and looked him fiercely in the eye, an act that had made some men lose control of their bodily functions. "Greenfellow is calling for you. Your armor is ready, your sword is at your hip, but your head is in the clouds!"

Jaron looked back at him, eyes wide in confusion or fear. It made Cord's heart sink. "I don't know if you're going to survive this, lad." He moved his hands to Jaron's shoulders. "You're going outside now, and you're going to fight. If this goddess we're here to honor had any decency to her, she'd come put a stop to it, but the gods don't intervene. Your fate is in your hands." He gave Jaron a friendly blow on the shoulder guards, and led him out of the pavilion.

The crowd was somber and spoke in low whispers; their festival had been darkened by scandal and the promise of bloodshed, and was sure to be talked about for years to come. Sir Earnold stood in the center of the jousting ring, leaning against the center railing, and an assembly of knights dressed in colored festival garb flanked him on both sides, creating a large fighting space.

The Reverend Sister Lyneth, Countess Corrina and Lady Cindra were seated in the high box, and the girl lurched forward as Sir Jaron exited the pavilion and walked uncertainly towards the makeshift arena. His eyes went to the high box and locked on Cindra, and she called his name. Mineth restrained her and the countess flashed her daughter a stern yet deeply concerned look. Lyneth wept inside, her faith in herself and her goddess shaken.

The herald, who had been on hand to announce the events, was returning from the high box. He had been in discussion with the countess regarding the rules for the upcoming duel and was now walking to the center of the designated area, preparing to deliver his proclamation. It was not shaping up to be a good day.

"By decree of her Ladyship the Countess Casselvane, Sir Earnold Greenfellow and Sir Jaron Dunlorden shall duel with arming swords until one of them lies dead."

A wave of gasps went through the crowd although it was what most had expected and why they had lingered. The herald waved his hands downwards for silence. "The argument is for the honor of House Corrina and that of Lady Cindra, daughter of the countess, and betrothed to the Duke DeKaard of Rokvynnar. Sir Earnold battles for House Corrina, having been pledged to defend the lady and her honor."

The herald approached Sir Jaron who had hardly taken his eyes from the high box. "Sir Jaron," he said in a low voice "You cannot claim innocence as this act was beheld by all in attendance. Do you have an intention you wish to make known?"

Jaron looked at the man before returning his eyes to Lady Cindra. "I fight for the truth of our love in the eyes of Selvina."

The herald repeated Jaron's intention to the crowd and it caused a clamor among the gathered faithful who were uncertain how to feel. The countess lowered her eyes, conflicted between her family's honor and that of her beloved goddess.

Lyneth placed a hand on the countess's arm saying, "Regardless of who is victorious, it is the hands of Selvina now." The sisterhood often had needed to interpret events in favor of political realities and they had learned to be flexible. Still, the priestess knew in her heart that this was partly her own doing.

Sir Cord took a place near the outer railing between the duel and the high box, not having the heart to stand with the men encircling the battleground. He watched helplessly as his friend and student took up a place opposite Greenfellow and with a professional eye, he appraised the combatants.

Sir Earnold was a big man, tall as Cord himself though not as broad. He was strong though not overly quick, and while he had trained at the Freekirk School in the *Daerbrik* fighting style, he had been raised with the *Maurbrik* style of his family's own disgraced school. Few men-at-arms in this province used that style anymore, but Greenfellow was quite proficient.

Maurbrik relied on strength and leverage, using an opponent's momentum against him. Typically the fighter used a short blade or buckler in the off hand, using it for close, vicious strikes or trapping the opponent's limbs. With a free hand they were more deadly, as was the case today. Earnold had a confident, bloodthirsty look in his eye, and he stood like he had won already.

Sir Jaron was shorter but well-built and quicker than Greenfellow. He had an advantage in leverage, being smaller, but since his opponent was schooled in both styles, there was little to exploit. Jaron was one of the *Daerbrik* adepts, a style which suited warfare over dueling, utilizing a shield to block attacks and mask counterattacks.

Without a shield, the fighter relied on quickness to sidestep and avoid blows, freeing the weapon to attack rather than parry. Jaron also incorporated an eastern style he had picked up somewhere, adding flourish and surprise to his arsenal. On a good day, he was Earnold's equal or better. Today was not a good day. The outcome seemed so very obvious, and it broke his heart.

Jaron was slouched and slack, his eyes wandering the field like a trapped animal. He kept looking to the lady as if it would help, and he would squeeze his eyes shut and blink as if trying to shake off a hangover. He looked defeated where he stood, and had no fighting spirit in him. Selvina couldn't have asked for a worse champion at her festival.

"Are you ready, Sir Earnold?" called the herald.

"Ready!" shouted the knight.

"Are you ready, Sir Jaron?" the herald asked with a hint of uncertainty.

Jaron looked at him, then to Sir Earnold, who sneered, and he gathered himself as best as he could, nodding to the herald.

"Then may the fight commence, and end when one of you lies dead!" The herald raised his arms and dropped them dramatically as he left the arena.

Earnold took up a fighting stance and closed on Jaron, who shook his head and readied his weapon. Greenfellow swung his blade from the shoulder, slashing at Jaron's head, making Jaron dodge to the left. But the swing was short and not meant to land, and Earnold swung the blade in an arc and stepped in, slashing at his opponent's chest. Jaron barely raised his sword in time to parry, and it sent him tumbling off balance. Earnold smiled and stepped back to watch.

155

Cindra was on the edge of her seat, her knuckles white on the rail as she tried to keep from crying out his name, lest it distract him. She had never felt so helpless in all her life and each time Sir Earnold swung his sword, Cindra's breath caught in her throat as if she were about to see the death of her beloved. Why was this happening? Why now, for the whole world to see? Couldn't they have been more discrete, showing their love in private yesterday under the tree? How had it all gone so wrong?

Jaron saw an opening and lunged, his thrust aiming for his opponent's forward arm, but it was a trick to draw him in and Earnold deflected the clumsy attack, grabbing Jaron's wrist and pulling him over his extended leg, tumbling him to the ground. He chuckled as the smaller knight pulled his face out of the dirt.

"Look at you, right where you belong," he said, casting a shadow over his fallen enemy. "Yours is a family of farmers, not knights. You should have been raised behind an ox's ass, plowing a field."

Jaron stood and swung a combination of blows at Greenfellow, which were blocked, parried, and dodged. Earnold stepped inside of Jaron's last attack and struck him in the jaw, felling him again.

"Plowing a field," he repeated, barely out of breath, "or plowing a peasant girl if you like. But no, you had to make a play for the count's daughter."

Jaron stood and rubbed his jaw, not letting his anger get the best of him. He waited for Earnold to make a move.

Earnold smirked and circled his prey, goading him further. "Your father's a bit too old to be a worthy opponent, but he won't live much longer by the look of him." Jaron restrained himself as he maneuvered and Earnold continued, "I doubt he'll be able to find a woman desperate enough to lie with him and squeeze out another spawn, so this day will mark the end of his line."

Jaron feigned an attack and reversed his sword, stepping in and striking at Earnold's face with the pommel. It was a glancing blow and Earnold grasped Jaron's arm instinctively, trapping it against his left shoulder and rushing forward, using the leverage to force Jaron back onto the ground with Earnold on top of him.

Jaron's sword stuck into the ground and was jarred from his hand and Earnold quickly adjusted his position, straddling the knight and poising his own sword point at his opponent's throat. He had Jaron's sword arm pinned and had disarmed him as well. He looked victoriously towards the high box and saw Cindra standing, screaming in protest. The countess could not bring herself to look upon the scene, and had her head bowed. The reverend sister beside her covered her mouth with her hands.

And Deliah, watching from the crowd, uttered a word under her breath.

Lady Cindra swooned and fainted into her chair.

Jaron, looking up at his impending death, became dizzy and felt the world go black.

Sir Cord, who had lowered his eyes to avoid watching the killing blow, saw wisps of smoke rising from the ground near his feet. He leaned over the rail and saw two roses trampled in the dirt beginning to burn and turn to ash and smoke, leaving behind a strange, sweet odor. They were immolated before his eyes and blew away. He looked up as he heard Earnold shout.

"Don't you faint on me, Dunlorden! I want to see your eyes when I finish you!" He shook the man's arm, striking Jaron in the side of the head with his own fist. "Wake up!"

Jaron's eyes snapped open and he blinked a few times, finally focusing on Earnold's face with a fierce intensity. Earnold saw the change but he had already won, so paid it no mind. He raised his sword over his head, point down, making to plunge it into his enemy's throat. With a shout, he struck.

The sword was too long for Jaron to halt the blow by grabbing the knight's arm. As the blade descended,

Jaron lifted his left elbow towards the sky so that the sword point entered the thick leather cuff of his dueling gauntlet. It cut his flesh and punctured the chain mail glove where it covered the back of his hand; the point would have pierced his throat had he not moved his head, but instead it gave him a rather deep, nasty scratch under his ear.

As Earnold realized what had happened, he released his weight on the sword and tried to withdraw it, but Jaron twisted his arm about and wrenched the trapped weapon from Greenfellow's grasp. The big knight had released Jaron's pinned arm and Jaron used his injured hand to grab Earnold's collar and pull him down into a savage punch. Earnold fell off the smaller knight and hit the dirt, stunned.

Jaron regained his feet and removed Earnold's sword from his wrecked gauntlet, its blade slick with his own blood. Earnold had scrambled to his feet and had taken up Jaron's sword. Jaron hefted the weapon and took a few precious seconds to get the feel for it.

It was a fancier design than what Jaron was used to, a sign of Greenfellow's family wealth. The blade was well balanced and light, and the brass pommel was stylized after the Jaydecean Wheel, representing the gods of nature surrounded by the all-encompassing presence of the World Mother. The Greenfellow family device featured three such wheels and a green diagonal bend on a field of gold.

Jaron thought it ironic that the Greenfellow heraldry honored the gods favored by the 'lowly' farmers they scorned. *All the better to strike him with*, he thought.

The blade was also more curved at the point and the edge was quite sharp, better for slashing than Jaron's weapon. His own sword, now being hefted by Greenfellow, was wide at the hilt and more narrowly pointed for the purpose of piercing chain mail from behind a shield. Battlefield tactics would be of little use in this fight, since he had no shield and his opponent was focused and freed from the chaos of war. A duel was an entirely different affair from a skirmish between soldiers on the field.

Jaron had often reflected on his previous duel with Sir Earnold, going over the movements in his mind. Sir Earnold, then a squire, had mostly trained in the *Maurbrik* style of his family and had little feel for the direct, agile attacks and economy of movement of *Daerbrik*. Jaron had been able to keep Earnold off balance and at a distance, negating the *Maurbrik* strengths.

Now Greenfellow was trained in both styles and knew to anticipate the direct frontal attacks and quick withdraws that denied an opponent a target. He would press the attack and get in close as he had at the start of this fight, keeping Jaron off balance and on the defensive. If Jaron were able to attack, Earnold would switch to the *Maurbrik* grappling and trapping, using Jaron's own limbs against him. It was an honest and grim assessment and it took Jaron all of three seconds to realize it and form a counter plan.

Sir Earnold swung Jaron's sword about before him, flourishing and testing its balance. Something had gone wrong, and his enemy was not as muddled as he had been at the start. The thought crossed his mind that this was Deliah's doing, a betrayal at the last moment in a sad, desperate bid for release.

Well, it mattered not. He would dispatch this farmer's son and repay Deliah for her treachery. He could not kill her, of course, but he could make her life *very* unpleasant. And he could do it with a few chosen words.

Focusing his mind on the battle at hand, Sir Earnold held his enemy's sword out before him, advancing in the quick steps of his adopted style. Using the longer piercing blade, Earnold made a series of thrusts and slashes designed to drive his opponent back to the railing, cutting off his retreat.

Instead of moving back, Jaron deflected the blows and danced sideways to his right, making a sidelong slash at

Earnold's undefended left flank as he passed. The blow scored a mark upon Earnold's mailed upper arm and chest; it did not draw blood, but it drew a shout of surprise and exuberance from the crowd who had lost hope for the young man.

Earnold regained his composure and glanced at his scored armor, smirking. It had been a good attack, but ultimately useless. He moderated his next attack, keeping himself more centered and able to answer another such attempt. Jaron stepped up and parried the blows, forcing Earnold's blade up and away as he stepped into the bigger man's left flank again, obviously making to cut across his midsection.

Greenfellow was ready for the move and stepped in to swing his fist down onto the man's head before skewering him. Jaron suddenly changed direction bringing his sword up and across the crook of Earnold's free arm, the blade biting into the mail and the impact damaging the joint and tendons beneath. Jaron bent low on one knee, redirecting his slash to the left across the back of Greenfellow's leg. He then rolled away and regained his feet in one graceful move, holding his blade before him in an Eastern style seldom seen outside of the theater.

Cindra clasped her hands before her and held back a cheer, keeping herself in check after her earlier display. This whole mess had been her fault, and she was not going to make matters worse by acting like an idiot as a man died over her honor. She had fainted when it seemed Jaron was about to be killed and when her eyes fluttered open, she saw the faces of Mineth and her mother and heard the cheering of the crowd.

She sat up, dreading to see Jaron's bloodied form upon the ground but instead found him circling her "champion" and looking more able than before. Now hope welled up within her breast as she waved off the worried words of her handmaid. She prayed silently to

Selvina to let love win the day, her family honor be damned.

Sir Cord slapped his hand upon the railing, shouting in approval at the sudden turn of events. His eyes flicked down to the burned remains of the two roses and a suspicion began to form in his mind. He spared a few seconds as the knights squared off, searching the faces of the crowd for an old woman in a kerchief and hood and a basket of roses. Not finding the face he was seeking, he resolved to continue the search after the fight, no matter its outcome.

Sir Earnold was furious. His left arm and leg had been slashed and while the blade of his former sword had not prevailed against his chain mail, the blows to his joints had left them feeling weaker and uncertain. Determined not to let his anger guide his attack, he circled the smaller knight, searching for an opening. When he had Jaron between him and the center railing, he attacked.

Jaron was ready for any number of blows, but what came was unexpected. Earnold advanced holding the handle of the sword in his right hand and gripping the end of the blade in his left. He held it before him as a man might hold a staff, ready to block any attack and release a blow from any quarter. Greenfellow was bringing the fight in close and if Jaron moved right or left, he could expect to meet either the point of his own former sword or be struck with the hilt or pommel like a club.

If Earnold were allowed to grapple close, Jaron's slashing blade would be useless. The center jousting rail was at his back, and he could not go beyond its boundary or he would be seen as a coward and loose the right to combat. Execution was not an option.

Earnold was almost within striking distance when Jaron turned and ran towards the nearby railing. Pushing off the wooden barricade with his foot, he leaped and reversed his momentum, twisting back towards his attacker in midair and delivering a sword thrust at the larger man's unprotected neck.

Sir Earnold instinctively turned his head and raised the sword to bar the strike, and the point of Jaron's blade was thwarted, cutting instead across Greenfellow's left cheek, crossing the scar he had received many years before at Jaron's hands. Jaron's body crashed into the large knight, bringing them to the ground in a heap, weapons flying from their grasps.

Rage driving him, Sir Earnold clasped his hands around Dunlorden's throat as the blood from his new wound began to sting his left eye. He didn't need a sword to kill the man, and it was time to bring this battle to a close.

He started to regret boasting and taunting Dunlorden while he was still under the spell, wasting opportunities. *If you mean to kill a man, then kill him. Leave the talk for the funeral.* It was one of his father's first lessons.

Jaron was right where he didn't want to be: in Greenfellow's powerful grasp and without a sword. All he could do was splay his legs on either side of the man beneath him, denying him the leverage to roll Jaron onto his back. His hands fought to break the larger man's hold, giving him just a few more gasps of air, but the mailed gauntlets were vice-like and unmoving.

He had perhaps ten more seconds before he lost consciousness... no, before he was *dead*. He had to do something inspired. He could see both blades lying out of reach where they had fallen, although the edges of his vision were becoming darker. He wouldn't be able to see them for long. They were so... shiny. His lungs burned for air.

This was not going well at all. He didn't want to die like this, certainly not at the hands of this man. What would his father think of that, as he buried his boy on the family farm? He could almost hear the old man's voice, gruff and hoarse from years of shouting and smoking harsh pipe leaf. *"If you die on me now boy, I'll box your ears!"* he seemed to say. Jaron's eyes drifted down to Sir Earnold's face. *Thanks, dad.*

Jaron balled his mailed hands into fists and slammed them into Earnold's unprotected ears, making his grip slacken just a little. Several times more he struck until blood flowed and mingled with the dirt. Finally Jaron was able to draw a rasping breath and he launched himself over Sir Earnold's head, out of his grasp and within reach of the swords.

He would have liked to grab one and finish his opponent, but he was too busy coughing and seeing stars. He kept an eye on Greenfellow, expecting him to leap to his feet and come at him again, but the man was just now trying to roll off his back, shaking his head and looking unbalanced. *Good,* Jaron thought, *I have some time.*

He staggered to his feet and walked over to where his own sword lay, groaning before bending to pick it up. Greenfellow was on his hands and knees, his head bowed as if he were begging for his life, but Jaron was sure he was just dealing with the loss of balance and the ringing in his head. Only *once* had Sir Fedrick Dunlorden boxed young Jaron's ears and only one ear at a time, and with a bare hand at that. Sir Earnold was no doubt in worse shape.

Sword in hand, Jaron swayed a bit as he watched his arch rival regain his composure. Shouts from the crowd reached his ears, including Sir Cord's deep voice, urging him to finish off the staggered knight. It seemed like a good idea but something held him back.

He realized then, when all was said and done, Earnold was in the right. As a squire, Jaron had stolen Greenfellow's betrothed and refused to kill him, scarring him instead. As a knight, Sir Jaron had charmed his way into Lady Cindra's company and had brought shame and scandal upon the very house he served. The man had reason enough to kill him without the matter between their respective fathers. Still, Sir Jaron was not about to be executed. Neither was Sir Earnold, for that matter.

He kicked Earnold's sword within the large knight's grasp.

The crowd gasped and went silent and Jaron thought he heard his big friend groan from the railing. *Damned fool*, he thought he could hear Cord saying, or maybe it was in his own head. *Probably right either way.*

Sir Earnold took up his sword and used it to raise himself up like a crutch until he wavered unevenly on his feet. His eyes no longer burned with hatred but they held a grim determination as he held up his sword and saluted his fellow knight. "I am going to kill you Sir Jaron," he intoned, no hint of malice present.

Sir Jaron returned his salute and said, "You are going to try, Sir Earnold."

The men faced each other for nearly a full minute, unmoving but for the breeze that threatened their precarious balance, snapping the ribbons in the air about the field.

They moved as one, lurching across the distance on unsteady legs, shoulders low and heavy with the weight of the steel in their hands. Sir Earnold slashed up across Jaron's raised blade, knocking it aside, and quickly reversed his attack, bringing the blade down upon the smaller knight's neck.

But Jaron's neck was not there. The smaller man had ducked under the second slash and darted to the side, driving the point of his sword under Sir Earnold's chin in a deft stroke, killing him instantly.

The large knight fell heavily to the field.

There was a momentary pause as the crowd took in what they had seen. The honor of House Corrina had not been recovered, but the love of the knight and lady was proven to be the stronger. Was it a sign from the goddess? What did it all mean? Not knowing what to make of the events, the crowd cheered for the victor.

Cindra leaped to her feet and clasped her hands before her mouth lest she cry out. Tears were in her eyes and her heart leapt for joy at the sight of her beloved standing there, alive and well. Yet, her passion was cooler and her feelings not as intense as they were before. Was it her shame that was stopping her from running into his arms again? Was her discretion so fragile as to be in place one moment and out the window the next? What was wrong with her?

The countess was also on her feet, a slight smile upon her face at her daughter's happiness, and nodding at the affirmations of her friend the reverend sister. Lyneth was in a state of rapture over the workings of her beloved goddess whom had surely been smiling down on the knight and lady.

A true love had won out over the odds, and the people had seen the strength of its power with their very eyes. It was an Omen, she was sure of it, and it foretold of a great destiny awaiting the knight, or the lady, or both. She clasped her hands in thankful prayer that she had been chosen to play a small part in the goddess's works.

Sir Cord hurried onto the field to see to his friend and make sure that none of the surrounding knights decided to take the honor of House Corrina into their own hands. He led the young man off the jousting field and sat him down on a bench, calling to the watchmen in festival garb. They approached, thinking perhaps he meant for them to take the lad into custody, but Sir Cord bid them to search the grounds for an old woman with milky eyes and wiry hair selling roses. The watchmen looked at the big knight as if he had been sampling the festival mead but did as they were ordered.

Countess Casselvane looked down upon the dear young knight whom her daughter loved. She had only meant for their time together to be a happy memory for them both, not to be realized in an affair that disregarded honor, bonds and station. Now one of her husband's knights was dead, and another marked as a disgrace.

The count was due back at the end of the month and she realized that in his rage, he might undo the victory this young man had won for himself. She did not wish to see her daughter mourn his loss, but something must be done. She would decide the young Sir Jaron's fate before her husband arrived and spare everyone the pain of going through this all again. But even as her daughter beamed down upon the handsome knight and he gazed up at her and smiled, the countess thought to herself, *this could have ended in a better way.*

She motioned for the victor to be detained as Sir Earnold's body was carried from the field.

Chapter Nine

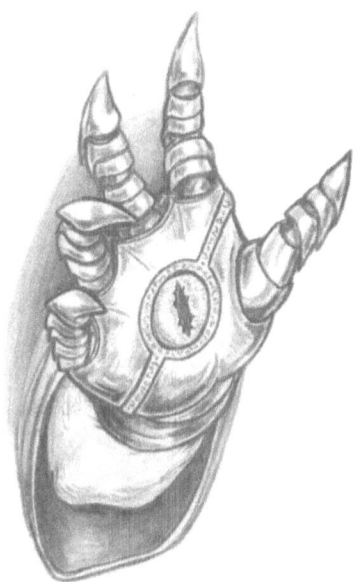

Questions and Gifts

"I should be dead," Jaron said solemnly, staring into the fire in his father's quarters.

"Boy, I'd get up and box your ears if I weren't so damned comfortable," said Sir Fedrick, his brow creasing over his watery eyes. "That'll be enough talk of death from you."

"If you'd like I could box his ears for you," offered Cord Freekirk, packing his pipe. "I don't mind getting up." He ignited a wick in the fire and lit his pipe with it, pulling in the flame and puffing out fragrant smoke.

The room was comfortable and well-appointed for a soldier's quarters in the castle, but as it was Sir Fedrick's sole lodging, it was not seen as an extravagance. Jaron sat in a plain wooden chair near the fire and Fedrick and Cord sat in high-backed, cushioned chairs opposite him. A table stood against one wall with the remains of a modest meal and a simple but comfortable bed was positioned against the opposing wall, smartly made and tidy. A few trophies of war were displayed on the walls with no great embellishment and the fire was the only light present.

Jaron sighed and rubbed his eyes, partly from the smoke and partly from exhaustion. "I've brought dishonor to House Corrina, father. The lady and I... it was scandalous."

Fedrick worked his lips around his own pipe, which rested in a large gap in his teeth. "I heard about it all by now, lad. Sir Cord here thinks there was more at work than just young love and he's told the countess as much. She doesn't understand the lady's actions either. Sounds to me like you were both out of your heads."

"Does it matter? We are both shamed and I have killed the man who was defending her honor. I've made a mess of everything." He went back to looking into the fire, avoiding the eyes of the other men.

Cord was getting frustrated. "I told you, it *matters* a great deal. If someone spelled you and the lady then it could have been a plot! Maybe some foreign scheme to spoil her betrothal and the alliance it will bring, or maybe..."

"Maybe if we hadn't had feelings for each other, it wouldn't have happened at all." Jaron said angrily. He had spent the last few hours in self-recrimination and he wasn't going to be talked out of it so easily.

Cord scowled. "Maybe not. But if there was magic, there was meddling. I intend to find out who was behind it and why."

Fedrick nodded saying, "I agree. If there's mischief afoot, then the count should know about it. Anyone casting spells on his daughter or his knights is an enemy of the realm as far as I'm concerned."

Jaron stood, raising his hands. "Fine. You go and ferret out the foreign wizard-spy and the old woman who passes out roses. I am going to walk the battlements and clear my head." He stalked out of the chamber and into the company of two armed guards, shutting the door behind him with a bit more force than was necessary.

Cord and Fedrick sat in the room listening to the crackling of the fire. Cord spoke first. "Sometimes I don't understand him."

Fedrick laughed in a puff of smoke. "*Sometimes*?" he cracked, his eyes wrinkling in mirth. "I don't understand him most times. He takes too much on himself when he bothers to take on anything at all."

Cord relit his pipe and said, "I remember when he first came to the school. He was so serious and focused, always trying so hard to fit in that he stood out." Cord extinguished the wick with a wave. "Then later he was so carefree, I wondered if he would ever pass his tests and achieve knighthood."

"Hah! I'd have kicked him from one end of the province to another if he hadn't," said Fedrick, gazing at the fire with his good eye. "After all, I'm not living here just because the rent is cheap." He motioned to the four walls.

Sir Fedrick had become a knight through a field commission but still had to pay for his own horse, armor and weapons. He had no family fortune or holdings to draw from, only his farm which had belonged to the county. The count had granted Fedrick ownership of the farmland and he had turned it over to a young, recently married couple to work, providing himself with an income, albeit a small one.

Sir Fedrick was a frequent visitor to the old farm and he was able to offer advice to the young family when times were difficult. He even brought them a goose or pheasant for feasting days so they didn't need to take from their own livestock and there was always a place for him at their table. He was perhaps the poorest and most beloved landlord in the realm, and that suited him.

He lived in the modest chambers in the castle in order to save for his son's future. The young man had no land of his own and would not be able to draw a rent until the farm passed to him. He had put the boy through the

Freekirk School and bought him his first sword, as well the horse he had named 'Vortigras.' The lad was given a stipend and had been purchasing his own plate armor piece by piece, and had half a set by now. Sir Fedrick wondered briefly if the lad would ever complete it and he cursed himself for the thought.

The men sat in silence, pipe smoke wafting about their heads. Eventually Fedrick said, "Do you think you can find the ones who did it? Is there really a chance? I mean wizards are a slippery lot. Even that 'Talon Finnael' character; and he doesn't pay the proper respect to authority, not to my mind."

Cord let the smoke trickle from his mouth as he asked himself that same question. "I don't know. I looked the woman in the face but can barely recall her." He shook his head, "The guardsmen at the festival found only an empty basket and a kerchief. No old woman with milky eyes, no roses. It's like she vanished. Can wizards make people vanish?"

"Don't know," said Fedrick. He cocked his head in question, "Where do you get roses this time of year? Seems too cold for them to bloom."

Cord nodded, "The Selvinian Sisterhood has a temple hothouse... no, not *that* kind," he smirked as Fedrick let out a guffaw, "a hothouse for gardening. They use it to grow roses year-round for their ceremonies. In the spring and summer their temple gardens are full of them."

Fedrick eyed him, "How do you know so much about their roses?"

Cord smiled and said, "I've had cause to seek a rose for a young lady in my time," he took another puff of his pipe, "There was a lass I met once during the colder months and I looked to give her a token of my affection."

Fedrick asked, "How did that turn out?"

"I'll let you know." Cord said with a smile. "Anyway it's best to start looking at the temple, perhaps even some local flower sellers. If we can find where the damned things came from we might learn much." He rose from his chair and knocked out the remains of his pipe leaf into the fire. "I'll report back when I find something. He's not going to take the full blame for this, not if I can help it." He donned his beret and cloak and gave Fedrick a salute before leaving the room.

The old knight placed the stem of his pipe between his teeth and sighed, releasing a wreath of smoke from the bowl. He had never liked magic and he liked those who tinkered in it even less. It took a peculiar kind of person to muck about with the forces of nature and power like that never led to any good, no matter what the wizards' guild or the Order might say. If you could play with fire and not get burned, why, there was no telling what you'd entertain yourself with next.

It was no wonder the gods had stopped interfering in people's lives, he thought, *We've found so many ways to do the meddling ourselves.*

Ildric Finnael left the Tower of Sight, locking the doors behind him with a few words of binding. Ivy vines from around the foundation twisted over the portal, obscuring the door from view. Ildric had chosen a robe with the Corrina colors of blue and gold, hoping to set the count's daughter at ease.

As for the peasant boy she had rescued, he knew not what would make the lad comfortable in the presence of a wizard, but he had decided it was time to interview the two children regarding their strange adventure and he would have to get the boy to talk openly. Maybe that was why he had brought along his little apprentice? After all, *he* seemed to have a way with children when he was of a mind to mingle with them.

Drahn sat on his haunches beside the wizard, watching the vines enclose the entryway. He had decided that he would walk with his master all the way to the castle, declining to fly or nestle in the man's backpack, comfortable though it was. Drahn had never walked the streets before, fearing the clumsy feet of much bigger things like horses or people, for he was only a little larger than a cat, excepting his long neck and tail.

Now he had his master to walk with and he had noticed on other occasions how the crowds seemed to part for him, not wishing to jostle the man with the silver hand. Drahn figured he could walk freely in Ildric's wake or by his side if they were conversing. It was so much easier to talk when both participants were at roughly the same altitude.

The strange pair set off from the tower towards a side street that bypassed the Market Square, which was bustling with activity in the late morning. The ocean breeze managed to carry over the tall block of apartments that lined the canal, but it was hardly refreshing since it bore odors from the fishing ward and the harbor stockyards. City life at street level was unpleasant to the discriminating nose; it was one of many reasons why wizards lived in towers when they could manage.

The Dweedragon glanced up the length of the man's silver-etched staff, which clicked a cadence on the paving stones as they walked. Every wizard had a *verge* of some sort, a specially prepared item that allowed the adept to pull upon the magic around them which they were otherwise unable to touch or feel. Most wizards of Ildric's ability carried a staff, but some used wands, rods or even talismans. Regardless of type and style, all verges contained small amounts of silver, and the etching of Ildric's staff caught the morning sun and sent little shards of light all about.

Long ago silver was found to have special properties in the presence of spirit wells, such as the one upon which the Tower of Sight and the Tower of the Silver Moon were built. These wells of magic, combined with silver, allowed humans to manipulate the fabric of the universe itself. It was later discovered that a verge could be made to safely draw upon magic outside of the spirit wells and as long as the silver conduit was safely enclosed in wood, there was no great danger.

Wood was a barrier of sorts, a balance of elements that shielded the wizard from the raw power he had to evoke to cast even basic spells. A verge took a long time to construct and attune, and a wizard could only use one he himself had constructed. It was a most prized possession.

Drahn had learned all of this in his studies, but he had no need of a verge himself. He was dragon-kind, the eldest of the elder races, and magic was in his blood. Still, Ildric's staff was very pretty and Drahn always liked to look upon it, dreaming of having his own someday. All practicality aside, a staff of dark wood and glittering metal would make a beautiful addition to his small horde. The little dragon's scales shimmered between red and purple as he pondered it.

The North River Walk was a wide street that ran southeast to the Sea Gate which separated the fishing ward from the city proper and northwest to the Temple Walk, the lovely thoroughfare that encircled the cathedral. Though the 'river' was actually a canal that emptied into the sea and the street had no real view of it, the North River Walk was still a popular place to take a stroll. Twin-orbed wizard lamps stood in a row down its length and the spillover business from the Market Square fed a number of shops and taverns.

Drahn took a while to reach his stride and Ildric's presence parted the crowd as usual, ensuring that the little dweedragon would not be stepped on. Accustomed to flying overhead, the small creature was getting many more looks than he had anticipated and was becoming a bit self-conscious. It seemed that people looked down far more often than they looked up. He decided to spark up a conversation with Ildric and distract himself from the odd looks. "So, we are going to give Lady Cindwa a gift, yes?" He asked, craning his neck upward.

Ildric started at the voice from his knee as if he had been lost in thought and forgotten Drahn was there.

"Yes, a belated birthday present. I shall also try to learn more about the attack upon the boy and her role in preventing it."

"You think it is important to your pwophecy?" Drahn asked, remembering his master's preoccupation with his visions.

Ildric shook his head saying, "It is not really a prophecy."

The dweedragon blinked and looked up at Ildric, puzzled. "It is a pwediction of the future. Isn't that what a pwophecy is?"

Ildric walked a few more steps before answering, "There has not been a true prophecy in over eleven hundred years. Not since the prophecy of Kraal's Return."

Drahn reached into his perfect dragon memory, recalling the passage he had read many years before:

The Blood Divine returns from distant lands,
And deathless ruler once again shall hold,
The providence of life in mighty hands,
As dark events will thrice again unfold.

The scion then must into danger leap,
And take the shard of heaven to contend,
With seed of bedlam in creation deep,
Sending one or both to meet its end.

Ildric nodded and smiled, always impressed with the mind of the scholarly creature. "That was the last true prophecy, for it was delivered by man but sent by the gods."

"Before they left the world to its own means," said Drahn, remembering his history lessons. "Then it cannot be a pwophecy unless it comes fwom the gods? You still had a vision of what will happen."

"But the interpretation, the significance of the vision is left for us to decide. What I saw may only be important to me, not to the course of human events. I cannot call it a prophecy if its meaning is vague and its worth is questionable." Ildric said.

"I see," said Drahn. "But if the gods meant for us to make our own destinies, then it would seem to me that divining the future is the best way."

"That would put wizards in the position of the priests of old, would it not?" asked Ildric.

Drahn considered and said, "Why not? If wizards can give people the knowledge they need..."

"Then what is to stop them from telling others what to do, from guiding the fate of kingdoms for their own ends? And if the gods will not come down and say otherwise, who is to argue with them?" Ildric shook his white head. "No Drahn, wizards must not seek such power. Divining brings knowledge but not wisdom. A man with too much knowledge and little wisdom is much more dangerous than his opposite."

"But, you believe that your visions are tied to the Lady Cindwa's destiny and that of the boy. Maybe even to the destiny of the kingdom. Is it not your place to tell them?" Drahn asked.

Ildric stopped at the bridge as a cart rolled past and considered his answer. "It is my place to seek answers to my own questions," he said finally. "To tell others about my visions is to deny them the search for their own destinies." He looked down at the dweedragon and smiled. "You may find that knowledge is not so great a thing as belief or hope."

Drahn considered this as they walked in silence across the bridge and through the Harbor District. The little dweedragon had a wealth of knowledge from his years of study with the city scholars, but there were many important things that were missing. As an egg, he had listened to his mother pass along some of the ancient stories and legends of his kin and she had given him his name.

But something had happened to her and his clutch mates, something terrible. He had been too young to understand all of what he heard through his eggshell, but his perfect dragon memory allowed him to relive it again and again. He had become separated from his mother, and his egg had rolled and tumbled about, disorienting him. There were voices of men and cries of draconic rage...

Drahn knew about the value of belief and hope. He believed he would find his family or what had become of them and he hoped with all his mighty heart that they were alive and well. He would not want Ildric or anyone else to tell him otherwise.

As they crossed a bridge from the Harbor District to the Lowcourt where the Tower of the Silver Moon was located, Drahn looked up at the tower and let out a little squawk. The pigeons had roosted again in his absence but there was no time to oust them now. His wings flapped in frustration, lifting his front claws from the ground, but he quickly regained his composure at Ildric's questioning look. The wizard was looking up at the patina edifice himself, but for different reasons.

"The council thinks I've lost my mind, you know," he said wistfully.

Drahn looked up at him in surprise. "What? Why would they think that?" He respected his master and was incensed that anyone would suggest such a thing.

Ildric cast his eyes towards the pavement as he spoke. "I have told them that a great war is approaching and that the end of all things is nigh. I have told them that we are living in the last days of our world, if it comes to that. What else would they think of me?"

Drahn cast an angry glance at the wizard tower and began forming a reproach, but then remembered what Ildric had just said about destiny and hope. "They... they are afwaid you are wight. They know your visions are the stwongest, and they don't want to face it."

Ildric nodded. "Tell a man it will rain and he will seek shelter. Tell him his house will wash away, and he may cling all the more tightly to the life he knows, defying the weather and the gods to do their worst." He looked up at the tower again saying, "I gave them too much knowledge and not enough wisdom. Some may act, some may panic, and most will do nothing." He smiled down at Drahn. "So much for Ildric the Prophet."

The wizard and the Dweedragon walked in silence to the gates of the Highcourt and climbed the road past the villas of noble families surrounded by bare trees and evergreens. There were no children playing on the lawns and only the groundskeepers were seen moving amongst the plastered walls of stone. For all of its wealth, it was a cheerless part of the city. The odd pair continued through the castle's outer gate, unhindered by the nervous guards.

Cindra had been informed of the strange visit and had dressed in her favorite pelice of fur-lined blue silk with a yellow gown beneath. Nixy had been told to attend as well and he had been scrubbed pink and given a clean linen tunic to wear. His hair, though combed and cut, still managed to retain its cowlick. He shuffled nervously around the room as the servants stoked a fire and arranged refreshments.

There was no real protocol for receiving a visiting wizard so the house staff did the best it could. Cindra sat on a comfortable couch lined with cushions, which was across from a large high-backed chair set out for their guest. A table was between them with an assortment of breads and crackers and various spreads like butter, honey, and goose liver paste. Goblets and pitchers of ale, cider and wine stood nearby at hand and servants were nervously trying to decide who would attend the lady and her guest.

Wizards of low stature were odd enough, but one as renowned as Ildric Finnael was bound to be problematic and no one wanted to be turned into a rabbit over a misunderstanding. They finished up and took their conversation out into the large hall, first placing a silver bell upon the table.

The room chosen for the audience was the castle study, an elegant room lined with beautiful and well-stocked bookshelves along the floor and upon the balcony which stretched along two walls. The outer wall contained two stained glass windows that, like all the others in the castle, were protected by spells to prevent them from breaking. The same could not be done for the walls, for they were so very thick; while they might crumble under cannon fire, the windows at least would remain intact.

A fireplace and various hunting trophies taken from the Shadowood Forest by generations of Cindra's forbearers dominated the fourth wall. Racks of antlers and snarling faces threatened her from above, invigorated by their recent dusting.

The occupants of the castle were startled by a single loud knock upon the main doors, an unnatural sound like the booming of distant thunder. The impact of a battering ram could not have been as unsettling as that single sound, which set the hairs on end and could be felt deep in one's chest. The doormen hurried to answer the knock before it struck again.

Cindra took a deep breath and folded her hands in her lap, awaiting the imminent arrival of Ildric Finnael, and Nixy quickly sat at her side, not trusting his knees to keep from going all wobbly.

After a few nervous minutes there could be heard the sound of footsteps and the clacking of a staff echoing through the large hall outside. The door opened admitting a servant, the countess, and the wizard. The children stood as they entered, Nixy doing so only after a hand motion from Cindra. The countess was attired in a simple housedress, since she was not meant to take a part of the meeting.

She smiled graciously and introduced their guest. "Master Finnael, may I introduce you to my daughter, Lady Cindra Corrina, and Master Nixyalderthor DuQuayne. Children, this is Arch Magus Ildric Finnael." She spoke with cool formality, but her eyes were uncertain. She had no fear for the children's safety but the visit itself was unusual enough to warrant apprehension.

The wizard was shorter than Cindra expected, perhaps a bit shorter than her father, but in his face was an age-worn wisdom and confidence. His white hair was brushed back and reached his shoulders and his beard was kept perhaps a half-finger in length and well-trimmed. She was expecting a long flowing one, and perhaps a hat. She knew him only by reputation after all.

"How do you do?" said Cindra, curtsying. Nixy mumbled something similar and bowed, not taking his eyes from the man.

There was a noise like a cough or throat clearing in the vicinity of the wizard's knees and from behind him stepped a small purple dragon, with large cat-like eyes, gracefully swept horns and iridescent wings which were folded at its sides. It moved around the wizard to where it could be seen and sat up on its haunches, winding its tail about its feet and folding its front claws together in a gesture of waiting.

The countess was taken aback for she had not noticed the little creature, but she recovered her shock instantly; a lifetime of hiding her emotions had made such a feat possible. She looked to the wizard for an explanation.

Ildric bowed to Cindra and said, "I hope the day finds you well, Lady Cindra." He nodded to the boy as well, "Master Nixyalderthor, how do you do. May I present my pupil, Drahn the Dweedragon." The small creature bowed his horned head to each of them, surprising them by speaking.

"How do you do?" he said in his light, high voice, raising eyebrows and drawing smiles across the children's faces. Nixy was too overwhelmed to utter anything embarrassing.

It seems my instincts were correct, thought the wizard.

The countess motioned to the table before them. "We have prepared refreshments, and if you have need of anything, simply ring the bell." She smiled and looked pointedly at the wizard's staff. "My servants shall attend."

179

Ildric bowed and pulled at his beard, saying with a laugh, "My apologies about the knock, Countess. It is an unfortunate habit for wizards to make an impression."

She nodded her acceptance and withdrew, leaving the servant to follow her out and latch the door behind.

Cindra, who had some training in receiving guests, gestured to the chairs. "Shall we sit?" She made an offer of snacks and drinks to the wizard who declined, and to the little dragon, who declined only after looking pleadingly at Ildric. "To what do we owe the pleasure of this special visit, Arch Magus?" she asked. She knew the answer but it was polite to ask.

"Please," he said, gesturing with his metallic hand as he set his staff aside, "You may call me Master Ildric if you wish."

"The Talon!" blurted Nixy upon seeing the hand, not meaning to speak aloud.

Ildric smiled at the boy. "Yes, I have heard that name too. Master Ildric will do." Nixy's face turned quite red.

"I have come with questions about the events that brought the two of you together, about the night of your birthday," he said.

"Very well," she said, folding her hands in her lap. "I had, er, left the castle, as you might have known, and I had my purse stolen," she glanced at Nixy, who smiled, "and I chased the little thief. It was after I caught him that..."

"It was Black Will," Nixy muttered, and Cindra nodded. The two turned somber as their minds turned to the night in question.

Ildric gave them a moment to collect themselves and asked, "Can you describe what you felt as he approached? I know this is difficult."

Cindra spoke first, "I saw him crawl down the wall of the temple. He moved... like a spider or a crab, feet first, with his back to the wall. He came up behind Nixy and I- I wanted to warn him, but I couldn't."

"We couldn't scream," Nixy said, "I tried, but it didn't make no noise. It was like we had our mouths covered or something."

Cindra said, "He was speaking in a strange voice, a horrible voice. He was saying something about Nixy's blood, about his father's blood."

Nixy stuttered, "B-b-blood Magic." His face was growing pale. Ildric and Drahn exchanged a worried look at the words.

"He began to drag Nixy into a dark alley... I was too scared to move; I wanted to run but didn't want to leave him..." Cindra fidgeted in her seat.

Drahn spoke up from the floor near the table, "What you did was vewy bwave," he said, and the girl smiled meekly at him.

Ildric nodded, "Yes, please tell us what happened next. You used your knife?"

"It was *my* knife," said the boy, fumbling with the sheath at his side.

Cindra said, "I took Nixy's knife after I caught him, and realized I still had it when he was being attacked, so..."

Nixy drew the blade and held it out for the wizard to examine. "*That* is the knife? *Your* knife?" asked Ildric, and Nixy nodded. The raven's head carving and white metal caught the light from the windows.

Cindra knew what Ildric was thinking, for she had the same thoughts. The weapon looked like it had belonged to a nobleman once; before somebody's sticky fingers had found it.

Instead of taking the knife, Ildric held his metal hand towards it and Nixy saw what looked like an eye embedded in the palm of the silver talon. The eye seemed to be made of polished stone of green and yellow with a black slit down the middle like the eyes of the little dragon before him. It was bigger around than a coin and seemed to shine with a strange light.

As the boy watched, the dark pupil of the eye flashed and widened and it moved to flicker its gaze over the knife, like a living thing. Nixy gasped and sat still as a stone, lest the creepy thing look to examine *him*. As the soft glow moved over the blade and the carved handle, Nixy glanced at the face of the wizard. Ildric's eyes were distant and unfocused, as if looking past him. Then the wizard's metal talon flexed and his eyes met Nixy's, his expression puzzled and uncertain. The stone eye no longer moved in its socket and the boy allowed himself to relax, holding the knife close to his chest.

Cindra had expected to see something strange and she had been delighted at the little dragon, but this display was... disquieting. "What just happened?"

Ildric sat back and looked at the children, nodding to himself. Drahn was curious too and waited expectantly for his master to speak. "I had suspicions," he said finally. "I had wondered how this 'Black Will,' had been driven off with only a minor injury. I suspected that the lady had carried a weapon of superior quality, possibly holding an enchantment. It seems I was correct, but the knife belongs to you." He looked at Nixy. "Tell me young man, how did you come by such a treasure?"

Nixy looked down at the blade, uncertain what he had just heard. Enchanted? "It belonged to my mum," he said, tracing a finger over the carved raven head. "She told my dad she wanted me to have it when I was old enough, and when I left home... well, I took it."

"Did you ever hear where she might have acquired it?" asked the wizard.

Nixy shook his head slowly, thinking back over the few times his father had ever spoken of the woman he loved.

"So," Cindra reasoned, "Black Will was driven off because I cut him with a magic knife? How did that help? It wasn't very deep..."

"I think," said Ildric, "that Black Will, as you call him, is a man possessed by a demnox." The word made Nixy squirm. "A demnox is a spirit of chaos and strife that has needs it cannot fulfill, for it has no material body. For this, it seeks a host among the mortal world with... similar needs. Together they are powerful but not invulnerable. The human host can be wounded so badly that the demnox can no longer heal him." Ildric pointed to Nixy's knife and said, "Or in this case, the demnox *itself* can be wounded with magic."

Cindra crossed her arms, looking vexed. "So I wounded an evil spirit. Splendid." Nixy didn't seem to think it was a good thing either.

Drahn reached up to sample the crackers and said, "It's possible that the demnox has existed for countless millennia without feeling pain. You gave it a sting it won't soon fowget!"

The dweedragon stopped chewing his cracker as he noticed they were all staring at him.

"That was hardly helpful Drahn," Ildric said. The children looked a little pale.

"Sowwy," Drahn said around a mouthful of crumbs.

"What do we do?" asked Nixy, "If the man is killed, won't the demnox move to a new body?"

"If it can find one willing to take it in," Ildric said, "What concerns me more is why it was after you."

"He talked about Nixy's father's blood, and Blood Magic. What kind of magic is that?" Cindra had seen the earlier looks traded between Ildric and Drahn and knew it was important. Also, she had no intention of letting her guests walk away with all the answers, leaving them with none.

Ildric and Drahn exchanged that enigmatic look once again but before Cindra could lose her patience, the wizard spoke, "Blood Magic is an ancient practice that has been forbidden in all civilized lands. Its origins go back to the days of the Sorcerer Kings."

Cindra frowned, "My education does not go back that far I'm afraid." She doubted Nixy's did either. The boy just blinked.

Ildric gestured to Drahn and said, "My friend here is the expert on ancient history. Give us a lesson Drahn, and make it light on details if you please."

The dweedragon climbed upon the table to make his presentation, situating himself within reach of the crackers and goose liver paste. "Many thousands of years ago," he began, "before the wise of the Celvestwian Empire, there were gweat families of many nations that had magic in their blood." He paused and gathered himself, taking care to pronounce his words more carefully and thus draw fewer snickers from the boy.

"The most gifted of these held powers beyond what we know today, and they ruled over their lands as Sorcerer Kings. They even held the blessings of Arathus the King God, who ordained that they should have divine protection to insure their rule. Thus, he sent legions of Kyraine to guard the Sorcerer Kings, should any seek to harm them."

"What's a Kyraine?" asked Nixy.

Drahn was happy the lad was listening. "Kyraine are the winged warriors and servants of the gods, most often depicted as beautiful women with clawed hands and feet."

The boy nodded his understanding and Drahn continued, "The Sorcerer Kings often made war upon one another, but they could not be undone, for the Kyraine would not allow harm to come to their charges, nor would they do battle against their sisters. It seemed as if the line of kings would endure forever in the care of the gods..." He paused for dramatic effect and hunched his shoulders, flexing his wings. "...But the forces of darkness had other plans. Lying in wait, they cwafted the downfall of the Sorcerer Kings..."

"No theatrics, Drahn," Ildric interjected, "just facts."

"Sowwy," said the little dragon, trying to maintain his dignity as the corners of his mouth drooped. Dragons were natural storytellers after all, and he was entertaining children, not lecturing old academics.

He defiantly took a finger-full of the goose liver paste and licked his claws clean before continuing. "Anyway, the magic in their blood was their stwength, and as it turned out, their greatest weakness. Minions of Llomaak, the Lord of Chaos, taught the Sorcerer Kings the secrets of Blood Magic, which allowed for the spinning of harmful spells against a person by using their blood, or the blood of a close relative.

"As the kings began to fall to terrible illness or calamity, there was a panic in the royal houses as the surviving sorcerers began rounding up all of their close relatives and imprisoning them, even slaying them, to insure that their blood could not be used by an enemy. Sadly, whether by the hand of a rival or by their own terrible precautions, the bloodlines of the Sorcerer Kings came to an end."

Ildric poured the dweedragon a goblet of wine for his trouble and Drahn said, "Why, thank you Master," before inserting his snout and gratefully lapping it up.

Cindra was puzzled. "If this Blood Magic was so effective, why isn't it used today? I am sure there are wizard assassins who would not hesitate to learn such vile things."

Ildric nodded. "This is true, and there are those darker elements that seek such power. But its uses are few in this age, thankfully. The Sorcerer Kings had magic in their blood, you see. Therefore, they were far more susceptible to that dark power than we mere humans are today."

Nixy asked, "But don't you have magic in your blood?" The man was supposed to be a wizard after all, wasn't he?

Ildric shook his head. "I am but a man who has studied the science of magic, what we call Wizardry. Like any difficult area of study, it requires years of practice, training, and the proper tools. Sorcerers, like the kings of old, had the power in their blood. They needed no staff or wand, no learning of tried and tested incantations and rituals. They are born to it, like a fish to water." He smiled. "Actually, the only one in this room with magic in their blood is Drahn here." He motioned to his little pupil who was dipping crackers in his wine goblet.

Drahn looked up and smiled weakly at them, hoping no one would ask. Cindra disappointed him by being clever.

"So why is he your pupil then?" she asked the wizard.

Ildric realized his folly and looked at Drahn with concern. He had not meant to bring up a sore subject, but it was one that came up often enough to those familiar with dragons.

Drahn finished his wine-soaked cracker and said, "Dwagons learn much while still in the egg. We are taught about our histowy and legends, even how to use magic. I was... sepawated fwom my mother before I hatched and... well, there is much I am missing."

"I'm sorry, Drahn. I meant no offense." She wanted to pet him but was not sure that would be a good idea. Did dragons like to be petted? Cindra knew *she* didn't care for it.

Drahn shook his head, looking forlorn. "It is alwight," he said, "I have learned much with Master Ildric, and I have studied with many gweat minds. I have even told the scholars much about dwagons, so that they might cowwect their books."

Nixy spoke up. "I didn't know my mother either. She died when I was born." He looked at the little dragon now like a kindred spirit.

Drahn said, "Oh, I knew my mother. That is to say, I never met her, but she taught my clutch mates and me, and gave us our names." He closed his eyes and then spoke a word in a voice deep and rumbling, sibilant and haunting. "*Drahnizhlomazhith.*" The children were taken aback, not expecting such a sound to come from the little creature.

"What was that?" asked Nixy.

"My name," said Drahn, opening his eyes and smiling, "As given to me by my mother."

"It is why we call him Drahn," said Ildric with a wink in his eye.

Cindra was still unsatisfied and wanted answers. "Something confuses me," she said, hating to break the mood of the moment, "If this Blood Magic is so ineffective, why use it on Nixy? Why do they want to hurt him and his father?"

"I wish I knew," said the wizard, pulling upon his beard. "It would be improper to speculate at this time, but I should point out that Blood Magic is by no means ineffective, it is simply much weaker on those with non-magical blood. It can still be used to cause illness or discomfort, perhaps worse." The wizard gazed at the table and asked, "Did the demnox say anything else before it fled, anything that might provide a clue?"

The children looked at one another, remembering the black bones of smoke and fire that had leapt out of the man, and the inhuman howling. Cindra grasped for anything she might have omitted from her written testimony of over a month before. "I think," she started uncertainly, "there was something. I'm not sure if it's important, but after Black Will fled to the rooftops and Nixy and I could speak again, I had the feeling that... that we were about to die. That running or screaming was hopeless and nothing would save us."

Nixy nodded in agreement. They had not spoken of this together, but each knew the other had felt it. It had been like a cold mist surrounding them, leeching away all hope and strength.

Ildric ran a finger over the cold metal of his silver hand. "Perhaps it was another power of the demnox, perhaps not. I think for now the castle is the safest place you can be." He began to rise, and Drahn used the time to hoard a small stack of crackers. "I thank you both for your willingness to share your story. I have much to consider, and more to look into. But first," he reached into the pocket of his robe as the children stood, "First I have a belated birthday present for the lady."

Cindra blinked in surprise, smiled and said, "Oh, it really isn't necessary, Master Ildric." Yet she was anxious to see what he had brought her. A gift from a wizard *had* to be something special after all.

The wizard presented her with a small wooden box with hinges and a latch. She took it, thanked him, and opened it carefully lest something pop out, explode, or begin to sing and play music. Instead it contained a velvet lining and a beautiful golden bracelet set with a sea stone of blue and green. It glittered in the light of the stained glass windows and begged to be examined. Cindra removed it from the box and turned it in her hand, admiring the craftsmanship.

"It's beautiful," she said, noticing the silver inlay in the shape of dolphins and glyphs. "Where does it come from?"

"It was crafted long ago in Celvestria, for the wife of a sea captain. It... will bring you good luck on your voyage," Ildric smiled as he gathered up his staff, "but only if you remember to wear it," he added with a chuckle. Drahn looked up from his cracker gathering, eyeing the wizard curiously.

"Thank you again, Master Ildric, I shall." She placed it on her wrist to admire it against her skin. It was kind of him to present her with such a lovely token, although she wanted nothing to remind her of her impending journey. She smiled and said, "We were honored by your visit this day. Know that you are always welcome in our house."

Ildric bowed as the interview was concluded, and Drahn hopped to the floor and bowed his head also. The wizard turned to the boy and said, "I brought a trinket for the young man as well. It is nothing as valuable as the knife you carry, but perhaps it will come in handy one day." He reached for a small crystal on a cord fixed about the top of his staff and unwound it, handing it to the boy.

"Thanks much!" Nixy said, as he examined the crystal. It was pale violet and painted with runes, and the leather cord was long enough to fit over his head. "What is it?"

"It is a glowstone," said the wizard. "You hold it gently, and speak the word '*Ilda*' to make it glow."

Nixy took the crystal in his fingertips and said "*Ilda*," as instructed, and the crystal flashed with a light that shone brightly in the windowed room, reducing gradually to a soft glow. The wizard nodded to himself as the boy grinned from ear to ear. "One never knows when a little light will come in handy." He straightened his robe and turned to depart, with Drahn hopping behind him, holding his stack of crackers in his forepaws. "Good day to the both of you, Lady Cindra, Master DuQuayne."

Drahn nodded to the children and tried to seem inconspicuous as he flapped to maintain his balance, waddling out of the room. Bipedal movement was not one of his strengths. *Perhaps I might have someone make me a belt and purse*, he thought as he toddled after the wizard.

The pair paid their respects to the countess and departed, walking through the gates and into the Highcourt before they spoke to one another.

Drahn piped up, "Why did you not tell her what the gift was for?"

Ildric turned to him and said, "Heard you nothing I said on the way here? I have done my part and given her a means of survival. I cannot tell her why or all may be undone."

Drahn, having achieved a hop-flap combination that allowed him to keep up with the man's pace, said, "But you did not even tell her what the bwacelet does. You needn't have told her about the accident..."

"Accident, you say? I do not know if it will be an accident." Ildric said as he marched down the steep road, his staff tapping the pavement. "All I know is that it *may* happen. The important thing is that we have new answers. The meeting was rather a success, I think."

Drahn asked, "What answers, exactly?"

Ildric looked into the distance, gazing at the dark mass of the Shadowood Forest that stretched into the horizon. "We know that the demnox and its allies are after the boy's father, and the father is not the man we think he is."

"Isn't he? Who is he then?" Drahn was confused.

Ildric explained, "I am not certain, but I think he is no farmer. My answers lie in the north, and so I must leave soon. In the meantime, I would like you to keep an eye on the lady and her young friend."

Drahn nodded and looked at the city skyline, which was his second home. He frowned and hopped before Ildric saying, "I will be happy to, but first I have business of my own to attend to. May I leave my cwackers with you?" He handed the stack to Ildric, who smiled and took them gently, putting them in his pocket.

Drahn took wing, flapping fiercely towards the Tower of the Silver Moon. His territorial instincts had taken over as he climbed high enough to dive on his quarry. The intruder pigeons had nested again, messing upon his precious tower, and he would make an example of them.

Cindra and Nixy left the study shortly after the wizard and the little dragon departed, and Cindra led the boy down to the ground level through the northeast stairwell and industry rooms. They walked in silence across the courtyard and into the bailey, Nixy tagging a few steps behind as Cindra headed for the outer wall. Chickens pecked in the cold dirt and cats watched them with mischief in their eyes and the sounds of daily labor echoed between the walls, bringing the comfort of familiar sounds.

Cindra had always dreamed of adventure but wounding immortal monsters and facing the threat of ancient and forbidden magic was a bit much to start with. She climbed the steps to the cannon wall and Nixy followed innocently, not noticing how warily the guards watched them, for they remembered the incident with the cannon over a year ago.

Cindra sat against the cold metal, looking out over the flowing river canal and across the far bank. A tree stump marked the place where she and her army of peasant children had broken a mighty and imaginary siege with a well-placed shot. *It had been worth the paddling*, she decided.

Nixy sat opposite her, his back to the outer wall. He had been holding the handle of his knife as it rested in its sheath and he drew it out now to turn it over in his hands, his blade, his *magical* blade that had wounded a monster and saved his life. It was no wonder he had never had to sharpen it. The white steel blade caught the daylight and sent little reflections around the dark masonry.

Cindra looked at his knife as well, wondering what it meant that the boy had inherited such a weapon from his peasant mother. She did not speak of it to Nixy, but she had a suspicion that his mother had met another man, likely a nobleman or wealthy traveler, who had given her such a gift.

The idea crossed her mind that the gift may have been in exchange for the pleasure of her company, but she quickly dismissed the thought. Such a magical weapon was worth much more than that, and would only have been given to a woman as a token of true love and affection. Or if she needed to fight off the denizens of the Abyss. The thought gave her a chill.

Nixy spoke first. "Cutter's *magic*," he said in awe, holding up the knife in a curiously heroic way as if he were posing for a statue, "My mam left me a magic knife. I wonder where she got it?"

Cindra kept silent, letting him work it out for himself. Or not. It was not her place to make him question his parentage.

Nixy held his glowstone in his other hand, looking with pride from one magical treasure to the other. The glowstone was nothing more than a useful bauble Cindra knew, for she had owned several of them herself. The knife however... She figured it would be prudent to give him some advice.

"I would keep their power to yourself," she said to him, "Magic objects are valuable and coveted. It will be better to let no one else know."

Nixy nodded, aware that greed and temptation were simply too much for some people to resist. "Don't worry," he said, "I know better than ta blab that I got heavy loot." His cheeks flushed a bit as he lapsed into his street talk; he wanted to show better in front of his friend.

They sat and stared out the gun port, watching the water flow out to the sea. Nixy, not liking the uncomfortable silence, asked about a rumor he had heard while working in the stables, "So, I hear yer supposed to... get married?"

Cindra lowered her head, wanting to stick the boy in the cannon and fire him off. Her nuptials were a sore subject *before* she had kissed Jaron and thrown her name into scandal. Now she wanted to bury her head in a hole every time the matter arose.

"I don't know what is going to happen," she muttered, looking wearily at the floor, "I was to be wed and sent away to another land, but after what happened three days ago at the festival..."

"Wha happened?" he asked, wishing he paid more attention when people gossiped. He preferred to talk to the horses when he was working.

Cindra looked at the boy like he had been sent to torture her. She sighed and resigned herself to answer lest he start pestering her with more questions. "My father arranged a marriage between myself and a Duke of Rokvynnar to form an alliance. I am to leave on the 24th of this month."

Nixy sat up and blinked, not having heard this before. Was that why stable master Gorin kept smiling and counting the days down at him? The realization made him feel ill. *'Just eighteen days more, boy...,'* the vile little potato man had uttered just this morning.

Cindra had not spoken of her departure date aloud before and the nearness of it felt oppressive. A thought had occurred to her several times since the tournament and it gave her no comfort at all. "Because of what happened at the Festival of Devotion... I don't even know if I will be leaving. The duke's family may call off the wedding. I may have ruined everything and my father will never forgive me."

Nixy said, "I heard that something terrible happened but I didn't know what ta believe. They said somebody died."

Cindra nodded. "Sir Earnold, my bodyguard died. He was killed in a duel with Sir Jaron Dunlorden."

Nixy blinked in surprise, "Wha-why? Why did they fight?" He had remembered them arguing the day he and Cindra visited the field but that big man had arrived to break it up.

Cindra held her head in her hands and sighed. "Sir Jaron and I... w-we kissed."

Nixy was appalled. "Eeew! He's old!"

"He's *not* old!" Cindra exclaimed, "And that's not the point! I am promised to be wed and I kissed him in public for all to see. I brought shame on my house and Sir Earnold was only standing up for my honor... It's my fault he's dead." Tears began to well in her eyes.

Nixy considered for a moment as the girl sniffled. "Seems ta me it's Jaron's fault seeing as he was the one what killed him."

Cindra was in no mood for the boy's stupidity. "Don't you see? Even the king was counting on this marriage happening. It's a disaster. A total disaster!"

Nixy didn't even want to think about an angry king. "What do ya think the count will do?" He knew that anger rolled down hill and he wanted to be ready if heads started to get lopped off.

Cindra stared out the cannon port, not caring to answer.

After a lengthy silence Nixy asked, "Do ya think the count will keep me here, after yer gone? If ya leave, I mean."

Cindra started to form an angry retort but realized that the boy had good reason to look out for himself. He was her responsibility now and she had to make sure his welfare was secured. It was almost like putting her affairs in order.

"I will bring it up with mother. I am sure it would be no problem." She knew she didn't sound very reassuring but it was the best she could manage. Without another word, she stood and walked out the portal and down the steps into the open bailey, startling a nearby guard who pretended to be minding his own business.

She didn't care if Nixy followed; in fact she preferred he wouldn't. She wanted to be alone for a while and suffer in solitude. Mineth would want to remain nearby, but even she would be no comfort today. She just wanted to sleep and have all her problems resolved before she woke. That might be a long sleep indeed.

Nixy had correctly sensed that she didn't want his company, so he stayed behind in the cannon wall. Girls were so confusing and strange, and they only seemed to get worse as they got older. So the mean-looking knight got killed over a kiss, and the count and the king would be in a fury if it meant no wedding.

That's girls for ya.

He looked out of the cannon port at the opposite bank of the river and saw two dark shapes there, milling about a tree stump in the afternoon sun. Big and black as night, the two wolves froze and seemed to look right at him across the distance. He could just make out their yellow eyes and lolling tongues, and he was suddenly glad to be surrounded by thick walls and running water.

Chapter Ten

Truths To Cling To

Sir Cord Freekirk figured he had been to every herbalist, apothecary, and florist in the city. His horse was tethered in a stable behind a nearby inn and he made his rounds on foot, asking at vendors around the Temple Walk surrounding the cathedral. He had decided to check the Selvinian Temple last, since the answers he sought were sure to be waiting for him there.

In the meantime, he had visited any place where someone might acquire roses out of season. At each vendor he had received the same answer, that the Selvinian Temple had a special license to grow roses out of season and no one wanted to risk punishment. Cord had asked at the first few places as a man seeking important answers, but tried thereafter to sound like a prospective customer, even offering bribes to those who might have a secret stash. It was really all a big waste of time, as he had been down this path once before, but he needed to be sure. Jaron's life might depend on it.

His wanderings finally brought him to the steps of the Selvinian Temple south of the cathedral. The temple was a simple marble hall lined with pillars and arched passageways and an ornate dome over the entrance. The dome was carved with the patterns of vines and flowers and a relief of the beautiful goddess graced the walls on either side of the tall doorway.

It was grand in design yet small and very feminine, and something about the structure made Cord nervous. No, not nervous, but on his guard. It was a place of female power and the subtle smell of incense and the delicate tinkling of wind chimes filled him with a peculiar awe. He wondered what it had been like in the elder days, when the goddess herself lived here and her presence could be felt within the walls. Was this temple even that old?

The doors were closed against the cold but unlocked, as were those of most temples during the day. He pulled with a bit more strength than was needed, forgetting how the heavy doors were so well balanced and easy to open. Looking within, he spied several gossamer shapes drifting amongst the light of candles; the flames and mist of burning incense danced in the sudden disturbance of the air.

He entered the temple as his eyes adjusted to the low light and was approached by a young sister of fewer than twenty years, wearing the simple white wrap of an acolyte. She had light ginger hair and a few freckles, and an innocence and simple beauty often cultivated by the sisterhood. She greeted him and smiled disarmingly.

"Welcome sir knight, to the Temple of the Beloved Goddess Selvina. How may we serve you?" She opened her arms in welcome, letting the long sleeves spread like wings, hinting at the curves of her body beneath the simple garment. It was a test Cord knew, to help the sisters separate the faithful from the curious adventure seekers. Nevertheless, he stared a bit more than he should have.

"I-I have come with some questions, sister. May I speak to a priestess?" He stammered a bit, clearing his throat. *Damned incense*, he thought, *that's all it was*.

The girl smiled and cocked her head as she lowered her arms. "Questions about love," she asked coyly, "or the act of love perhaps?" Her eyes twinkled in the candlelight.

Cord gulped, feeling his mouth suddenly dry. *She thinks I'm here for some cheap titillation*, he realized. He frowned to cover his blush. "Er, my questions have to do with... roses. May I speak to a priestess about the hothouse flowers?"

The girl blinked once and nodded, bidding him wait upon one of the floor cushions near the walls. Sir Cord preferred to stand. Men, women and couples sat on the cushions, some talking, some pointedly not talking. They were here for matters of the heart, seeking or repairing their loves, or for blessings of fertility, each waiting to speak to a priestess who would guide them through one of life's greatest mysteries.

The temple floor was covered in rugs and pillows and the sisters sat with their parishioners at low tables, taking tea with them and conversing over candlelight. The voices were low and respectful and did not carry very far. Just as well, for some came here with rather delicate matters to discuss. Soft laughter accented the distant banter and soon the acolyte returned with a priestess before her, making Cord relax. He did not wish to wait long in this place.

The woman bowed to the knight in greeting, introducing herself as Sister Avyth. She was an older woman with a kindly face and full figure, her gown was airy and comfortable and she wore a silver circlet upon her brow. "Welcome sir knight. I understand you have some questions about our gardens?"

She led him towards the back of the temple where they occupied a more private alcove, seating themselves upon cushions about a low table. The acolyte served them tea and departed, drawing a curtain closed behind her. Such spaces were used for the private matters of the nobility or whoever might make a suitably large donation to afford the privilege. The walls of the alcove were draped with tapestries, some of a more explicit and informative nature and besides being terribly distracting in their graphic depictions, they helped to keep voices from carrying.

"Spelled?" asked Sister Avyth in a hushed voice. "Surely you don't think the sisterhood is involved?"

Cord raised his hands to reassure her saying, "No, no sister, I suggested no such thing. Whoever enchanted the roses could be an enemy of the crown, meddling in the count's affairs. My sources tell me that such a spell would take perhaps a day or more to prepare. Might someone have acquired two roses before the festival, from anywhere but the sisterhood's gardens?"

She thought carefully before answering, knowing her response might carry deep implications. Finally she shook her head saying, "No. There is no reason to believe so. Our prices are not exorbitant and the penalties for growing them illegally are too steep. The law was made so for the sake of the faithful, so that they may have genuine sacred roses without fear or false claims."

Cord nodded, hearing the answer he had come to expect. So the roses must have come from the temple's hothouse and whoever spelled the lady and Sir Jaron must have had access. This was going to be a delicate matter. He asked, "Could someone have stolen a flower or two without the caretaker's knowledge?"

The sister shook her head again. "No, the bushes are secure within the hothouse and the caretakers sleep nearby in the dormitory. If anyone were to try and enter, an alarm would sound and alert anyone on the grounds."

Sir Cord had not heard of this before but was not reassured. "An alarm? A good thief could avoid an alarm."

Sister Avyth said, "This is a *magical* alarm, an enchantment put in place by the Casting Guild's Ward

Masters." She straightened her back proudly. "It was a spell woven by many wizards and it would take just as many to unravel it."

Cord noted the pride in her voice. It must have been very expensive. "Is there no way," he began, "that anyone *other* than the caretakers might know how to pass the alarm?" He really did *not* want to sound like he was accusing the church of assisting in treason. A formal complaint from the Selvinians would not help Sir Jaron or himself.

Sister Avyth narrowed her eyes and folded her hands on the table. The candlelight gave her an ominous quality as she leaned forward. "Sir Cord," she said, her voice thin, "the order grows winter roses for the sacred Festival of Devotion and keeps a tally of the sales. You may look over the festival accounting if you wish, but if you have questions about the effectiveness of our security, you would be wise to ask the Casting Guild. We have nothing to hide."

Cord's face turned red, and he was glad for the low light. Perhaps that was one reason for it: to cover embarrassment? He said, "Forgive me. I did not mean to imply that the sisterhood was involved in anything improper..."

"No, of course not," she said, sitting back. "You are only being diligent and acting on behalf of the count and your comrade, Sir Jaron."

"He is my friend, Sister Avyth," he said.

"So much the better," she smiled. "Your devotion to him may be enough to uncover the truth. I hope it is. We will give you any assistance we can, for if there was any wrongdoing against the temple, we would wish to know of it."

Sir Cord sat back and nodded. He had always considered his own brand of diplomacy to be good enough, but he was a bit of a blunt instrument after all. The sister had guided him away from his clumsy inquisition and set him on the path of mutual assistance. Anything he uncovered must help the sisterhood safeguard their reputation, for they were possibly victims as well. Why hadn't he thought of that approach? *Because you've got a spiked mace between your ears*, he thought to himself.

He got to his feet as Sister Avyth stood, signaling the end of the meeting. She motioned for the young acolyte to join them and said to the girl, "Thyssa dear, please take Sir Cord to the accounting chamber and provide him with the ledgers for the last week. Also bring a reading light and a tea service," she bowed as she turned to leave them. "He has much to research. Please give him all the help he needs."

The ginger haired acolyte Thyssa looked up at him and smiled. "This way, sir knight," she said in an innocent voice, gesturing to a side door. As she led him down the corridor, Cord noticed the slightly embellished swaying of her hips. *It is going to be a long night*, he thought.

———

The funeral rites were performed at the Temple of Balkon on the northern flank of the cathedral and the procession was assembled in the late morning for the march to the cemetery. Sir Earnold's body was adorned in finery and ceremonial armor and borne upon the shoulders of eight Knight Fellows. The flat litter upon which he rested was dressed with a banner of blue and gold, and white lilies trimmed the borders. An honor guard was assembled to lead the way, marching to the sound of drums and mournful bagpipes. Black sashes hung across their chests and each man had a red ribbon draping from the side of his blue beret. It was a procession for a fallen hero.

Jaron had given his solemn word to return to the castle walls after the burial and the countess had been kind enough to rescind his house arrest. He now followed his brothers in arms from a distance, not wanting to shame the proceedings with his presence. A letter was sent from the Balkonitte priesthood making it known that it would be improper for him to attend the rites since his honor was besmirched, and while he had no stomach for the ceremony and had been detained at the time, the exclusion still stung him.

Besides, there might be family members of the fallen warrior in attendance, and the last thing he wanted to do was bear their hateful stares. The feud between their two houses was far from over he feared, so long as there are Dunlordens and Greenfellows to carry it on.

The morning traffic was bustling, for it was an overcast day already and many hoped to finish their errands before the clouds released their burden. It was a fittingly gray and gloomy day to match his mood, and the crowd made it easier for Jaron to go unnoticed.

He wore a hooded woolen cloak against the cold air and his attire was simple and discrete. He bore no device of his house or the house he served, but wore upon his sleeve a black armband in deference for the occasion, should anyone question his intent. The crowd closed back upon the street in the wake of the procession, making progress a bit difficult. Jaron was in no hurry however.

The cemetery was just northeast up the street from the jousting field and though there were buildings blocking it from view, the neighborhood was unmistakable. The Winter Palace and its walled gardens loomed in the distance at the foot of the mountain and the smell of wet earth was strong here. It had rained late last night, probably making it easier for the gravediggers to excavate the cold clay. Sir Jaron stopped inside the gates of the cemetery, looking through the trees as the funeral procession made its way to the Warrior's Rest.

The Greenfellow family had a plot in the city they had served for so long, and once enough time had passed, Earnold's bones would be exhumed and stored in a stone crypt that housed the remains of his ancestors. Jaron wondered what would become of his own body in the near or far future, when he met his fate. Would it be carried to rest in such a manner? Would he deserve such honors?

The pipes began a wailing hymn called "First on the Field," a traditional warrior's burial dirge, and the honor guard raised their swords in salute. Jaron was so moved by the music that he barely heard the soft footsteps behind him and flinched at a gentle hand on his shoulder.

"Will you not go inside, Sir Jaron?" A soft feminine voice asked. Jaron turned and was surprised to see the haunting beauty of Deliah, Greenfellow's once betrothed, standing at his shoulder.

He blinked away the memories that rushed into his mind, the lingering feel of her lips pressing against his own, her body caught in his embrace, that fateful and magical lapse of reason that had led to this dark day. He found he had no greeting for her; no words for bridging the gap of years that separated their last meeting. He simply replied to her question.

"My presence was neither required, nor desired," he said, "I'm here to... pay my respects. And you?" He looked at her questioningly, more than a little confusion in his eyes. "I thought you were married years ago."

She looked at him with her storm-cloud eyes, irises gray and flecked with fire and ice. They had a way of making his stomach quiver, as if they could see into his very soul. He had once found them irresistible, but now they made him wary.

"May I not pay my respects as well? My marriage has not erased my past." Her voice was gentle, but her gaze was full of unspoken implications.

Jaron relented and returned his eyes to the burial. "I suppose you have as much reason to be here as I. We share the same guilt."

She stepped forward, wrapping her cloak about her woolen dress to ward off the damp. "My guilt is greater," she said, and Jaron offered no argument. *Who had killed him first*, he wondered?

"I suppose that is the reason we are both here," he said, "To bare our guilt. He was defending the honor of House Corrina after all."

"But surely the priestesses of Selvina will speak on your behalf?" she said, turning to him. "It was fought in the name of love, at the goddess's own festival. Does that mean nothing?"

"Things are not so simple," he said, folding his arms and watching the litter bearers lower the body to the ground. "It seems I have a talent for disrupting betrothals, and this one was arranged by my lord and endorsed by my king. I will be lucky if the count sees fit to let me live."

"But," she began in protest, then more calmly, "But there was talk of a spell, some sort of enchantment. There are rumors..."

"I can't explain what happened between us," he said, looking at the wet grass. "All I know is that it happened and it can't be undone. Cord Freekirk is looking into it, bless him, but what can he hope to do? He's no wizard or spy catcher."

"Good Sir Cord, school master and loyal hound of Casselvane," she intoned respectfully. "Do not underestimate him. He has a reputation for seeing things through."

"To the bitter end," Jaron said.

The pipes had gone quiet and the sound of mourning could be heard from the Warrior's Rest, whether professional or not, Jaron could not tell. A boorish part of his mind wondered who would miss Greenfellow to weep so, and he reminded himself not to think ill of the dead. Besides, paid mourners were still in fashion among the merchant class, who had not yet gotten over the novelty of hiring people to enhance any gathering. He supposed it did not matter.

Sir Earnold has being lowered into the ground and Jaron and Deliah watched in silence, each reflecting on the moment in their own way. Jaron imagined one of the war god's Kyraine, a female form with talons and downy wings, grasping the soul of the fallen knight by his *tipok* knot and lifting his spirit into the sky for its journey to Balkon's Field. What the man's final judgment would be, Jaron could not imagine, but that was for the gods to decide after all. There had been no love lost between the men, but that meant little in the grand scheme of things.

Deliah, for her part, was content to see him put to rest. She had remained at the tournament long enough to watch him die, and being here today gave her the closure she had sought. She knew the man in ways others could not and did not mourn his passing; in fact she secretly celebrated it. He was among the last that knew, and he could threaten her no more. Her life here would be on her own terms, and it would end when *she* chose. *Nothing lasts forever*, she thought bitterly.

———

Sir Cord Freekirk awoke early in the morning in the temple dormitory after a night of pouring over names and numbers by the light of a wizard lamp. Thyssa the acolyte had been more than helpful, offering to read the ledgers to him and decipher the columns of figures. Once she realized that Freekirk was actually literate, she offered to take notes on his findings, stopping only to serve him stimulating tea and cakes from the temple kitchen.

Once he became too tired to continue, she offered him a place to sleep and the warmth of her company. Chastity was not required of Selvinian Sisters, only discretion, and Cord was in no condition to resist.

The small lodgings were cold and austere and lit by a high window that admitted the pale blue dawn. Cord untangled his limbs from the sleeping young woman and made sure she was bundled under the blankets before he set about getting dressed.

As he donned his clothes, he reflected on the results of his search. The ledgers were fairly simple and straightforward and revealed that the sisters made quite a nice profit from their flower sales, but more to the point, they were sold out of season only by members of the order and not by outsiders. The old woman who gave the roses to Lady Cindra and Jaron was defying the law, but no one had seen her save Cord himself, and her victims.

As he entered into the hall of the dormitory he encountered a few sisters and acolytes going about their duties, and they met his eye with knowing smiles and covered giggles. *Damn it*, he thought, *Jaron would be proud of my efforts on his behalf.* Guilt quickened his steps as he left the dormitory and walked the grounds.

The hothouse was towards the back of the temple property and was constructed of wood and glass and surrounded by a low stone wall. There were shapes to be seen moving inside in the morning light, although the fog on the glass made it impossible to see details. He walked about the long structure, looking with an untrained eye for some obvious flaw to reveal itself. Finally, he came across a sister who was emerging from the outer door and he waved to get her attention.

She carried an empty bucket and her gown showed signs of the warm damp from which she had come. She smiled and bowed her head to the knight saying, "May I help you sir?"

Sir Cord nodded in greeting, "Might you know anything about the wizards who spun the wards for the hothouse?"

The sister fluttered the hem of her dress to cool her legs as she spoke, "I know the spells must be reapplied every few years, but for their names, I know not. The Ward Master's device is upon the door, by way of warning to those might try to enter unbidden." She pointed to the doorpost near the latch where a small brass coat of arms was displayed.

Cord approached and examined it. The device bore the symbol of a tower encircled by a dragon, the head of a cat emerging from the ramparts. The letters "Sy" and "Wy" were engraved on either side of the tower. Cord thanked the sister and left the grounds, heading for the inn where he had stabled his horse.

Those who owned heraldic devices were usually well known and he only needed to ask enough people. He wondered briefly if he was qualified to question a Ward Master about his spells, but decided that it was better him than no one. He could only do what he could do.

An innkeeper, it so happened, knew of the owner of the device and directed Sir Cord to the man's building. It was only a few streets away from the inn and had the look of a well-kept property, with newly painted walls and neat gardens. Cord rode into the courtyard, hitched his horse and walked about the doorways looking for the heraldic device he had seen earlier.

The home of Syvin Wyngaard, Ward Master, was marked with a brass knocker bearing his personal crest. Sir Cord straightened his jacket and beret and rapped on the knocker, sending an echo through the cold air of the courtyard. He hoped it was not too early to call and wondered suddenly what hours a wizard might keep.

The door latch clicked open and a man with a nightshirt and house robe answered, looking a bit rumpled and unsteady. He was tall and a bit lanky; his face was long and narrow. He had a pronounced nose that only added to his birdlike visage, but his eyes were keen and bright even as he squinted against the cold morning air. They were the kind of eyes that improved the look of his whole face, lending him a romantic quality. Cord was surprised at his age as well, expecting someone much older and bearded. This man was perhaps in his early thirties; young for a Ward Master? Cord did not know.

"Yes?" he asked warily, taking in the knight's beret and the sword he wore.

Sir Cord bowed and said, "Master Wyngaard, I presume?" The man in the doorway nodded and Cord continued, "May I enter? I have some questions about an important matter."

Syvin nodded and let him in. Cord was shown to a chair by the fireplace which had burned out in the night. Syvin took some fresh wood from the stockpile and dropped them onto the grating, wrinkling his large nose as the old smoke and ash were kicked up. He spoke as he fumbled with a box of flint and tinder.

"Does this have something to do with the count's problem, the man he was having us look for? I'm afraid we have made little progress." The fire began burning slowly and Syvin sat in the opposite chair. "If he truly is possessed by a demnox, then finding the man himself may not solve the problem, you see." He wrapped his robe about his waist and waited for Cord to start asking foolish questions.

He was surprised however, for Cord had an entirely different set of questions. "I am not here on the matter regarding the attack on the Lady Cindra. Rather, I am here about some work you performed for the Selvinian Temple; the hothouse in particular."

Syvin frowned and looked confused. "Th-the hothouse? You mean the *Posthe Clamorus* spell?" He saw Cord's blank expression and explained, "The Alarming Ward?"

Cord was not sure if he was truly out of his depth or if the man was using magical jargon to be difficult. "Yes, the alarm spell. I was wondering..."

A movement behind Syvin's chair caught the knight's attention and Cord saw a woman in a house robe come down the stairs to see what the noise was about. Syvin saw Cord's distraction and stood to introduce her.

"Ah, may I present my wife, Deliah. Deliah, dear, this is..." he looked to the knight as Cord stood, realizing he had not gotten his name.

"Sir Cord Freekirk," said Deliah Wyngaard, her cheeks going a bit white as she recognized the big man standing before her. She could see he recognized her as well.

"Oh, do you know him?" asked the wizard.

Cord did not know what to say. Deliah *Wyngaard*. He had forgotten the name of the man she married, for he had only heard it once from Jaron a year after the school's most famous scandal. *'Deliah went and married some wizard, can you believe it? Name of Wyngaard,'* Jaron had said incredulously.

Deliah, Cord thought, *who was once betrothed to Earnold Greenfellow. Deliah, whom Jaron and Earnold fought over long ago. And now Earnold was dead and Jaron was doomed because of some roses, which were protected by... What was going on here?*

Deliah answered her husband but watched the play of thoughts across Cord's face as she spoke, "Yes, he is the master of the local Daerbrik Fighting School. A man I was to marry was a student of his. You remember what I told you of that terrible experience?"

"Ah," said Syvin uncomfortably, "Ah yes, dreadful matter." Cord wondered what version of the story she had fed her husband but said nothing. Did the man even know Greenfellow was dead? Deliah did, surely.

"Perhaps I can start some tea?" Deliah said, removing herself from the scene. As she entered the kitchen, she took a deep breath and shook her head. It was only yesterday she had told Sir Jaron not to underestimate Cord Freekirk, but that had only been to bolster the poor man's hopes. She did not imagine he would be so hot on the trail! Her mind spun as she wove a mental web of lies and alibis, trying not to ensnare herself. She would have to take the initiative before Cord could establish his suspicions. Too soon, too soon!

The knight sat down opposite the wizard and tried to regain his composure. What was he going to ask again? *Could anyone else have the knowledge to pass the alarm spell.* That was it. *Like your wife,* he thought, but dismissed the notion.

"You were asking about the alarm spell cast upon the hothouse," said Syvin, getting back to business. He sat back in his chair and looked expectantly at his guest.

Cord blinked. "Er, yes, I was wondering how the spell is disarmed by the garden's attendants."

Syvin raised an eyebrow, "You realize I cannot divulge the specifics," he said, "but I can tell you that it involves a password combined with a series of mental pictures. That is," he explained, "one must imagine three specific images as the password is spoken."

"So no one can simply overhear a password and get inside," Cord concluded. "Might anyone but the sisterhood know these secrets? Besides you, I mean."

Syvin thought for a moment and said, "There were three other guild wizards involved in the spinning of the spell but they only knew their own parts. Each wizard contributed to the crafting of a... a magical lock, so to speak. I was the one who designed the locks, so that I might bind them all together. Their secrets are known to no one but me, and the client of course."

A clattering from the kitchen caught Syvin's attention and he called to his wife, "Deliah, dearest, are you alright?"

She appeared briefly in the doorway and said, "Yes I am fine husband, just a bit clumsy this morning. I will have your tea presently." She ducked back inside, wondering how to bring their conversation to an end before the web got too tangled.

Syvin was looking a bit distressed and leaned toward Sir Cord. "Am I to assume that someone has entered the hothouse without permission?"

The man's reputation was at stake and Cord was hesitant to share his suspicions, even the most basic ones. Nevertheless, he owed him an explanation. "I am investigating the use of two roses in a spell to ensnare the count's daughter and one of his lordship's knights." His face was grave as he spoke, "It is believed that the roses could only have come from the temple hothouse and their records reveal no sales prior to the festival."

"Stolen?" said Syvin in alarm.

"Stolen, or sold in secret by one of the temple gardeners," Cord said, uncomfortable with giving voice to the prospect.

Syvin considered for a moment and asked, "What manner of spell was used?"

Cord had no proper name for it; he only knew what he had witnessed. "They were each given roses by a mysterious old woman, and soon afterward they took leave of their senses," he said, recalling the day vividly. "Sir Jaron was in a great distraction over Lady Cindra, and she herself was overcome with the same malady for him. It was more like madness than love.

"He was forced to fight in a duel because of his behavior, and Sir Jaron was almost killed because of his state. Then upon the ground, I witnessed the two roses as they burst into flames. The change was immediate and Sir Jaron recovered in time to prevail." Cord sat back. "I would say it was a love spell, if such a thing exists."

Syvin nodded in agreement and said, "They do exist. One must have ingredients from the intended, such as hair or blood to be used in the spell. The effects are not as you describe them however. Such charms amount to potent suggestions; they don't create such... overwhelming behavior."

"Do you know of anyone who can create such a spell, even a lesser one?" Cord decided to follow this road to see where it might lead, but he also wanted to see how much the man would change the subject.

Syvin shook his head, "There are not many in the Casting Guild that pursue a trade in Charms. There is no market for such skills, not a legitimate and legal one, anyway."

"So the list must be small," Cord said, folding his fingers. He would see if the man aimed suspicion at another, telling Cord much of his character.

Syvin looked into the growing fire, his brow knitted in thought. Cord waited for a sign of nervous guilt or diversion but Deliah's return interrupted them both.

"I have your tea ready," she said, bringing in a silver tray and serving them on a low table between the chairs. "Oh, and husband, I don't mean to be a bother, but it seems that the firestone refuses to be extinguished." She held out a short wand topped with a crystal, waiting for him to take it. "I don't wish to burn down my kitchen," she said as she smiled sweetly.

Syvin excused himself and took the wand, examining it as he walked into the kitchen to extinguish the 'firestone,' whatever that might be. Cord felt a tingle of warning as Deliah leaned in and whispered in his ear.

"My husband knows nothing, but I must talk to you alone."

She smiled and withdrew as her husband returned, handing her the wand and kissing her cheek. Cord sipped his tea and sat in uncomfortable silence, wondering what she intended to reveal. He barely heard as Syvin gave him half a dozen wizards who specialized in Charms, including an endorsement of their character with each name. He half listened as the man babbled about his notes and security measures, assuring the knight that his precautions were more than sufficient. He never made a single allegation and Cord was more inclined to believe Deliah that he was blameless. He waited for a lull in the man's dialogue and used it to conclude the interview. He thanked the wizard for his time and stood to leave.

"I notice you have an herb garden out front, is it yours?" Cord asked.

"It is tended by my wife," Syvin said, "She uses them in her cooking and medicinal liniments."

Cord brightened at his luck and said, "May I speak to her about it? I have taken up cooking in my spare time and would like some expert advice."

"Of course," Syvin said with a slight frown. He called to his wife and Deliah came from the kitchen and he relayed the knight's wishes before retiring upstairs, bidding him good day.

Deliah and Cord made a slight show of examining the garden in the courtyard, pointing to this and that, until she spoke in a low voice.

"I heard about what happened at the festival and I heard what you told my husband," she said, "and I feel terrible." Cord waited for more. "I... I am afraid I had a hand in this affair, though I thought I was doing a great favor."

"A favor to whom?" Cord asked.

"Sir Earnold," she said quietly.

"What?!" His voice echoed about the walls, so he lowered it. "Sir Earnold?"

"He asked me to take two roses from the temple. At first I refused, but he seemed determined. He said," she looked at Cord pleadingly, "he said I owed him for breaking his heart, and he had found a love to make him happy. He said he wanted the roses for a love spell... a spell for him and the object of his affection." She hung her head in shame.

Cord put his hands on his hips and scowled, "How did you pass the alarm at the hothouse?" This was too much.

"I... you mustn't tell my husband! I was able to read his notes and learn the keys of the spell." She looked back and forth as if she might be overheard in the garden. "I can read some of the old languages; Earnold knew this. I went through Syvin's library while he was away." She pleaded with the knight, "If he or anyone in the Casting Guild learns of this, it will be a horrible scandal!" She dropped her eyes to the cold ground. "It would ruin him. And me."

"So," Cord tried to put it all together in a way that made sense. "Sir Earnold approached you to gain two roses because he knew you could read your husband's writings. You entered the temple hothouse and stole the roses... did you cast the spell upon them as well?"

By law women were not trained in the magic arts and could not legally use them. Cord was not sure why, but it was an ancient tradition. Witches were rare, and learned outside of the accepted bounds of the universities, making them suspect of all kinds of things. A love spell such as this reeked of witchcraft, at least to Cord's mind. If Deliah was a witch, he could not save her.

"No! I cannot cast spells!" she shook her hands before her. "I only know some of the old Celvestrian tongues, such as those used in magical research." Many people learned words of command, so they may use magical trinkets, or alarm spells like the sisters of the temple did. "The spinning of magic spells is forbidden for women," and she said more quietly, "in this land."

She turned to look at the door of her house and the life she had made. "I do not know who was to enchant the roses for Earnold. He would not tell me his name, or the name of the woman he intended them for. He only pressed me for help because of the debt I owed him, for being unfaithful with Jaron Dunlorden and causing him so much pain." She sniffed back newly summoned tears. "Had I known... had I known what his true intentions were, I would never..." She covered her face with her hands and turned away, hoping she was being convincing.

Cord listened to her sobs, wondering what he was to tell the countess. There were scandals within scandals here, and no one would come out unscathed. Had Sir Earnold, seemingly a loyal knight, actually arranged for this disaster? Cord had imagined a foreign wizard or spy that lurked in dark corners, scheming against king and crown. Now if Deliah was to be believed, *Deliah* of all people... it was some kind of revenge for an old family feud and wrecked marriage.

Why would Greenfellow involve Lady Cindra in such a plot, bringing disaster on his lord's name? It would be better to die than dishonor the lord's house and jeopardize a treaty. And then there was the matter of Syvin Wyngaard, the Ward Master responsible for so many protection spells across the city, even within the castle itself. What would become of his reputation if it was learned that his *wife* had bypassed a powerful spell and stolen from the temple?

Cord had heard enough. He had expected to spend days chasing shadows and hopefully find something that could help Jaron. Now he had more information that he knew what to do with.

Deliah was still sobbing into her hands. Cord approached her and held his beret in his hands, not sure

213

what to say. Did she realize what she had admitted to? He would have to report this and let the countess decide how to prosecute the matter, after all that was what higher authorities were for. He had wanted to save Jaron's good name, but not at the cost of another knight's honor. It was like searching for a thief and finding your brother holding the loot.

Cord took a few steps towards his horse and turned to the weeping woman, "I can put in a word for you, but your fate will be for others to decide."

Deliah rubbed her eyes and nodded, sniffling sadly. "I understand. Please," she strode forward, pleading, "tell her ladyship that my husband is blameless in this horrid affair. Do what you wish to me, but save his good name." The words surprised Deliah as she spoke them, even more so that she meant them. She had truly come to care for the man in a way she had not expected. He was a rarity in the world, soft-spoken, modest despite his accomplishments, gentle, loving and kind. It would be a crime to drag his life into the mud.

As the knight mounted up and rode away into the city streets, Deliah turned and looked up at the window above the door. The shutters were partially opened, as they were each morning, and beyond she saw the sleeve of her husband's robe as he moved from the window.

Chapter Eleven

A New Home

Cindra walked the battlements of Casselvane Keep, pacing back and forth near the chimney that serviced her father's bedchambers. He had returned from his annual visit to the northern reaches of the province only hours ago and by now was soaking in a bath. It was her mother's idea, thinking it would be best to break the news to him if he was relaxed and naked in a tub. He would be less likely to storm about in a rage if that was to be his impulse.

She pinched a piece of dried meat from a pouch at her waist and fed it to the Ember Swallow perched on her arm, a thick leather gauntlet protected her skin from the bird's sharp talons and searing forked tail feathers. Gavagul had been the family's special messenger for nearly four generations. He lived within a stone aviary above the castle's center gate, nesting in a bed of charcoal and porous stones. It was hoped that someday a female would come along and nest with him for a while, leaving a precious amber egg in his care. Ember Swallows were known to live for well over a century, but it didn't hurt to have a young one to carry on if something happened.

Gavagul took the offered meat in his beak and worked it down, hardly tasting it. His tail feathers let off a bit of smoke and his rich orange plumage ruffled with pleasure. "More!" he said in whistling but melodious voice.

"You're going to get fat," Cindra scolded, but she gave him another strip of meat anyway.

"You're going to get fat!" said the bird, mimicking her voice perfectly.

Cindra let him perch on the battlements where he wouldn't scald anything. She headed over to the chimney and leaned over to listen, hearing very little over the sea breeze and the call of gulls. She didn't expect to pick up much at all really, unless there was yelling. No yelling yet.

It was a week to the day that the treacherous Sir Earnold Greenfellow had been laid to rest, and only three more days until her ship departed. She could see it anchored in the harbor now; its blue flag with white stripes marking it as a ship of Rokvynnar.

Its smaller escort was moored nearby, also taking on supplies and delivering what was to be the first of many trade goods for the region to sample. They had been notoriously punctual, arriving on the day and hour arranged. Cindra wondered if they had left home early and anchored out of sight, waiting for the day just to make sure they would arrive on schedule. It had made an impression anyway.

The last week had been truly difficult, but all seemed to work out for the best. Sir Cord Freekirk had brought back evidence of a plot by the knight who had sworn an oath to protect Cindra's safety and honor with his life. The traitor Greenfellow had pressured his once betrothed to steal two roses from the Selvinian Temple so that he might have a love spell prepared in time for the festival. She agreed, not realizing he meant them for Cindra and Jaron and not for himself and some fictional sweetheart. Cindra assumed the rose thief was this 'Deliah' that Jaron had mooned over and she wondered just what kind of woman she must be. Not a very well-bred one, she decided, thief of hearts and flowers.

Greenfellow apparently had the roses enchanted with a powerful charm, meaning for herself and Jaron to lose control so that he might call him out and settle old feuds. But the spell didn't last. Sir Jaron had won and Greenfellow paid for his broken oath with blood.

Cindra had heard many details that disturbed her and there were still many unanswered questions but her mother seemed content to leave such stones unturned. Worse than a foreign plot for which faceless enemies could be blamed, this conspiracy was bred within the ranks of House Corrina itself.

If everyone involved was brought before the court and punished for their part, it would affect not only the people's faith in their leaders and protectors, but also in the Casting Guild and its magical safeguards, and in the Selvinian Temple who failed to spot an old woman selling tainted sacred roses at their own festival. She could forgive her mother for the decision she had made, for ultimately it saved Jaron's life and many reputations in the process.

The young knight had been banished from the province of Casselvane for a period of two years. He was to wander in other lands, trying to redeem himself through deeds of worth and virtue. At first, Cindra was told, for she was not present, the young man had begun to protest, insisting that his shame was too great to bear. But the countess had been forewarned of his melancholy and reminded him that it was his duty to overcome his weaknesses so that he might return to House Corrina a stronger warrior in heart, mind and body.

Jaron accepted his sentence and swore to better himself, taking his leave to prepare for his exile. Cindra had not expected him to ask after her, nor did she risk contacting him, yet there was so much left unsaid. Luckily she had a pet bird that could speak for her, and in her own words.

She went over to Gavagul who was preening his feathers, and addressed him. "Gavagul, I need you to deliver a message."

The bird looked up and blinked with large red eyes. "Who to?" he asked, sounding a bit like an owl.

"Sir Jaron Dunlorden," Cindra replied. "You may find him to the west, about a six day ride from Portshia."

The bird seemed to look through her, its avian eyes going blank. No one really understood how Ember Swallows were able to find the intended recipients of the messages they bore, but they did so with amazing accuracy, especially if given good directions. They were even known to see through disguises, delivering secret messages to spies and people in hiding. This had made them a bit of a detriment, for they had no sense for the arts of subtlety, and combined with the flash of their fiery arrivals, were just as likely to expose the addressee to his enemies. Since only important and wealthy people used the rare creatures, anyone receiving a message from one was probably someone important, or in the employ of someone important.

The bird fluffed its feathers again and looked at Cindra. "Ready," it said.

Cindra closed her eyes and took a breath, preparing the message she had composed over the past week. It helped her to envision Jaron's face as she spoke and made her feel less silly to be articulating her feelings to an orange bird.

"Dearest Jaron," she began intimately, "I regret that I could not see you before you left the city, and I fear we shall never meet again. But I shall always hold you dear as my first love, and I will carry the memories of our time together into the lands of my new home.

"Should you ever sink into despair, use the remembrance of my love to bear you up, for I shall do the same. Had we more time and fewer obligations, then the world would have been ours to share and the gods themselves would have envied our happiness. I bid you farewell and send my love, so that it may guide you as a ship that follows a star."

She nodded and spoke the bird's name, so that it would know she had finished. "Gavagul, deliver this message to Jaron with all speed. Try and be back in three days or my ship will leave without you."

Gavagul whistled and spoke an avian reply, saving his words for the message. He leaped from the battlements in a flapping of orange wings, blowing like a hot summer breeze on the girl's face. He circled as he climbed over the castle ramparts, finally turning west as his plumage began to glow with heat. His form now like a fiery comet, shot over the cliff wall and the river, leaving a trail of white smoke in the clear afternoon sky.

Cindra watched as the radiant creature vanished in the distance over the southern-most boughs of the Shadowood, and her mind began to wander. She looked at her feet as she walked about the battlements, pacing back and forth. Lost in thought, she just about jumped out of her skin as the voice of her father shouted from the depths of the chimney.

"WHAT?" the count bellowed, just about jumping out of his tub. Water sloshed over the canvas lining and onto the floor as the bath servant reared back in fear.

The countess, Sir Fedrick, Sir Cord and Constable Fingelm were situated across from the bath, the knights standing to either side of the noble lady as she sat in an elegant chair. The constable, who was trusted council, stood nearer the tub. He looked down in distaste as the water stained his velvet shoes.

Countess Casselvane repeated herself, keeping her face impassive. "Sir Earnold has been slain and Sir Jaron has been banished for a period of two years." She folded her hands in her lap and continued, "There was an incident at the Festival of Devotion that led to Greenfellow's death. It was later revealed that treachery was involved and Greenfellow himself was behind it."

Before her husband could muster another outburst, she added, "In the interest of avoiding an even greater scandal, I have let the details remain publicly vague. Sir Jaron Dunlorden shall bear the disgrace for the part he played, although he was not truly to blame." She looked to Sir Fedrick, who had heaved an unsteady sigh, and she placed her hand on his arm to comfort him. "His own honor demanded a sentence, and his absence will help the scandal to diminish."

Sir Fedrick's voice cracked as he spoke, "I lent him *Valdiroth*, my lord. My hope is that stewardship of the honor sword will hold him true to his duty and bring him home."

The count, who had settled back into the bath, stared at them with exasperation. "One of House Corrina's Honor Swords?" He shook his head and looked to his wife, "What... what manner of *incident* could have led to this catastrophe? And how was Greenfellow behind it?" The count had chosen Greenfellow as Cindra's bodyguard for the man's strong sense of duty and loyalty, knowing that it was in part to compensate for his sullied family name.

The countess had decided she should be the one to relate this news, seeing as she was partially responsible. "I had allowed Sir Jaron to escort Cindra to the theater and to take her riding, all under Mineth's supervision, of course. He and Sir Earnold had a history, of which I am sure you are aware, but I never imagined that it would drive him to such measures.

"Sir Cord has learned that Greenfellow acquired two roses which he had enchanted by an unknown wizard, to drive Sir Jaron and our poor daughter to... unseemly passions before the festival crowd. They shared an embrace and a kiss," the count started at this, "for which Greenfellow challenged Sir Jaron to a duel."

"My daughter kissed a..." he looked at Sir Fedrick who was looking at the floor in shame. "Before a crowd?" He sank a bit in the tub and looked at the ceiling beams as if they might fall upon him at any second. "This could ruin everything. All my work... the marriage..."

"To the best of our knowledge, the marriage pact is secure. The ships wait to carry Cindra to her new home." said the countess. "If anything, this incident will show that our enemies fear our alliance with Rokvynnar and will resort to the most puerile mischief to prevent it."

"Our enemies?" asked the count, running a water-wrinkled hand over his face.

Constable Fingelm spoke up, "The story we are encouraging points to unnamed foreign or domestic adversaries, such as the Dissenter Houses that oppose the king. We are posting notices about the city advising that the 'Festival Incident' was the work of wizards who remain at large. This much is true, for we do not know who Sir Earnold had dealings with."

"Sir Earnold..." the count muttered to himself, still unable to believe he had misjudged the man so completely. Treachery seemed to run in the Greenfellow family, or at least it was so fostered by the feud with the Dunlordens. Still, for the knight to use his lord's daughter in such a way, it was unthinkable.

The constable continued, displaying his shrewdness, "The notices may help us learn the identity of Greenfellow's accomplice, but more importantly, it will help mitigate the damage caused by this incident," Fingelm strode about the tub as he spoke, stroking his reddish beard thoughtfully. "This disgraceful act can be used in our favor, both to curry sympathy here and abroad. Victimizing a lady so..."

The count sloshed in his tub. "Do not be so quick to use my daughter's shame for political gain! Her betrothal and the alliance were to be my legacy. I am not eager to use this disaster for the same purpose."

221

The constable was unmoved. "Winds of change propel the ship of state, my lord, and we must be ready to steer whether they be favorable or no."

"Yes, yes, lest it sink or run aground or whatnot," said the count, waving off further allegory with a sprinkling of water, "I don't need a lecture, Fingelm. I need some time to consider things further." He turned to his wife who was still sitting impassively, "And don't think that ambushing me in the bath will make things easier for you. I intend to be just as upset when I dry and dress."

The countess only raised an eyebrow.

Cindra had been unable to sleep the night before her voyage. She had tried not to wake Mineth with her pacing but the handmaid was ever attentive and managed to stir, mumbling her concern. She eventually moved her pacing into the cold dayroom and went to sit in the window nook to watch the day break.

The light of the morning could be seen upon the waters out of her window, the tide carrying the glittering waves into the shade of the mountain or breaking upon Lighthouse Point. She wondered if her new room would look upon the rising sun, drawing her eyes towards home each morning.

Mineth awoke and checked on her mistress, making sure the girl was alright before she began the final packing. She had spent the last week sorting through Cindra's possessions, hoping to reduce their baggage by getting the lady to part with some of her older things. At first Cindra was inclined to take all of her dresses but Mineth reminded her that fashions being what they are might be different in the new land, and perhaps she should leave some of her Calilonian styles behind.

There were enough things given up by week's end that if sold, would provide for many poor families. It pleased Cindra that someone should benefit from things she no longer needed. After dressing in a warm and simple gown, she called for the porters and left her room for the last time.

As her luggage was carried out of her room and loaded onto waiting carts, she ventured down to the base of the grand stair. There was a doorway under the stair that led to the lower depths of the castle and Cindra took a glowstone from a shelf just inside the entrance. *"Ilda,"* she said and the stone began to shine with a soft radiance. Holding it before her, she proceeded down the spiral stair past the entrance to the wine cellar and the hall that led to the seldom-used dungeons.

She barely noticed the damp and chill of the deep chambers, so preoccupied was she with her thoughts. It was rare that she came down here anymore, save for the one day a year. It had been how long? Four years since his passing? Her dear little brother, whose life had been the center of her family, had sent them all scattered and adrift upon his death. Cindra had known that he would be more cherished than she, since he was to be the heir, but still she found joy in holding him and listening to his laughter, his little hands gripping her fingers and the faces he made.

As he grew older, he would learn to know her face and reach for her when she visited. She watched him take his first steps, she picked him up when he fell, and made up games for them to play together. On his third birthday, she took him about the whole castle, carrying him in her arms or letting him walk beside her when he wished. She showed him all the good places to hide when called for, showed him where the secret doors led, and where the cats liked to raise their kittens. There had been a litter that summer and the little feisty one who would be named Rufi was the most entertaining, making the small child clap and squeal.

Then the fever came, the coughing, day and night. The Lelonethan Priests were called for and the smell of their brewed medicines and herbs filled the nursery. There were prayers said in the chapel, prayers to any god that would listen, but long had they been silent and heedless.

Her father and mother were closer in that week than she had ever seen before or since, and Cindra witnessed a deep well of feeling between them as they gave one another strength. Late one night, she was awoken by her mother's wailing cry of despair.

She came to the entrance of the catacombs. The door was unlocked, for there were no treasures within, only the bones of her ancestors. Her light shown upon the carved crown of Arathus set over the doorway, runes of blessings and peaceful rest adorned the frame.

She entered the still chamber and held the glowstone before her, following the light until it fell upon the raised slab of granite where her brother's little stone sarcophagus rested. The beatific image of a young boy was carved on the surface, the curls in his hair looking almost soft and yielding. A robe of chiseled finery covered his frame, and his tiny hands were held as if in supplication. A necklace of pearls draped his hands like prayer beads with the seashell and pearl symbol of House DuMaylione still unmarred by the dust of four years.

"Hello Argie," she said, laying a hand upon the boy's stone curls. "It has been awhile since I've come to visit you; in fact, this may be the last time." She placed the glowstone next to the effigy and its light caught the gold of the seashell ornament. "Today I leave on a ship for Rokvynnar and I do not know if I will ever return." Her fingers traced the curl over his brow and she allowed herself a smile. "I will be a duchess, you know. Big important title; a lot of power and responsibility." Her smile disappeared as the irony in her voice fell upon deaf ears.

"I've envied you the life you might have had. I always wonder how it would have been, if I'd be happy for you or bitter. I like to think I would be happy... if you had lived. If I could see mother and father be proud of you, see your smile." She blinked at the dust and found her eyes were moist. "But you didn't live, and things have been... bitter. You'd think that I'd be leaving all that behind now but I think I'll be taking it with me. My marriage isn't what I had hoped for, and as for love... well, at least I can say I knew it once.

"Listen to me, little brother," she smiled and shook her head, "Here I am in your tomb, mourning *my* life. I should know better. Mineth would scold me, I'm sure." She straitened and collected the glowstone, "Rest, little Argus, and be at peace. Carry our love with you always." She touched her forehead to make the sentiment a prayer, and left the tomb. She had one more boy to visit, and he was to be found outside in the sunlight.

The little statue was engulfed in shadows as the dim light receded, and once again the air became still and cold as stone.

Nixy had dreaded this day. He only had one real friend in the world and she was leaving forever. To make things worse, Gorin the stable master was looking forward to the day when the daughter of the count was no longer shielding the lad. Nixy realized that it may have been a mistake to taunt the man while at Cindra's side. He just figured she would always be there. *Stupid*, he thought. *No one is always there for you.*

So now the boy would have to be on edge, listening for the potato man's foot falls in the mud and his raspy breath. It would be his only warning before receiving a foot in the rear or a slap on the head. Gorin had learned not to shout so much if he wanted to get his hands on someone as slippery as Nixy. Still the nasty little man, who was only a bit taller than Nixy and shorter than Cindra, would probably get tired of picking on him so long as Nixy played the part of the whipped dog. It was his defiance that had gotten him in trouble in the first place.

He had watched the carts making their way out the gates bearing what were surely Cindra's worldly possessions to her waiting ship. Crates of furniture and chests of clothes rumbled by and one cart that was covered and escorted by at least a dozen men-at-arms. *Must be something nice*, he figured.

Still, there was no sign of his friend, although he did see a few members of the castle staff that he had come to recognize. Minerva the kitchen woman was seeing to a selection of eggs and chickens from the coops and she would wave in Gorin's direction when she walked by. He would wave back in a pleasant way and then glare at his boys to make sure no one was gawking.

The constable was seen talking to the men who escorted the covered cart, giving instructions or something. He even saw Mineth making sure the luggage was loaded properly but she didn't notice him even though he waved. Still no Cindra.

It was almost noon before she came out of the castle gate and walked across the bailey to the stables. Gorin grumbled something indistinct as she approached, but left for another part of the yard to give the boy and noble lady some privacy. Nixy kept working until she got closer, not wanting to act overly sad or silly, but when she stopped a few paces from the stalls, he put down his brush and went to meet her. Gorin had been kind enough not to make him slop the stables today since the girl's nose was delicate.

"Hey," he said awkwardly, not sure what to do. He had never learned much in the way of manners but remembered to give her a low bow.

"Hello Nixy," she said, smiling, "I have come to say goodbye. I will miss you, you know."

Not sure what to say, he squinted up at her in the noon sun.

She looked down at his leather shoes and fidgeted a bit. "I've told my parents that it would make me happy if they saw to your education," she looked for a reaction, not sure what he would think. "They can arrange for you to learn letters and numbers and other things that may help."

He looked up at her, confused. "Help with what?"

"Well, you don't want to be a stable boy all your life, surely? You could... learn a trade or something. Perhaps become a navigator and sail up the coast to visit me?" She wanted to believe it was within the realm of possibility, however unlikely.

He shrugged and shuffled his feet. "I never thought that far ahead. Guess I was too busy looking for my next meal. I... I wanna thank you fer all ya done for me, m-milady." He stumbled on her title, feeling silly.

"It was my pleasure to do so, Nixy. Besides, you gave me someone to look after and I had missed that." She stepped forward and gave the boy a hug, not caring if it was unbecoming. Who did she have to answer to here anymore? She said in his ear, "And you may always call me Cindra."

Nixy returned the embrace weakly, his arms trembling. "Goodbye Cindra," he said, and realized he was crying.

She smiled and stepped back, holding him at arm's length. "Goodbye Nixyalderthor DuQuayne, Prince of the City." She felt a warm tear fall down her cheek and she turned and walked back to her waiting carriage.

The household servants and all of the available guardsmen were turned out to line either side of the path between the castle gate and the outer gate which led into the Highcourt. Nixy was there too, along with anyone else who could be spared. From his position, half way to the outer gate, he could barely see the count and countess come down the stair to the courtyard and enter the waiting carriage. Mineth and Cindra were already inside, having said their goodbyes. The carriage was underway now, rolling towards the line of people as they cried their farewells and waved their hands high, some holding kerchiefs, some saluting. Many younger ones were standing solemnly, remembering the little girl, beloved General of the Children's Army and Head Troublemaker, their leader and herald of a time that would not come again.

As the carriage rolled by, Nixy put on a brave smile and waved his hand until his arm hurt, catching a glimpse of his friend's face as she saw him and broke into a wide, happy grin. It was the last he would see of her and it was good. No tears, no sadness. Just good.

———————

The *Indisputable* was by far the largest vessel Cindra had ever seen, dwarfing its escort, the *Wesvyyn Gull*. Most ships of the Rokvynnar were small and fast, with narrow hull and lightly armed like the *Gull*. The *Indi*, as its captain called it, was long and tall with sixteen guns in full, twice as many as the average Calilonian warship. Cindra had some basic knowledge of sailing ships, since she lived in a port city and had been curious enough to ask after books. As grand as the *Indi* looked however, she was not sure if she was keen on making it her home for the next few weeks.

"Where is that blasted bird?" said the count, searching the skies. No one had bothered to look for Gavagul until today when he was meant to accompany Cindra to Rokvynnar. Arrangements had been made at some expense to insure that the bird had a warm place to sleep that would not create a fire hazard for the ship.

Cindra looked innocently at her parents, acting indifferent. Nothing gave away a caper like taking too much interest. She pretended to examine the ship some more.

"She is a beautiful sight, yes?" Cindra turned and saw two men approaching, dressed in Rokvynnar naval regalia. They wore long yellow coats with black trim and black sashes at their waists, and tall black leather boots polished to a shine. Black gloves were tucked into the sashes, and each man wore a fencing sword at his waist, bound to the scabbard with braided leather straps called 'peace knots,' preventing them from being drawn. The men bowed low to the count and countess and again to Lady Cindra as the retinue of Corrina men-at-arms shifted their positions, looking intimidating.

"Captain Gawyyn of His Majesty's *Indisputable*, at your service," he said in thickly accented Calilesh. He turned to his companion and introduced him as well. "This is Commander Ryynard of the *Wesvyyn Gull*, which will serve as our escort on the voyage."

The count, who had met both men after their arrival, nodded his head and gestured to his daughter, "May I present Lady Cindra Corrina of Casselvane, and her attendant Mineth, who shall be your guests for the voyage."

"Milady Cindra, who shall be our duchess, it will be a pleasure to welcome you aboard." Captain Gawyyn was obviously used to dealing with nobility and was probably from the nobility himself, if naval customs were similar between the two countries. He had an easy manner and charm that Cindra found comforting. Perhaps he had been chosen for this voyage because he was part diplomat? It would make sense. She decided she liked him, and that was a good way to start.

The captain made polite talk and answered a few questions for the sake of the count and countess who, despite their position, were still worried parents. After soothing their minds, he took his leave to return to his ship. Commander Ryynard, a quiet man who was wary of everything, also took his leave and headed down the dock to where his smaller ship was moored. A company of local oarsmen awaited the lady and her handmaid patiently, trying not to eavesdrop.

Cindra had been so preoccupied with packing and planning that she had overlooked this moment when she and her parents would part ways. In her mind, it was a moment charged with emotion and depth, when all she had felt would come forth in the most eloquent way possible, layering meaning upon meaning, breaking hearts and raising spirits at the same time. Yet now she could think of nothing to say. 'Goodbye, I'll miss you both' seemed so empty and trite. What does one say when leaving behind everything she knows?

The count spoke first. "It is time for you to depart, but before you go..." Cindra braced herself for the imminent fatherly advice and words of wisdom that always sounded so self-serving, amounting to 'Don't embarrass me,' but they didn't come.

Instead he said, "I want you to know that, in spite of all that has happened... I am very proud of you. If the law would allow, you would be my heir." He smiled sadly and the light on the water seemed to gather in his eyes, "You have the Corrina spirit. Carry it with you into your new home and enrich our allies with its fire."

Cindra was struck dumb. She stared at him for a moment, her jaw quivering, not certain of what she had heard. Blinking back the sudden tears from her eyes, she embraced her father with a fierceness and sincerity she had not felt since she was very small. He returned it with an almost crushing firmness, making her squeak.

She turned to her mother and hugged her as well, too choked-up to speak. The countess whispered in her native tongue, telling Cindra all would be well and happy and that she was loved, like she had done when the girl was little and afraid of thunder storms. Cindra sniffed back her tears, tickling her nose with the fur lining of her mother's coat.

"I-I will miss you both," she said weakly, wiping her eyes dry. "Carry my love with you always, and I shall carry yours." She stepped away and did her best to smile as her lower lip quivered against the attempt. She gave a little curtsey and turned towards the water.

Mineth had said her goodbyes to her mother before leaving the castle. It was her intent to be a steady rock for her mistress if emotions ran too high, but now she found herself weeping openly, and was no help at all. She bowed and said her farewells to the count and countess, and took her lady by the arm to guide her to the waiting boat.

They walked down the steps to the jetty and the men helped them aboard, and with a gentle shove, the boat was cast off and moving towards the ship. Cindra turned on the bench and waved to her parents, who were arm-in-arm, flanked by guards and servants. They held their hands aloft in parting and Cindra felt the first thrill in her belly of embarking on a new adventure. She had been dreading this day for so long that she had neglected to see the possibilities. A wave struck the boat and she turned her attention back to her course.

Sea spray misted her face and the salty air filled her nose, as her eyes took in the enormity of the *Indisputable*. Painted with white and blue trim, it had no less than three masts along its length, which was easily over a hundred feet from stem to stern. The side of the ship boasted eight of its sixteen guns, all very diplomatically stowed behind watertight doors. A web-like network of ropes called 'shrouds' ran from below the railings to the tops of the masts, holding them in position and also allowing the crew to climb like little spiders up to the yardarms.

The sails were being unfurled and Cindra saw they were striped with white and blue, each stripe as wide as a man was tall. Two great square sails were hung on the fore and main mast and a triangular sail at the rear. Cindra was amazed at the sheer number of ropes and pulleys that made up the rigging and wondered how the sailors kept them all from tangling. She supposed she would find out in the next few weeks.

As the boat approached the side of the ship, a hoist was pushed over the railing and a sling was lowered, presumably to assist the ladies aboard. Mineth gave Cindra a worried look, already seeming a little green about the cheeks. Cindra put on a brave face and allowed the sailors to help her into the sling, smiling assurances to Mineth as she was secured in and raised up to the deck. The captain was there to greet them both and offered to show them to their quarters, when one of the men shouted for his attention. It seemed that a fiery missile was heading straight for the ship and everyone stopped to watch with mounting fear.

Everyone, that is, but Cindra who silently praised the bird's impeccable timing. Gavagul circled the ship twice, letting his trail of smoke and flame die down before landing on the railing near the ladies. The captain, who was expecting this extra passenger, enlisted the aid of a cabin boy to fetch the bird using a belaying pin as a perch and bring it along to its special fireproof accommodations.

The crew was slowly returning to work now that they recognized an Ember Swallow, but they kept an eye on it just the same. It was bad enough that they were sailing with two women aboard but a flaming bird amidst all the wood and canvas was a bad omen.

Cindra and Mineth were led to the rear of the ship and into a rather narrow room that was situated below the stern deck. The stern cabin, as it was called, was formerly the captain's quarters, but he had arranged for the ladies to use it for the duration. Cindra gave the man her thanks, wondering what his new quarters must be like if this was where he usually slept.

The cabin was increasingly narrow towards the aft and two thin bunks were set against each wall, meeting head to head at the rear of the room. Above the bunks on either side of the cabin were the room's only redeeming features: windows that extended out like turrets, glazed and gilded, providing a lovely view in the enclosed space. They even opened, explained the captain, for the sake of assisting in sanitation. Having her most important question answered, Mineth relaxed visibly.

The rest of the space was taken up by a pair of small chests containing clothing and bedding and by Gavagul's special cage which was mounted to the ceiling beam. It was like a strange merging of an iron pot and a gibbet, creating a tall barred enclosure with a sealed base to contain charcoal and fresh wood chips. A thick leather glove was near at hand, like the sort used for falconry, but the cuff was boiled and hardened to guard against heat. The bird was being placed in his cage by the cabin boy, who was more than happy to be relieved of it. It squawked and chattered something, obviously worn out from its flight.

Captain Gawyyn gave the ladies a bow as he excused himself. "I must attend to the departure, but I would be honored if milady and her attendant would dine with the officers and me tonight." When Cindra hesitated, he said, "It is a tradition, but it is by no means required. You may attend another night, if it is more suitable."

Cindra nodded and said, "It would be an honor, captain. We shall attend tonight." She used her best voice and bearing, seeming not at all the nervous girl and every bit the future duchess.

The captain said, "Splendid! I shall have my boy call upon you at sunset. And now, I take my leave." He and the boy left the cabin and closed the door, leaving the women alone with the sound of creaking wood and men shouting muffled orders in a foreign tongue.

Gavagul broke the silence with a whistling chirp, "Lady Cindra Corrina," said the bird in Jaron's weary voice. Cindra's gaze darted up at the cage, and then looked pleadingly at Mineth, who shook her head and stepped out of the room, clucking her tongue in disapproval.

Cindra stepped near the cage and felt the bird's warmth through the bars. "Speak," she said anxiously. Gavagul ruffled his feathers and summoned his message from memory.

For more than an hour Mineth waited for her lady to come out of the cabin. At first, she wouldn't answer the knocking, but when Mineth said she would get the captain, Cindra relented and opened the door. She had obviously been crying but she would not discuss it. Mineth tried to comfort her but since she did not know what Sir Jaron had said in his message, it was difficult to find the right words. When in doubt, Mineth found it was best to just sit quietly and be there for her lady. It seemed to help.

After a bit of coaxing and freshening up, Mineth brought Cindra up on deck and together they watched the Casselvane Range recede in the distance. The walled keep that had been her home for so long was not visible without help, and the captain was kind enough to offer his glass to the women. Looking through the lenses, Cindra saw the white stones of the castle atop the cliff outcrop, looking so much smaller than she had imagined. Only the tallest structures were visible over the western hills, and the Winter Palace itself seemed to blend into the carved face of the mountain. Cindra returned the spyglass to the captain as her city passed out of sight; her feelings and thoughts she kept to herself.

Captain Gawyyn was standing near a large wheel upon the quarterdeck which Cindra assumed steered the ship. A crewman was keeping it steady, making slight changes as the wind and seas demanded. The captain gave orders in a strong, steady voice, and the other officers relayed them to the men, shouting to be heard over the noise of the wind, sea, and sail. It was difficult trying to understand the nautical jargon of a crew speaking Calilesh, but hearing the words in Rok was taxing Cindra's limited vocabulary. She watched the men hauling on ropes and trimming the sails, trying to ignore the women in their midst. It had occurred to her that she and Mineth would be an oddity aboard a ship, but had not bothered to ask further. Now, as she watched the averted gazes and nervous eyes, she decided it might be best to limit their time on deck, and the captain agreed.

After the initial excitement had worn off and the women had time to settle in to their new surroundings, they began to truly feel the motion of the waves and the rocking of the ship. The waters were not rough or choppy but the constant motion was beginning to take its toll. Cindra was taking deep breaths through her nose and out through her mouth like she had been taught once while sick in a carriage, and Mineth was lying on her bunk with an arm over her eyes and moaning occasionally. Both windows were open and secured, letting in a cool sea breeze and giving the women a place to visit if their stomachs took a turn for the worse. So far, no one had needed to befoul the ocean with her breakfast.

Cindra had, in her more steady moments, practiced walking up and down the cabin as the ship moved under her. Being but five or six steps in length, it was not much room in which to gain her sea legs, but it was better than stumbling about in front of the crew. She had already bruised her knees against the bunks, but her balance was improving. She tried to encourage Mineth to walk about as well, but the handmaiden was hearing none of it.

The smell of cooking meat was wafting in through the windows, and Cindra noticed that sunset was approaching. If she could engage Mineth in some duty, she thought, that might rouse her and end her overdramatic moaning. "Mineth, we should dress for dinner. It is almost sunset."

Mineth just rolled over and faced the bulkhead. "Oooh, you go, milady. I could eat nothing tonight."

"I *shall* go, but I will need your help getting properly dressed," she said patiently.

Mineth groaned as she turned and sat up, looking about the room with bleary eyes. "Yes, milady," she mumbled, and pitched her legs over the side of the bunk. A few moments later, she rose to her feet and began wobbling over to the dressing chest. Cindra backed against the bulkhead to give her room to maneuver, steadying her by the elbow just once. She did not intend to spend the rest of the voyage babying her handmaid, if it could be helped.

Mineth brought out a few folded dresses that would do for a formal meal at sea, setting them on the bunk for Cindra to choose from. Cindra picked one that was green with yellow trim, and bared her shoulders. It might be a bit distracting for the crew, but since she would be dinning with the captain and his officers, she figured it would be appreciated. She had no idea what was fashionable in Rokvynnar, but while she was still in the warmer latitudes, she would try to dress comfortably. Besides, she felt the need to be complimented and fawned over a bit.

Cindra opened her jewelry box and took out one of the pearl necklaces her mother had given her, these being adorned with the Corrina cat and sun/moon symbol instead of the seashell of DuMaylione. It was fitting that she had such a reminder of family and it made her happy to put it on.

There were other items she could have worn as well but Mineth told her not to be so eager to show off her wealth and finery. Trinkets could be stolen or lost, and the less seen, the better. Cindra agreed; it would be bad enough to be stolen from but to have the crew turn out their pockets and face whipping or worse... best if they weren't tempted.

The cabin boy came knocking as the sun dipped below the waves and Mineth was given a second chance to attend. The handmaid was in better spirits, but still pale and unsteady, and so declined. Cindra bade her goodnight and followed the boy down a steep stair below decks.

Forward of the stair was a wide deck with a ceiling not much taller than she, and many lengths of netting and cloth hung from the ribs of the ship, some upon one hook and some stretched between two. At first she thought they were something with which to catch fish, but then she witnessed a crewman climbing into one and pulling a bedroll over himself. He rocked with the motion of the ship, and seemed to be quite comfortable, though he looked a bit like a stone in a sling. *Curious*, Cindra thought. She also noted the rows of cannons and crates of shot that stood by at the ready, and wondered if the captain might let her fire one off...

Aft of the stair was a narrow corridor made of hanging linen, like a maze of laundry. She could hear laughter and voices coming from the far end of the deck, and the boy led her to a makeshift curtain behind which the captain and his officers were seated about a table; candle light and wizard lamps providing a merry ambiance and a bottle of port supplying good cheer.

The men stood as she entered, stooping under the low ceiling and bowing as the captain introduced them. Cindra smiled and nodded to each man in turn, taking her chair opposite the captain. It was indeed the most confined table she had ever attended, having room for each person's plate and goblet and little else.

A boy filled her cup with port and she watched the dark liquid move to and fro with the motion of the ship. The deck had a musty odor, a mixture of sweat and mold and wood. The hanging linens that provided a measure of privacy for the officers also cut down on the air circulation, making the space warm but stuffy.

Delicious scents came from somewhere forward and made the experience more bearable, allowing her to ignore the feel of bumping knees and cramped legs. She did not have long to wait, for the meal was served shortly after she was seated.

The food was a combination of cultures, mixing the fancy breads and sweet, tangy sauces of Calilon with the seared, spiced meats and vegetables of Rokvynnar fare. The drink was heady and rich and left a smoky trail down the throat, as good port should.

"My compliments to the chef," said Cindra after tasting some of the blackened meat, which was slightly crispy outside but still tender and juicy. *At least I might like the food in Rokvynnar*, she thought.

"I shall pass that along," said Captain Gawyyn, nodding in approval. "And may I say that you are looking quite exquisite this evening."

She gave a little blush as the men agreed, raising their goblets.

The captain's first officer, a man named Bayell, spoke up. "Milady Cindra Syn Casselvane," he began, using the Rok term 'Syn' to denote her lands, "have you been on a sea voyage before?"

She replied, "I have not, in fact, this is my first time out of sight of Portshia." A thought occurred to her and she asked hopefully, "Do the noble women of Rokvynnar travel often, at sea or otherwise?"

Bayell seemed amused but remained respectful, "Women do not travel by ship unless there are no other practical means," he saw Cindra's disappointment and added, "but the dowager duchess has been known to go abroad from time to time. I think she has even visited your sovereign's royal court in the north."

Cindra wanted to ask 'was that before or after her husband died?' but decided against it. She asked instead, "What is the dowager duchess like? I have heard very little."

The captain grinned and said, "Ah, your ladyship's mother-to-be. She is a stern and formidable woman, with an iron constitution." The officers nodded in somber agreement as his grin faded. "It is said that when the young duke Hammyd passed beyond, gods keep him, she kept to her schedule and refused to lock herself away in mourning." Gawyyn paused to take a drink, "She was resolute to be an anchor for her people in their time of need. It was an amazing thing."

Cindra watched as the other officers paused in their eating and drinking to reflect on what must have been a national tragedy, like the passing of her own dear brother. Yet the duchy still had another male heir, though he was only twelve. She sighed mentally. At least he wasn't terribly old, like some of the men that less fortunate maidens had to marry. Cindra had a cousin across the bay in Aurilon who was married to a man as old as Count Casselvane. She was in her twenties, but there was still a difference of decades between the lady and her lord.

Cindra wondered which was worse in the end, to have a husband that was too old to play with his children, or to be older than him and think of him as a child. The young duke wouldn't be a boy forever, and perhaps he would give her reason to respect him, besides it being her marital duty.

As for the dowager duchess, she wondered what kind of woman refused to mourn in private for her own child. It seemed that such a person was either a devoted leader of her people, or a stonehearted troll. *With my luck, she will be both*, Cindra thought bitterly. It was doubtful she would be winning the woman's heart any time soon, to say nothing of proving herself worthy of the duchess's surviving son.

"What of the young duke?" She asked as she forked through her meal. She tried to make the question sound casual yet interested, but thought it came off as worried and fearful, and she cringed a bit.

The captain seemed to interpret it as the nervousness of a bride-to-be, and pretended not to take notice of her discomfort. He played up his lord in a way that had likely been crafted and practiced for just this question. "His grace Duke Haynyyd is a marvelous young man, with a bearing beyond his years. His manner, I am told, is like unto that of his late brother, and indeed the burden of assuming the title under such circumstances has given him a solemn resolve to live up to his family name.

"That being said, he is also known to be a lad of good nature and thoughtfulness, and is one of the few who can bring a smile to the face of the dowager duchess in these harsh times." The captain finished his oration with a dramatic weight, taking another sip of port.

Cindra considered. So he's a mother's prize cub that plays at being his departed older brother, and probably deals with his troubles by shouting 'I am the duke!' at his servants and advisors.

"How charming," said Cindra, smiling politely and sipping a bit more port than was advisable.

Captain Gawyyn seemed pleased and returned to his meal.

Chapter Twelve

Night Capers

It had been a long week and Nixy was tired; more tired than usual since Cindra had left on her ocean voyage. Master Gorin had been harsh, but seemed to have relented a bit when the boy didn't provide as much sport as he was hoping. Nixy didn't care. He just wanted to go to bed and collapse.

The stables had been given an extra good cleaning and Nixy had been chosen to take the first and last of the duties. He had shuffled to the well afterwards, drew water into a bucket, and stripping off his tunic, washed himself down with a clean groom's brush. He was used to smelling a bit like horse, so he didn't mind the scent the bristles left on him. Next, he gave the tunic a good soak and wringing, and swung it around a bit to dry it. He would hang it on a line in the stable quarters later where the rest of the lads were probably throwing dice and chatting before bed. The sun had almost set and Master Gorin would soon be heard stomping up the stairs and the chatter would die down and the dice would disappear, and beds would be filled before the door was flung open. Same thing every night.

But this night, the potato man had an extra chore for his favorite whipping boy. Gorin came from the castle gate carrying a bucket full of mutton bones and called to Nixy before the boy could climb the stairs over the stables. Nixy looked back, ready to be smacked or hollered at, but the stable master seemed to be in a decent mood.

"Boy!" he said, just loud enough to be heard, not his usual skin-bristling bark. "I got one more thing for ya." He waddled over to the lad and set down the bucket. "Minerva's been good enough ta provide the lord's hounds with some treats," he said as he rubbed his neck in an odd way. "Be useful and pass these out, but make 'em sit still for it, no whining or biting."

Nixy nodded silently and waited for the little man to wander into his little cottage, rubbing the bruise on his neck and smiling. He didn't understand grownups. Nixy didn't like to be bitten, but why the little man was smiling about it, he couldn't imagine. He picked up the bucket and wandered over to the kennels on the other side of the main gate.

It was after sunset by the time he had finished because he could never visit the kennels without petting and visiting each hound in turn. They smelled the mutton on him and were restless but he made sure they each settled down and sat patiently before he rewarded them. Gorin would have done it himself, except that the hounds almost never obeyed him and had bitten him on several occasions. Nixy knew enough to get all of the pats and playfulness out of the way first, because even he was not immune to the ill nature of hungry dogs.

Now smelling like horse and dog and his eyes stinging with fatigue, Nixy wandered towards the stables. The night seemed darker than usual and he looked up to see if the moon was out. It was just a sliver of light, but bound to get bigger over the next week. The stars were out and there were no clouds, but still Nixy felt the weight of the night on his shoulders. The torches at the castle gate were flickering weakly and the guards were talking and paying him no mind. He quickened his pace towards the stairs.

The sound of wings caught his attention and he looked up into the darkness, eyes wide and straining to see. It sounded like a big bird, maybe an owl, and it was close. He saw a flickering of movement near the roof of the stable quarters and stood still, trying to hear something more. He saw a dark shape and heard claws on the shingles, but the roof was not steep enough for him to see clearly without walking further into the bailey, out in the open. With the stairs and his bed so close, he decided it would be better to be indoors and in the company of the lads than to know what was perched above him. He started up the stairs, stomping his feet a bit in the hopes that he would frighten whatever it was away. He heard no flapping, so it seemed the bird wasn't afraid of him. He wished he could say the same. Something was gnawing at his spine, quivering in his stomach, making the ordinary sounds of the night seem ominous. He reached the door and panicked just a little as the latch stuck, but it opened with a shove and he hurried inside. Something brushed the back of his head as he passed through the entrance, tickling his hair, like the legs of an insect or the stroke of grasping fingers. He shut the door with a bang and brushed the back of his head, rubbing the feeling away.

The other stable boys were all looking at him with mild amusement, some half into bed, laughing to cover their own panic. "We thought you was Gorin!" said one of the boys, who was still dressed under the covers.

"Nah," said another older lad. "Gorin makes the stair creak something fierce. Nixy was having you on."

"Nixy, you pisspot!" said a boy who's leg was tangled in his sheets in his haste to cover up. "I thought I was gonna get my ear cuffed again!"

The Gold Cat's Daughter

"I wasn't trying to be Gorin," Nixy said, "There was an owl or something, I was trying to scare it off."

"Looks like it scared you off instead," said a boy Nixy's age, who slept across from him. The boy giggled and the laughter spread around the room, turning annoyance into good humor. Nixy laughed in spite of himself, happy to be forgiven. He hung up his wet tunic and climbed into his cot, settling down for the night.

Nixy awoke in the dead of night. His bladder was full, and he felt the blanket, relieved to find it dry. He must have been dreaming, for he remembered urinating out the window until the pressure went away, but it kept coming back stronger than ever. He hated those dreams, but they had their purpose, he supposed. He threw off the covers and placed his feet gingerly on the cold floor, trying not to wake anyone. As he moved towards the door, making the floorboards squeak, he heard the scratching of clawed feet on the roof tiles again. He froze and listened, a tingle in his spine making his bladder ache, but heard nothing more. He thought to wake someone to watch him just in case, but the thought of asking a friend to guard his back while he relieved himself seemed rather silly. Instead, he took his glowstone from its hiding place behind his cot and put it around his neck. The light would offer little protection but was a comfort nonetheless.

He grasped the latch and pulled the door open gently, bracing as the chill night air washed over him. He looked at the wall for telltale shadows, trying to see if anything was lurking on the roof, but the moonlight was too dim to be of much help. He stepped onto the landing, wondering if he should just pee over the side of the stair, but he was still so close to whatever had been scratching the tiles... best to go further down.

The boys weren't given the luxury of a chamber pot and had to make do with the common outhouse in the bailey. The little shack stank worse than the stables, so Nixy used the stables whenever possible. They would do for tonight and the horses wouldn't mind. He reached the bottom of the stairs and picked a dark corner to relieve himself in. After a moment he felt much better and all but forgot about the noise on the roof. He fastened up his trousers and headed back to the stairs, trying to be quiet. The horses stamped and whinnied in protest of something, making Nixy flinch, and the whine of the hounds in the kennel pricked at his ears.

He was on the fourth step when he looked at the top of the landing. Blocking the way to the door was a dark shape, stooped and hunching forward as if about to descend the stair. It was bigger than any of the stable boys and stood slowly on thin legs, rising higher still. Nixy froze in terror, his breath catching in his throat. The thing looked as bony and gaunt as a starving man, but a deep sense of dread shone from it like a cold dark sun. Its head was the wrong shape, as if it wore a horned mask. Something moved above its shoulders like extra limbs, a sickly wet popping could be heard as they flexed. It exhaled, like the soft hiss of a cat, which sent tendrils of steam curling about its head. Nixy's hand shot to his chest and his heart thundered with raw fear as he felt the glowstone around his neck. His fingers curled around it and he struggled to speak the word but his jaw was clenched shut. The thing on the stairs took a step down making the wood creak, the smell of stagnant water and rot emanating from it as the night air became colder. The magic word raced through Nixy's mind like panic, like fire. *Ilda! Ilda! Ilda!* He must have managed to speak the word through his fear, for a light flared up in the darkness from his clenched fingers, the glowstone shining like a bright star and illuminating the shape on the stairs.

The figure flinched and recoiled, a low growl escaping its throat. A pointed nose and chin parted to reveal a toothy grimace and angry eyes returned the weak glow with a fire of their own. Grey-green skin was pulled tightly over its skeletal frame and the creature blocked the light from its eyes with a horrible clawed hand. A gristly pop followed as it extended a vein-covered wing, like that of a bat or dragon, shielding itself from the glare. The skin stretched horridly and glistened as a toad's, sickly and corrupt.

Nixy ran. He didn't remember choosing a direction or even moving his feet but he was running for his life across the bailey, putting the structure of the stables between him and the thing on the stairs. For the first time he thought of his knife, but it was wrapped up in the extra blanket he used as a pillow, safe and useless. No way to get to it, no place to go. He wanted to shout for help but it would use precious breath. The ground stung his cold feet but at least it wasn't muddy and slowing him down. He chanced a look behind and saw the thing was pursuing him, spreading its wings and beating the air as it bounded forward, lurching closer with every stride. In seconds it would be on him, probably lifting him into the night like an owl with a mouse. He hated being a mouse.

Nixy dodged to the right, heading towards the outer wall and the structures built up against it. He ducked between the support columns of the smithy and ran towards the opening into the cannon wall; if he could just get under cover, the beast wouldn't be able to fly off with him. He could evade it in the narrow confines of the cannon wall, reach the outer battlements and maybe find a guard. He was beginning to think now, recovering some of the wits that kept him alive on the streets. The glowstone had extinguished itself and bounced wildly against his chest as he ran. Only the whitewashed walls provided any sense of space, catching light from the stars and dim lamps in the castle. The stair into the cannon wall was just ahead. He would have to reverse his direction to climb them, giving him a chance to see his pursuer before ducking into the passage.

He reached the foot of the stone stair and turned to race up to the archway when a shadowy form stepped forth, blocking his way. It was the shape of a huge wolf, featureless and black in the darkness, with only its yellow eyes and fangs glowing in the night. Nixy pressed himself against the wall, a new terror gripping him. He had always feared wolves from the stories his father told. Now he was staring up at one as it growled fiercely. A second growl was heard at Nixy's side as another black wolf emerged from the shadows, blocking his escape, close enough for the boy to feel its breath on his arm.

The skeletal creature stopped in its tracks with a beating of wings, buffeting the boy with its foul odor. It uttered something in a hoarse voice, and blackness overtook Nixy. His father's face appeared in his head, telling him he should have never left home. He fell to the cold earth and the last thing he heard was the howling of the wolves.

The next thing he knew he was lying in a comfortable bed covered in linen sheets and a thick blanket of down, the smell of broth seeping into his nostrils. Minerva, the kitchen mistress who had the stable master's affections, was bringing in a bowl on a tray to set by a low table at the bedside. She squinted at his face a bit too closely and smiled, drawing back in relief.

"You had us worried for a time, young man!" she said in a jovial voice. "We thought you was done for this morning." She sat him up and placed the soup tray on his lap. It was chicken broth with bits of vegetables and a wooden spoon.

"Where am I?" asked the boy, looking around at the open chamber with its columns and sturdy stonework. On either side of the bed were wooden blinds about as tall as he was, giving the bed space the look of a stall in a stable. Across the room were several such beds and stalls, providing a bit of privacy for whoever slept there. Each contained a few personal belongings, mostly devotional in nature. Statues of gods and goddesses carved of wood, or sticks woven and arranged into the Jaydecean Wheel adorned the small shelves over each bed.

"Servant's quarters in the castle," she said, "You were found late last night by the west wall, all fevered and shivering, poor thing." She shook her head with pity. "It was Master Gorin who bade me to take care of you, saying you owed a debt to the departed young lady and he would see you pay it." She smiled and added, "He was so worried."

Nixy couldn't believe it. The little man must have been aware that the boy was under the count's protection, and had panicked when he turned up hurt. Was he hurt? How did he wind up by the west wall anyway? He felt well enough, just a bit fuzzy and tired, but they were feeding him broth, so it might be worth his while to take a rest and enjoy the attention.

His memory was coming back little by little. He had needed to pee last night, and got out of bed to go down stairs. He remembered the cold ground, the cold air, and a cold feeling about him... Had there been something on the roof? An owl, probably. He remembered the scratching noise on the roof tiles and thought himself silly for being so afraid of nothing. In the light of day, the fears of the night were like a distant memory.

He ate his broth in peace, and enjoyed the soft bed while he could. Soon enough he would have to go back to work.

———

Dexer stepped off the gangway and onto the pier, happy to be home but anxious still. He had to deliver the package before he could relax, certain that even now unfriendly eyes were on him. The Boss never left anything up to chance and he probably had people spying on Dexer during the entire caper, just to make sure he did the job and brought back the prize. Dexer found he was more worried about his own cohorts than the city watch or the count's men. Maybe that was what the Boss had in mind. Either way, he had never sought to test his luck. If there were spies watching him, then let them watch. Maybe they'd learn something about a true professional. He let his mind wander a bit as he walked, recalling the work he had just finished.

The caper had gotten off to a shaky start. The ship had arrived two days late due to a storm and the ride had made Dexer a bit sick. Once they got into port at LuQuivost, very little improved. The authorities in Aurilon were more cautious than usual and questioned the passengers and crew, giving the ship a thorough inspection before letting anyone disembark. Dexer had to use every bit of the identity he had concocted, giving his false name and intentions, showing forged credentials, even recounting a story of his recent travels which he had cooked up for just such an emergency. The port inspectors had been satisfied and let him off early and once more Dexer was convinced that his priest disguise was his best.

The priesthood of Obamir, Red Hats as they were called, were often found along trade routes and places where commerce thrived, so the comfortable robes and broad-rimmed red hat made for a perfect cover. Obamitte priests could make a decent living by blessing the fortunes of merchants and tradesmen and receiving charitable donations in return. Since Dexer was under no obligation to pay a tithe to the temple, the donations were just a nice bonus. To his mind, the priesthood was a scam anyway, since the gods no longer spoke to them directly or seemed to mind what went on in the world. A priest could lead a less than devout lifestyle and few would be the wiser. Fewer still would care to stop it, lest their own vices be endangered. There was only that pesky bit about judgment, if that was to be believed; most feared the judgment of the afterlife enough to keep them in check, but Dexer had ceased to worry about such things.

The Boss had given him orders to fetch an item he had arranged to buy, before the money exchanged hands. It seemed like something a small time criminal would do and the Boss could surely afford to pay for what he wanted and keep it legitimate. Still, he must have his reasons, and Dexer knew better than to ask.

He checked into a modest inn and began to ask the local merchants about ships bound for Minael, hoping to learn more about his quarry. One of the local businessmen who dealt in precious stones mentioned the name Dexer had been looking for: Feyn Hathiid. A Minaelese jewel merchant who traveled the Emerald and Gozhian seas, Hathiid was currently in LuQuivost and staying at a fine inn near the garden square called DuVizhan Druz, the Blue Badger. Dexer still had his priest disguise on and wondered why the man had described the infamous Blue Badger as a 'fine inn.' It was, to all outward appearances, a decent establishment, but it was known to keep a generous selection of company girls for the wealthy patrons. It seemed the visiting Red Hats from Calilon were inclined to be a bit less pious while in Aurilon. He'd heard things about these foreigners and their frivolous ways and it sounded like something he should look into when he had the time. For now, he was working.

He chose more local clothing to observe the Blue Badger that evening. He had checked with the harbormaster and learned that the next ship for Portshia left at high tide the next day and he cursed his luck for the storm that had made him late. Still, it could have been worse. Obamir was the god of luck and fortune, so he may not have smiled upon Dexer's impersonation or intent, but Dexer cared little for Obamir. He gave what little devotional thought he had to Tavenji, the Trickster and Lord of Lies. Dexer made his own luck and turned fortune to his favor by whatever means necessary, so he would take what fickle fortune gave him and make the best of it, by knifepoint if needs be.

There was no sign of Hathiid, but a pair of his errand boys were leaving the inn and heading for the dock. They had the dark skin and curly hair common to Minael islanders, and wore trousers and jackets of voluminous fabric dyed in red and blue. They returned bearing what looked to be a leather tube containing large feathers and a small chest of hardwood. The chest probably contained something fragile and likely to spill by the way it was carried. Dexer could see that both boys were armed with daggers and kept their eyes on the shadows. Either what they carried was trivial or the boys were more dangerous than they looked.

He sat and watched the entrance for a while longer while he formulated a plan. The Boss wanted the jewel merchant unharmed, so he could not simply break in and dispatch him in his room. He would have to dig deeper into his bag of tricks and cover his trail. He could not afford to be seen by the man in case they met again in the near future. Dexer hated to rely on flunkies to carry out his plans, but they had their uses as well.

He had been to the Blue Badger once before while on another mission several years ago. That had been an easy job, just a slip and slice, but he had needed to learn the layout of the place to plan his escape. He doubted the inn had changed much. It was three stories high and built in the style of Aurilon; its wattle and daub walls and wooden frame showed off the beauty of the structure that was lacking in the plastered faces of Calilon's southern architecture. They were also a bit easier to climb with the right gear, since the frame provided hand and footholds. The windows were shuttered and unglazed, for which Dexer was thankful. Also, the roof was steep and thatched, which was a much older style but had its advantages. Wooden or clay tiles were noisy to clamber around on, but a hook landing in thatch was nice and quiet.

He finished his surveillance and pulled up the tunic's deep hood, which had a long trailing tail that fell to his waist. He hid a bare dagger in the tail of the hood, just in case he needed a surprise weapon. He made sure his purse looked fat and hung in plain view as he entered the inn. He made a show of hiding his face, which was not uncommon in the famous DuVizhan Druz. He entered the foyer and was met by a large clerk with a friendly face who asked him his business. He played a hunch and mumbled something about a recommendation from 'the red priest,' wondering what the man would say about that. The clerk seemed taken aback but then relaxed his shoulders and showed Dexer into the main chamber. *Quite the scam*, he thought, and wondered if he should have worn his priest disguise instead.

The air was thick with the smell of perfume and alcohol as well as the wisps of smoke coming from exotic pipes and incense, and buried under it all like a dirty secret was the sweat of eager men. There were no women to be seen in the main area, for this was a place to relax and unwind before making a selection. When a man made known his desire and ability to pay for it, he was escorted into the 'showroom,' where the house mother showed him the selection of young ladies, or lads, if that was his taste, and then adjourned to more private accommodations on the upper floors. It seemed that Feyn Hathiid was still present and had yet to make his selection. Dexer took a seat on a floor pillow and took out a pipe, watching his quarry through the fragrant smoke.

The Minaelese jeweler was reclining on a couch decked with fat pillows, smoking a long-stemmed pipe with a large bowl. His dark moustache was waxed and curled at the ends and the rest of his curly mop of hair was hidden beneath a long hood, its train twisted about his head in an elaborate fashion. He wore a silk jacket and trousers of deep blue and orange and a red sash about his waist, which bulged with years of good living. His fingers were clad with gold rings and jewels, and he wore earrings of gold as well. No doubt he kept his guards well-paid and happy, for the man was a walking fortune. Three hefty bodyguards were seated around him, talking quietly and eying the other patrons as their master puffed happily on his pipe.

The Boss had dealt with the man on numerous occasions and knew a little about his security precautions. Hathiid disliked being away from his prize merchandise and mistrusted others. It was not unusual for him to wear the goods on his person, though not openly. The glittering jewels that adorned him were a distraction, in case he ran afoul of thieves. His ,real treasures were under his rich clothing. Dexer saw an odd bulge in the man's waist as the jeweler leaned over to speak to a servant boy and confirmed that the red sash disguised another belt beneath, probably a hidden purse.

The servant boy rose and went to fetch the hostess, who soon joined them and took them back to the showroom. Sliding doors parted to reveal a collection of beauties dressed in soft finery, and the jeweler and the hostess entered, along with a bodyguard, and closed the door behind. The glimpse of the women sent a murmur about the room, as the remaining patrons grew more eager. Dexer wondered if the man would get greedy and take more than one. He hoped not, for the fewer people in the way, the better. He reached for the leather pouch that contained his pipe leaf and opened a side compartment, taking out a cone of incense that he had specially-made in Portshia. He just had to wait.

The doors opened a few moments later and the merchant emerged with a young woman on his arm, blonde hair and fair of skin, with large blue eyes. She was taller than he and full of figure, very local Dexer decided. The hostess led them upstairs, followed by the errand boys and the packages they had retrieved, and two of his bodyguards. The third stayed below taking a place near the front door. At the call of an alarm, that man would either run upstairs or outside to catch someone fleeing the building. Dexer smiled around his pipe and relished the challenge.

The boys came back down empty handed and wandered towards the front door, probably to get some fresh air. Dexer waited for a moment and rose, stumbling out with his head down past the remaining bodyguard. He saw his opening now and needed to summon up his most charming aspect. This was hard, since he spent most of his time trying to intimidate people. He nodded to the clerk in the foyer, and faking an irritated throat, coughed and headed outside. The two boys were standing in the street talking in their native language as passersby took in their clothing and foreign faces and gave them a suspicious distance. One boy soon left; his friend calling reminders to him as he called back reassurances. 'I'll be back soon, yes I'll bring that too, sure, sure.' The tone was easy enough to comprehend, though the words were strange. Dexer waited until the other boy was out of sight before approaching the remaining lad.

"Excuse me," he said, trying to sound polite and harmless, but the boy jumped and spun. Dexer opened his hands to show he meant no harm. "Speak Calilesh?" he asked, hoping he could use the boy. The fewer people he came in direct contact with, the fewer witnesses.

The errand boy looked the tall gaunt man up and down and said, "Of course!" in a thickly accented voice. He seemed to be in his mid-teens and placed his hand on a dagger in his sash. "What do you want?"

Dexer smiled and the skin about his eyes and face crinkled with the strain. "I think we can help each other," he began. "I notice you serve a rich master."

The boy just glared at him warily.

"I think he would like what I have to sell, but he seems to be busy at the moment..." He held up the incense cone between his fingers. "This incense... is rare and special, made by the love priestesses of Tribilia." He smiled at the made-up name as the boy looked confused. "Burning it will prolong the act of love and make every moment more intense than the last." He palmed the cone and looked suddenly uncomfortable. "Of course, you're probably too young to know about such things..." He shifted on his feet as if to leave.

The boy got defensive. "I know about women! I have had many myself!" He crossed his arms, his dagger forgotten.

Dexer held up the incense cone again, "Then you understand! But you're young and strong and need no help. Your master is older and uh... might have need of this." He allowed a little desperation to crawl into his voice as he continued. "I wish I could have sold this to him before he took that woman upstairs, but now... maybe... If you could burn it and place it in his room, I promise he will have the time of his life. You could tell him afterwards where you got it, and he will already know its worth." Dexer's eyes burned with an intense eagerness, willing the boy to take up his offer. Anyone who knew him would have feared for their life under that gaze.

"This can make him *very* happy, and in return he can make me rich. You won't regret it, in fact," he took a handful of gold coins from his purse; "I'll give you a share for helping me." He held the coins out to the boy, whose arms were still folded. "What do you say?"

The boy looked at the coins and Dexer watched as his greed overcame his caution. He reached out and the gaunt man dropped the coins into his hand along with the incense cone. Pocketing the coins in the folds of his sash, the boy looked at the cone and gave it an experimental sniff. He blinked and wrinkled his nose at the odd scent. "You are not lying to me? The master will whip me if I ruin his night, but I will tell him about you."

Dexer raised his hands in surrender, "I wouldn't lie to a young man who kept such company! I'm not a fool. Tell you what, when you place the censor in his room, meet me in back of the inn by the alley. I'll pay you another seven crowns for a job well done."

The boy eyed him suspiciously again, "Why should I meet you back there?"

Dexer leaned in closer and explained, "You want to share your good fortune with the others, that's your choice. If you work alone, you keep all the profits yourself."

The boy considered and nodded in agreement. "I will meet you in back of the inn."

Dexer laid his finger beside his nose and then pointed at the boy with it, the Circle of Gold's hand sign to keep a secret. He patted the boy on the cheek and walked into the shadows behind the inn. There were a few preparations to make while he waited.

The boy took longer than expected and Dexer had the ill feeling that his plan had hit a snag. He checked the position of the moon, marking perhaps a half an hour since the boy took the incense and reentered the whorehouse. He wondered if the boy would come back at all, or worse, be accompanied by suspicious bodyguards. He really didn't need to deal with that tonight.

His fears were eased when he saw the lad slip out the back of the inn and creep towards the stables, peering cautiously into the shadows. Dexer was sitting on one of a dozen barrels that were arrayed in the courtyard, along the wall between the stable and the alleyway. They were all full of something heavy; he knew, he had checked. He hopped off the barrel and motioned the boy over into the dark courtyard.

The errand boy walked over eagerly, his hands in his pockets. Dexer looked for the telltale signs of tension in the lad's shoulders and the angle of his forearms, but found no sign that the boy was pocketing a weapon. His dagger was still at his waist in the sash and his eyes spoke of success. He strode with confidence over to the gaunt man and raised one hand to wave, keeping it ready to accept his payment.

"Did you get it into his room?" asked Dexer, his hand upon his purse.

"I did," said the lad, "I had to convince the guards at the door but they allowed me to slip inside and place the burning censor within." He looked about in the dark, "My master questioned me, and I told him that it was a special gift for his pleasure. He let me place it by the window."

Dexer nodded with approval, "That's good, that's good. And you came straight back?" He needed to know how long the concoction had been burning.

"The master had me bring him wine, but I returned after leaving it in the room." The boy related his success with some pride, perhaps trying to increase his reward.

Dexer smiled, his yellowed teeth looking sickly next to his pale skin in the dim light. He jingled his purse to undo the drawstrings and leaned towards the lad a bit saying, "I never got your name, boy."

The young man tensed a bit, but raised his chin and said proudly, "I am Mar Javem."

"Mar Javem," Dexer repeated, "well done, well done."

He struck like a snake as he drove his dagger under the boy's sternum, piercing his heart. The lad's eyes widened in surprise and quickly lost focus as he slumped into Dexer's arms.

Mar Javem's pocket was relieved of his earlier payment. His body was dumped between two barrels in the back row, and a nearby wooden crate was placed over the space to conceal it. Dexer checked the ground for dark stains and covered any blood he found by kicking dirt over it. He had removed the dagger just before dropping the boy into his final resting place, preventing the spilling of more blood on the ground or his clothes. It never helped to make a mess of things.

After making sure he had not been seen, Dexer left through the alley and made his way around to a narrow gap between the inn and the neighboring structure. It was lit only by starlight and wide enough for two men to walk side by side, and was the home to a number of rats. No one noticed his ascent up the side of the inn, using the exposed wooden frame as hand and foot holds. If he were not so far from home, he would have prepared a toolkit for scaling walls. As it was, he had to make do with his own underused skills.

The climb took a bit longer than he had intended, much to his private embarrassment, but he succeeded in reaching the thatched roof and pulling himself onto the yielding straw. He took a few moments to recover his strength before continuing his ingress. It would be difficult without a length of rope and harness, but he had one trick up his sleeve that should make life much easier, at least on the way out.

He began walking along the rooftop, keeping low to avoid detection. The rooms on the third floor had windows facing north towards the street and south towards the stables. The second and first floors had only false, windowless shutters, making them stuffy, private, and cheap. Someone of Hathiid's means would prefer the finer rooms above with their larger spaces, airy windows, and stone chimneys for colder nights. The night was not very cold, but the chimneys served another purpose. Dexer stopped at each one to check for a particular smell, sweet, cloying and heady.

He found it at one of the north-facing rooms, near the building's front door. So close to the entrance, he would have to be extra careful to avoid being seen by striders in the street, and if the alarm was raised, the bodyguard waiting downstairs would make a getaway much more interesting. He worked his way down the slope of the roof towards the eaves above the window ledge. He slowly leaned down to descend face first towards the edge, securing his gloved hands into the thatch as he prepared to ease his weight off the roof and over the street below.

He had examined the ledge and the roof from the street earlier, planning his movements in advance, but it was always different when you were looking down from the heights rather than looking up. He took a breath, checked his handholds one last time, and swung his legs down in a controlled arc.

His trailing boot caught the window ledge and he gained his footing, pressing himself closer to the wall. He transferred his grip to the eaves and listened at the shutters, making sure he was unseen and outside the correct room. There was silence within and without and the smell of his special incense could be detected through the slats. He took a gulp of fresh air and held it.

He opened the shutters carefully and looked inside, taking in the unmoving bodies on the bed; a long, colored feather was clutched in Hathiid's hand as he lay across the legs of the sleeping whore. A small hardwood chest containing vials of strange oils was open on the nightstand, in easy reach. The man had removed his silken jacket and trousers, leaving himself in a loincloth and his red sash. Dexer looked for the burning censor and retrieved it, opening the lid and tossing the smoldering incense out the window. Only after the air cleared a bit did he let out his breath and take another. The smoke was clinging near the ceiling and made him swoon slightly, even though he had worked with the substance often and was not as affected as others. Hathiid and his companion would sleep for hours, awaking with a drunken feeling and a powerful hunger. By that time, Dexer would be long gone.

He turned the sleeping man over gently, feeling under the sash for a hidden pocket or purse. He found it at the man's side where he had noticed an odd bulge before. It was a thick deerskin purse that was sewn shut and a leather belt secured it to his waist. The buckle was a cunning little puzzle that required some combination of pressure on certain hidden levers, but Dexer had no patience for such an obstacle. He decided to cut his way through the sewing.

He removed the prize from the man's safe-purse and marveled at the sight. It was the largest amethyst Dexer had ever seen; it was roughly cut and as large as a boy's fist, with unfinished edges and bits of stone still embedded in it. Yet as it was, it was probably worth a small fortune. It had a deep, rich color and no internal flaws that he could see in the low light. Dexer was only familiar with jewels that could fit on rings or necklaces. This was out of his league.

Hathiid snorted in his drug-induced slumber, bringing Dexer's mind back to the job. He had the stone, he had a patsy, and all he needed now was to make a clean getaway with no traces left behind. That was why he had forsaken a grappling hook and rope, because it would be too obvious. He was in a foreign land and unable to go to ground, so when the theft was discovered, he would need plenty of time to clear out and keep them guessing. He headed back to the window and climbed out onto the ledge, closing the shutters behind him.

Reaching up his sleeve, he retrieved the tool he had commissioned for this caper. There were wizards in Portshia that were happy to experiment with unorthodox enchantments, especially for a purse full of coin. Dexer had found one who had sold him on an idea that could revolutionize the housebreaking profession, although that was not the man's intent. The wizard had given a promising demonstration, and Dexer had ordered one to be made immediately.

It was a dowel of wood, probably elm, about eight inches long and over an inch thick, inscribed with silver inlay. There was also a crystal of quartz imbedded in the middle of its length with runes scribed about it. Dexer gripped the wood on either side of the crystal, holding it like the rung of a ladder, and after making sure the street was clear of prying eyes, stepped off the third story window ledge.

The dowel began to grow warm in his grip as he fell, slow as a feather, towards the shadowed street below. He was hanging by the magic handle as if it were tied to a rope. He could feel his weight straining on his wrists so he held on tight but his fall has beautifully slow. He would have to pay the wizard extra for this, and order many more. He was only halfway down!

Halfway down the handle grew hot. Were he not wearing gloves the heat would have seared his skin. Looking up, he saw the quartz glowing brighter and brighter as he picked up speed. "Pig shit," he whispered and instinctively bent his knees and braced for impact. The ground came racing up and he hit with a thud, rolling and wincing as the jolt shot up his legs and rattled his teeth. The crystal flared and popped, sending little shards flying about him, some striking his face. He shook his hands to free them of the smoldering handle which had blackened his leather gloves along the palms and fingers. Recovering his wits, he rolled to his feet and limped into the dark alley he had used earlier. He had no broken bones but there would be bruises and scrapes. He would have to pay the wizard a visit for this. Just one visit.

Dexer still had a bit of a limp as he walked through Portshia's Harbor District looking for a cab. The cramped quarters on the boat ride home had not allowed for him to exercise much and his ankles were still stiff. Nevertheless, it had been a great caper. The news had reached him the morning after as he boarded a packet ship for Portshia; the sailors were all talking about the scandal that had struck the harbor town last evening.

A wealthy merchant had been at the Blue Badger, having it off as they do, when his own servant boy stole something precious from him in the night and disappeared. They were searching the town for him and checking the ships heading out to sea. Dexer figured his ship had been halfway across the bay by the time they discovered the lad's body among the barrels near the stable. Would the merchant continue his trip to Portshia, to explain to DuChat why he could not sell him the promised stone? Dexer hoped he would just for his own amusement.

After finally getting a cab to take him on a roundabout path to the Boss's manor house, Dexer hobbled with dignity across the courtyard and into the foyer where he was taken to DuChat's study. He adjusted his cloak and jacket before he entered and removed his hat, making sure his ever-present hood was straight beneath it. No sense in looking like he had just gotten off a ship. The house servant knocked on the door of the study and opened it for Dexer, flicking a nervous glance into the room as he did. This put Dexer on edge and he brushed his arms against his body to double-check for the daggers hidden about him. The Boss was not alone.

Sitting across the desk from DuChat with her back to the door was a woman hooded and cloaked. The hem of her dress draped over a pair of light boots of leather and she wore dark blue gloves to match her attire. The cloak was so blue it seemed black in the low light. Dexer approached the desk cautiously and removed a wrapped bundle from his vest as DuChat stood and looked, expectantly.

"Ah, welcome back Dexer. I trust all went well?" DuChat said as the gaunt man stood beside the seated woman, eyeing her nervously.

"I imagine if things had not gone well, he would have had the good sense to never return," said the woman in a strangely muffled voice.

She turned her head to look up at him and Dexer suppressed a shudder. Beneath her hood was a pair of somewhat pretty eyes, but she wore a mask over her nose and mouth which resembled the grimacing maw of a beast out of nightmare, a troll or bloodthirsty wolf. The mask was painted much like her own complexion, making it look like her own face. It took him a moment to recover himself as he glanced at the Boss, which brought a smile to DuChat's face.

"All went well," said Dexer, his desire to elaborate on his adventure now quashed in the presence of this unnerving woman. "The merchant lives, and he thinks one of his own servants stole from him." He handed the bundle to DuChat who took it reverently as the woman rose to her feet. Dexer didn't think he was going to be introduced and he didn't care to be either.

DuChat unwrapped the bundle and took out the enormous amethyst carefully, holding it up to the light. A hungry look was in his eyes that went beyond the admiration of treasure; it was almost as if he was beholding his life's pursuit. He handed the gemstone to the woman, who took it gently in her gloved hands.

"So..." DuChat said softly, "Do we have it?"

The woman held the stone closer to her masked mouth as if to whisper secrets to it; she closed her eyes and spoke in a language Dexer had never heard before. *"Kwaath nahg vaash ol thamaz, a Mash bah havaath gnen.*" She held the stone a moment longer and opened her eyes. "We do not," she said a bit dejectedly. "It seems we shall have to deal with the Mad One after all." She handed the stone to DuChat as if it were a river rock covered in slime.

The Boss opened his desk drawer and removed a coin purse, hefted it, and passed it to Dexer. He then placed the stone upon a map of the Red Coast that was spread upon his desk. "It seems so," he said, "Are the alternate arrangements in place?" He dismissed Dexer with a wave of his hand.

As Dexer bowed and turned to leave, confused by the odd exchange, he overheard the woman speak behind her hideous mask. "Yes, Ghethas is prepared to leave immediately and deliver this rock as payment. They will meet on the coast after it's done."

"Good," said DuChat, "there are a few more details to discuss before we proceed..." Dexer opened the door and left the mysterious meeting behind. He had his money but it wouldn't do to count it here. It was a job well done, wasn't it? They seemed to be disappointed by the prize he had gone through so much trouble to bring back. It was what he had asked for, was it not? Dexer shook his head and adjusted his hat, pocketing the coin purse. *I got paid for my work, and that's all that matters*, he reminded himself. *I don't need a pat on the head, don't need no explanations, let my betters do what they will, long as I get paid.*

Dexer left the mansion and climbed aboard the waiting cab, looking about him for signs of deceit as he departed. One could never be too careful, especially after completing a job. There were a number of times Dexer himself had 'rewarded' a flunky who had seen too much or asked the wrong questions, taking the payment from his still-warm fingers. Double-cross was an unfortunate part of the game and you could only trust someone as long as they didn't try to kill you.

He climbed into the covered carriage and ordered the driver to take him to the Market Square as he opened the coin purse to check his payment. He took a special dagger from his jacket pocket and used the blade to poke around inside the purse. No scorpions or venomous insects. He flipped the dagger around and inserted the pommel into the purse. The end of the handle was set with a lodestone, with which he sifted through the coins, but it picked up no needles or spring traps with its magnetic grasp.

Satisfied that the payment was not to be his last, Dexer sat back and relaxed a bit, wondering when he would next have something so diverting to do. The creak in his joints reminded him that more regular training was in order and the pain in his ankles reminded him that he still had to visit a certain wizard and offer some constructive criticism on his latest invention.

Dexer had a special dagger for that too.

Chapter Thirteen

The Lady's Last Voyage

She was long serving before the mast, a weathered sailor on a turbulent sea. The wind had etched her face and bosom and her dress had faded into dull shades of its former splendor. As she looked out over the Emerald Sea; the falling sun gave fire to the ripples on the water that heralded another calm evening. The Lady of the *Indisputable* gazed calmly ahead of the vessel as she had since its launch, her carved and painted features bringing good fortune and comfort to her crew.

Cindra stood on the foredeck over the wooden figurehead and watched the sun setting on her eighteenth day at sea. The evenings were so eerie after nightfall, when only the stars and moon and the sails of their escort gave any sense of the surrounding vastness. There was nothing to be seen from horizon to horizon but the bejeweled darkness, and sometimes it seemed as though the ship were sailing through an ocean of stars, with only Lieutrella's radiant face revealing the waters beneath. Her light had waned of late however; the moon was only a sliver the night before.

The wind was in the west and the weather was favorable, yet it was the evening of the new moon and the captain would not risk sailing without its guidance. Cindra knew that it was possible to navigate by the position of the stars somehow, but had not had the opportunity to learn. On this voyage, the captain had explained, they would try to keep in sight of the shore as they sailed up the Red Coast towards Rokvynnar. On a night so dark, he had said, it would be safest to drop anchor and wait for morning.

The captain ordered the men to hoist signal flags to inform the *Wesvyyn Gull* of his intentions. Cindra did not mind the stop, for she always felt more at ease trying to sleep knowing they weren't going anywhere. *Besides, there's less of a chance I'll miss anything interesting*, she thought.

Mineth had finally gotten her 'sea legs' after the first week and was a constant companion when Cindra went above deck. The captain had acquiesced to allow the women about an hour at morning upon the deck and again at dusk so long as things were favorable, and Cindra and Mineth had made a habit of greeting the sun each morning and bidding it farewell that evening. The hotter part of the day, for hotter it was in the open sun with the glare on the water, was spent inside their small but cozy cabin reading what few books they had brought for the passage.

They usually took their meals in their quarters and the cabin boy was at their service, should they have any needs. Pinn was his name, and he was a ruddy-faced little character who spoke very little Calilesh, but did so with such enthusiasm and eagerness that he always brought a smile to the faces of the ladies. Mineth especially liked to try new words on him, pantomiming what she could not pronounce. He reminded Cindra of

Nixy, though a bit older and less sly, but with the same shock of blond hair and ready charm.

She found she missed her friend, though she had spent little time with him since their fateful meeting. Nixy was after all the only friend she'd had who was neither chosen as her playmate nor drafted from among the servant children to fill the ranks of her Army of Mischief. They shared a bond she did not fully understand, yet it was likely she would never see him again. This line of thought inevitably led her to Jaron, whose name and face had haunted her each day since he departed on his long exile.

Ah Jaron, he was her first love and possibly her last. *Where was he now?* she wondered, *and does he regret the message he sent to me?* She went over his last words to her, spoken in his own voice by the courier bird Gavagul. He had wanted her to forget, as *he* wanted to forget. He must have been feeling very alone and helpless wandering out of his homelands, towards an unknown future. *As though I were not?* He had told her to go on with her life and to leave old shames behind (*Oh, that was infuriating!*), focusing on her bright future. *Bright! What did he think I was getting into?* she thought in a hot fury. He wanted to do the same, putting his feelings for her behind him like a tragic, grand mistake. *Selfish, thickheaded fool!*

It had taken all this time for her to think about it without crying, without getting red in the face, yet still Mineth could tell she was troubled. The handmaid stood beside her and felt the lady stiffen as the unshared message weighed once more upon her mind. Mineth put a hand on her shoulder to give her support. Though her lady still would not speak of the details of Sir Jaron's last words, she had sense enough to guess that they were not pleasant and happy. "There, milady," she offered, "time is what you need."

Cindra wiped the tears from her eyes; not bothering to pretend the sea air caused them this time. She looked into the red sun, barely a fiery thumbnail above the darkening waters, and spoke. "He wanted me to *forget* him, Mineth. As he wants to forget *me*." Her throat caught on the last words and she felt choked.

Mineth put her arm around her lady's shoulders and gave her a comforting hug, saying, "He may say so milady, but he never will, you mark me." She leaned closer lest a nosey sailor were not minding his own business. "Men will bury their feelings down deep rather than deal with them, and it does them more harm than good. They think they are being brave and strong and putting a weakness aside, but it is not so.

"Sir Jaron, if you pardon me, will never forget you. He might make a new life for himself in his exile, but he will never forget." She sniffed back a tear for the pain her lady was feeling and the suffering ahead that she had yet to experience.

"But why did he say so?" asked Cindra, her voice shaking. "Why be so cruel?"

Mineth thought on this a bit and answered, "I believe he wishes you to feel as little for him as he feels for himself. That way, it makes the parting easier."

Cindra looked puzzled at her handmaiden. "What do you mean?"

"Well," Mineth said, her eyes on the darkening water, "I imagine he thinks it was wrong to love you the way he did, and he thinks he is unworthy of you; so as long as you still love him and cherish him, he cannot be free. If there is even a chance that you might one day find your way into each other's arms..." Mineth lowered her chin, "...he will cling to that hope, though he die a little each day for it." Her voice faded and her gaze turned inward.

Cindra looked into Mineth's eyes, seeing something she had not noticed before. "How do you know this, Mineth?" How well did Cindra know the troubles of the woman who had been at her side all of her life?

Mineth sniffed and smiled reassuringly, saying only, "I read those silly romantic stories, milady." She said no more on the matter and the women watched the sun fade beneath the waves.

They took the evening meal in their cabin, enjoying the cheese and bread despite having to pick bits of mold from it, and they sipped at the vintage of wine that had been brought for their private use. They also had a bit of meat from the game fowl that were kept for the officers. The voyage was all but half over, and hopefully the decent food would last them until they made port. Cindra did not ask what the common sailors were eating and drinking, but did not imagine it would be as 'nice' as their nightly fare. Best not to learn the particulars, since it was beyond her influence and beneath her concerns besides.

At any time the ship could make for shore and take on fresh supplies at the villages that sparsely lined the coast, no more than a few days apart. The buildings were too small to make out from the deck of the *Indisputable*, but the sails of the local fishing boats could be seen when there was a settlement nearby.

As they traveled on, the fishing villages had become farther apart and Cindra had not seen another sail for days. Still it did not feel as though a mutiny was imminent and she had no reason think that a lack of good cheese on her account would so enrage the crew.

Mutiny at sea was one of the many things she had read about before departing and while she had no wish to be in the middle of one, it was an exciting prospect to consider. She wondered what sailors did to alleviate the boredom of life at sea, for aside from the wind in her hair and the sea spray, it was rather dull. But then again, the men all seemed so busy most of the day and the officers made sure there was no time to sit about and plot mutinies. The men also sang and chanted a lot to the music of a squeezebox. Mineth made the mistake of asking young Pinn what the men were singing about and the resulting translation, partly in pantomime, made her sputter and blush furiously.

After finishing their meal and having young Pinn clear away the remnants, the women sat under the lantern to read to each other as they had done since Cindra had learned her letters. One of the books they had taken for the voyage was the Tome of Deep Mysteries, the scripture of Obesh, god of the sea. They had learned a few prayers for safe travel and good weather and had recited them each night, and they read about the making of the waves and waters, and the stories of the ancient faithful and the Souls of the Spray, and the Great White Dolphin that was the favored shape of Obesh, and how he would chase in anger the great sharks Masha and Mektha, and the seas would roll in their wake.

The men had taken up their music and singing again this night, earlier than usual since the anchor was dropped and there was no need to work the rigging or steer the ship. It would likely run later than usual too, and Cindra wondered how they could revel so long after working so hard. Not that it mattered to her, for she had been able to fall asleep to the noise after their first week at sea. Mineth grumbled and complained about it, but Cindra would hear the handmaid snoring softly before she herself drifted off into slumber.

The night's dreams were strange, as she had come to expect since taking to sea. The creaking of the hull and the rise and fall of the waves, the songs of sea birds and even those of the great whales made their way into her dream world and she felt herself adrift on the water, sometimes even under the water, floating and moving with the slightest whim and effort. She dove deep into the blue ocean and visited her father's castle, which for some reason had been submerged, though no one seemed to mind. She walked with Nixy and her mother through the great hall, chasing fish as they swam by. Her father sat on a throne made of a great seashell, and he spat out large pearls for Cindra to wear as a necklace. She laughed and blew bubbles that floated to the high ceiling.

Then she was on the deck of a ship, like the *Indisputable*, but crewed by the children of the castle she had left behind, her Army of Mischief. They followed her orders as she had them roll out the cannon and fire on an approaching pirate ship manned by Norsican raiders of old, with horned helmets and shields, just like in the ancient carvings and pictures from her family histories. Then her ship became her bed, and the masts and sails became the posts and curtains, and she drifted on towards the dawn, feet kicking in the water and her chin on her pillow.

She awoke on her stomach on the narrow cot, her back and hips aching. She rolled in her sleep more often now and wished for a return to a large feather mattress. Mineth was stirring and bleary-eyed and they both blinked at the foggy morning sky through the windows. Grey and featureless was the morning and naught could be seen of land, sky, or sea. Cindra sat up and leaned against the bulkhead while Mineth poured water in a bowl so they might wash their faces. They both wore nightgowns of white linen that clung to them in the damp air. The first order of the day was to freshen up and dress, then prepare for breakfast and their morning stroll upon the deck. Soft footsteps sounded upon the ceiling of their cabin as the watchman took his post.

Mineth opened the dressing chest and laid out simple garments for Cindra and herself, moving some items so she may repack the books they had read from the night before. Cindra uncovered the cage that housed Gavagul and made little chirpy noises to stir him from his sleep. Mineth was now stacking some things on her cot to reach their cloaks near the bottom of the chest, for the morning was cold.

"Tsk, I wish we had more trunks, or at least more space to put them in milady. This is much like living in a closet, but less practical." Mineth was complaining, which meant she was fully awake at last. Smiling, Cindra took a piece of dried meat from the feed pouch and offered it to the bird who fluffed his feathers and took it, warming the air as he did so. The smell of ash and warm coals filled the cabin.

"What is this?" asked Mineth as she repacked the chest. She was holding a small box of cherry wood hinged and latched with delicate brass fixtures. Cindra did not recognize it until Mineth opened it, revealing a velvet lining and a golden bracelet within.

"Oh!" Cindra exclaimed, "It's my birthday gift from Arch Mage Finnael. I'd forgotten." She took the box from Mineth and removed the bracelet, working it over her wrist as the blue-green stone, silver-etched runes and dolphins flashed in the dim light. "What do you think?" she held her wrist near her hair and posed, setting off the gold against her auburn locks.

Mineth nodded in approval saying, "I don't know why you never mentioned it before, milady, for it is a lovely thing." Cindra shrugged and made to take it off, but Mineth stilled her saying, "Oh, do leave it on. It will go well with the dress I've picked."

Cindra left the bracelet on her wrist and said, "I guess I never showed it to you because it was meant for my voyage, and I did not wish to think on it at the time. But now I am here, so I don't see the harm in wearing it." She looked over Mineth's dress selection.

There were calls in the fog as the watchmen tried to raise the attention of the *Wesvyyn Gull's* crew. Shouts of "Heeeeyohoy!" rang through the mist and at first Cindra thought little of them but as they continued and were raised by more voices, she put her cloak over her shoulders and left the cabin in her bedclothes, much to Mineth's chagrin. The handmaid donned her own cloak and followed shortly after.

Captain Gawyyn was standing upon the quarterdeck and Cindra went to speak with him. He gave her a nod of his cap and returned his attention to the watchmen in the rigging as they called into the fog. "Is everything alright, Captain?" she asked, though it was obvious things were amiss.

The captain looked back over the larboard stern where their escort ship was supposed to be anchored, but could see and hear nothing. He shook his head and said in a low voice, "The *Gull* is not answering our hails, nor can we find her in this fog. She should be about there," he pointed into the wall of grey mist, "about an arrow's flight away."

Cindra looked about her to the faces of the men who had noticed her presence on deck. Some were already murmuring to each other and giving her strange glances, as though she had something to do with this ill fortune. It was not at all comfortable and she considered returning below decks.

Mineth came up behind looking worried and wrapping her cloak tight about her, partly against the cold, but partly to cover her lack of proper dress. Cindra relayed the news about the missing escort and they were about to start down the stairs again, when one of the watchmen called out from the shrouds.

The women looked up and saw the man pointing to portside into the fog and when they turned to see, they witnessed a shape emerging from the mist; a sound could be heard as well, like the rhythmic splashing of water. The shape resolved into a ship, but it was not the *Wesvyyn Gull*. The vessel was smaller and lower to the water, and ranks of oars could be seen dipping and lifting out of the sea, driving the ship nearer. To Cindra's untrained eye it seemed as though the other vessel was coming right at them...

Many voices were raised in alarm and the captain put his hands on Cindra's shoulders and nearly pushed her towards their cabin, telling her to make fast the hatch. She stumbled into Mineth, who quickly made her way to the door, supporting her lady as best she could. Cindra gained her balance and steadied herself against the railing, looking out at the ship that had caused such terror amongst the crew.

The red sail was furled on the lone mast and the ship bore no flag. The bow seemed to be thick and carved in the manner of a charging beast with two great horns sprouting from its head, capped with metal piercing tips. Working the oars were dark figures in the mist with horned helms like the Norsican pirates of her dreams. She saw spears and shields lining the gunwales, ready to be taken up in a moment. There was a figure that rose up to stand behind the bow, bracing itself for the impending impact, and Cindra saw its face.

The foreign words being flung about her made more sense and her mind locked in an instant of disbelief. *"Waan Dal! Minzaan!"* she heard from the frightened sailors. The words formed in her mind as she grabbed Mineth, *'Bull men! Minozhians!'* Gods, Minozhian raiders!

Of all the spawn of the Time of Chaos, the beast men were the most legendary and the most feared. It was said that there was a god known as Ko'Baash the Beast Lord, and he was worshiped in many lands and in many different aspects. The people of Minozhia, who valued strength and ferocity, revered him as a mighty bull. During the Time of Chaos, Ko'Baash brought about a change on his followers and made bestial atrocities of them. Some said the Beast Lord was none other than Llomaak the God of Chaos, and the beast men were his latest attempt at creating horrid life.

Cindra pushed Mineth ahead of her into the cabin and locked the door, looking frantically for something to bar it with. Mineth was pale with fear but she had the presence of mind to help her lady stack the dressing chests in front of the hatch. Cindra rushed to the port window and looked out in time to see the enemy vessel strike the side of the *Indisputable*; the jolt of the impact nearly threw her out the window and she had to grab the bulkhead to steady herself. Gavagul squawked in his cage as it swung back and forth and Mineth fell onto a bunk, shrieking in fright.

Cindra could see the bestial invaders taking up spear and shield and moving forward over the bow as the *thump-thump* of heavy feet fell upon the deck outside the door. The sounds of battle rang out as the men fought for their lives, screams filling the air and deep roars of animal rage chilling the blood. The ship listed to port as the bodies converged there, pressing and repelling the attack. There were loud stomps up the stairs, which disturbed Gavagul greatly, and the ceiling shook with the clash of arms in the small space. Dust and paint chips fell on the ladies' hair as a body struck the deck overhead, and they grabbed each other in terror as a great spearhead was driven through the planks, fresh blood starting to drip from its point.

There were splashes in the water outside the windows, and sailors could be seen trying to swim away, to lose themselves in the fog and take their chances with the sea but spears were flung at their thrashing forms and they soon drifted, crippled or dying, to await the sharks or the embrace of the cold waters.

Mineth withdrew from the horrid sight when her eyes suddenly fixed on Gavagul's cage. Rushing forward, she flung the cage door open and withdrew the anxious bird, setting him on the nearest cot as his flapping and clutching began to burn her hand. She shouted quickly at Cindra over the sounds of men dying before the cabin door, "Send a message, milady Cindra, send for help!"

Eyes wide as she nodded in comprehension, Cindra picked up the bird about its body and lifted it to the sill, opening the window wide. "Gavagul, take this message to my father! We are attacked!" The door shook under the impact of a large fist and the sound made the women jump. Gavagul chirped in distress. "Minozhian pirates are killing the crew, we lost our escort in the fog, they..." Another pound on the door brought a shriek from Mineth as she pushed with her meager weight to brace it. "They're breaking in!"

A roar and a crash made Cindra scream as Mineth was shoved aside in a pile of wood and baggage. She saw the huge form of a nightmare creature in the doorframe; what she had earlier thought to be a horned helmet were its own natural horns, if natural they could be called. Its snout was flared in anger and its shaggy head came into the room, supported by a thick muscled neck and broad shoulders. Its musky stench filled the cabin and its thick leather armor creaked about the joints as it kicked the chests aside. The beast man carried a large wicked knife in its grasp.

Mineth wrenched herself from the tangle of wreckage and stood before the creature, arms spread wide, barring his way as she faced her lady. Her face was intense, almost furious; her eyes were wide but focused on Cindra's, her body rigid and steady as it had ever been on the rocking sea. She cried in a loud voice, "Get away, Cindra!"

Then the wind was knocked from her body as the monster struck, the point of his blade protruding from her breast as a blossom of crimson spread there like a rose, staining the pure white of her nightgown. Her large brown eyes still looked at Cindra but lost their focus and her arms hung limp at her side.

Cindra screamed in horror as her lifelong friend was taken from her. Mineth's body was shoved off the great knife to make a heap on the deck amidst the wreckage of the room. Cindra shook with fury, helpless to act, as the monster stepped over his victim. She saw a flash of color out of the corner of her eye and remembered the ember swallow in the window. "Fly!" she screamed at Gavagul as the bull man raised his knife, seeing the bird for the first time. A moment of indecision crossed his face and he chose his target.

Cindra launched herself out of the portside window as Gavagul took off in a flash of fire and smoke out the starboard opening. The creature flung his great knife at the bird, missing and shattering the window as it spun out into the sea. Cindra fell in a shower of broken glass and metal framework, shrieking in pain until she hit the cold water where her breath left her, frozen in shock.

It took her a moment to open her eyes and begin to move, the nightgown tangled her limbs and her hair was in her face, drifting like an auburn curtain. She kicked at the emptiness beneath her, struggling to reach the surface which shimmered just out of reach overhead. She heard the thunder of cannon fire, saw the flash over the water issue from the bulk of the ship, and could almost make out movement at her cabin window when a spear broke the water and pierced her gown, scratching her flesh below the ribs. She fanned at the water frantically, unsure of how to maneuver, trying now do go deeper and avoid being skewered like the hapless sailors that floated nearby. The spear was tangled in the side of her robe now and she tried in vain to free it.

Her lungs were burning and she desperately wanted to breathe but she had never been a swimmer and could only thrash about in the darkening void, sinking for lack of air. Seawater seeped into her nose and she reflexively tried to expel it, using the last of her precious breath in the process. Her vision began to go black and she heard something like a ringing in her ears, almost like a song. She looked up at the gray surface of the water as it receded above and the tension left her limbs as she felt herself fall ever so gently to a new home she would never see.

Gavagul beat his wings with all his might to escape from the whirling blade, leaving the ship behind in a trail of smoke and flame. It was not the first time someone had tried to kill him in the course of his duties and it was not the best attempt by far, but this was an important message and he would not be thwarted. Once he was out of range of arrowshot, he banked and circled twice about the ships. The fog was beginning to burn off now and he saw the masts of the *Wesvyyn Gull* in the distance, much farther than it should have been, and the men were scrambling at the rigging to set sail. *Indisputable* was impaled upon the horns of the enemy ship and the large beast men swarmed about the deck, flinging open the cargo doors and tossing the bodies of the crew overboard.

Cannon roared pointblank at the enemy ship, sending splinters into the water but doing little harm. Gavagul saw his family's daughter drifting under the sea, saw the ghostly fanning of her gown as she struggled, and saw a bull man emerge from the portal and pierce her with a spear. He circled again and saw her white gown fading like a wisp of cloud as she sank, saw men drifting or drowning as the currents bore them eastward, he saw the forms of distant sharks.

A sad twittering escaped his beak as he broke off his search and turned towards Casselvane Keep, leaving a double ring of smoke high in the air to mark the site of the attack for the escort which would doubtless arrive too late. There would be no need for food or rest, for he had received enough of both while enclosed in his cage. The wind was at his back and there was no need to follow the coast, so much of the flight could be made over land. Gavagul would arrive home before midday, but any help he could summon would come far too late. Therefore it was his duty to deliver the daughter's last message, so that her parents would know her fate. His kind were only gifted to understand and repeat, so he would not be able to offer any details on what he had witnessed, but what he bore was explicit enough.

A burst of flame and smoke punctuated his trail in the sky as he put on all the speed he was able to muster.

Chapter Fourteen

The Red Coast Road

The tide was returning, moving steadily up the shore with each wave as white foam rolled and spread across the red sands. The crashing of waves on the rocks echoed up the coast as the seawall rose to the west, its craggy face looming over the narrow beach. Seaweed and pieces of rotten wood were deposited upon the shore, only to be rearranged as the ocean made its endless changes to the land. The sun was falling behind a line of trees that crowned the dark cliffs, while gulls perched in the nooks and crannies of the rock face to look down upon what might be their next meal.

Cold sea foam washed up the girl's pale legs, making her twitch. Her skin was still numbed by the waters, but the afternoon sun had dried her a bit, and the return of the waves stirred her out of her sleep. She wore the tatters of a white linen nightgown, which had been torn and twisted around a spear that lay beside her. Her skin

278

bore many scratches and bruises, though most had closed in the salt water or were caked with red sand. Another wave rushed up to her hips and she gasped, opening her eyes.

Cindra's face was half in the sand and covered with her tangled auburn hair, but as the wave returned she woke up quickly and coughed, spitting out grit and seawater as she crawled up the small beach to escape the cold foam. Her arms were weak and shook as she tied to support her weight, and something was pulling at her clothing. Looking around her back, she saw the spear entangled in her gown, a big heavy pole of hewn wood bound with leather strips and topped with a long broad spearhead of black iron.

The sight brought back memories with a rush of pain and fear, and she saw Mineth, her dear handmaid and lifelong friend, impaled on the knife of a savage Minozhian beast man, saw the blood spread across her chest, remembered the life fading from her eyes. A tiny whimper escaped Cindra's lips and soon she was wailing at the empty sea, her chest clenched in pain as her body gave and gave to the cry and took nothing in. Finally a racking sob allowed her to breathe again and she wept for a long while, trying to free the offending spear from her gown with numb fingers.

She pulled herself up to sit upon the stones, just out of reach of the tide. She looked with hatred at the weapon that had almost killed her, trying to remember what had happened after it struck. She was under the water, sinking and flailing to avoid the surface lest another spear find its mark. There was pain, pressure, her head pounded with the need to inhale, but to do so would mean her death. There was a noise, like a song... She had gulped a mouthful of air. Was that right? She remembered taking a breath *under* the water, filling her lungs with sweet relief and not the cold death of the ocean. Had she imagined it in her panic? She was here safe on the shore, wasn't she? Just how did *that* happen? She rubbed her eyes as dry as she could.

Cindra looked around and felt her skin, as if to make sure she was not dead. *Not that I would know how to tell*, she thought, and she noticed the scrapes and felt the cut on her side, the linen clinging to the wound with a crimson stain. It hurt a bit as she pulled the cloth away, but it bled little. *I can't be dead and drowned if I'm hurt and bleeding,* she decided.

She looked down to examine what was left of her nightgown. It was in tatters and barely hid enough for modesty by anyone's standards; worse than its condition was the fact that the fabric was both wet and thin, and a breeze was already chilling her. When the sun sank it would be very cool indeed, if the nights aboard ship were any indication. *Might I make a fire?* She looked about for kindling but realized she had no idea how to start one, even if she had a stack of wood and a pile of dried grass. She had no flint or tinder, no magic tricks that could spark a flame.

The surf reached her toes and she knew that she needed to reach higher ground at any rate, fire or no. The watermarks on the cliff face made it plain that this beach saw waves higher than she, and there was little time to find a safer place. Luckily the cliffs became lower to the southeast. She started to head that way when a thought struck her and she went back for the heavy spear that was being buried in the sand. Lifting it out of the surf and looking it over with disgust, she began her hike towards the lower rocks using the weapon as a walking stick, wondering if she would be forced to defend herself with the vile thing.

Her thoughts returned to Mineth and she wondered what the Minozhians had done with the captured ship that had been meant to deliver her to her wedding. Did they take what they wanted and leave on their own vessel, or did they commandeer the *Indisputable*? If it was the former then maybe her dear handmaiden had been found by the missing escort and received a respectful burial at sea. The other alternative was something she didn't want to consider. Her sorrow extended to the captain and officers, to silly little Pinn the cabin boy, and all the sailors who had left families behind. She stopped walking for a moment and gathered herself, for there was no time for grief now. Daylight was waning.

The cliff face became a collection of boulders further down the beach, which was choked with small stones and debris that made walking quite painful. The sands hid many sharp stones that Cindra had the misfortune to find, and she made her way more and more slowly, testing the path before her as she stepped. To make matters worse, the beach was home to many crabs that clambered along sideways across her path and she had to knock them out of the way with the butt of the spear. Some did not appreciate this and scampered back to try and pinch her, but Cindra leaped away, braving the sharp rocks over the snapping claws of the little monsters. Her breath came in sharp hisses of discomfort as she pushed on.

The boulders that made up the beachfront were precarious, smooth in spots and sharp in others, and Cindra gained several new scrapes as she climbed them. She thought she might have to abandon the spear, for it was hard to climb the steeper slopes with it, but she managed anyway. *Better for it to be a burden now than to want for it later on*, she thought. Besides, she was nearing the top of the bluff and there were trees and bushes that would make climbing a bit easier. She was at least able to toss the spear up the slope to wait for her as she struggled up the rocks.

As she reached for a handhold on the branch of a nearby tree, a twig caught on her bracelet. She took a moment to dislodge it, leaning against the slope of rock and soil, and another memory came into her mind. A song, a wailing twittering, almost bird-like song reached her ears under the water. She was borne up by something smooth of skin and strong, and she held on for dear life. *Was there more than one?* She could not remember, she only knew she was moving far and fast, her breath becoming harder to draw as she passed beneath the waves. Finally her head broke the water and the cold air whipped her hair and she breathed once again as she always had. Smooth gray skin was under her fingers as she had lapsed into sleep.

The memory faded and she looked at the bracelet with its luminous sea stone and silver dolphin figures that adorned her wrist, glittering in the failing light, and she marveled at the gift of the arch wizard Ildric Finnael. She wondered if he had known of the attack, or if it was simple prudence that inspired him to give her such a treasure. If she ever made it back home, she would have to ask. *Had he known Mineth's fate as well?*

Pulling herself up by the tree branch, Cindra made it to the top of the bluff and rubbed her arms and legs for warmth. She was high enough above the tide, but there was still the matter of food, shelter, and making it through the cold night. The breeze and her damp gown were robbing her skin of feeling, and her fingers and toes bled from the climbing and rough terrain.

She picked up the spear and looked into the thickening trees and brush, wondering if there was a village nearby. Her stomach rumbled at the sudden thought of a fireplace and pot of stew, the vision giving her strength to press onward into the copse of trees. The ground was easier on her bare feet but there were brambles and nettles to be avoided and the bushes snagged on her tattered gown. She took the long trailing remnants of the garment, wrapping it under and around her waist to get it out of the way. Her legs were freer now but were acquiring many more scratches and bug bites and they began to itch.

The trees became thicker as she went on and the land sloped upward slightly, forcing her to rest every few moments. She had never walked over wild ground before and was not in any condition to do so for long. Her legs felt wobbly and her arms were weak, the trees blocked out the fading sun and the creatures of the forest were stirring. She had the sudden realization that she would make a fitting meal, even with the heavy spear at her side. She doubted she could make much use of it if confronted by wolves or hill cats. There were stories of worse things in the wilderness besides.

Cindra walked steadily on for what seemed like hours, heading north as best she could reckon. She remembered old maps from her studies and recalled a road that ran along the coast for much of its length, almost unto the borders of Rokvynnar where her ship had been bound.

The Red Coast Road was built during the centuries between the old empire's conquest of Calilaar and Orthicus the Great claiming the throne. Then came the Hundred Year Reign and the Time of Chaos, when all manner of strange things were let loose upon the world. The lands became more perilous and people gathered closer together, shunning the wilder regions. A strange cry sounded in the distance and Cindra forced herself to think about something else.

Birds had been settling in the trees, vying for the most comfortable branches, and their squabbling had grown dim. There was little daylight left and Cindra was no longer sure if she was heading in the right direction. The sun had been out of sight for some time and the shadows no longer gave any clues. The forest canopy obscured the stars and the moon had not yet risen above the horizon. *It would be a sliver of a moon anyway*, she thought sullenly. She could no longer smell or hear the sea and there was no breeze. The smell of woods surrounded her and became oppressive. She sniffed for the telltale scent of cooking fires or livestock but only detected the musty earth and the moss of surrounding trees.

The woods seemed to absorb all sound, for she could only hear her own footsteps and labored breathing. Snapped twigs were like whip cracks in the darkened woods and even the birds had grown quiet. She had imagined that the forest at night was full of the noises of its creatures; owls, deer, foxes, squirrels, boar, and whatever else was supposed to prowl the night. Mice, even. She heard nothing.

She held her breath for a moment out of some buried instinct and it was then that she heard a soft rustling from the bushes to her right. She spun towards the noise and caught the glare of two predatory eyes before they moved out of sight. Her heart leaped and she gasped in fear, her pulse started pounding as she realized she was being stalked by something not a stone's throw away. She gripped the spear defensively before her and tried to see deeper into the shadows, her eyes wide and staring. A cold sweat broke over her skin and a snarling sounded from the brush as the thing began moving slowly around the foliage, for the hunter knew it had been spotted. It was now hoping to maintain the prey's terror before it could act. Cindra saw a dark form against the shadows of the forest floor and her blood froze.

The beast was like a large wolf in size and form, but its snout and jaws were far too long and its head was surrounded by a shaggy mane of reddish hair. Its shoulders were hunched; it raised its black hackles and it seemed to become larger as Cindra watched. Its waist seemed overly thin and its legs ended in big thick paws with wicked claws. A long bushy tail completed the nightmare image as it circled around to her right, looking for open ground. Its tongue lolled and the overlong muzzle wrinkled in a grimace as it bared its many teeth.

Cindra held the spear out before her, a spike of panic energizing her limbs. The spear was heavy and unwieldy but comforting as she clutched it to her body; pointing it towards the yellow eyes of the creature, she turned her head quickly from side to side to check her surroundings.

There was a small clearing to the left up the hill a few paces; the trees were thin enough to allow her some freedom of movement to defend herself. She backed towards the clearing, keeping the spear point between her and the wolf-thing. It changed direction, shifting back the way it had come, and began circling to her left up the rise of the hill. She hesitated for a moment, wondering what it was up to. Her legs began to shake and the strength left her arms as the panic took its toll on her weary body.

The beast was moving in a wide circle, its dark body pacing behind the trees like shadow blending into shadow; the ruddy markings of its mane and tail danced in the low light as powerful muscles rippled underneath the coarse fur. It was gaining the high ground, making sure that its prey was between the sea and its jaws.

Cindra continued up the gentle incline to the clearing, thinking it was the best place to make a stand. If the horrid thing wanted to attack her, it would have to leave the safety of the trees and come into the open, where it would meet the sharp iron of her spear. The warm spark of bravery in her heart told her this, but the cold reality of her situation spoke differently. She could not run far before collapsing or falling to the beast's fangs; there was no safe place to go. She had very little strength left in her arms and possessed no skill with a spear; the beast probably weighed as much as she did, if not more, so she might fend off one attack but not a second. Its jaws looked powerful enough to rip her spear away or snap it in two, and soon it would be too dark to see. She wondered why she had been spared drowning in the sea only to be eaten on the shore.

"I will see you soon, dear Mineth," she muttered as the creature snarled in answer.

She stepped towards the center of the clearing and tried to hold the weapon steady. There was a large patch of soft clover on the ground and it was cool under her feet. Little fireflies began to appear over the grass and brush, their dim dancing lights distracting her from the glowing eyes of the beast. She strained to see its dark bulk in the shadows, but the sun was falling too low and she lost its eyes amongst the fluttering of fairy bugs. She held her breath and her heart skipped a beat as the hunter eluded her sight. She gripped the spear with white knuckles, a cold sweat breaking over her skin.

A few heartbeats later the monster exploded from the brush in a rustle of dead leaves and undergrowth, black claws dug into the earth and ripped up the grass as powerful limbs propelled it forward. It had snuck about to Cindra's left and was making for her unguarded flank, angling its jaws to rip at her soft pale thigh and snap the bone. Cindra stumbled back and to her right as she brought the spear to bear, but the butt of the weapon struck a tree and halted her defense. She shrieked as the animal's hot breath and spittle flecked her leg. She smelled the blood of a recent meal on its yellow fangs, caught the scent of carrion and death.

There was a snap and a sound of whipping branches and the beast's charge was brought up short; it yelped in anguish as the clover patch trembled and snarled about the animal's back leg, revealing a snare that pulled it off the ground and hurled it towards a thick tree. Cindra dropped the spear and fell on her backside as she shivered and quailed at the sight; the beast was whisked through the air into a large patch of moss on the side of the tree. Instead of a soft thump, there was a sickly ripping noise and the creature thrashed in pain; hidden spikes of sharp wood were beneath the moss and the predator had been impaled upon them. It howled and struggled but to no avail as rivulets of dark blood ran down the bark and pooled at the roots. Cindra didn't move until the beast had ceased its struggle and grew silent.

She shook as she got to her feet, taking up the spear from the ground and sweeping the clover around her, lest another trap be set nearby. Satisfied that the wolf-creature would be the only victim, she examined the snared animal more closely. There was a woven rope about its leg and it ran taut through the crotch of the large tree, the rest of the length was tied to a strong sapling nearby, which had been bent to the ground before being set off. It was too dark to see much more, so she made her way back to the clearing to get her bearings. With luck, she might see stars above the thin trees. She came around the deadly tree trap, examining the way the wooden spikes had been bound to a flexible mat and tied to the trunk. *Who had set this*, she wondered?

A bark and a snap made her jump in terror as the wolf-creature made one last vengeful attempt on her life, its head and long jaws swung and clamped on the air inches from the girl's ear, sprinkling Cindra with the beast's dying blood. She backed up hurriedly and took up the spear, determined to make certain the thing was truly dead. *As I should have done before*, she thought. She lifted the spear point to the creature's neck, placing the point in the shaggy mane and after closing her eyes for a moment to gather her composure, thrust it in with all her might.

Her might did not amount to much, as it seemed, and the creature flinched at the blow, kicking its front legs to dislodge the new pain. Not wanting to cause the monster any more suffering, Cindra hefted the spear again and pushed into the shaggy neck until new blood sprang forth, running down the iron blade and onto the leather wrappings. The creature stopped moving and was still.

Too exhausted to feel fear or anger, only the need to sleep, Cindra stumbled away up the hill. The stars she could see did not guide her but she figured the way she was heading was just as good as any path. The dark woods were daunting and she did not want to wander blind into the trees, but neither did she want to rest near the smell of so much blood and carrion. The dead thing would draw other flesh eaters to the spot for an easy meal and Cindra would not be a side dish if she could help it.

It occurred to her then that whoever had set the trap might return to see if it was sprung and that she might be rescued, but something warned her against waiting. She was after all a girl alone in the woods, dressed in tatters and more or less helpless. She knew little of who might live in these parts and was not quick to trust strangers, be they noble or base. It would be best to search for a village or town where kindly souls might take pity on her, rather than take her chances with someone in the wilderness, far from the boundaries of civilized conduct.

The night stretched on and she struggled through the brush and branches for what seemed like hours, though she doubted she had the strength left in her for such a trek. The moon was unseen and the stars were bright but veiled by the forest canopy, only winking between the leaves and no help at all. The ground had leveled out and the going was easier, though her feet were cold and bleeding from dozens of cuts and scratches and her shivering made it hard to carry the spear so it dragged behind her. If another fell beast of the night reared up before her now, she would fall and be devoured, of that she had no doubt. The forest noises had returned at least, and the hooting of an owl was her only company in the darkness.

The cold was overcoming her limbs, her extremities were growing numb, her nose was running and useless, her ears hurt, her fingers felt stiff and stone-like, and the tatters of her gown did nothing to protect her from the faint breeze that constricted her chest. Miserable and feeling despair at ever seeing another dawn, she stumbled into another clearing and tripped upon a hard stone, falling to her knees. The shock of impact along her limbs was intensified by the cold and she cried out, collapsing into sobs.

The ground felt frozen beneath her and was as hard as stone, and she knew that to lie where she fell would mean certain death. The breeze was stronger here, blowing through the clearing in little gusts, chilling her to the bone. She could not make her fingers recover the spear but she managed to crawl on her hands and knees across the cruel stones towards the comfort of a patch of grass and loam she could see in the starlight just across the clearing. She looked neither left nor right, but focused on the soft patch ahead as if it were a feather bed with a thick blanket by a fire.

The cold stone gave way to a shallow ditch that she had to cross, but just beyond that was her reward. Mud squished under her knees and soothed her tortured skin, her fingers felt yielding grass and leaves and her body curled into a shivering ball upon the soft foliage, tears of hopelessness mixing with the joy of this little victory, for at least she would be comfortable as she slipped into a deep sleep.

Her dreams were brief and troubled. She twitched with exhaustion and fear, kicking away at the snapping jaws of an unseen animal. The sea swallowed her and spit her out on a barren shore where every step held danger; every soft patch of grass hid a snaring deadly trap. Mineth was calling her name, telling her to flee lest they catch her. She heard voices murmuring in the dark and she felt hands upon her, shaking and rubbing her skin. The sensation was all too real and she awoke with a start, shapes surrounded her and shadows danced in the light of a torch, which seemed as bright in the darkness as the noon sun.

"*Ga-te-shon'a le,*" a masculine voice spoke near her face, Cindra inhaled the scent of smoke from a campfire mixed with leather and sweat.

"*Anshó'a le?*" said a female voice near the flickering torchlight.

Cindra's eyes focused and she threw off the hands on her shoulders with a flailing of her arms, but the man was the only thing holding her upright and she fell back into the soft grass.

"Do not be afraid!" said the man, backing away and giving her room. "All is well, we will not hurt you." He stood and moved towards the woman holding the torch.

Cindra saw their dress and features in the light and a shock ran through her; they were Galindri, the nomads who had lived on the continent of Gartetha long before her own people came to these shores. Dark of skin and bright of eyes, with hair braided and tied above their heads; leather and linen were their clothes and they wore furs and cloaks against the cold.

The man was perhaps twice Cindra's years but wore no beard, and the woman was shorter than he and sturdy, the torch she bore illuminated the bright colors of their garb, and her many-layered skirt shone with the colors of springtime, yellow, green and blue. His shirt was greenish blue and his breeches were red, with leather boots wrapped to the knees. Their emerald eyes caught in the torchlight and reminded Cindra of the wolf-thing that had almost killed her. She had only seen their kind up close once before, in the Portshia Market Square on the night of her birthday when she had slipped from the castle to explore the city.

Another figure moved from the shadow of the trees and stepped near to the frightened girl. Cindra looked up and beheld what seemed to be a Galindri hunter carrying a bow and quiver of arrows in one hand, a fur-lined cloak in the other. The hunter looked down at her with eyes like chips of green ice; an impassive face gave her no sense of comfort. Short, layered skirts swayed at the knees and a linen wrap wound about the hunter's waist and torso, crossing her breasts and passing behind her neck. *The hunter was a woman!*

Cindra stared in wonder and looked again at the huntress, sure in her stance and unmoved by the cold. The woman had the same dark skin as the other two, her hair was bound up and braided as well, but her clothing was coral and red and she wore a dark crimson band of cloth across her brow. At her waist was a leather belt bearing two knives, one with a handle of horn, and the other handle wrapped with metal wire; a brass pommel glinted in the firelight.

The woman held out her cloak to Cindra, who was still wary under the woman's cold glare. "*De-petha*," the woman said and she shook the cloak. Waiting just a heartbeat too long, the shivering girl reached out for it but the huntress had already dropped it on the ground and was walking past the couple and into the darkness. Cindra wrapped the cloak around her and began to weep, for this was the first comfort she had felt since her last moments on the ship. The woman with the torch handed it to the man and she approached the girl with arms outstretched saying, "Come with us, child. There is a fire and food if you are hungry."

Cindra's stomach grumbled in answer and she rose to her feet, aching with every step. The woman put an arm around her for support while the man led the way with the torch, walking between large gaps in the trees. After many steps on the hard ground, Cindra realized that she was walking on a road paved with flat stones and that she must have tripped in the gutter on one side, crawled blindly across the paving stones, and dragged her exhausted body through the opposite gutter before falling asleep. She had crossed the Red Coast Road! Had she stopped any earlier in the woods she might have never been found.

Ahead in the darkness was a campfire glowing behind a caravan, just a little ways off the road in a clearing. The trees and bushes served to shield it from the winds but they also hid the campfire from view just a short distance down the path. Cindra might have wandered past it in the darkness, never seeing or smelling it, since it was also downwind from where she had fallen.

Now as she approached she saw a large campfire and some people moving about and she heard noises from within the covered walls of the caravan; its sides were painted with crossing patterns and images of horses and of trees and valleys rendered in bold color. Baskets and bound parcels hung from the sides and a short stair led up to the door in the back. A goat was tethered nearby as well as two horses, and she smelled smoke and food, wonderful food seasoned with spices she could only guess at and she saw a cook pot suspended near the blaze.

There was an old man with braided gray hair sitting near the fire. His face was worn and etched with many winters; a bright woven blanket covered his shoulders and he watched with bright eyes as the couple approached with the foundling. The huntress was standing near him, watching impassively, and out of the caravan came a younger woman closer to Cindra's age, flawless skin and hair the color of dark honey, braided but unbound and draping down to her waist. She bore a bundle of clothes in her arms and wore a wide-eyed look of wonder as the visitor was helped into camp. Her skirts were long and colorful and she wore a wrap about her torso like the huntress, but also a long-sleeved blouse that was tied above her midriff, leaving it bare.

She deposited the clothing in a neat pile on a log and watched as Cindra was seated before the fire. The older woman who had helped Cindra walk to camp sat beside her and said to the staring young woman "*Gebeh, g'ólena.*" The young one jumped at the words and went to busy herself with the cook pot and Cindra again felt her stomach grumble and pull at her waist as though it were trying to eat itself.

"I am Luka," said the woman to Cindra, leaning forward to present herself. "Luka Volda-Goro. What is your name, child?" She spoke in an accent that carried a strong cadence.

Cindra was soaking in the warmth of the fire and was learning how sore she truly was now that her skin had feeling again. It took her a moment to respond and she said weakly, "Cindra Co- er, Cindra." She had begun to say 'Cindra Corrina,' but caution told her to leave the name of her noble house behind in the wilderness, surrounded by strangers. There was something about these people that bothered her, something she could not place. They seemed kind but wary and the huntress, if that was what she was, did not seem to care much for her presence in their camp. It was as if they had brought a dangerous animal into their midst and the stern woman was looking for an excuse to kill it or chase it away.

Luka smiled and said to the others, "Our guest is Cindra," to which they answered "*El-á'tra-beh,*" nodding to her and smiling. "Welcome," said the old man, his voice was deep and rough but had a kindness about it. Luka stood and walked around the fire to stand behind the old man, putting her hands on his shoulders and saying with much respect, "This is Majii Sula-Koro, father of my husband and his sisters." Cindra bowed her head as she would for a nobleman of higher station, just to be on the safe side. She knew nothing of Galindri ways but it would be best to be respectful, especially if they were going to feed her.

Luka placed a hand on the arm of the huntress who stood nearby. "His eldest is Teya Haana-Majii, who leads our wanderings." Cindra nodded her head and blinked at the comment. *She is the leader?* Teya only glanced at her.

Luka then moved to the man who had awoken Cindra on the road. He had a ready smile for his wife and placed his hand over hers as she presented him. "His son is Navo Haana-Majii, and he is my husband." Navo had a friendly face and he seemed to smile a lot, and Cindra noticed that Luka seemed to feed him well enough; he may have been thin once þut married life had filled him, as the saying went back home.

The younger woman now had a bowl in one hand and a cup in the other and she presented them to Cindra gingerly. Luka said, "And this is little sister Haani Jalara-Majii."

Cindra nodded and took the food, her hands shaking as she did. She set the warm bowl on her knee and drank from the cup, filling her mouth with warmed milk sprinkled with nutmeg. The bowl contained a stew of vegetables and meat in a hardy broth and the smell of spices tickled her nose.

Haani smiled at Cindra as her dark honey hair fell like a curtain beside her face. "Eat. Share the fire," she said with a smile.

"Thank you," Cindra said, nearly too choked up to speak.

After her meal Cindra changed into the clothing Haani had brought for her and with little strength left, she laid down by the fire. A blanket was provided for her to sleep upon and she used another for a pillow; with the crackle of the fire and the quiet foreign conversation of her hosts as the only nightly noises, she drifted into a deep slumber. Her dreams were many and confused, but she was too exhausted to even pay attention to them. She had no sense of time; it seemed like the whole of her life was relived in this one night of rest, right up to the last morning on the ship and the horrors that awaited her thereafter.

She heard a snuffling and felt hot breath on her cheek and opening her eyes she saw a great brown snout with two gaping hairy nostrils hovering inches from her face. The gentle laughter of her hosts told her she was safe, but the shock of it still made her squeak. One of the horses was leaning over to examine her as she slept; the wetness on her face told her he had stolen a kiss as well.

"He likes you," said Luka who was sitting nearby tending the fire. Teya walked by and took the horse's reins, leading him back to the front of the caravan. "I have made a morning meal for you if you are ready," Luka held the bowl in offering, waiting for the girl to sit up. "I have used less of the spices we eat to make it easier for you."

Cindra sat upon a stump and took the bowl, smelling the yellowish porridge with interest. "How do you say 'thank you' in your language?" Cindra asked.

"*B'á-ja*," said Luka with a smile, and Cindra repeated it the best she could.

The others were about as well; Navo was helping Teya pack the caravan and harness the horses, while Haani was fetching water and tending the goat. Majii was walking out of the trees opposite the road, his step was a bit uneven due to his age but he seemed hardy and at home in the woods. Cindra ate her porridge and watched the preparations. It seemed they were moving out this morning.

Luka began cleaning the cook pot, for it seemed that the others had already eaten. The morning was blue and cold and the smoke from the low fire permeated her hair and clothing. The sun was too low to be seen yet, but its light struck the tops of the trees overhead. Birds abounded in the branches, greeting the dawn, and squirrels scampered up and down the trunks of nearby trees, spying on the intruders and making loud claims to anything good that might be left behind.

Majii returned to the fire and sat near his daughter-in-law, sighing heavily as he bowed his head. Luka, as if responding to something unspoken, turned to Cindra and said, "Father Majii wishes to know how you came to be here alone."

It was not exactly a question. Cindra knew she was required to explain herself so that they might decide what to do about her. She decided that the truth was best, or at least half-truths as they applied to her identity.

"Well," Cindra began, "I was on a ship bound for Rokvynnar. My-my friend and I were traveling to a new home and..." the fresh memories were flooding over her like the tide, "...and our ship was attacked. My friend was killed and I jumped overboard to escape." She stirred the porridge slowly, her appetite abated. "I don't know how I managed to make it to shore." She looked at her bracelet but did not speak of it, did not mention the wizard who gave it or the powers it seemed to have. She supposed it was a good sign that she was still wearing it; these people were not thieves at least.

Luka placed a hand on Cindra's shoulder, said, "I am sorry for your friend. Pirates are growing bolder by the season."

"It was Minozhian raiders!" said Cindra with a bitter tone. She clenched her hands into fists and began to tremble. "They killed everyone on board, dumped them into the sea. Mineth saved my life, but..." She sniffed back a tear.

"Mineth was your friend, then." Luka said, "You spoke her name in your sleep."

Majii was looking into the fire, but the others had gathered to hear the tale. Only Teya kept a distance, listening but trying to seem busy.

Navo spoke. "Minozhian bull men! So they have returned to these shores. There will be trouble in the coming months; they raid villages, striking quickly and vanishing before help can arrive."

Teya walked by the fire and said, "It has always been so. At least they go back where they came from."

Navo was not deterred, "It has been tens of winters since they last struck the Red Coast. Not since I was a small boy." He turned to Teya, "You were a girl then, not yet a man." She kicked him with a pointed toe and he winced, accepting the price for his joke. Cindra dared not smile.

Luka continued the gentle questioning, not letting her husband's musings steer the talking elsewhere as he often did. "Where are you from Cindra? Where is your home?"

Cindra wondered that herself. If she spoke truthfully, her new home was in the ducal palace in Kyshmeryyk with a twelve-year-old duke as her husband. If she had her way she would be returned to Portshia in Casselvane, but would her father not send her off again? If not by sea, then by land surely, and she would pass this campsite yet again on her way to a belated wedding. At least she could answer the first question truthfully without doubt. "I am from Portshia in Casselvane Province."

There was a murmur among the Galindri and Navo spoke, "We were just in Portshia this last winter! *Bo-thé Ga-yá-toh!* Must we go back?" Cindra wanted to beg them to return her home but she remained silent. She knew enough to know that it was much to ask of strangers.

Majii lifted his head and blinked, looking at Cindra as if he had noticed her for the first time. She looked back at him and she gasped as the pieces fell into place. *She had seen these people before, in her own city!* The night of the Great Escape, the night she met Nixy, she saw Galindri, *these* Galindri! Why didn't she realize it earlier?

Majii smiled and his face creased and wrinkled, but his eyes shone like glittering emeralds. "You were the girl in the market!" He pointed to her and looked to his family, "I know her eyes; I've seen them before! In the city market, in the night, she walked by our camp; a girl alone with a hood and cloak but with these eyes, this face!" He looked at Cindra, who had begun to laugh and asked her, "Am I not right?"

Cindra nodded and closed her eyes, remembering the night months ago. "It was the end of Kraamoth, the 28th day, and I was walking in the Market Square. I saw your fire and caravan and wanted a closer look. I'd never seen Galindri before. I got too close and..." she looked up at the huntress and laughed, "...and Teya frightened me away!" The others laughed at this, the memory returning of a meek little girl in the night, but Teya only stared at Cindra with a puzzled expression as if trying to see a deeper meaning.

Majii chuckled and poked at the dying fire with a stick, "It is settled," he said and Haani clapped her hands, Navo and Luka smiled at each other and made ready the wagon. Only Teya was still standing there, looking as if something had passed her by. She stepped towards her father and started speaking in their language very rapidly, obviously arguing about what had been 'settled.' Majii silenced her with a raised hand and said, "It is settled. She may travel with us until her way is known. A chance meeting twice is not a chance; it is the will of the Mother."

But Teya was not convinced. "Father, we can take her to the next village, but we should leave her with her own people! It could bring trouble on us. Besides, we do not have food for another mouth."

Majii looked up at his daughter and gave her a measuring stare then said, "She is meant to be with us for now. In her own time she may leave, but that is for the Mother to judge." Then he motioned to Cindra as he returned his attention to the fire, "As for food, you may teach her to hunt." Teya stared at this, but said nothing.

"I can teach her to cook," said Luka.

"I can teach her to sing, dance and speak!" Haani said cheerfully.

"And I can teach her to dodge Teya's temper!" said Navo, who this time managed to duck away from his big sister's foot.

For all the horrors she had experienced and the danger she now faced alone in the wilderness, the last thing she expected was the kindness of these exotic strangers; people she had only heard of in stories and rumors. Seeing them in the Market Square had been a rare thrill but being among them, under their care and protection, if that's what it was, could not have been dreamed of.

She was nobility and these people were outcasts in their own land, forced to live the existence left to them after her ancestors had claimed the country for their own. Cindra decided it would be best to keep her identity secret for now, not knowing how these wanderers might feel towards a member of the ruling class. She especially mistrusted the tall, stern huntress Teya, for the woman seemed to need little reason to hate her.

For now she would play the meek and simple girl, calling no attention to herself but for the color of her skin. Whether for good or ill, the old man had offered her a place among them for a time and she thanked the silent gods for it.

The Author

Mark Rude, also known as Markalf the Going-Gray, is a wizard from Phoenix, Arizona, deep in the land of Mordor. He studied the Arts at Northern Arizona University, in the age when painting was done with paint, not pixels, and a photo shop was a place where you worked with something called 'film.'

It was in this age that he forged the story of Cindra Corrina, intending to make the story into a graphic novel, though it was not overly graphic, and not entirely novel. The comic book he called *Passage* kindled the spirit of the story. Three issues were forged in the land of Mordor, in the fires of Phoenix, before the effort was abandoned; yet the spirit of the story endured.

Cindra's tale was of epic proportions, untellable in quarterly comics that came out only once a year. Yet there was hope. Using fewer graphics, and with more emphasis on words, Cindra's story grew like the light of dawn over a darkened land. Markalf was able to spin his yarn as never before, making a nice sweater, some hand warmers, and a scarf.

Markalf the Going-Gray lives alone in a high tower, where he plots the doom of characters great and small.

www.markrude.net
www.facebook.com/markrude.net